VALENTINE
Texas
Butter My
Biscuit
LYLA PARISH

VALENTINE
Texas

MEET THE VALENTINES

Beckett Valentine
Kinsley Valentine
Harrison Valentine
Remington Valentine
Colt Valentine
Fenix Valentine
Emmett Valentine
London Valentine
Sterling Valentine
Vera Valentine

in order from oldest to youngest

**Each book in the Valentine Texas Series
is a stand-alone with rom com vibes and
a Happily Ever After.**

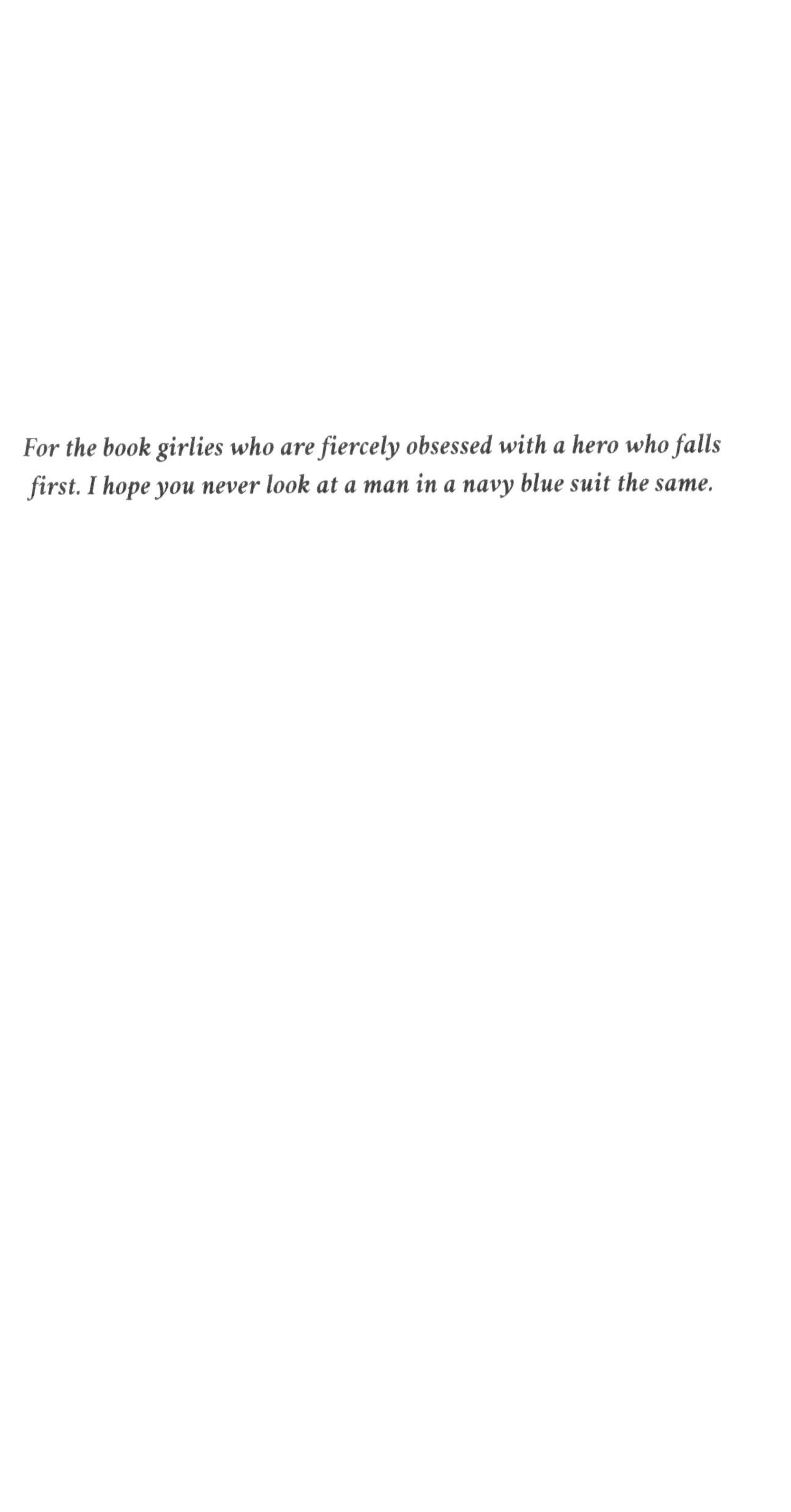

For the book girlies who are fiercely obsessed with a hero who falls first. I hope you never look at a man in a navy blue suit the same.

HAVE YOU EVER THOUGHT JUST
MAYBE YOU BELONG WITH ME?

—TAYLOR SWIFT

CHAPTER ONE

GRACE

My bestie and I have been driving for nearly twelve hours straight, only stopping for bathroom breaks, shitty coffee, and to grab lunch. If you can call it that. I'm still not sure what was inside that fried tortilla I ate from a random middle-of-nowhere gas station. I didn't ask.

When the Houston skyline finally comes into view, I pull out my phone and try to capture a picture of the buildings downtown, but it comes out in a smudge of colors. So, instead, I take our signature road-trip selfie of Harrison and me as he drives, and then I turn my attention to the sunset. My day has gone full circle as the fading light glows against the reflective windows of the skyscrapers.

Fifteen minutes later, we finally arrive at the house I rented for the weekend. The owners decorated the place with Christmas lights, and they glow red and green against the windshield of the truck. It's early December, and the holiday season is in full effect.

We counted the number of red reindeer noses and antlers on vehicles during the drive. Once we rolled over thirty, neither of us could remember how many we'd seen. Texans really like dressing their cars up for the holidays.

When my feet press against the pavement of the driveway, I'm relieved. We might've driven all day, but we made it. Then again, traveling anywhere with my bestie is a guaranteed good time.

Harrison throws his duffel bag over his shoulder, then grabs my suitcase, and like a gentleman, he wheels it to the door.

Then, we glance at the keypad at the same time.

"Shit. I forgot to save the code." I unlock my phone and search for the confirmation email the host sent after I booked this place. But when I receive a text from my boyfriend, I'm fully distracted and smiling like it's my birthday.

JOEY

Hey, lover.

I *LOVE* it when he calls me that.

GRACE

Hey! How are things?

HARRISON CLEARS HIS THROAT, shifting his weight from one leg to the other. "So, you gonna unlock the door or leave me standing here while you text your boyfriend?"

JOEY

Thinking about you. Can I call you in a few minutes?

GRACE

Sure, I'll be around

I'M ONLY ten minutes away from him. And tomorrow, when I fall into his arms at his doorstep, he'll be surprised. Showing up unannounced on the day of our anniversary is my way of saying I want to take our relationship to the next level. I'm ready to be all in with him … *I think*.

"Save your sexting for later."

"Sorry, totally distracted." I click out of my messages and look up into my best friend's sea-blue eyes.

He shakes his head, and his perfect lips transform into his signature Valentine smirk. The only reason he's here is because I can't drive that far alone, and he's the best travel buddy.

Eventually, I find it, take a screenshot of the email, and text it to Harrison in case he needs it when I'm occupied with Joey for the next few days. I punch in the four-digit code, twist the knob, then push the door open. Vaulted ceiling, fake plants everywhere, and a breakfast nook for two … it's adorable.

Harrison sets down his bag as I walk down the hallway, giving myself a tour.

"Uhh," I say, meeting back up with him.

"What's up?" He stretches, lifting his arms above his head.

I open the booking app and read the description of the place before I look at him. He crosses his arms and waits for me to speak with his brows raised.

"There's only one bed."

He glances at the brown leather couch that's seen better days, and even I know his six-foot-three body will not fit on it comfortably.

"We used to share beds all the time when we were kids. We can go back to that," I explain.

Harrison shakes his head. "Nah, it's fine. It's just for a couple of days. The couch will work … if I even come back after hittin' up downtown."

Him going home with someone after a night of fun isn't anything new. Considering his reputation, if he didn't, I'd be shocked. But that's just the way things are, the way they've always been. He's a wild mustang, at least for now, and whoever he ends up with will be one lucky lady.

He continues, "Plus, I don't want your boyfriend gettin' jealous."

"For the last time, Joey doesn't care about us. But how about this? What if I promise *not* to fart on you and swear that I won't try to snuggle?" I hold out my finger for a pinkie promise.

He makes a face and playfully slaps my hand away. "Okay, but what if I like your farts?"

I snort. "See, and this is why we're friends. You're only here for the toots."

"You know it. But honestly, I probably won't see you once you're with *Joooeeeeey.*" He says his name in the high-pitched voice he uses when he's trying to impersonate me.

"You're right because, once I'm there, I don't plan on leaving his house—or rather, his bed. Especially since I got waxed from front to back *just* for this weekend."

"Thanks for sharing with the entire class. We all learned something today." His sarcasm is on point.

"It just shows that I care about personal hygiene. A girl has to landscape."

"Was happy, livin' my best life, not knowing your butthole is silky smooth. Remember that talk we've had a million times over the years? There are some things I absolutely, one hundred percent do *not* need to know." He holds up his hand and counts. "That includes menstrual cycles and sex shit. And, no, I don't want to guess dudes' dick sizes either. Some things are *off-limits*."

I notice how he says the last word. "Just remember, *you chose me* as your best friend. Now you're stuck with me, and you're kinda forced to listen to me talk about all the things I want to talk about, including Aunt Flo and butt plugs. BFFs *forever*, remember?"

"And somehow, you made our friendship sound like prison."

"Well, being with me *is* a life sentence." I glance out the back patio door into the backyard. "Oh, I forgot to tell you, there's a hot tub. We should get in it tonight." I reach forward and grab my suitcase.

"I'd be down for that. Lucky for you, I packed my swim trunks."

He gives me his signature boyish grin, the one that melts panties and snatches phone numbers from thin air, and I fully understand the allure. Harrison Valentine is like a mythical creature because men like him don't exist. But I'm the lucky one who gets to call him my BFF.

"Wouldn't have mattered. You'd have just skinny-dipped."

"You're fuckin' right about that." He shoots me a wink. "So, what's the plan tonight?"

When his ass hits the couch cushions, it sounds like he plopped down on pure plywood. "Shit. It's hard as a fuckin' rock."

"We're sleeping together. And it's not up for discussion."

"Gracie, if you want to share a bed with me, all you have to do is ask. You don't have to come up with these big, elaborate plans like this just to get me between the sheets with you. You know what I mean?" And the devil smirks again.

I playfully swat at him, missing because he predicted it. He's always predicting my moves like we're playing a game of chess.

"That's it. You're absolutely getting all my snuggles tonight. I don't care how much you complain or say you hate it." My voice lowers to a dangerous level as I threaten him. "My leg is getting wrapped around yours, and there is nothing you can do about it other than take it. You're *fucked*."

"So help me God, if you even think about crossing that invisible line in the middle of the mattress, I'll tickle you until you scream bloody murder and piss your pajama pants. And I won't apologize for it either."

I shrug. "I'm more than willing to take my chances."

"You've been warned," he says. "Not to change the subject, but I'm starving. Wanna order in? I'm getting hangry."

It's just past six, and my stomach is growling too. "Yeah, that'd be great. Whatcha in the mood for?"

Before he can answer, my phone buzzes in my back pocket, interrupting the conversation. I pull it out and see the name flash on the screen.

"Just choose something and order. You know what I like. Gonna take this." I show him Joey's picture that I saved from his online dating profile. It's what I saw for months before we made it official and decided to go for the long-distance thing.

Harrison gives me a thumbs-up as I walk down the hallway toward the bedroom. I sit on the edge of the mattress and then answer.

"Hey, baby," he says as I kick off my shoes.

We talk every day on his way home from the office. It's quickly become one of our traditions, something that I look forward to Monday through Friday. Sometimes, I feel like it's the only time we can talk.

"Hi. How was your day?" I grin, knowing just how close I am to him, and if I weren't exhausted, I'd pop over tonight.

"It was good. Had a lot of meetings. I'll be happy when this month is over. There is so much work to complete before the end of the year." He pauses. "I just wish you were here with me right now."

When the words leave his mouth, my heart flutters.

I lean back on the bed. "You do?"

"Yeah. I can't stop thinking about you."

"Aww. I've been thinking about you too. Whatcha doin' tomorrow?"

I stretch out on the mattress. It's soft, and I know tonight I'll sleep like a baby. Especially if Harrison isn't stubborn and actually sleeps beside me. He's always so warm.

Joey continues, "I've got a few errands to run in the morning, but I'll be home after then. I might read a book."

"Well, if you're bored after lunch, call me. I'm not doin' much." *Except for driving to your house.*

His tone turns gravelly. "Maybe we can FaceTime?"

"Yeah, I'd love that." I know exactly what that means. Lately, we've been sexting and fooling around together on camera. It's been fun, but it's just not the same as being with someone physically.

Several times over the past year, we've tried to meet up, but it hasn't always worked out. Just once, but we couldn't be together because he was in a rush.

After this weekend, I hope he realizes what he could have every day.

"I miss you," I say, wishing we could spend more time together.

He laughs. "I know. I miss you so damn much. If only you were closer."

"What if I moved to Houston?" I ask with my eyes closed, knowing he can't leave the city because of his job and position.

I can hear the excitement in his voice. "Oh, so is the option on the table now?"

"*Maybe.* While I love Valentine, I'd move for my forever person." As I'm staring at the ceiling, I hear the bathroom door click closed. Valentine is my hometown in West Texas, and it's named after Harrison's family.

Moments later, Harrison walks out, wearing a pair of swim trunks that hang haphazardly on his carved waist. Muscles cascade down his body as he leans against the doorframe and mouths, *Hot tub.*

Swallowing hard, I pull my gaze away from him and nod, returning to my conversation. "I was hoping you'd be able to come visit during Christmas. My mom and stepdad are dying to meet you before the end of the year since our one year is tomorrow."

"I didn't forget." His voice lowers. "And I'll check my request on Monday and will confirm. But you know it's a very busy time at the office, so I'm sure it will be denied."

"You never know." I sigh, trying to stay hopeful.

"Good news is, I've already got approval for your sister's wedding. I can't wait to be your plus-one, baby. Me and you in Hawaii. We're going to have a good time."

"I'm looking forward to it. I seriously cannot wait."

I daydream about walking the beach with him, making love in our balcony room, and just spending time together. Maybe watch the sunset, view the moon over the water, walk the beach hand in hand, dance barefoot in the sand—all the *movie magic* things that couples in love do.

"Me neither." He quickly changes the subject. "Sorry to cut it short, babe. I think I need to let you go because the traffic is getting heavier. I just wanted to call and tell you how much I love you."

I laugh. "I love you too. Hope you have a good night."

"Chat tomorrow?"

"You'd better believe it," I say, knowing I have the perfect plan in place.

"Good night, Grace."

I end the call and set my phone down next to me on the bed. I've been trying to imagine the look on his face when I see him. I like to think he'll be happy, and I'll fall into his arms, and we'll make love until the sun sets.

Or maybe I'm a hopeless romantic, and we'll fuck right there on the floor. At this point, I don't care. I crave intimacy and not from a stranger. Whoever I'm with next, I want them to know me and love me.

When I return to the living room, I grab my suitcase and then change into the two-piece bathing suit that accentuates my curves, which I've learned to appreciate over the years.

As a teenager, I wouldn't have been caught dead wearing something that showed my stomach, but years ago, I decided to step outside of my comfort zone and not care what anyone thought anymore. All thanks to Harrison questioning why I gave two shits about what anyone thought. Something he reminds me of often.

Since then, it's been crop tops, miniskirts, bikinis. Nothing is off-limits for my body. *Not anymore.*

As I make my way through the kitchen with a towel tucked under my arm, I notice a bottle of wine on the counter. I wrap my long hair into a top bun, snapping the ponytail holder from my wrist, then pick up the note.

"Aww," I say, seeing the host left this as a welcoming gift and take it outside with me.

Before I open the sliding door, I catch sight of Harrison with his muscular arms stretched out as he relaxes in the hot tub with his eyes closed. I drink him in and ask myself how the boy I used to eat mud pies with became *this* man.

Harrison Valentine is tall, handsome, and stacked with muscles from working with horses all his life. He even has a cute little dimple that's buried in his right cheek that only makes an appearance when he genuinely smiles. With his dark, messy hair and go-with-the-flow attitude, Southern charm and manners, and the ability to make anyone laugh at the wrong time … well, he's the catch of the century.

The only problem?

No one is catching him.

Not even me. But that's because of our pact. The unspoken one, where we don't cross the line regardless of how many drinks we've had.

His long, dark eyelashes flutter open when I step outside, and his smoldering gaze pierces through me. Harrison's sexiness, without even trying, wounds me.

"I brought this." I hold up the bottle. Feeling the brisk winter breeze, I shiver. It's in the upper forties, and my nipples are so hard that they could cut glass.

His eyes dart up and down my body, and he grins, but he doesn't say shit. "Come join me. It feels amazing."

After setting down my towel, I climb in and move next to him. The jets spray against my tense muscles. I hand him the wine, then roll my neck around. It cracks a few times.

"Want me to rub your shoulders?"

"Oh God, yes."

I move in front of him, and his strong hands are on me. His thumbs dig into my neck and knead the knots away. I close my eyes, enjoying how well he works me, how he knows *exactly* what I need.

"You're tight." His breath brushes against my neck, and goose bumps form.

"Mmhmm. But, damn, do I like it hard." I laugh, fully melting into his touch. "If training doesn't work out for ya, you should look into becoming a massage therapist. You'd be fully booked."

He snickers, his hands sliding up my neck, and he digs his fingertips into the base of my head, adding more pressure as he turns me into putty. "I'll keep that in mind."

It grows quiet, other than the breeze through the trees and the sound of the jets moving water around us.

He softly clears his throat. "Can I ask you a serious question?"

I glance at him over my shoulder, barely meeting his eyes, but he doesn't stop massaging me. "Sure."

"Are you moving?"

He gives it to me a little harder, and a breathy moan escapes me.

"Ah." I try to recover. "So you heard that?"

He clears his throat. "I wasn't eavesdropping. I just—"

"No, it's fine. Real talk? Sometimes, I think about leaving Valentine. And for *love*, I would."

He doesn't say anything.

I smirk over my shoulder, the bun in my hair nearly smacking him. "Would you miss me if I left?"

He rolls his eyes. "Don't make it weird."

I fully turn around and face him, placing my hands on his thighs. The lights from the hot tub cast reflections on our faces. "You would. You have fun with me. Just admit it."

Harrison exhales. "You know I'd miss you, Gracie."

I smile. "Me too though. Sometimes, you're the only reason I stay. I mean, because who else is going to watch sappy '90s rom-coms with me?"

"You're right about that. I'm kinda irreplaceable, babe." He smiles. "So I guess that means you two are serious?"

I hand him the wine. "Yeah, it's been a year, and if he wants to progress the relationship forward, then I want to give us a real chance. My lease doesn't expire for another six months. So I have time to think about it."

"Why didn't you tell me?" He looks hurt.

"I didn't want to talk about things until I knew for sure. No use in worrying about something until it's reality, ya know?"

"Right. But I'd still like to be prepared. And not find out, like, *two weeks* before you leave or something."

"Well, since we're on the subject, can I count you in for helping me pack my shit?"

Harrison shakes his head, removing his hands from me, and I roll my neck around.

"You just want me for my muscles and my truck. It's all I'm good for."

I laugh, giving him a smile. "Doesn't every woman?"

"Point taken."

"But I'm sure there are many other qualities you've got goin' for you." My eyes slide up and down his body. "Like—"

Just as I'm about to say something, a loud *ding-dong* sweeps the moment away.

"Was that the doorbell?" I ask.

"Oh shit, yeah. The pizza. Hold on."

He quickly stands, water sloshing around, and steps out of the hot tub. He runs through the backyard barefoot and opens the side gate. Moments later, he returns with a large pizza box in his hand. When he opens it up and the meaty aroma wafts my way, my mouth waters. I see cheese and a thick crust with pepperoni, mushrooms, and black olives.

"You're speaking my love language!" I stand with the wine held tightly in my grip.

Harrison holds out his hand, helping me down so I don't bust my ass. While I was nearly sweating in the water, now that I'm out, I'm cold. He hands me the pizza then wraps a towel around me before doing the same.

"Let's light the fireplace," I tell him once we're inside.

"Good idea."

Water drips down his chest, and he hurries and dries off before walking through the house. I set the box down on the coffee table, grab two cups for our wine and napkins.

With one click of a button, the flame immediately catches on the faux logs.

"This is cheating. A gas fireplace."

Once everything is set up, I turn to him. "I'm gonna change into my pj's. I'll be right back."

"Me too," he says, unzipping his duffel.

My stomach growls as I remove my swimsuit, dry off, then change into my silk cami with matching sleep shorts.

When I walk into the living room, Harrison's wearing dark-gray joggers and nothing else as he flicks through the channels.

His eyes scan my body. "Should you be saving that sleepwear for your boyfriend?"

"He gets my birthday suit. But why? Do you think it makes me look hot?" I sit next to him and elbow him.

He bumps his body against mine. "If my girlfriend was wearing that around another man …"

"Oh, so you're the jealous type?"

"When it comes to *my* woman, *you'd* better believe it."

He meets my eyes, and there is no doubt he means every damn word. But … I swallow hard, knowing there absolutely is not a deeper meaning in his words. Because there can't be.

"What were you going to say outside?"

"Don't remember. Remind me what we were talking about." I reach forward and open the box, happy for the distraction.

"I don't remember either," he says.

But I have a feeling neither of us forgot as we slide our fingers under fat slices and take a bite.

"This is so good. Oh my God," I say around a mouthful. My eyes widen.

Harrison laughs. "The place had incredible reviews. Like thousands. It's a mom-and-pop shop, been around for forty years or something. Originated in Chicago, I think."

"It's"—I moan—"better than sex."

He nearly chokes on the bite he's swallowing. "That tells me you haven't been with anyone worth remembering."

"You're right about that, but hopefully, that will change tomorrow. Cheers."

We tap our pizza slices together and eat while we watch TV.

When an episode of *Yellowstone* ends, Harrison asks me if I want any more.

"Nah. I've got a food baby," I say, patting my belly.

He chuckles, then reaches forward, brushing his thumb close to the corner of my mouth. When he pulls away, there's marinara on the end. And suddenly, it feels like we're twelve again, having a slumber party at his parents' house, eating pizza and watching rated-R movies. Neither of us would turn our heads during the sex scenes.

"I'm gonna miss the fuck outta you if you move away."

I smile. "Now, don't be getting all soft on me. You can always come visit."

He stands and takes the rest of the pizza into the kitchen. I hear the fridge door open and close, and then he washes his hands. Immediately, I start yawning. I turn and look at the time on the microwave. It's just past eight.

"I kinda wanna watch TV in bed. Wanna join me?"

He smiles. "You promise not to trample over that invisible line?"

"I don't make promises to you that I can't keep."

And he knows that's the truth. I stand and stretch, then make my way down the hallway.

As I flick on the light in the bedroom, I yell, "Come on, bestie. Don't be as stubborn as a mule. Your back is gonna hate you tomorrow if you choose that shitty couch!"

As I'm pulling down the comforter on both sides, Harrison stands in the doorway, all man and muscle with those joggers on his waist. "Pick your side and then follow the rules."

"That's real rich, coming from the number one rule breaker I know."

CHAPTER TWO

HARRISON

Grace climbs under the blankets and pats the opposite side of the bed. "You know you can't deny me."

She gives me that confident look of hers, the one where she knows she's right.

"Are you gonna play nice?" I cross my arms over my chest, not budging.

Her brown hair is splashed across the pillow as she sinks into the mattress, letting out a relieved sigh. Grace closes her eyes. "So comfortable. Would be better if my bestie were here. After he turned off the lights."

This isn't the first time Grace and I have ever shared a bed, and I'm sure it won't be the last. When we were kids, we bunked together on trips until we were teenagers, when hormones were raging. As soon as Grace got boobs, our mothers refused. Probably for the best.

It's not even a big deal now, but I like to poke at her about it because her last boyfriend lost his shit. I mean, I get it. I wouldn't want my woman sharing a bed with a man like me either. But with me and Grace, it's different. We are *just* friends who talk about farting, buttholes, and everything else. And because we've experienced every embarrassing thing together, we're overly comfortable.

She knows me better than anyone. But it goes both ways.

I climb under the sheets and tug the blankets over my chest, then realize how cold it is in this house. I sit straight up and turn on the lamp next to the bed.

"Where are you going?" Grace opens her eyes.

"I'm turning on the heat." I place my feet on the floor and stand.

"Good idea. I thought it was just me."

"I'll be right back."

I make my way down the hallway and spot the thermostat on the wall. It's not on. I flick on a light, and the inside temperature reads sixty degrees. I click a few buttons and then wait for the furnace to rumble. Nothing happens. So, I slide the temperature gauge to eighty. Still nothing.

I go to the bedroom. "It's broken."

"What?" Her voice goes up an octave.

"Yep. You'll have to call the host tomorrow and let them know."

She groans. "That sucks. I'm gonna be an ice cube tonight."

"Let me see if I can find some extra blankets."

I grab my phone, turn on my flashlight and search in every closet. There's a quilt folded in the linen closet and a throw blanket draped over the back of the couch, so I swipe them both. It's better than nothing.

I place them on top of the comforter, then crawl back between the sheets. Grace stretches and touches me with her cold-as-fuck toes.

"Holy shit, woman!" I jolt away from the icicles. "Your feet are frigid! Get those things off of me!"

"They're going to fall off! Help me!" She stretches her feet out further and presses them against my thighs.

"Ow!" I try to wiggle away, but I'm also laughing my ass off.

"This is another reason why I didn't want to share a bed. You make me sweat. Plus, your fingers and toes are always like this!"

"You're going to mistreat my poor tootsies like that? I'm finding a new bestie to share a bed with who doesn't mind if I touch all over them. I don't have cooties." She playfully pouts.

I get up and walk out of the room. "I can promise you, no one is going to ever want those icy nubs on them. No one."

"Oh, come on! Don't sleep on the couch. I need your body heat tonight. Don't make me beg."

I chuckle as I search for my duffel bag in the living room.

As I unzip it, she continues, "Okay, fine. I'll beg if that's what you want."

"Waiting."

I stop digging for a brief moment and wait. Silence. Then, I reach in and find the thick socks that I like to wear with my boots in the winter. I grab them in my fist and go back to the bedroom, but I stop at the doorway.

"Oh, I'm sorry, I didn't hear you *begging*."

"Pretty please with cherries on top. I will play nice." Her nipples are rock hard and poking through the silk tank top she's wearing. She notices me take a peek. She clears her throat. "I know. I seriously have tits of mass destruction right now because it's so cold. Imagine how cold my toes are. My nipples aren't any better."

"You didn't ask me to warm those up," I say, my words very clear.

When she gulps, I burst into laughter, walking toward her. Then I pull the comforter down and grab one of her ankles.

"Hey!" She kicks. "You'd better not be tryin' to hog-tie me!"

She yelps with laughter as I slide a sock on one foot, then the other. Then I rub my hands across them, trying to create some sort of friction. I used to warm her feet up like this when we were kids.

She sighs with relief, and I help reposition the blankets on her.

"Good night, princess. Keep your body parts to yourself."

"I'll try." She snickers. "Thank you."

"Welcome." I climb back into bed and roll over on my side. With my back facing her, I close my eyes.

"You're too good to me," she whispers.

If she wasn't taken and I wasn't chickenshit, I'd be good to her in other ways, too, but I keep that to myself.

My body relaxes, and I slowly begin to drift off. Right before I fall asleep, she speaks.

"Do you remember the first time we kissed?" she asks.

"Yes." I laugh with a sigh. "I distinctly remember you telling me that you needed to practice before homecoming because you were nervous about kissing your date."

That was the *only* time we've ever crossed the unspoken off-limits line. However, Gracie has tempted me on more than one occasion.

She rolls over, moves in, and wraps her arm around me. Her breasts are pressed against my back, and her warm, hot breath flutters against my skin.

I turn and try to look at her, but she's too close. "You agreed to *no* snuggling."

"Shh." She squeezes me tight.

"Gracie," I groan.

She sighs and then rolls away from me. "Fine. I'll freeze over here instead. Nice knowing you."

Of course, I feel guilty, but I also know we won't be able to do this forever. One day, we'll be married and living our own lives. I can't imagine her future husband would ever allow this, so I'll take what I can.

I move in close to her, wrapping my arm around her waist and pulling her into my body.

"You're toasty," she says, relaxing against me. She releases a contented sigh.

"I hope you know you're the *only* woman I spoon with." I think I feel her smile. "Good night, Gracie."

"Night, Harri."

And then I'm left wide awake, holding her, until her breathing slows.

Tomorrow, she'll be with her boyfriend with hopes of moving their relationship forward.

In six months, she might move to the other side of the state.

While I'm exhausted, I lie awake. I take it all in, knowing that we're growing up but hoping we're not growing apart.

It's in the silent moments when I hold her like this that I wish things were different.

I WAKE up without an alarm because I'm sweating. I don't know when I rolled over in the middle of the night, but Grace is holding me, lightly snoring like a Disney princess in my ear. She's also sleeping in the middle of the bed, hogging all the space, with her leg wrapped around mine, like usual.

When I slide out from under the blanket, it feels like the middle of July. I grab my phone, noticing it's a few minutes before five. Of course it is. Working on the ranch all my life has ruined my internal clock.

Going back to sleep won't happen, so I get up and curse the thermostat before turning it off. Guess it's not broken; it's just cranky.

I grab a cup of water and chug it, needing this headache that I can feel coming to go away. Probably dehydrated, but it doesn't stop me from brewing a pot of coffee. I pour a cup of coffee, leaning against the counter as I glance at notifications on my phone. I didn't check anything yesterday while we were driving.

The first person I text back is my brother. Beckett is several years older than me, and we're business partners. We've been training horses and teaching people to ride them since we were young teens. After he purchased the Horseshoe Creek Ranch with the love of his life, we built a large training facility. I called in several favors and did tons of begging to be able to join Grace on this trip.

Once I press Send, his text bubble immediately pops up. Of course his ass is awake. His internal alarm clock is like Old Faithful too.

BECKETT

Oh, lookee, you're actually alive. I texted you yesterday and heard jack shit from you.

HARRISON

Sorry about that. I was occupied. You know, driving across the fucking state.

HE LOVES to give me a hard time, but it's a two-way street with us.

BECKETT

How's Houston?

HARRISON

The traffic makes me want to never drive again.

BECKETT

Sounds about right. So, today is the day? You
gonna meet him?

THE SITUATION WAS HEAVILY DISCUSSED before I left, and he knows exactly why I'm here—to make sure Grace is safe. She met this fuck on a dating app and has seen him a few times over the year. He's practically a stranger.

Then, I think back to our chat last night. I didn't realize how serious she was about this man, and none of it is sitting well with me. While I want to meet—threaten—him, I don't want to do anything to influence her relationship.

HARRISON

Nah, I'm gonna drop her off, then head to
the bar.

BECKETT

I hope you have fun. Wear protection. And try to
make it home in one piece.

HARRISON

Will do.

BECKETT

It's gonna work out.

HARRISON

Thanks, bro.

TODAY MIGHT BE one of the longest days of my life. I voiced my concerns when she invited me on this trip, but I was told to stop acting like an older brother. No matter how hard I try, I can't do that. Protecting her, making sure she's safe, is something I've been doing since we were kids. That ain't changing.

After I finish one cup of coffee, I open a dating app to find my next distraction. Gonna be honest—this part of Texas has some attractive women. If their profile makes me laugh and they're attractive, I swipe right.

Just as I'm going for cup two, I hear feet walking across the floor, and moments later, Grace enters the kitchen. Her dark, long hair is a mess, and she smiles up at me. Then she chugs a cup of water.

"Thirsty?" I ask, laughing.

"For more than just this," she mutters.

I glance down, noticing she's still wearing the socks I gave her.

She looks at them too. "These were cozy. Instantly fell asleep once my toes were warm."

"You sure it was the socks?" I lift a brow, looking at her over my mug.

A sly grin meets her lips, and there's an underlying current streaming between us. Or maybe I'm just tired.

"Could've been little Harri pokin' my back all night."

"Pfft. Little? *Please.*"

She snorts and sits on the stool. "Show me then. Prove me wrong."

I meet her eyes. "You sure about that?"

"Nah, I was kiddin'. Don't want to see your sausage this early in the morning."

My phone vibrates, and I get a notification from the dating app.

Grace glances down at it. "You should let me pick your dates."

I unlock it and hand it to her. "Go for it. You know what I like."

She starts swiping and stops. "Oh, she's really pretty."

Grace turns the phone around and shows me.

"Gorgeous." I meet her eyes, knowing for damn sure I ain't talking about that stranger on the app. "Want some breakfast?"

Her eyes quickly slide up and down my body. "I had them stock the fridge with food. Should have some bacon and eggs in there. I can cook for us."

"I got this," I say, opening the fridge and pulling everything out.

Grace yawns, and I pour her a cup of coffee and add the perfect amount of vanilla cream.

She sips, then hums. "Nailed it."

"The color of caramel."

I grab a skillet from a lower cabinet and place it on the stovetop. Once it's hot, I carefully put slices of bacon on the bottom, and it immediately sizzles.

"That smells so good," she says.

When I turn around to meet her gaze, she's looking down at *her* phone, smiling. Joey must already be awake and texting her.

After the bacon is crispy, I start the eggs. Grace loves hers cooked over easy, so I carefully flip them so they don't get rubbery. A minute later, I hand her a fork and a napkin and then sit beside her at the little nook.

She bumps her body against mine.

"Thank you, Prince Harri."

"You're welcome, Princess Grace."

It reminds me of the moment I *officially* made her my best friend in first grade. Our class dressed up for Halloween, and I was Prince Charming and Grace was Cinderella. Of course, our mothers coordinated it because they're best friends.

Six-year-old me wanted her to be my princess forever. I even told her as much.

Grace cuts open her eggs, and the yellow yolk runs out. She mixes the white with it and takes a mouthful. I do the same.

She locks her phone and then slightly turns her body toward me. "I'm actually nervous about today."

"Are you sure it's not excitement?" I meet her brown eyes.

"It might be."

"He's gonna be thrilled to see you, especially knowing you drove all this way to be with him. Men love that."

She laughs. "True. I was thinking I would do the whole *knock on his door, wearing a coat*."

"And?"

"And when he answers, I'll open it and show him the lingerie I picked out just for him."

"Like a flasher?"

"Exactly like that. Would you be surprised if that happened to you?"

"If a woman that I love and haven't seen in months shows up on my doorstep, wearing sexy-as-fuck lingerie …"

She nods.

I smirk. "I'd be fuckin' thrilled. Probably wouldn't make it off the porch though. Ain't nobody got time for that."

"I don't want it to seem like the start of a bad porno though. Tell me the truth. Is it *too … cheesy?*" Her nose squishes.

"I mean, it *is*, but it's also so adorably *you*. So, I say, go for it. Be yourself, princess. Who gives a shit if it's cheesy?"

A wide smile fills her face, and I see that twinkle in her eye. I know that look—it's the in-love one. I hope this one lasts, but if it doesn't, I'll pick up the shattered pieces of her broken heart and help her glue it back together again.

She's a hopeless romantic, still searching for her fairy tale, and I want her to have her happily ever after. But with *me*.

"Thanks, Harri. I needed that pep talk."

I smirk, then bring my attention back to my food. She's the only person in the world I've ever allowed to call me that.

It doesn't take long before we're finished eating. I wash our dishes and then doomscroll on social media to busy my mind as Grace quietly works on her laptop.

She's the receptionist at the local newspaper, but she's also been helping my older sister, Kinsley, with a new weekly article that's launching the first week of January. It's called Dear Kinsley, and my sister is answering anonymous questions from the townsfolk.

Hours pass, and we have lunch, and then Grace rejects Joey's call. And I know it's him because of the number of vibrations her phone does. I look over my shoulder at her, hoping she changed her mind.

"It's a part of my plan. We were supposed to FaceTime and get naked … which means he's ready for me."

"Eww. *Way* too much information. Keep that shit to yourself."

"I've got to get dressed!"

She's giddy, and I love seeing her this happy.

"Nothin' to worry about at all. Promise ya that," I confirm, trying to be as supportive as possible. My lower back hurts from sitting on this concrete couch all day.

She stands and rushes to the bedroom. "I'll be right back."

When the door closes, I lean my head back, knowing I need to snap out of this funk. I take in a few deep breaths and promise myself that I won't barge through his door and ask him a million questions before I leave her there. I will not bash his face in. I will not sit outside of his house and wait like a stalker.

I run my fingers through my hair.

When Grace returns, she's wearing a long black trench coat over her curvy body. The waist is cinched with a tie, and her hair is in bouncy curls. Her high heels match the ruby-red lipstick she's wearing, and I can see the black fishnets. If I had to guess though, I'd say they're thigh-highs. More her style.

My mouth slightly parts, and she nearly steals my damn breath away. My best friend is fucking gorgeous.

"Too much?" She chews on the corner of her plump bottom lip—something she sometimes does when she's nervous.

"No." I clear my throat and stand. "Not at all. Give me a spin."

She does and then tucks hair behind her ear before breaking eye contact.

"He'd better never let you go."

She grins. "I hope he doesn't."

There is more I *want* to say, but the moment passes by like a warm summer breeze. So, I change the subject. "Give me five, and I'll be ready too."

As I pass her, I stop and place my hand on her shoulder. "You've got this."

She shoves her hands in her deep pockets. "I do."

I grab my duffel from the floor and pull out some jeans and a polo, and then I go to the bathroom. I lean against the door for a few seconds, knowing I need to stop the turmoil swirling inside of me.

I'm just afraid of losing my bestie.

I've been warned about this over and over—that one day, one of us would find a partner and forget about the other. I've seen it with a lot of my guy friends who get married. Hell, even my brother, Beckett. His life now revolves around Summer. And Grace's will revolve around Joey's while I'm still fucking around to forget.

I almost feel guilty for being so … *selfish*. For wanting to keep her all to myself. But my intuition is hardly wrong, especially when it comes to her.

I splash cold water on my face, hoping it will jolt some sense into me. It doesn't, so I push away the nagging thoughts and plaster a cocky-as-fuck smile on my face. I'm good at pretending. Well-practiced.

Once I'm dressed, I meet her in the living room. As I slip on my boots, I steal glances at Grace.

When she looks at me, I laugh and shake my head.

"What?"

"Nothin'."

"You'd better tell me," she warns.

"Was just thinking about what Sadie said yesterday when I stopped to get us donuts."

Sadie is the bakery owner who used to babysit me as a kid. She always gives me a hard time about Grace. But then again, who doesn't?

"Well?"

"It wasn't nothin' she hasn't ever said before."

She lets out a sigh. "You're doing that thing where you kinda tell me what someone says, but not really."

I walk past her. "Let's get goin'."

"No, no, no." She walks toward me, her heels clicking on the floor, then playfully pokes her finger into my chest and presses me against the door. "You're gonna tell me, mister." Her face goes from semiserious to a smirk. "Oh God, you're wearing that cologne."

I lift a brow. "I always wear it when I go out."

"Seriously brought some weird memories."

"Weird?" I make a face.

"I should've said *good* memories, but it was weird they came to mind."

I lift my brows, and she takes a step back, removing the space between us. I wonder what she remembered. Our history is decades long, so no telling.

She narrows her eyes. "You're distracting. What were we talking about?"

I shrug, and she follows me outside, holding her coat close to her body just in case the wind blows it open. We climb inside the truck, and I immediately turn on the heat. Dark, ominous clouds hang over us, and they meet my turmoil.

"Is it supposed to rain?" she asks, looking out the windshield.

I realize I didn't check the radar this morning. "Kinda looks like it, doesn't it?"

She pulls her attention away and navigates us to the destination.

On the way there, my body temperature rises, and I try to find the right words to say before I drop her off.

After one last turn, we arrive at a two-story home with a fountain in the front. The neighborhood is ridiculous, with cobblestone driveways and bushes that are stories high.

I lean forward, staring at the double oak doors of this man's mansion.

Then she looks at me proudly. "This is it."

I meet her eyes, finding it hard to let her go. "It is. Good luck. Make sure he wears protection."

"Oh God, you sound like my *mom*."

"If you need me, please call me. Okay? I don't care where I am or what I'm doing."

"You're still going with the parent thing."

I zero in on her. "I just want you to be careful. I know how *some* men are. I am one, okay?"

"Okay." She nods, fidgeting with the hem of her coat. "Did you figure out what you're gonna do tonight?"

"Not yet. It's gonna be a *choose my own adventure, fuck around and find out* kinda night."

"Same." She licks her lips like she's going to say something else but doesn't.

"Go have fun. Get outta here. *Joooeeeeey* is on the other side of that door." I force a laugh.

"Yeah, he is. I'll see ya."

I give her a wave and watch her get out of the truck.

Grace struts down the sidewalk like it's her runway, swinging her sexy hips in those heels. Before she makes it to the door, she turns and gives me a thumbs-up. Then she takes a few steps forward and rings the doorbell.

CHAPTER THREE

GRACE

It's colder outside than I expected, and the cool draft sneaks its way up the bottom of my coat, which falls right above my calves.

After I give Harrison a thumbs-up, I reach forward and ring the doorbell, admiring the stonework on this gigantic house. I looked up his place before visiting and saw a picture of it online. Even though I knew what to expect, it's larger in real life.

Through the glass, I see someone walking toward the door. My heart rate increases because I know Joey is just feet away. So I carefully untie my coat.

When the door swings open, I smile, then open both sides, revealing the red lingerie I bought just for him. *"Surprise."*

He pulls me close and kisses me, stealing my breath away. Our tongues slide together, and I wrap my arms around his neck. I hear the mean roar of Harrison's truck as he drives away.

"You're so sexy," Joey mutters against my lips, leading me inside. He shuts the door, pressing my body against the cold wood. "What are you doing here?" He searches my face.

"I came to surprise you for our anniversary."

He takes my hand, leading me down the hallway that opens

into the huge living room with plush white furniture. I look around, amazed, but he's staring at me. I meet his gaze, and then I see he's hard for me.

Our mouths find each other again, and we stumble to the couch. He pops my breasts outside of the bra and sucks on my nipples, then licks my neck before sucking my earlobe.

I sit up, reaching for his belt, desperately needing to feel him inside me. This will be our first time together. The anticipation nearly kills me.

"I told you I didn't like surprises, but, baby girl, I'll take you any day."

I desperately unzip his pants, needing him. And just as I lift my ass to pull down my panties, I hear the doorbell.

Joey looks pissed, and all I can think is Harrison decided to act like my big brother after all. Then, seconds later, I hear a beeping, like someone is punching in a security code.

"Get up," he says. "Hurry."

I pull up my panties, and he leads me to a closet, then pushes me inside. Like I'm a mop.

"Joey!" a high-pitched female voice says as he closes the door.

It's dark. I'm cold and confused. My heart rate is ticking so hard it causes my head to pound. None of it makes sense as I try to understand what the fuck is going on.

"Sweetheart, you're home. I missed you so much. What a surprise!"

Even though it's pitch black in this small space, I see red. Emotions flood through me as I realize I've become … the *home-wrecker*.

The *other* woman.

His younger *mistress*.

I can hear their loud kisses and smacking.

"You're so hard for me," she says and laughs.

I want to throw up.

"Always, baby. It's 'cause you're always on my mind."

Tears form on the brim of my eyes, confirming he recycles the same lines between us. I cry because I've become exactly what I was so scared of being after my parents' divorce—the other woman.

For most of my life, I blamed my dad's second wife for destroying our family. My therapist believes that divorce is the root of all my relationship problems. I'd agree. But for the first time in my life, I realize Tanya never deserved my anger; my father did.

"Joey, yes!" she screams out.

I wrap my arms around my body as I listen to them fuck. Her cries, his groans, and their bodies clap together all the way to the dramatic finish.

"You think we made another baby?" She giggles, and I cover my mouth so my sobs aren't heard.

As I blink away tears, I want to text Harrison and tell him to come get me. But my goddamn phone is in my coat pocket on the living room floor.

"I hope so. I love you."

"I love you too. What's that noise?" his wife asks.

The timing is remarkable. Iconic even. Couldn't have been planned any better. I want to disappear.

"Shit, the cleaning lady must've left her coat. Didn't even notice. I was in my office working. Probably trying to find where she left her phone." His lie comes so fast that my head spins.

I hear him stand and zip up his pants.

I can imagine them on the couch, the place where I would've given myself to him had she not interrupted. And I'm so damn relieved. At least I'll leave with some dignity, knowing I didn't sleep with a cheating bastard.

The woman yawns loudly. "I want a bath. Join me?"

"Yeah, go draw the water, sweetie. I'll be right there."

"Not too long, okay?"

"Not too long," he repeats.

I hear footsteps come closer, and I nearly stop breathing, but thankfully, she keeps going. A minute later, the door opens, and Joey looks at me with sad eyes.

"I can explain everything."

I push him with every bit of my weight. He stumbles back.

"Fuck off," I spit out, and that's when I notice the ring on his left finger. He must've taken it off when he let me in, then put it back on when she arrived. "You're married."

"Yes, but—"

"I don't want your excuses. Leave me alone." I rush past him, quickly grabbing my coat and making my way to the door.

"Grace," he hisses. "I love you, baby girl."

I reach for the handle. "Tell that to your wife. Oh, wait, you just did."

I walk outside, rushing down the steps, holding my coat tight against my body. As soon as I turn onto the sidewalk, thunder rolls.

Tears flood down my face as I frantically call Harrison. It goes to voice mail, and I panic, but I keep walking even if my vision is blurry.

"Harrison, please." I'm nearly sobbing. "*Please* come get me. I left his place. I'm walking. You'll find me."

I hang up and text him, and that's when I notice my phone has one percent.

"No," I whisper, and when the rain starts falling, I'm scared I won't survive heartbreak again, not when my fairy tale quickly turned into a nightmare.

My coat and hair are soaked, and I'm so cold as the winter wind stirs.

When I round the corner, I spot a bus stop that's covered. I sit on the wet bench and sob until my throat is raw. The only thing that pulls me away is my phone.

I answer.

"Gracie, are you okay? I'm on my way to you right now. Where are you?" He's panicked.

"Please be careful. It's raining really bad."

"Now, who's being the parent?" he asks. "Where are you, princess?"

"I don't know. At some random bus stop. And my phone is about to—"

The call ends, and I look up at the sky, the rain pelting hard against my skin.

"Why?!" I scream out.

I place my face in my hands, hoping to God that Harrison arrives quickly. He'll find me. He always does.

Knowing I'm on a different block, I return to the main road, where he'll have a better chance of running into me. I walk for blocks in stripper shoes and not one Mercedes stops to ask if I'm okay. I feel like Julia Roberts in *Pretty Woman* when they wouldn't sell her clothes.

I hate Houston. This would never happen in Valentine. I feel stupid for even considering moving here for that *bastard*.

"Gracie!" I hear from behind me.

I turn to see Harrison walking toward me with an umbrella outstretched. He left the truck running in the middle of the road with the lights on and the windshield wipers sloshing the water away.

When I see him, relief floods me, but I notice the way his jaw is clenched tight and see the anger in his eyes.

He moves the umbrella over me, placing his opposite hand on the small of my back as he stands in the rain. "Did he hurt you?"

I shake my head, unable to form a complete sentence.

"I need to hear you say it." He swallows hard, getting soaked.

"No, we didn't ..." *Have sex.* I can't finish my sentence. I don't need to.

"Okay, okay." His voice lowers as he leads me to the truck. "I'm here. You're safe."

He opens the door, escorting me inside. It's warm, and it smells like his cologne. I see the cup of coffee in his cup holder.

Harrison closes the umbrella and slides inside. He reaches behind the seat and gives me one of his old T-shirts. "It's not much, but it might help some. I wish I had a towel."

I slide off the soaking wet coat, toss it in the back and sit miserably in the expensive lingerie. Instead of using it to dry off, I put it on. At least I feel less naked.

Harrison kicks the truck into drive, and he grabs the coffee and hands it to me. "It'll help you warm up."

I take a sip. "What is this?"

"White chocolate Christmas something. I couldn't make up my mind, so I let the barista choose."

I place both hands on the outside of the cup, tears streaming.

He glances at me. "You want to talk about it?"

I take another drink and shake my head.

Harrison finds a side street and pulls over. "Come here."

He unbuckles and opens his arms, and I fall into them. He holds me and pets my wet hair.

"Why does this always happen to me? What is *wrong* with *me*?"

He gently moves me so he can meet my eyes. "Nothing. There's nothing in the world wrong with you. I don't want you to think that for a damn minute, okay?"

My bottom lip quivers, and he pulls some tissues from his glove box and hands them to me. I blow, making a noise.

"I feel like a cheap whore. I'm so stupid. This is all my fault." I shake my head.

"He's married, isn't he?"

My mouth falls open. "How did you know?"

"Just a feeling. Fucking asshole." Harrison breathes in, and his hand balls into a fist. "I'm sorry, Gracie."

"For what? You didn't do anything wrong."

"Oh, I know. I'm pre-apologizing."

Then, he puts the truck in drive, and we zoom off.

35

CHAPTER FOUR

HARRISON

I see red as I grip the steering wheel.

I should drive us back to the rental, but I can't do that when she's heartbroken again. This time, I can't sit by and do nothing, not when she's blaming herself. Luckily, I'm good with directions, and I remember exactly where the dickwad lives. I take another left, and I slow down in front of his house.

"Harrison." There's sadness in her eyes.

I honestly thought my intuition was wrong. At least, I hoped.

I reach over and brush my thumb across her cheek. "You're too dang pretty to be crying."

She says my name again, but I get out of the truck, walk down his driveway, crack my knuckles, then knock on the door. A busty blonde in a fuzzy house coat answers the door. Her brows lift, and she smiles.

"Howdy, ma'am," I say. "Is your husband here?"

"Are you two friends?" Her eyes move up and down my body.

"Acquaintances."

"Joey," she hollers over her shoulder. "Baby, there's someone here for you."

"Who?" he asks, rounding the corner.

Not a flash of recognition meets his face as he looks at me, trying to figure out who the hell I am. And that's because he never cared about Grace, her friends, or her family. He never tried to meet anyone from Valentine. Makes me wonder how many women he has waiting in the wings.

Joey's brow creases as he moves to the doorway. "I'm not buying anything."

"Oh, I'm not selling you anything. Just wanted to tell you how much of a piece of shit you are." I swing and slam my fist right into his face.

His wife screams and covers her mouth. "Joey?"

"Call the cops. I don't even know who this man is."

"If you ever message or call or even try to see Gracie again, I swear to fucking God Almighty, I'll cut off your dick and shove it down your throat." I spit on him.

"Who's Gracie?"

"A kind, beautiful, funny woman he never fucking deserved."

I turn my back and walk away just as she kicks him in his balls.

"I don't know what he's talking about," he pleads as she screams something.

It's raining harder now, and I rub my knuckles as I make my way back to the truck. When I'm inside, we sit in silence for a minute before I make a U-turn.

She shakes her head. "You shouldn't be fighting my battles."

"Never. Being *my* bestie is a life sentence, babe. Goes both ways."

Grace doesn't say anything the rest of the way back to the rental. She stares out the window, wiping tears away. Knowing she's in pain makes me want to go back over there and beat the shit out of him. But I'm sure his wife is making his life hell. She deserved to know.

When I pull into the driveway, Gracie gets out of the truck, wearing my T-shirt, and I smile when I see the thigh-highs.

She walks in the rain and goes inside. I grab her wet coat from the back seat and follow her. And just like that, the happy-go-lucky girl in love, who was laughing and making jokes yesterday, has vanished, and the toxic cycle of another shitty relationship ending continues.

Classic case of looking for love in all the wrong places.

I'm tempted to burst into the bedroom, pull her into my arms, and tell her it's going to be okay, but I know she needs alone time. Maybe not a lot. Maybe the rest of the night. If she were home, she'd be stress cleaning.

I peel off my wet clothes and change, and then I wait thirty minutes. Then, I go to her. When I walk into the bedroom, she's lying face down on the bed, still in her lingerie, crying.

I walk over to her and sit down, rubbing her back. "Wanna watch your favorite movie?"

"No."

I nod, respecting that. "I'm here for you if you want to talk, and if not, I'm still here. I'm sorry this happened."

"Thank you, me too. I think I just need to be alone."

"Okay."

I walk back into the living room and stare at the blank TV, giving her space. Then, I text my older sister.

HARRISON

Queen Kinsley!

KINSLEY

Uh-oh. What kind of trouble are you in?

HARRISON

I'm not in any trouble. But I have a question. Is it possible to manifest evil?

KINSLEY

How much did you focus on it?

HARRISON

A lot.

KINSLEY

Did anyone die?

HARRISON

Jeez, do you think I'm a monster?

KINSLEY

Do you really want me to answer that?

I SMILE. I don't mind her giving me a hard time. I can take it because I dish it too.

HARRISON

Point taken. Well?

KINSLEY

To answer your question … no. The universe absolutely doesn't respond to negative energy.

HARRISON

Okay, but what if it's a positive for me but a negative for someone else?

SHE IMMEDIATELY CALLS ME, and I answer.

"Did Grace and her boyfriend break up?" She doesn't say hello or anything. No, she just cuts straight to the chase.

"It's not my place to say." I keep my voice low.

"That means they did."

"Hush."

"Welp, little brother, I guess this is your chance to *finally* ask her out before she finds someone else." I hear her shuffling cards.

"You didn't pull out the tarot."

"I sure did. I'm also pulling in all of your energy right now for a love reading."

"I'm letting you go now. Love ya, sis!"

She gasps loudly, being dramatic but also trying to grab my attention. "No way. You're never gonna guess what card I pulled."

"*Goodbye!*" I end the call, not allowing her to pull me into her woo.

While I love her, I don't want to get mixed up in her *told you so* about the cards always being right. Hanging up does nothing though.

She sends me a text, and when I open it, I see a picture of The Lovers card on her coffee table. Then she sends another text.

KINSLEY

This is a twin flames card. It's one of the most powerful cards a person can pull for a love reading! This is HUGE! It talks about complementary energies, raw truths, and a balance of forces.

HARRISON

Now you sound like a Jedi. Stop texting me before I block you.

KINSLEY

I dare you. Because if you do, I'll use one of the many, many favors you owe me and easily get myself unblocked. So try me. This card doesn't represent new love either … friendship moving to something deeper.

HARRISON

BLOCKED!

KINSLEY

ACE. OF. WANDS. OMFG.

HARRISON

Kinsley.

I LET OUT A SIGH. I should've never texted her, even if she's the perfect distraction because she's not helping. Not at all.

KINSLEY

You don't understand. It's I CRAVE YOU energy.
This is huge.

HARRISON

This could mean anything. There are a lot of people who crave me.

KINSLEY

I CHUCKLE.

KINSLEY

The next card. No way. NO FREAKING WAY!

SHE'S BAITING ME. Something she's perfected over the years.

KINSLEY

Oh, come on. You know you're dying inside
because you don't know.

I IGNORE HER.

KINSLEY

Well, I'm gonna tell you anyway. Four of Wands.
This one is all about commitment. Marriage
even. This is deep. Really deep. Wow, next year
is going to be wild for you.

HARRISON

Keep your manifestations to yourself.

KINSLEY

I need to light a love candle for you. Keep me
updated. Rooting for you.

HARRISON

BYE!

I LOCK my phone and set it down, replaying everything that happened. As shitty as it is to admit, I'm relieved it didn't work out. I don't ever want her to experience heartbreak, but she deserves a man who puts her first.

After an hour passes, I take a deep breath and pour two shots of whiskey into glasses.

When I open the door, Grace is where I left her. Her lingerie and high heels are in a pile on the floor, and she's wearing her fuzzy pajama pants and a T-shirt.

"Gracie," I say, sitting on the edge of the bed. "Brought you something."

She glances at me, and I smile, handing her a glass.

She sniffles. "You filled this full."

"Of course I did. Thought you could use a hefty dose of the *I don't give a fuck* syrup."

I hold up my glass, and she does the same.

"To friendship and always being there," she says, then clinks her glass against mine.

"To always being there," I repeat.

Her nose and cheeks are red, and her eyes are swollen from crying.

We shoot down the shots, and she does a little wiggle at the end.

"Will you bring me the bottle?"

"You might feel like shit tomorrow," I warn.

"I feel like shit right now."

I nod and make my way to the living room. I change into something more comfortable, then I grab the whiskey and return to Grace. I slide in next to her, handing her the bottle. She chugs. Then I open my arms, and she falls into them.

"It's gonna be okay. I know you're hurting, and I'm fucking livid over it, but it's better to learn these things now."

"Why does this happen? Why am I the queen of failed relationships?"

I keep my hold on her as she cries on my T-shirt. "I'm probably not the best person to give advice. But I'll tell you this, it ain't you, princess. You're not the problem."

"I am."

I pat her arm, and she pulls away.

I tuck her hair behind her ears and study her pretty face. "You're a bit too gullible."

She crisscrosses her legs, leaning her head against the headboard as our arms brush against one another.

"How did you know he was married?" She takes another swig and then hands me the bottle.

"It was all the red flags."

She sniffles. "Tell me."

"He never went out of his way to visit you. I'd drive across the fucking world for someone I was in love with. I'd literally walk five hundred miles over hot coals. Oh, and how he canceled on Halloween and didn't come to the party. That was bullshit. And even though you told me he might visit for Christmas, I knew he wouldn't. That's not love."

When he canceled visiting her on Halloween, she was devastated. So, I found her a Princess Peach costume to match me and my younger brother Colt's Mario and Luigi costumes. Had she and I planned it together, I'd have probably been Bowser because Lord knows I will steal Grace away from any man and fight them for her.

Her bottom lip quivers. "Oh." Then, more tears fall. "He was supposed to join me for my sister's wedding. Guess I'll be going to that alone, too, like always. I was hoping next year would be different, that I'd be in an incredible relationship. I was looking forward to Hawaii. Now, not so much."

"I'll go with you."

"Really?" She looks at me.

"Yeah. Why not? I don't think I have anything going on other than work. What do I need to do?"

"Nothing. It's all paid for. I just need to change the reservation."

I smile. "We're gonna have a blast. Plus, I've never been before, so it will be a whole-ass experience."

"Toes in the sand, margaritas on the beach. Also, we're staying at a really nice resort." She starts to cry again.

"Hey, hey." I wipe her cheek with my thumb. "Don't think of it as the end, but rather the beginning of something else. Something better."

"At this rate, you're gonna get married before me," she says, and this causes me to burst into laughter.

"Doubt it."

"Why? You can have anyone you want." She makes a face. "You have zero issues finding a date for anything. Right now, you could unlock your phone and pick any phone number in your contacts, and they'd meet you anywhere you asked. I wish I could switch places with you."

I shake my head. "No, you don't."

"One-night stands. Random men tripping over their dicks for me. The ability to walk into a room and command it. I haven't had sex in almost two years. Fuck." She drinks more whiskey, and I think I see her eyes blink at different times.

"Gracie, one-night stands don't fill the void."

"Will you coach me?"

"What?"

"Be my dating coach. Teach me how to be exactly what men want. *Please*?" When she blinks, more tears stream.

"That's really what you want?"

"Yes," she whispers, not waiting a beat. "Right now, I'm not living. And I'm not getting any younger. So it's either that or I need to start adopting cats when I get home; otherwise, I'm gonna be lonely as hell."

"Okay."

"Okay, as in yes?"

"Sure." I shrug, gulping whiskey down, feeling the burn from head to toe.

Grace wraps her arms around me and squeezes me tight. I hold her for a second, kinda hating myself for agreeing, but I'll do whatever it takes to make her happy.

"Know that being the woman every man wants isn't full of shits and giggles."

"I just want choices. Right now, I have zero."

"Zero?"

She pulls away. "Yeah. The only person who wants to hang out with me is you."

"Thanks. You make it sound like—"

She places her finger over my mouth. "It's not meant as an insult. You're great. But I want to be swept off my feet. I want my fairy tale." She chokes out the last two words.

I wipe a tear away. "I'll do whatever I can to make sure you get it."

"What would I do without you?" she asks.

"Adopt a fuckton of cats."

This makes her laugh.

"I think I'm drunk." She hiccups. "And suddenly, nothing really matters. I just don't understand why most men aren't like you. Sure, you're a fuckboy, but I know you'd never cheat."

"Never. I respect relationships. And marriage? The fact that he disrespected something so sacred? Piece of shit. When I'm with someone, I'm one-hundred-percent dedicated to them and only aim to please."

She nods. "Too bad I'm not your type."

"What does that mean?" I ask her, not fully understanding.

She lifts a brow. "You have a certain type of woman you *always* go for. Blonde. Tall. Thin. Opposite of me."

She noticed.

"Yeah, well, you have a type you go for too … dweeby. You can do better."

"I will, now that I have a dating coach who's gonna teach me to have game."

"What have I agreed to?" I shake my head.

She laughs. "You're going to create a monster."

I set the whiskey on the nightstand and grab the remote, then flick through the channels. "Look."

"Aww," she says, leaning her head against my shoulder. "I love this movie. Tom Hanks. Meg Ryan. A bookstore. The scene in the coffee shop. I need this kind of romance in my life."

"They're enemies," I remind her. "Hated each other."

"But the connection is undeniable. You can tell they care about one another. That means something." Her words are slurring.

I've watched this movie with her more times than I can count over the years and have the lines memorized.

"I think it's kinda unrealistic."

She shakes her head. "No way. Could still happen."

At some point, I get up and grab toilet paper so she can blow her nose, and we eat leftover pizza in bed.

We watch the movie to the end, and when Tom Hanks and Meg Ryan meet at the park, Grace bursts out crying—again. And then the credits roll.

Grace pulls the covers over her body. "Will you snuggle me again tonight? I don't want to feel alone."

I turn onto my side and then wrap my arm around her waist. "Only because you asked so nicely."

"Or maybe it's because you love me?"

"You know it."

CHAPTER FIVE

I wake up to an empty bed with my head pounding. The whiskey was an awful idea, but in the thick of it, drinking that much seemed like a fab idea. Right now, I have no idea what time it is and contemplate rolling over and going back to sleep until I realize the sun is up and it's bright. When I sit up and look at my lingerie on the floor, I'm reminded of what happened yesterday.

My phone is dead on the nightstand. I plug it in, then walk into the main area. On the counter, there's a note with a large cup of coffee from a local shop.

Went out. Coffee is for you. Be back in an hour.

—H

I take the lid off the top, and it's still warm. After I take a tiny sip to test the temperature, I smile. Tastes like Christmas in a cup. The same flavor he had yesterday.

As I drink my coffee, I walk to the patio door and look outside. The sun is high in the sky, and it's bright as hell out—a total difference from yesterday's weather. This is sunshine after darkness, and I hope that's a metaphor for my awful dating life.

I trusted him.

That familiar emptiness fills the pit of my stomach again, and it's followed by that Negative Nancy voice in my head, telling me I'm not good enough. How I'll never have the type of love I crave with anyone. It's harder for kids of divorced parents, and somehow, I always fuck it up.

After how badly things ended with every one of my partners, it makes me wonder if I'm just not capable of having a healthy, long-term relationship, *just like my parents.*

Then I think about my sister and her relationship with Chip. They seem happy, like they can't breathe without the other close by, and that's why they're getting married. It gives me hope that maybe our parents didn't completely fuck *us* up. Maybe it's just *me.*

My heart thumps hard in my chest, and I have that overwhelming urge to cry again. And instead of holding it in, I let it all out. Loneliness appears, and I'm mad at myself for thinking this time would be different. I tried to be perfect, even though there was distance between us, and it wasn't enough.

Tears splash on my T-shirt, so I go to the bathroom to grab some toilet paper to blow my nose. That's when I hear my phone ringing.

I pick it up to unlock it and see it's Haley, one of my friends from high school. Her parents own Main Street Bookstore. She's an angel, but she also has the worst luck with relationships, just like me.

"Hi!"

"Hey! Just calling to see if you're going to the New Year's Eve party at the bed-and-breakfast?"

I laugh. "Harrison and I are always together on New Year's Eve. Have been since we were kids. So, if he's there, I'll be."

"Well, I just wanted to make sure you weren't planning to spend it with your boyfriend."

The lump in my throat that the whiskey couldn't wash away last night grows to the size of a golf ball.

"We broke up."

"What?" She sounds as shocked as I still feel.

"He was married."

"What?!" Now she sounds angry.

"I know. He shoved me into a closet, and I listened to them … *fuck*." I can barely get the words out. The humiliation I felt—still feel.

She gasps. "No. I'm so sorry, Grace. Seriously. That's messed up."

"It was. I was so excited and then …" I try to speak, but the words hang up in my throat.

"Hey. This is a good thing. That guy gave me the creeps."

"Even you saw the red flags?"

"Yes. We all did," she admits. "You just weren't listening to anyone. You didn't hear what Harrison said to you on Halloween?"

I try to replay the memory, but it's not coming to me.

"He told you to dump Joey's ass for canceling because he wasn't committed to you. We all agreed."

"He says things like that about everyone I date." I huff.

"Because he's right. He's always right. He even warned you about Mikey and Justin. Girl, we could go back to high school with Matt. I think you're so blinded by the thought of love that you refuse to see what's right in front of you, even if someone is pointing at it."

My bottom lip quivers as I think about all the warnings he's given. She's right. Harrison has been telling me for months, bringing it to my attention when I was ditched or stood up or when Joey couldn't talk or was short.

"If the red flags were snakes, they'd have bitten you."

I clear my throat. "I asked Harrison to be my dating coach. And you telling me that just confirmed my decision."

"He's gonna teach you how to date?" She doesn't sound convinced.

"He agreed. But I'm also going to let him pick the men."

She gasps. "Why don't you just date him?"

"Because we're just friends."

"Who roll in the sheets together."

"We haven't slept together. Ever. I mean it."

"Maybe you should?"

"I just got out of a long-term relationship. The last thing I need to do is mess up the one healthy relationship I have with someone of the opposite sex by fucking him."

She laughs. "I'm just giving you a hard time. Anyway, I gotta go. Mrs. Yancy just walked in, and I know she'll ask the premise of every single book on the new release table. Let's have dinner when you get home and catch up!"

"Sounds good."

"Oh, and I'm sorry about your breakup. I know you're probably hurting. Just remember, your heart always mends."

"But what if it doesn't this time?"

"It will."

"Thank you. Bye."

I check my text messages and turn around to see Harrison is back because the bathroom door is closed and the light is on. Just as I walk out of the bedroom, I hear the toilet flush and the door opens.

"Found your coffee?"

"Yeah, I did. Thanks. It was awesome."

"Who were you talking to?" he asks.

"Don't be nosy."

"It's kinda my business to know who thinks we're fuckin'."

"*Everyone.*" I give him a look and then laugh because it's the truth. "So, does it matter?"

He shrugs. "Maybe we should then."

"I know your rules. Just one night, and that's it."

"Yep. I'm sure that's all it would take to know it was a mistake."

I narrow my eyes at him. "It wouldn't be a mistake."

Then he laughs and points his finger at me. "No?"

"That's a trick question. Not talking about this. It would be weird. Like doing my brother."

"Luckily, you don't have a brother."

"Yeah, because he'd probably have kicked your ass already."

Harrison rolls his eyes. "Nah, he and I would probably be best friends. Go lady huntin' together."

"Yeah, right."

"You're just scared he'd be cooler than you." He snickers.

"*I'm* gonna kick your ass. Sometimes you're annoying, like a sibling."

"I take that as a compliment," he says, and that's when I notice he's dressed nicely.

"Wait, where did you go?"

He's wearing black jeans and a collared shirt with a gray sweater over it. Then I smell the hint of his cologne. It was a date.

"I met up with someone."

"Really? That's awesome. Hope it was one of the hotties I swiped right on."

"It wasn't, and you'll never guess who it was."

I make a face. "Wait, it's someone we know?"

He chuckles. "Stephanie."

"*Prom queen* Stephanie?"

"Right."

"Wow, I'd never have guessed her. I didn't realize you two still spoke."

Harrison and Stephanie were high school sweethearts too. She took his virginity. Not that I was jealous or anything. Or was I?

"We check in every once in a while, but it's been years since we've sat down and talked. I posted a photo of the hot tub the other night with a caption that said something about a starless sky in Houston. She messaged me early this morning and asked if I wanted to have brunch. I'd forgotten she had an office here."

"Wow. I did too. But that's amazing. Well, how was it? How is she?"

He opens the fridge and pulls out the milk jug. Notices it's soy then returns it. "She's great. Looks the same. Still has the same sense of humor. It brought me back." He pauses for a brief moment, smiling like he's recalling a memory. "She broke it off with her fiancé."

"Whoa. Wasn't he some big lawyer at a firm or something? I remember her mama telling me in the grocery store over the summer."

"Yeah. He was. Apparently, it only lasted three months. Seeing her was a happy surprise."

"Oh God, did you hook up?"

"Not yet. I *might* see her later tonight though."

"You should, for old times' sake," I encourage. "I mean, isn't she the one who got away?"

"I don't think I've ever said that."

He pops a brow, but I know he hasn't dated anyone seriously since they broke up and she moved away for college. After her, his bedroom rules began, and he's avoided commitment like the plague. Like he's waiting for someone.

"Hmm, I guess I always thought it was her."

"You know what assuming does?"

"Hush up. She's the only girl you dated for a long time."

"It's been nine years," he reminds me.

"Yeah, it's worth seeing if there's still something there, somewhere. Try to rekindle an old flame."

He shrugs. "We'll see what happens. Would be wild though. After all these years, getting back together? Oh, we took a selfie."

Harrison pulls his phone from his pocket and unlocks it. Then he walks over and shows me.

"Oh my God. She's gorgeous."

A blonde-haired, blue-eyed woman with a pearly-white smile grins at the camera. Harrison's dimple is out.

"You two look like the perfect couple. Like Hollywood stars."

He laughs.

"I just ask that you don't get married before me. I don't think I can handle sitting at the singles table."

"I doubt that will ever happen," he says. "But anyway, what are your plans tonight?"

"I'm having a half gallon of Blue Bell delivered and eating the whole tub while watching a true crime documentary."

He shakes his head, opens the freezer, and pulls out some peppermint ice cream. "I already got you covered."

"Is it sad that you know my breakup traditions?"

He doesn't even answer. "But I was thinking we could go out, my young Padawan."

"Are we really starting today off with the Star Wars stuff? Who does that make you then, Obi-Wan?"

"No, I'm Master Yoda, and you're Luke Skywalker. And I'm gonna teach you how to be a man-eater, so then all your wishes of fucking around and finding out can come true."

"But I thought you were hanging out with Stephanie tonight?"

"I said it was a maybe. You and I have plans first. I made us a reservation on the island."

My eyes widen. "*Baymont Island?*"

He laughs. "It's only an hour away, and I remember you mentioning you'd always wanted to ride the ferry."

"We were kids when I said that."

"So? I didn't forget, and we're already this close. Plus, the weather is amazing, so I thought we could make a night out of it. Then we can head to this fun bar that's on the seawall. Do some dancin', flirtin', and who knows? Maybe you'll even get some phone numbers."

"Or maybe I'll go home with someone."

He crosses his arms over his chest. "Maybe you will."

"But I have one rule …"

"What's that?"

"Apparently, I don't see red flags. So, if you think someone is a creep or married, then let a girl know?"

He meets my eyes for a few seconds too long. "That's a deal."

I hold out my hand, and he takes three steps forward and shakes it.

"It's confirmed then. Want to pick out what I'll wear tonight?"

He smirks. "That might be a bad idea."

"I trust you."

HOURS LATER, after my shower, I walk into the bedroom where Harrison has laid out my clothes. I packed several outfits, thinking that Joey and I'd have a night together in the city. Another reminder of how fucking stupid I was.

There's a pair of high-heeled leather boots, slacks that make my ass look fabulous, and a dark-green baggy sweater that swoops down low. I close the door, drop the towel, and slide them on. Then I look in the mirror and smile.

A moment later, there's a knock on the door.

"Come in," I say, and Harrison opens the door.

"Daaaaaaamn, girl." His eyes slide up and down my body, and he gives me a mischievous grin. "You look amazin'."

"Only because of you. I've never paired these things together before."

He meets my eyes. "Oh, I know. And I'm happy to take full credit."

I laugh. "Keep it up, and you'll become my personal stylist too."

"Wouldn't be the worst job I've ever had. I muck shit often." His smile doesn't falter. "Are ya almost ready? We gotta get goin' if we're gonna make our dinner reservation."

"Yep." I grab my phone and then follow him to the truck.

The sun has already set, and the temperatures have dropped from the cold front that moved in yesterday, but it's enjoyable.

On the way to Baymont Island, we pass tons of buildings decorated with Christmas lights. Holiday music plays low in the background, and we talk about nothing. I'm glad for the mindless conversation though, and I'm happy to be with Harrison instead of being alone. I've always had a good time with him, so I know tonight will be fun. It's what I need.

When we pull into the restaurant, Harrison turns to me. "Maybe we can watch the moonrise tonight. It begins at midnight. Will come up over the horizon."

"Yeah, I'd like that."

I guess that means Stephanie is a *maybe*.

We get out of the truck and walk into the old historic building that was previously a speakeasy during Prohibition. This restaurant was featured on TV, and there are nicely framed pictures of Guy Fieri in the waiting area.

The lights are low, and a pianist is playing in the corner. The high ceiling is tiled with decorative gold tin, and a gigantic crystal chandelier hangs from above.

I chew on the corner of my lip as Harrison gives his name, then returns to me.

"You had a reservation?"

He smiles. "I've had this planned since you asked me to join you."

"With me?"

"Yes." No hesitation.

Before I can ask any questions, the host interrupts us with two leather-bound menus and directs us to follow her. We're seated by the windows so we can watch the tourists walk the street. We also have the perfect view of the beach. The candlelight casts a warm glow between Harrison and me, and I look around, amazed that I'm here with him.

"This place is like ..."

"A movie?" Harrison laughs.

"Yes! How'd you know?"

"I saw the pictures online and watched some videos on YouTube. Thought you'd like to visit."

"It's incredible," I say as a bottle of rosé is delivered.

A man with a cloth over his arm pours our glasses and then places the wine in the bucket of ice.

"What brand is this?" I ask, taking a sip.

"Gaslighter. Taylor Swift's favorite."

"I don't even want to know how you know that," I tell him.

"London told me."

London is his little sister, who is obsessed with Taylor. She even learned how to play the guitar because of her. To be honest, she's really good too.

"Of course she did," I tell him. "It's amazing though. I love it. Might be my new fave."

My eyes scan around the room again, and then I lean forward and whisper, "It's romantic in here."

"Perfect place for a date."

He glances out the window, and a woman meets his gaze. She immediately smiles, and he gives her a side grin.

The woman takes a second glance over her shoulder, and he doesn't break eye contact until she's out of view.

"That's what I want to learn. You did it so flawlessly."

"What?" He takes a sip of wine, bringing his attention back to me.

"You have the *female gaze*," I say.

"No idea what you're talking about."

My mouth falls open. "It's hard to explain. It's a certain look that some men have mastered. It makes any woman seem like they're the only person you see."

"Please. You give me too much credit."

"You have to teach me how to do that."

"It's basic flirting, princess. You just give the person your undivided attention, like your world surrounds them."

He relaxes his shoulders, tilts his head, then leans a little closer. "Then you ask questions because you're actually interested in what someone has to say."

The candle flickers as he picks up his wine and sips. After setting his glass down, he licks his lips, then activates that cute little side grin as he stares into my eyes. Slowly, his gaze slides down to my bottom lip, then back up again. "If you could have one wish in the world, what would it be?"

I ask myself why my heart is fluttering as I swallow hard. Somehow, he's stolen my breath away as I look for my words.

"Wow, I felt that," I whisper, realizing I was mesmerized for a brief moment. "Yes, I need to learn these skills."

"Yes, teach you I will."

I snicker at his Yoda talk as he leans his back against the booth and relaxes.

When the conversation has a brief pause, the server walks over.

"I'm sorry. I haven't even looked at the menu yet. Can I have another minute?"

She smiles between us and nods before disappearing into the large room. I focus on the words on the page, wondering what the alcohol content is in that wine because my head is swimming.

"I think I'm gonna have steak and shrimp."

I close the menu. "I'll have that too."

"Medium rare," we say in unison.

"Only way to eat it," he confirms.

When the server returns, he orders for the both of us and then we're back to the conversation.

"What do you want in a relationship?" Harrison asks me. "I want to make sure I'm picking the right dude."

"Someone attractive, hardworking, and not married. Seriously not that picky. I just don't want another dud. I need a man who knows how to wine and dine but also isn't afraid to commit."

"And what's *attractive* to you? Give me an actor."

"Easy. Scott Eastwood."

He laughs.

"Why is that funny? He grew up riding horses, fishing, and hunting. He's just like one of us but happens to be the son of a legend. I feel like if he came to Valentine, I'd win him over, and he'd never leave. I fell in love with him in *The Longest Ride*. Lord have mercy …" I fan myself.

"Didn't we watch that together? The bull rider movie, right?" He pours more wine into both of our glasses.

"Yeah, that's the one."

"He could easily be a cousin. Though I read he didn't ride in the movie. They used a stuntman."

"Don't care. Let a girl dream."

Our food is delivered on a platter and set in front of us. Harrison and I exchange a smile and cut open our steaks.

"It's perfect," I say, my mouth watering with anticipation. I take a bite and let out a moan.

He nods. "Incredible. Maybe the best steak I've ever had."

"Yes, I agree." I take one of the shrimps off the skewer and cut it in half. "Oh my. I think I'm moving here just to eat this once a week," I tell Harrison, and a smile touches his lips.

"Glad you're *not* moving. I was sad thinking about that."

"Because you can't live without me."

"You're right about that. Can't imagine a world without you in it."

"I'm sure you could find someone to replace me, considering all those numbers you have in your phone."

"Nah, it's not the same. You're irreplaceable, babe." He sucks in a breath. "You know I would've supported your decision. I just want you to be happy."

"I know, thank you. I want you to be happy too."

He takes a drink of his wine and then grins. "I am."

CHAPTER SIX

HARRISON

After we eat dinner, Grace and I walk over to Whiskey River, a country bar with fifty different whiskeys, dancing, and mechanical bull riding. It's four blocks away on the opposite end of The Strand.

Before we walk in, I set an alarm on my phone so we have plenty of time to watch the moon rise over the horizon. When we walk in, we're both carded and glow-in-the-dark bracelets are snapped to our wrists. I'm shocked at how large the place is and how it nearly takes up an entire city block.

Grace turns and looks at me, and she's smiling. We make our way around the perimeter of the room because the middle is a large wooden dance floor, where a lot of people are two-stepping.

"Want a drink?" She reaches out her hand, and I take it. She drags me through the crowd with her until we push our way to the bar.

A woman with bright-red hair walks over to me and leans across the wood. "Whatcha havin', sweetheart?"

"Tequila," Grace says.

"Make it two. Patrón. Salt and a lime, please."

"Tequila in a whiskey bar, love it." She smirks, turns, grabs two shot glasses, then tosses them in the air before fixing them how we asked. They're set in front of us. "Want to start a tab?"

"Sounds good." I hand her my card, and she asks for my ID.

"Your birthday is two days before mine. Taurus."

"Same year too?"

"Yep, same exact year. Twenty-seven. Gettin' old."

Grace grabs her shot and turns away as I continue chatting, "What's your name?"

"River."

She holds out her hand, and I take it.

"Harrison. Nice to meet you."

Someone taps the bar a few seats down, and she gives the guy a look.

"I hope to see you around, *Harrison*."

"Yeah, you will."

She keeps my gaze for a brief second before walking away. Then I grab my shot and mirror Grace's stance, leaning against the bar.

I hold my glass in the air, and so does Grace. Then we clink them together and shoot them back. She does a little wiggle, and I smile just as "Crazy" by Patsy Cline plays.

"Wanna dance?"

"Another shot first," she says.

I turn, and River is already pouring them and sliding them to us.

We toss them back, and then I take Grace's hand, leading her onto the dance floor. I wrap my other hand around her waist and pull her close, falling in line with everyone else who's two-stepping.

"I feel like this is my theme song."

It makes me chuckle.

"Hey! Don't laugh!"

"I'm tryin' really hard not to." I smile.

"Dinner was amazing. Thank you. I needed a night out."

"You're welcome. I knew you would."

"What if I'd been with Joey tonight and missed that entire experience?"

I shrug. "Things always work out the way they're supposed to."

"Yeah," she says.

"And I'd have found someone to join me; don'tcha worry your pretty little face about that. Or I'd have gone alone. Doesn't bother me in the least to go out and have dinner by myself. Do you know how many numbers I usually get when I do that?"

She meets my eyes. "Hundreds."

"Close." I spin her around.

"So, tonight, what do I need to focus on, Coach?"

"Depends. What're your goals?"

A sly smile slides across her lips. "A number. A kiss. Or to be dicked down. Any of them would make me happy."

"You sure you're ready for that after your breakup?" I ask.

"If that's where the night leads me."

"I guess we'll see," I say, holding her, smelling the sweet vanilla scent on her skin. It brings back memories, all good ones.

The song ends, and another starts back up.

"You're the best dance partner I've ever had," she says.

"Because we used to practice in my parents' livin' room," I say with a laugh. "We were supposed to be world famous, remember?"

Her head falls back into laughter as I bring her out, twist her slightly, then add another spin. Every single beat is met with precision. Dancing with her as a kid meant holding her, and, fuck, sign me up any day of the week.

It's more upbeat, so we slightly change our stance, picking up our pace with the crowd as we dance. Just as I'm getting ready to say something, a guy wearing a cowboy hat meets Grace's gaze. She smiles at him, and I even notice the sparks.

"What about him?" she asks me, and then I spin around to get a better look.

He's wearing a black cowboy hat and a black shirt with pearl buttons. His eyes dart in the opposite direction, and then I turn back to Grace.

"You think he's good-lookin'?"

"I think I need to double-check that. Spin me again."

So, I do. Grace and I used to go dancing every weekend after we turned twenty-one at Boot Scooting—the local bar in our hometown.

We move fluidly together as if our brains were connected.

She giggles. "Yeah, he's cute. I just hope he's tall."

"For your sake, me too."

Grace once dated a guy who was five inches shorter than her, and after they broke up, she swore she'd only date men who were at least her height or taller. She's kept that promise to herself for the past five years.

"Ooh, he's standing," she whispers. "And he's coming this way."

"Yeah?" I suck in a breath.

A second later, I'm being tapped on the shoulder. The guy is eye level with me.

"Scuse me, may I?"

"Oh, sure," I say, handing Grace off to him. "Have fun."

I walk straight toward the bar and grab another shot, whiskey this time. It makes River smile.

Grace and the guy seem to be hitting it off because she's laughing hard at whatever it is he's saying.

"Your girlfriend leave ya?" River asks when she hands over my drink.

"Not my girlfriend. We've been best friends since we were in the womb," I correct, taking a sip. "I'm single as a Pringle."

"Really? Harrison, the single Taurus." She grins.

"That's right, sweetheart."

"So, whatcha do for a livin'?"

I lick my lips, meeting her eyes. Maybe I have perfected the female gaze over the years. "Guess."

She takes a step back and places her hand on her chin like she's trying to unravel life's mysteries. "Are you a lawyer?"

"Hell no. It takes a certain kind of person to do that work." I laugh and immediately think about Stephanie.

"You're a financial adviser."

I shake my head. "You're ice cold, River. Maybe I'm a bartender like you?"

"Bartender?" She laughs. "Babe, I *own* this place."

"Shit, girl. You're a boss babe?"

"Better believe it. This was my dream."

"Ahh. Whiskey River makes a lot more sense now. But, wow, that's … incredible. I'm impressed."

"What about you? A rodeo clown?"

This makes me snort. "While that would be a fun-ass job, Me and my older brother are horse trainers in West Texas. A little place called Valentine, about twelve hours that way." I point behind me.

She narrows her eyes. "Wait. *No.*"

"What?"

"Are you that guy who went viral, like millions and millions of views?"

I give her a puzzled look, even though I know exactly what she's talking about.

"There was this video of this guy who was teaching this influencer how to ride a horse, and she totally made him into a thirst trap. Wait a second."

She opens her phone, scrolls, and then she opens the video. I hear my voice, and her eyes widen.

"It *is* you!"

I shrug. "I guess it is."

"I'm shook right now," she says. "One night, I stayed up and read the comments on that post. Nearly pissed myself. Did all that exposure change your life?"

"Business ain't *ever* been better." I give her a shrug and down the rest of my whiskey. "I had a few talent agents contact me, but bein' a cowboy isn't a costume to me; it's a way of life."

"Wow. I cannot believe we have a celebrity in here right now. Can I take a picture with you?"

"Sure."

River pulls out her phone and takes a few pics, then turns it around to let me see. "I can't wait to show my sister."

"Oh, stop. You're gonna make me blush." My tone drops as she hands me her phone.

She wrote *Harrison, the Cowboy* for my contact, and the cursor is in the space where I need to put my number.

I meet her eyes. "Distance ain't an issue for you?"

"Nope." She tucks her lips into her mouth.

I program it in and hand it back. She immediately texts me.

"Got you," I tell her.

"So …"

Before she can finish, Grace comes to my side. She's laughing and smiling. "Landon, this is my best friend Harrison, who's basically like my brother." Then Grace looks at me. "This is Landon."

I hold out my hand. "Hey, Landon. Nice to meet ya."

His handshake is firm, and he's dressed nicely. "Good to meet ya."

"So, what do you do?" I look him over from head to toe, noticing his nice-as-hell boots and the huge-as-fuck buckle he's sporting.

"He's a bronco rider." She's beaming. "And he trains horses."

I tilt my head. "Really? Landon … Wells?"

He looks at me curiously. "Yeah? How'd you know that?"

"Dude, I've watched you ride on the internet. Damn. You're a champ." I give Grace a slight nod, and she grins, understanding. "Can I get you a drink?"

"Nah, I'm good," he says. "Just wanted to come introduce myself. Grace told me about you and your brother's business. I'm gonna have to look it up."

"You should," I tell him. "Come check it out if you're in the area. My older brother is a huge fan."

"I might." He glances at Grace, who is looking at him with googly eyes. "Nice meetin' ya."

He wraps his arm around her, and she looks over her shoulder at me. I give her a thumbs-up, and when I turn around, River is gone, chatting with someone on the other end of the bar. I notice she's refilled my whiskey though; maybe she knew I'd need it. I sit on the barstool, not paying any attention to anything that's going on, lost in my thoughts.

Eventually, River returns, and she makes a face at me. "Why do you look so … *down?*"

I shake my head with a smirk. "I don't."

"Yeah, you do. You look like someone knocked your tricycle over."

"I barely know you, and you're giving me shit. I feel like I'm at home."

"All small towns are the same, you know. Some have beaches. Others have mountains. At the end of the day, same old shit," she tells me, then looks out to the crowd of people dancing and sees Grace with Landon. "Ahh. Got my answer."

"What?" My brows squish together.

"You have a thing for her." She grabs the towel and wipes off the bar.

"No, I don't."

She slides me another whiskey. After this one, I'll stop. Sober up.

"I grew up workin' in a bar. I own the most successful one on the island. We see millions of tourists in here during the summer. You really think you're the only man I've ever seen look at a girl like that when she's dancing with someone else?"

I roll my eyes.

"Hardheaded Taurus."

"I'm not sitting here and having this cliché-as-fuck conversation with some bar owner who acts like she knows everything about relationships."

She snickers and wrings out her towel, cleaning off the empty glasses sitting next to me. "If this were like in the movies, the conversation we're having right now would be the one that changes your entire life."

"So tell me something so good that I'll never forget it," I suggest, knocking back the rest of my drink.

She leans her elbow against the bar. "If you don't tell your best friend, who is *just like your sister,* that you have a thing for her, you'll lose the fucking opportunity. Trust me on that one."

She looks past me, and I turn and zero in on them together, having a good time.

When I turn back, she meets my gaze. "If you haven't already lost your chance."

"I'm good, actually." I pat the bar.

River shakes her head and places a glass of water on the counter. It's like she knew I was thirsty. I dance with a few women to pass the time. Exchange some numbers. Just as I'm closing out my tab, the alarm on my phone goes off, reminding me about the moonrise.

Grace and Landon are on the other side of the room, sitting at a bar top that overlooks the dance floor. He's close, but he's been respectful all night. I'd know—I've barely taken my eyes off of them.

My alarm goes off for the second time, and I text Grace.

HARRISON

Moonrise?

I SEE her face light up across the room, and she smiles.

GRACE

Yes. I'll meet you up front in five minutes?

HARRISON

Don't be late.

I STAND, wave goodbye to River, then fall into the shadows as Grace leans in and kisses Landon. He's a national champ. One of the best riders I've ever seen, and if I recall correctly, he went to the same college as my younger sister Fenix. I think he's older than her though.

Honestly, he'd be perfect for Grace, and he understands ranch life. He hands her his phone, and I know they're exchanging numbers. One more kiss, and then she walks away and makes her way through the crowd, wearing a cheesy grin.

I move toward the exit and wait outside. I'm happy for the fresh air. For a second, I felt like I was suffocating.

Grace walks out, and she's humming some song. When she sees me, her smile widens even more.

"Was it stuffy in there to you?" she asks, falling in line next to me as we make our way down the sidewalk toward the street crossing.

"Yeah, I thought it kinda was," I admit. "Thought it was just me though."

"No, it wasn't. I felt like my heart was gonna race out of my chest. Maybe he was just … turning me on."

I let out a laugh, but it almost feels forced. "You can go back if you want. I can wait out here."

"No way." She shakes her head. "Absolutely not. I've never seen a moon rise over the water. You think I'd miss doing this with you for some *D*?"

"Yes," I say.

"Okay, you're right. I would, considering how long it's been. Ugh." She lets out an annoyed growl. "But we're besties. I wouldn't want you doing things like this alone. I want to experience them with you," she says, pulling me in.

"Good. Because a one-night stand doesn't fill the void. Being with the real deal does."

"You're right." She smiles, and we cross the road and take the stairway that leads to the beach.

Before our feet touch the bottom, Grace bends over and takes her boots and socks off, then steps into the sand with her hand held out. I take it and fall in line beside her.

As we kick wet sand between our toes, Grace speaks up. "Most men are searching for a booty call. Maybe Landon is different from all the fuckboys. Maybe he'll give me a real chance."

She trips, and I'm quick and catch her before she falls.

She looks up into my eyes, smiling. "You were just like a Marvel hero."

"You mean a Jedi," I say, lifting her to her feet.

She snorts, smoothing her hands down her sweater. "I'm so clumsy sometimes."

"You mean tipsy. I hope you always stay like this," I tell her.

"Clumsy?"

"Happy," I say.

We move toward the resort lawn chairs that are facing the

sea. Gracie sits on the edge of one, and I nudge in right beside her.

She turns to me. "How much longer do we have until it rises?"

I pull my phone from my pocket and check the time. "Fifteen minutes."

"Oh good."

Grace scoots closer, lifts my arm and places it over her so we have more room. Then she leans her head against me, and I can smell her perfume and her flowery shampoo.

A few stars are twinkling in the distance, but it's nothing like what we see at home, where there's hardly any light pollution. The wind blows slightly, and Grace shivers.

"Take my jacket."

I move forward, sliding my arm from behind her head and removing the jacket from my body. When I hand it to her, she happily takes it.

"Thank you. If you get cold, tell me, and I'll give it back."

"Nah, it's fine. I've got on layers." And plus, my body is on fucking fire.

We return to how we were before. We sit in silence, just enjoying the sounds of the waves crashing on the shore as we sit in the dark. A couple walks by, and they're laughing about something, and then it's just us again.

"One minute," I whisper.

Then, as if we invited the moon to visit, it peeks over the horizon.

"Wow," she whispers.

We're mesmerized by it as it slowly drifts over the horizon. Moonlight dances across the rippling water and waves. At first, it looks red, then transforms into a bright white. Wisps of clouds float across the top.

Once it's high in the sky, Grace sits up and looks at me. "Tonight wasn't so bad, was it?"

"No, I had a great time."

"All because of you," she says, wrapping her arm around me, listening to my heartbeat.

"One day, you'll find someone who makes you happy," I tell her with a promise.

"Maybe I already have," she whispers into the night, and the only thing that pulls me away is my phone vibrating.

A part of me thinks it might be River, but I unlock it and see a text from Stephanie. And I know Grace sees it.

CHAPTER SEVEN

GRACE

Harrison's phone buzzes, and he pulls it from his pocket. With one glance, I read the name across the top. *Stephanie.*

I swallow hard and remember how things were in high school when they were together. Honestly, when they broke up, I was happy. For years, I'd thought maybe Harrison was going to marry her. I guess that's still a possibility, considering she broke it off with her fiancé.

"Ready to go?" he asks, patting my arm, sitting up.

And just like that, we're walking away from the line, the one we never cross.

"Yep, let's head back." I stand.

As we walk, our hands brush against one another, but I don't take his this time. When we do that, it's only ever done in a friendly way anyway. Nothing romantic.

When we make it back to the street level, we take the sidewalk to the tourist parking area. I still feel the alcohol coursing through my system; honestly, it's probably the only reason I kissed Landon. Liquid courage. I don't typically make moves like that, but I'm trying to do better, be better, have more fun, take more risks.

"So, are ya gonna meet up with her?" I ask once we're in the truck.

"Who?" Harrison cranks the truck, and we take off.

"Stephanie."

He glances over at me. "Maybe. I'll see how I feel once I take you back."

"I can stay at a hotel on The Strand. I'm sure there are rooms available because it's offseason."

"Absolutely not. I'm not leavin' you in Baymont when we have to be up early to leave tomorrow. Beckett already told me I couldn't extend my vacation a single day."

This makes me laugh. When I look out the window and pay attention to where we are, I'm a little confused why there's so much traffic.

He smiles. "We have to ride the ferry while we're here."

"Seriously? For a second, I thought you'd forgotten."

He glances at me. "Never."

More cars fill in behind us, and there's no escaping. We're actually in line to load onto a ferry. I look outside at the seagulls flying overhead. By the water, there's someone throwing pieces of bread for them.

The boat arrives, and soon, cars are flooding off of it. After the toot of a horn, we're being directed to move. Traffic guards wave us forward, pointing for us to go in the outside lane. I turn around and look over my shoulder to see how many other vehicles are boarding.

"This thing might be full."

Once we're parked, he turns off the engine as the vessel gently rocks. There's an announcement playing overhead, telling us to stay in our vehicles until the boat is loaded. I'm all smiles.

"We have to go upstairs so we can see from above," Harrison says.

"Yeah, let's do it."

Eventually, the ferry is loaded and slowly starts moving across the water. We get out of the truck and walk to the edge, looking over. Then Harrison follows me upstairs, and we step outside onto the upper deck as the salty sea air kisses my cheeks.

We go to the front, and I look up at the moon. "This is incredible. I think this is one of the best nights I've had in a really long time."

"So the trip wasn't a complete waste?"

I shake my head. "Not at all. You made it worthwhile."

"Per usual," he says.

"Over the years, I've lost count of how many times you've saved the day."

He's standing right beside me, leaning against the railing, staring out at the dark sea that surrounds the boat.

I glance over at him. "Landon asked me if we were into each other."

"Why?"

I shake my head. "I dunno. I had to explain our history."

This makes him chuckle. "Yeah? And how did that work out for you?"

"Not sure. He still didn't seem too convinced. Maybe you being my coach won't work." I laugh. "You'll scare all of my dates away."

Harrison breaks eye contact and gazes out at the water. "He doesn't have to worry about *me* stealing *his* potential woman."

"As if you could," I say.

He lifts his brow. "I could."

"Too cocky." I shake my head. "I'm not fallin' for that. I'm immune."

He shrugs. "Whatever you say. All it takes is one kiss, and women fall in love with me. It's not called the Harrison Valentine Kiss of Death for nothing."

Now, I'm laughing. "Really? Let's test your theory then. I'm not scared."

"What?" He smirks, taking a step closer.

"If you're so confident, let's see. I'd love to be able to deliver you a good old-fashioned Valentine *I told you so*."

"Nah. I'm good. Maybe some other time," he tells me, shaking his head.

I'm not sure why I feel rejected.

I shrug. "That's fine. Just didn't think you'd be such a chicken at the chance of a lifetime."

"No one—and I mean, no one—calls me a *chicken*."

Harrison straightens his stance and turns toward me. Then he brushes his thumb across my cheek before dipping down and sliding his mouth against mine. I open my lips a bit wider, and his tongue darts inside, massaging mine. The kiss deepens further, and my control slips as I thread my fingers through his hair. I moan against him, feeling weak in the damn knees as he slowly pulls away. He creates space between us, and I place my fingers over my lips as he smirks.

Right now, I'm too stunned to speak; my throat is dry, and my thoughts are a tangled mess in my mind. "I, uh … I …"

"Cat got your tongue?" He's not even fazed by the hum of electricity streaming between us.

"I think you've still got it." My body is on fire, and the only thing I can blame is the alcohol. "I don't think it was supposed to feel like that."

"Like what?" He doesn't meet my gaze, and right now, my heart is racing too fast for me to articulate the right words.

Were there fireworks?

I shake my head. "Nothing. See, not madly in love. No cupid eyes. Here's your *I told you so*."

"We'll see," he mutters, and I see the hint of a smile on his lips —the lips I kinda want to kiss again.

"I guess we will." I swallow hard, holding on to the railing.

He tilts his head, his eyes still scanning over the water. "Ya see, the thing about me is … I *linger*. I crawl under your skin and bury myself there. It starts slowly, and you don't realize it until I'm always on your mind. Or at least that's what all the women who've demanded I see them for the second time say. So it's official; you got the Harrison Valentine Kiss of Death. Maybe I'll be delivering you a good ole Valentine *I told you so*."

I playfully roll my eyes. "I am not an option. Even you know that, especially with my track record."

"Yeah, and the last thing I want to do is prove all those rumors right since people around town are so convinced there's something going on between us." He laughs.

"You're absolutely right." Though I can't deny how fast my heart is pumping blood right now.

I'm trying to act normal. It was nothing, right?

I remember when we were fourteen and kissed, but we were kids with overactive hormones. What's my excuse now?

"So, how long until your Kiss of Death fully activates? I want to put a calendar reminder in my phone."

"Six months usually. But your guess is as good as mine."

Now I'm laughing, but my palms are sweating. "So it's a ticking time bomb. Got it. I'll, uh … keep a lookout for that. I'll give it six months."

"Forgot to tell you. There ain't no antidote either, so good luck, princess." He shoots me a wink. "You're so *fucked*, but just remember, you begged for it."

"I did *not* beg."

He chews on his bottom lip. "That's how I remember it. The night Grace came up with an elaborate way of getting me to kiss her *again*."

"I did not! I called you chicken, and then you devoured my mouth like you liked it. But it doesn't matter because I'm gonna be just fine, trust me. Totally immune," I explain, noticing the goose bumps forming and prickling all over my skin.

"I liked it." He shrugs. "No shame from me."

"Shut up," I say. "And don't use your *female gaze* stuff on me."

He bursts into laughter as the ferry glides across the water, and I allow the breeze to cool me off. When land finally comes into view, we're instructed to go back to our vehicles. My lips are numb, and I'm trying my best to keep the conversation going and not give a hint of it being awkward. Harrison opens my door for me, and when I look up into his eyes, I feel sick.

"I think I'm gonna …"

He quickly leads me over to the edge of the boat, where I puke up my guts. I lean against the railing, keeping my eyes closed because the last thing I want to do is see it. The smell is enough, and I know everyone is looking at the stupid drunk girl.

"Gracie, you okay?" Harrison places his hand on my back. He sounds worried.

I feel clammy and break into a cold sweat.

"Take your time. Breathe," he tells me. "I think you drank too much."

"And the rocking of the boat isn't helping." I'm so embarrassed that I keep my eyes on the ground as he walks me to the truck. Once I'm inside, I remove his coat and lean my head against the cold window.

"Need some napkins?" He opens the glove box and hands me a stack.

I wipe my mouth, wishing I had something to remove that taste on my tongue. "Thank you. I'm sorry for being a hot-ass mess."

"Don't apologize. You were just having a good time. I'm proud of you. Can't remember the last time you got sloppy drunk."

On the way back to the house, I fall asleep and only wake up when we're pulling into the driveway. I think I drank more than I realized.

Harrison opens the door to the truck and helps me unbuckle.

I place both feet on the ground and feel the world slightly tilt on its axis.

"I've got you," he whispers. "If I need to carry you, I will."

I stop walking and give him a look. "You *cannot* carry me."

With one swoop, he slides his arms behind my legs and lifts me. I wrap my arms around his neck and hold on for dear life.

"Oh my God. You're such a caveman. And fucking strong. You can't just pick me up like that."

"But I did. When you gonna stop underestimating me, princess?" he mutters.

"I guess starting now," I whisper.

He chuckles. "Good."

The sidewalk seems like it's stretching on for miles, and time feels like it slows down. I can smell the faint hint of his cologne on his shirt and feel his hot breath against my skin as he holds me so effortlessly.

"Gonna set you down so we can unlock the door. Ready?"

I nod, and he gently places me on my feet.

"Next time we go out and I'm tired, that's my method of travel."

"I gotchu, babe. But it might mess up your game." He shoots me a wink and leads me into the bedroom, where I fall back on the bed.

Carefully, he unzips my boots and removes them, then helps me crawl under the blankets. I close my eyes, and when I open them again, he sets a gigantic cup of ice water and a pot on the nightstand.

"You need to drink this."

I sit up and take a sip. "Thank you."

As I lie back down, I start sweating and wiggle out of my pants, then throw them on the floor. Then I remove my sweater and toss it over his shoulder before I sink back down.

"How much did you have to drink?" He leans over and tucks loose strands of hair behind my ear.

"I don't know. I had shots with you. Shots with Landon. The wine at dinner. Maybe I just mixed too much. I'm not a spring chicken anymore."

He chuckles. "That's true. I thought you were fine on the beach."

"Was the motion of the ocean, I think." I can barely keep my eyes open, so I close them. I'm exhausted from emotional overload. I've had a long weekend. Too many ups and too many downs. "Will you stay with me until I fall asleep?"

Because I know he's going to see Stephanie.

"Sure," he says.

He kicks off his shoes and slides under the blankets with me. Once he's there, my body relaxes, but my mind will not shut off. It's rushing through so many thoughts and emotions, from Joey to dinner to kissing Landon and then losing control on the ferry with Harrison. I need to check myself before I wreck myself.

Just as I'm falling asleep, Harrison's phone vibrates hard on the side table. The noise brings me back to reality. The mattress moves slightly, and I know he rolled over to grab it. The light from his phone brightens the room as he types back.

I keep my breathing slow, wishing I could fall asleep. After he locks his phone, I hear him suck in a deep breath. Then, moments later, he slides out from under the blankets. A few minutes after that, his truck cranks.

I try to ignore that old pang of jealousy that creeps up. Don't get me wrong; Harrison and Stephanie are great together. They always have been, but I also know she didn't like me that much. I was a threat to their relationship, but I never got in the way.

Maybe things have changed. It's probably nothing.

I try to relax and not think about the two of them together. Then I laugh, realizing I should've bet him that he'd see her tonight.

If I had, in the morning, I'd be fifty dollars richer.

CHAPTER EIGHT

HARRISON

I wake up in Stephanie's bed with her naked body pressed against mine. The last time we were together was nearly ten years ago, and while we're different people with different life experiences, it was like we were eighteen again. That was the last time I dated anyone seriously.

"Good morning." She holds me tight, squeezing me.

I roll over with a grin. "Mornin'."

"Last night felt like old times, didn't it?"

She draws circles on my chest with her finger, and I lift my arm, pulling her in closer.

"Yeah. Brought me back to high school when we would skip class to fool around."

She laughs. "Oh goodness. I'd almost forgotten about that. Wow, I really could've benefited from you being around when I was in law school."

"I bet. You always said sex helped you think straight," I remind her with a chuckle.

Stephanie sits up, looking into my eyes. "Do you remember that pact that we made all those years ago?"

"Remind me. It's been a while." I tuck straight blonde hair behind her ear.

"We promised one another that if we weren't married by twenty-seven, we'd give each other a real chance."

"Why did we choose twenty-seven?"

She gasps. "You don't remember?"

I try to dig up all of our old conversations, but my brain isn't cooperating. It's still in a fog from all the shots I took last night or from kissing Grace. I shrug.

"Because all the greats don't make it past twenty-seven."

"The 27 Club," I whisper, and it all comes flooding back. "Janis Joplin, Jimi Hendrix, Kurt Cobain, Amy Winehouse."

"We're twenty-seven now." She holds up her bare ring finger.

I laugh because she is a little bit superstitious at times. I think we all are. Kinda happens when you grow up in the West.

"And we're gonna make it to twenty-eight."

She sucks in a deep breath, and we lie in silence for a few minutes as the moonlight splashes across the marble floor of her penthouse. She's done well for herself, and I'm proud as fuck of her.

This was Stephanie's dream—college, moving to the city, becoming a successful criminal defense lawyer with a heart of gold. Oxymoron, I know, but it's true. She cares about her clients. She has too much empathy at times for people. And at one point in our young lives, we desperately cared about each other.

"I've got a confession to make," she says.

I nod, and she continues, "I've kept up with you over the years, especially after you went viral after training that girl to ride. I think I gave the video a million views myself. Did you really have to ride shirtless?"

"It was hot as fuck outside. You know how it gets in the dead of summer."

She gives me a smirk that says *yeah, right*. "I also know you haven't been with anyone long term since us."

"You're a little stalker." I waggle my brows.

"No. Maybe a little, but not in a bad way. I just always felt like you were the one who got away, and I think it's why I couldn't commit to my fiancé."

I sit up in bed. "Steph, it's been so long. We'd have to try to get to know each other again, and it's obvious we've both changed."

I hold out my hand because her bedroom is extravagant. The woman in front of me isn't the cheer captain that used to suck my dick after every Friday night football game.

"But back in the day, we were good together—the quarterback and head cheerleader, Danny and Sandra Dee, prom king and queen. We had something special, Harrison. Everyone knew it. Even Grace and you still trust her with your life. I haven't been able to find what we had all those years ago, and I don't want to live my life with regrets." She's confident. Knows exactly what she wants.

But she is right in all aspects.

"We were good for each other."

"And you never said goodbye," she whispers, and I'm brought back to the memory of when she moved away to college.

"I never do," I remind her, and she tilts her chin so she can meet my eyes. "Unless it's the actual end."

After graduation, we spent the entire summer together and were glued at the hip. We made love on the hay in the loft of the barn, slept in each other's arms in the tree house behind my parents' house that my little brothers and sisters played in, and drank underage until we passed out. The days turned into nights, and when the leaves started to fall, I knew it was time for her to move to Austin—the party university, one of the best in the entire state. She'd gotten a full-paid scholarship and cheered, and she was ready to leave it all behind for me. But I told her to go. I wouldn't be the man to stop her from fulfilling her dreams, and I told her if she stayed, I'd break up with her. To protect her future. I wanted her to be sure that I was what she really wanted. And then a decade later …

"Do you remember that time I snuck out of my window and jumped off the second story of my parents' house to meet you in your truck at the park?"

"Ahh. Yeah. Teenage you was dumb as hell and didn't think about how you'd get back up there, and we had to sneak into your dad's garage for the ladder. Then I nearly got busted when I was putting it back."

"I was an only child! I didn't get to learn how to sneak out from my older siblings like you. I had zero practice!"

I chuckle. "We had a lot of fun together, didn't we?"

"What I'd do to go back in time," she says with a sigh.

I smile, replaying old memories like a movie in my head. Stephanie and I were adventurous and insatiable for each other. My mama was convinced I'd knock her up before we graduated high school, but I was responsible. That's one thing I am. No accidental pregnancies for me, regardless of how many people are convinced I'll be the one.

My alarm goes off, the first reminder that I need to get going, and I reach over and silence my phone. "Shit. I gotta go. I wish we had more time."

"Me too."

I slide out from between the sheets and place my feet on the floor. She clicks on the side lamp, and I see several silver condom wrappers on the bedside table.

"Can we see each other again?" She sits up and presses her hand against my back, lifting the comforter with her to cover her perfect breasts.

"I've got rules, babe." I look over my shoulder and meet her gaze.

"Yeah, I heard about them online. You know there are fan pages."

"Are you runnin' one of them?" I shoot her a wink.

She shrugs. "I just know your rules aren't valid because you just broke them with me." She taps her finger over her plump lips. "Last night."

"Guilty as charged." I slide on my clothes, and she lies in bed and watches me.

"You know I'm right though." She's grinning. She's *flirting*.

"No denying it." My socks and shoes are on the other side of the room, and I stand, plucking them from the floor. I want to make it back to the house before Grace wakes up. Not that I care if she knows, but because she's going to encourage me to go for it. "Let's play it by ear."

She gives me a nod and smiles, almost as if she knows something I don't. "As long as it's a maybe … I'll accept it." Then she smirks. "Mmm, Mr. Valentine, you've gotten so much better with age."

I chuckle, leaning across the mattress to kiss her. "I hope to see you again."

"You will," she promises.

As I walk across her large bedroom and reach for the door, I look over my shoulder at her sparkling blue eyes. She's a beautiful woman. Gorgeous. Smart. Intelligent.

"See ya."

"Still not a goodbye." She blows me a kiss, and I smirk before leaving.

We always did have a good time, rolling in the sheets together. The attraction between us is still very much alive. But we're not dumb teenagers anymore.

Revisiting that relationship is tempting because she's one of the women in my two-woman category that I think I could spend the rest of my life with. Grace being the other one.

As I crank my truck, I think about this weekend. Half of the shit that happened, I could've never predicted. Maybe this weekend will change the entire trajectory of my life.

How fucking cliché would that be?

The sun is rising, but there is a lot of fog on the road from the steadily changing temperatures. I'm almost surprised there is so much traffic this early in the morning, but then I remember that Houston is big as hell. When I make it back to the house, I walk in and grab my bag. I hear the shower running.

I move through the living room and down the hallway, noticing the door is slightly cracked. While I should keep my gaze forward, I turn and see Grace standing under the stream, rinsing her hair. I swallow hard and force myself to keep walking. I wish she realized just how gorgeous she is and that she literally holds all the cards; she just can't see them.

Pushing the intrusive thoughts away, I toss my duffel onto the bed and open it wide. When I glance over at the time, I calculate the drive. I don't think we'll make it to Valentine before dark, which is a bummer, considering I have to be at work around five tomorrow to catch up from this little vacation.

The water shuts off. As I bend over to pick up my clothes, Grace enters.

When I look over my shoulder at her, she screams, and her towel falls to the floor. I turn my back as she hurries to pick it up.

"Shit. Sorry! I didn't mean to startle you."

"I didn't hear you come back! You should've warned me!"

"You were in the shower, and I didn't want to interrupt!"

"This weekend just keeps getting better," she huffs.

My back is still facing her. "Listen, it's nothin' I've never seen before. Your body is beautiful."

"You don't have to lie," she mutters.

I cross my arms over my chest and turn to face her, knowing she had enough time to cover herself. "I wouldn't lie about that, okay?"

I'm being serious as fuck, and she knows it. Her breath hitches, and then she breaks our intense eye contact, her face softening.

"Okay. I just—"

"I won't listen to you talk down about yourself, Gracie. Some of the things you say just aren't true. Bruce Lee once said something about how one shouldn't speak negatively about one's own self because the body doesn't know the difference."

"There are just days when I don't feel … pretty. Or wanted. I'm seriously Jan. In real life!" She shakes her head, and it's hard for me not to laugh, mainly because I'm confused.

"Jan, like in *Grease*? The musical we did in high school?"

"Yes, exactly like that. The awkward, fat friend who doesn't have a boyfriend and is forced to go to public events as the third wheel."

I walk over to her and let out a breath, placing my hand on her shoulder and squeezing. "Well, I'm not datin' anyone, so that ruins the entire third wheel theory. You're a good person. Smart. Attractive. Funny as hell. When *she's a ten, but she dates douchebags* kinda energy."

She snickers. "Oh, like, *he's a ten, but he won't commit* kinda energy?"

"Okay, I deserved that. But know that if you were a sucky, negative, unfun person, I wouldn't be around you. So, have a little faith in my choice of people. Especially my best friend."

She cracks a smile, then laughs. "We became besties when we were six. Your brain wasn't even fully developed then. Maybe you don't see how awkward I am because it's normal to you."

"You're not. But the resting bitch face sometimes."

"I don't have an RBF," she says.

And she doesn't. It's just something I tease her about because she always says she doesn't want to look mean. She never has. Grace is the approachable, fun friend who loves to throw a party.

"Now you don't," I say, lifting her chin when she smiles. "Cheer up. Being single gets worse."

She playfully smacks me. "I'm just in a mood."

"No? Really? Had no idea," I say sarcastically, but it makes the smile return. One thing I've always been good at is making her laugh.

"Joey texted me this morning. It's thrown me off."

I remove some jeans and a T-shirt from my bag so I can change into some clean clothes, then stuff my dirty clothes inside. "Do I need to drive over to his house and beat the fuck outta him before we leave?"

"No," she whispers. "He was nice and apologized for disrespecting me. He also weirdly thanked me for everything. Then he mentioned that he and his wife are moving forward with their divorce after this weekend."

My brows are raised as I listen to this bullshit because that's all this is. "And then I hope you blocked his stupid ass."

"I did."

I don't want to listen to her blame herself for this. "Look, what happened shouldn't have, but don't discredit what you just went through. There's loss there, and you need time to heal. That shit hurts."

"He apologized, and most men don't do that so it makes me think that maybe he does have an empathetic bone in his body."

She removes the towel from her head and dries her long hair while the other one is still tightly wrapped around her body. When she digs through her suitcase and pulls clothes from inside, I turn my back.

We can communicate without speaking at this point.

"I've always wanted the best for you, Gracie, and I want you to be happy. I think you dodged a bullet with this one."

"Increasing my body count is what I did."

"You need someone who will give you that *movie magic* romance that you obsess about."

I hear the towel drop and the rustling of material.

"But what if I'm searching for something that doesn't really exist?"

"Do you believe that?"

She laughs. "Based on my past relationships, kinda. I dunno. Between the hangover and my intrusive thoughts, I'm just in a weird mood today. Ignore me."

"I don't expect you to break up with someone you talked to nearly every day for a year and be over it in a weekend. That'd make you a psycho."

She chuckles. "Dressed."

I turn back to her. "Finding the *one* sometimes takes time. I've heard that when you stop trying for love, that's when you tend to find it. So, just go with the flow. I believe it's the secret recipe for a happy life. Maybe try out your single era. Could be your best one yet."

That earns me a popped brow.

"You're so good at gassing me up."

"It's my hobby," I say, looking under the bed to make sure nothing got pushed out of sight. I lost one of my favorite belts that way.

Grace runs her fingers through her wet hair and doesn't take her eyes off me. "You know, your sister keeps asking me what my word of the new year will be. I've been thinking about *fearless*. Maybe my single era will be incredible. Why check out when I haven't shopped the whole store?"

"I like that. Fearless." I finish packing and zip my bag. "Not to be a Debbie Downer, but the last time she *forced* me to choose a word of the year, something overly dramatic happened, so I don't do that anymore."

"Sounds superstitious to me."

"Call it whatever you want. I learned my lesson, and now I don't fuck around with that. Too much bad juju. It's like when you pray for patience, and you're stuck in traffic for five hours. I'm good."

"Well, I guess you still have three weeks to change your mind."

"Oh, I won't. Trust me on that."

THIRTEEN HOURS LATER, we finally make it to Grace's condo. My back hurts, and I'm exhausted from staying up all night, but I haven't complained about it once. I chose it. And I can't say I regret it either.

While we took turns driving, it rained half the time, so it made the trip almost miserable. Would've been if it wasn't for the company.

We talked about everything, but Stephanie was never mentioned. I'm sure Grace knew I was with her though, especially when Stephanie tagged me on social media and most of our mutuals commented some words of encouragement. By the time I get back to Valentine, everyone will know me and my ex were together.

Distance doesn't mean shit. News and gossip travel fast.

When I pull into her driveway, I kill the engine and turn off my lights. I grab her suitcase and then carry it to her door. When she walks inside her place, she gasps.

The place is nearly *empty*. Like, it's obvious that something happened.

There's a note taped to the front of the fridge. It looks like it was written in permanent marker. Grace peels it off, and her eyes scan over the pages so fast.

When she finishes, she crinkles it in her fist. "Just when I thought this month couldn't get *any* better."

"What's it say?"

She hands it to me.

"Julia moved out while I was gone. What am I going to do? I just renewed for another six months."

Her emotions bubble, and I open my arms.

"I can't afford to live here without a roommate."

"I'll do whatever I can to help. Got it?"

"I feel so stupid for signing that lease. I should've just moved back in with my mom and stepdad. And if not, I guess I'll have to move in with you. Sleep on your couch or something."

It honestly wouldn't be the worst suggestion she's had.

"If it comes to that, deal. Colt won't mind."

We've lived together for five years and he's used to my shenanigans. Plus, he likes Grace's company. Everyone in my family does.

She sniffles. "You mean it?"

I draw an *X* over my heart. It's how we've made unbreakable promises to each other since we were kids, and we only pull them out in serious situations.

CHAPTER NINE

GRACE

Harrison gives me a hug. "Do you need me to stay with you?"

"No." I shake my head. "I know you gotta get home. I'll be fine. I promise."

"If you need me, call me, okay? You can fall asleep with me on the phone, like old times."

"I will." I walk him to the door and watch him climb into his truck. He gives me a wave before backing out and leaving.

Once I'm inside, I lock the dead bolt, then lean against the hardwood as I look around. The artwork that Julia had on the wall, two of the chairs from our unmatching dining room table, and the recliner are gone.

I make my way toward my room and notice her door is cracked. All that's left are the indents of where her bed and dresser once were, along with thumbtack holes of different photos she had hung. We weren't super close, but I at least considered her a friend. Probably didn't see the red flags in her either. Maybe I'll learn that some people just suck.

As I stand in the space, tears fall in drops on the floor. It feels like everything in my life is falling apart.

I walk to my room, flick off the light, and crawl into bed. I think about Joey. I think about Harrison and Stephanie. That stupid kiss. And Landon.

Just as he comes to mind, my phone buzzes.

LANDON

Did you make it home okay?

GRACE

Yeah, about an hour ago. Thanks for asking.
Did you?

HE TOLD me he was flying back to Fort Worth today.

LANDON

I did. Thought about you.

GRACE

Aww. That's sweet.

LANDON

It's true. I'm gonna try to come visit you after the
new year.

GRACE

I'd really like that. The West Texas mountains are
gorgeous.

LANDON

Like you.

I BLUSH and find myself smiling, even if it's a bit cheesy. I look at the time and see it's just past eleven, and I'm exhausted.

. . .

GRACE

Call me tomorrow night. I'd love to chat with you more.

LANDON

It's a date. Good night, Grace!

GRACE

Night.

BEFORE I LOCK MY PHONE, Harrison texts me.

HARRISON

Made it home. Sweet dreams.

GRACE

Sweet dreams.

I LIE AWAKE, staring at the ceiling, replaying the last year, and know I have to make changes in my life because I don't want to be in the same place I'm in this time next year. The thoughts haunt me, and I toss and turn, knowing I have to be up at seven for work.

Just as I kick one leg out from under the blankets, my phone buzzes, so I reach over to see Harrison calling. I quickly unlock my phone and answer.

"Hi."

I smile. "Hi."

"Why aren't you asleep yet?" he asks, and I can imagine him at his house, lying in the dark, talking to me.

"I'm trying." I keep my eyes closed, wishing my body would let go, wishing to lose the fight to Mr. Sandman. "Why aren't you?"

"Just restless. Making sure you're okay. I know how you get in your head."

I softly laugh. "Are you whispering so your lady of the night doesn't hear?"

"No, I'm alone, but you know I wouldn't care."

"You don't have to worry about me. I'm just so tired, and I can't sleep."

"Maybe you should put on a pair of socks?"

"Hmm. That's a thought. But I don't feel like gettin' up." Just having him on the phone with me is enough to help me slowly relax.

"When you stop talking, I'll end the call. Just like when we were teenagers."

"Okay," I whisper, remembering when we'd stay up all night talking and then fall asleep on the phone together. Usually, I'd be the first to snooze because his voice is smooth, like honey. "I like listening to you breathe."

"Like this?" He makes the Darth Vader sound effects. "Luke, I am your father."

"Exactly." I place him on speaker and put my phone next to my pillow as I pull the blankets over my shoulders. "Harrison?"

"Yeah?"

"Tell me a bedtime story. Like old times."

"Okay." He chuckles. "In a land far, far away, there was a beautiful princess ..."

"And she just wanted to be somebody's someone."

"How was your trip?" Kinsley leans over my desk, twirling her brown hair around her finger.

"It was fine."

She's sipping on a large coffee that she got from the coffee shop on the corner. It smells like sugar and spice and everything nice.

"Where's mine?" I immediately smile.

A few months ago, I was hired as the front desk clerk at the newspaper. It's a fancy way of calling me a receptionist. This job is a stepping-stone for me while I work on my wedding planning business. It's not somewhere I'll work forever.

"You can have this one," she offers, and even though her lips are pink, there isn't a smudge on the lid. "So, zero updates?"

"Zero."

I log in to my computer and flip my planner to December. Just a few weeks ago, I was asked to help Kinsley sort through all of the entries for her weekly Q&A column. The two of us have a lot of work to do before Christmas to get ready for the launch in the first week of January. Kinsley is the only reason this job is tolerable. She at least makes it fun.

"So Houston was just *fine*?"

She patiently waits for me to give her more information, but I don't feel like talking about it. Honestly, if I could snap my fingers and erase Joey from my life, I would.

"Yep." I meet her eyes. I told her how excited I was to see Joey. It was all I talked about since Halloween. "Do you know something you shouldn't know?"

"Nope," she says. "Did you *do* something I should know about?"

"Absolutely not."

She snaps, and her shoulders fall. "Damn. Was hoping you and my brother finally got over your shit. Guess there won't be a Christmas miracle where you two admit your feelings."

"I know you're just trying to give me a hard time out of habit, but it's not happening, Kins. We're really just friends."

She glares at me.

"Oh, I was reminded about the Harrison Valentine Kiss of Death."

She snorts. "He's not *still* calling it that."

"You know about that?" I give her a puzzled look.

"Everyone does. It's why so many women are *obsessed* with him. Out of all people, I thought you'd know about the curse."

"Totally forgot about it until then."

"Wait." I almost see the cogs spinning in her brain. "Did you two kiss in Houston?"

Immediately, my cheeks heat and give me away. Dammit.

I try to act unaffected, but it's nearly impossible. I'm a bad actress, and everyone in town knows it.

She leans across the counter and whispers, "Oh my God, you *did.*"

"You'd better not tell anyone. It was a joke. Do not feed the rumors about us."

I keep my voice low and look over my shoulder, making sure no one else can hear our conversation. There are three other journalists in the office, plus our boss. The last thing I need is this spreading throughout the office because gossip always makes its way around town.

Something said in passing can easily get inflamed into something it's not. There is no stopping a runaway train when drama is involved.

"Your secret is safe with me, but tell me, has the Kiss of Death started to work?"

"I'm completely immune," I say, something I've been repeating since the moment our lips crashed together. "Are there any planets in retrograde right now? Everything feels *strange.*"

"Nope," she singsongs as she walks to her desk. "I knew my reading was right."

"What reading?" I get up and follow her as she logs in to her computer.

"The love tarot reading I did for Harrison when I guessed that you and your boyfriend broke up."

My jaw clenches. "You're too good at this."

"At what?" She types away and then looks up at me.

"Getting information out of people."

"As easy as squeezing juice outta oranges. It's why I became a journalist. Plus, I've had lots of siblings to practice on over the years." She looks up at me. "I heard about your roommate."

I shake my head. Nothing is private here. "Who told you?"

"Vera saw Julia moving furniture out of your condo on Saturday."

Vera is the youngest Valentine sibling. She just turned seventeen and graduates from high school in June.

That's the thing about small towns—someone is in your business without even trying. That's just how it is. Most of us try to keep our business to ourselves, but you just gotta assume someone saw something. And people talk.

I sigh.

"So whatcha gonna do?"

"I need to find a roommate by the end of the month, or I'll have to move back home with my mom. Something I cannot do." I keep my voice low.

Kinsley stops typing. "You know, I think Remi is looking for a place."

Remi Valentine is a year and a half younger than me and Harrison. She's also twins with Colt. There are a total of ten Valentine kids—Beckett, Kinsley, Harrison, Remington, Colt, Fenix, Emmett, London, Sterling, and Vera. I've hung out with all of them throughout the years.

"Really?" This is the best news I've heard all week because we get along so well.

"Yeah, she said she wanted to move out of my parents' house

after the start of the year. Maybe *she* manifested this." Kinsley claps her hands together. "Want me to ask? We have a lunch date, and I can chat with her then."

"Please. She would be perfect. We don't hang out like we used to, but we've always gotten along."

"Yeah, you two would be lucky to have each other as roomies. I'll keep you updated. Put some feelers out there," Kinsley says.

Debbie enters, wearing dark glasses over her face, and her hair is a mess. Kinsley and I both give her a look as she sits at her desk. She's worked at the newspaper for decades and knows everything about everyone. The woman also takes no shit from anyone, not even our boss.

Before we can say anything, she lifts her hand. "Don't speak. I drank too much yesterday, and I'm dealing with a hangover. Also, mind your business."

When Mr. Anderson, our boss, comes out of his office and glares at us, I take that as my cue to return to the front. I unlock my computer and scroll through my email, deleting all the junk and flagging what's important. Once I've sorted through it all, I text Harrison.

GRAOC

Good morning! Hope you got some rest.

HARRISON

Didn't. Stayed up way too late. Couldn't sleep.

GRACE

Maybe you needed some forced snuggles.

I LAUGH, thinking about how much he hates them.

GRACE

Oh, thought I'd give you a fair warning. Kinsley
might know we kissed.

Just typing that causes a surge of adrenaline to course through
my veins. I look at the message and read it a few times before I
press Send. Last thing I need is her blindsiding him at a family
event.

HARRISON

WHAT?!

GRACE

I don't know how she got it out of me.

HARRISON

This is your fault. Drunkie just had to call me a
chicken!

GRACE

I'm not sorry about it.

His text bubble appears and then disappears. Then, he doesn't
type anything for what feels like an hour, though only a minute
has passed.

HARRISON

No?

GRACE

No. What about you?

. . .

ANOTHER LONG PAUSE.

I might have pushed it too far this time. Then my phone dings.

HARRISON
Hell no.

A SMILE TOUCHES my lips as I think about how he kissed me.

GRACE
Would you do it again?

NOW, I'm getting too brave, but I kinda want to know if it feels the same when I'm not three sheets to the wind. Butterflies swarm me as I anticipate his answer.

HARRISON
Depends. I prefer it when girls don't puke after
my mouth is on theirs.

THAT RESPONSE IS good enough for me.

GRACE

Oh, yeah, true. Going into my cave and hiding
now before I get in trouble.

HARRISON

Whatcha doing for dinner?

GRACE

Nothing. Julia might've taken all the food out of
my fridge, considering she took the shower
curtain.

HARRISON

I honestly never liked her.

GRACE

Can you start warning a girl?

HARRISON

Absolutely. I'll be at your house at 7.

GRACE

It's a date!

I REREAD what I typed and bite my lip, realizing my error. Or
maybe I'm too in my head.

GRACE

Not a real date. I didn't mean it like that.

HARRISON

Maybe it is. See ya then.

MY BODY HEATS from the inside out, and I know my cheeks are
beet red. They always give me away. I turn my head to make sure

no one notices, and Kinsley is standing in Mr. Anderson's doorway. She's smiling.

Busted.

I wouldn't put it past her to ask her brother if he just texted me. She means well.

GRACE

Wait. Do I need to pick up anything?

HARRISON

Nah. I gotchu, babe.

Babe.

I read the word. He's called me that a million times. Has he always been this flirty? I scroll up to last week and reread our messages with the blinders turned off. I scroll back further, and it's still the same. Have I been oblivious?

"Yes," I whisper and lock my phone, "I have."

With my fingers on the keyboard, I stare out the window as I replay old memories.

"Ahem." Debbie knocks on the counter. "Baby, you were on a different planet."

"I feel like it too. Sorry. Whatcha need?"

"Can you help me change the toner?"

I nod, standing, happy for the distraction. When I pass Kinsley, she nods and goes into the break room. I don't follow her. Once I'm finished with the printer, I keep my gaze forward, not bringing any attention to myself as I pass all the journalists.

The day passes by quickly, and when I clock out, I'm shocked that it's already dark. It's the one thing I don't like about the winter months. I want more sunshine.

As soon as I step outside, Kinsley stops me. "I talked to my sister. She's in. She said she'd text you this week so you can meet up and chat. Roommates!"

"Oh my God," I say, giving her a hug. "Thank you!"

Then I text Harrison and let him know the good news.

HARRISON

Told ya it would work out.

GRACE

You're always right! Not sure why I doubted ya. Excited!

ONCE I'M HOME, I make sure I have pots and pans. Thankfully, I do.

And then I bide my time until Harrison arrives.

CHAPTER TEN

HARRISON

"**W**hy are you walkin' with a pep in your step like that?" Sterling asks when I turn the corner. He's carrying a shovel full of shit.

Sterling is eighteen and my youngest brother. After he graduated high school earlier this year, Beckett offered him a job at the training facility. We've been teaching him the ropes and giving him more responsibility. He works hard, shows up on time, and follows instructions. It's been great having him around, even though I give him a hard time.

"Must be going on a date," Beckett says from the hayloft as he throws a bale over.

"What the hell?!" I yell up at him as it drops right in front of me.

He chuckles and throws another one. "I ain't got time for you to be walkin' like a slowpoke. Go on vacation for a weekend and come back with no fucks to give."

"Oh, he actually had fucks to give?" Sterling chuckles, and I turn to glare at him.

"I remember when you didn't work here and Beckett couldn't gang up against me with anyone."

"The good ole days," he says with a snicker. Beckett climbs down the ladder and grabs a bale in each hand. "Wait until I get Fenix training here and Emmett too."

He's talking about our younger sister and brother. Fenix had a barrel racing scholarship at A&M and is a great teacher and rider. Emmett is working the cattle on our parents' ranch, but we're trying to swipe him to help us train horses. Dad already warned us about stealing his workers from the facility.

When his boots hit the ground, he glares at me. "You just gonna keep standin' in the way, or you gonna help?"

I growl, picking up the other one, and follow him outside.

"I got somewhere to be." The twine I'm holding digs into my hands.

Beckett's wearing his leather gloves.

"I do too," he says. "My future wife is waitin' for me."

"Yeah, same," I mutter under my breath, and I know he doesn't hear me because he wouldn't have let that one slide.

"What's been goin' on with you?" he finally asks. "Something is up."

We spread the alfalfa around for the horses, and they immediately mosey over.

"Not sure what you're talkin' about." *Deflected.*

"You've been in your head all day. That's all." He pulls the gloves off his hands and stuffs them in the pockets of his Carhartt jacket.

"Just tired from driving across the state," I say because it's not completely a lie. But he's right; I have been thinking a lot today. On the way back to the barn, I turn to him. "You know how Mama always says she can feel change in the air?"

"Yeah."

The sounds of our boots crunching over gravel fill the silence.

"For some reason, I get it. Feels like something big is happening right now."

He pats me on the back. "I hope you didn't knock someone up."

"Fuck off," I tell him, the conversation perfectly ruined. I make a beeline toward my truck. "See ya tomorrow."

AFTER I SHOWER, I stop by the grocery store and then go straight to Grace's. As soon as I park, she opens the front door for me. Her hair is down, tucked behind her ears, and she's wearing shorts and a T-shirt.

"Need me to grab anything?" she asks as I carry a few bags in each hand.

"I got it, thanks."

As I pass her, the light hint of her perfume lingers. She follows behind me, and I set them on the counter.

"This is gonna be so good," she says, unloading the bags.

Different-sized pots and pans are on the counter, along with an assortment of knives and a cutting board.

"Oh, you got wine?" She reads the bottle. "Sweet red. How'd you know I was thinking about picking up a bottle of this?"

"Because I can basically read your mind these days."

"Really?" She lifts a brow. "What am I thinking right now?"

Her eyes meet mine and trail down to my lips.

"You're dirty," I say with a laugh.

"What?! I wasn't thinking anything like that!"

"You sure? You basically just eye-fucked me." I meet her gaze.

She gasps. "No, I didn't. *This* would be eye-fucking you."

Grace takes a step back and does the same thing, but instead of stopping on my lips, her gaze trails down my body as she nibbles on her lower lip.

"Okay, that's enough. I feel like you undressed me."

She snorts, pouring us two glasses. "What, you don't imagine your best friend naked twenty-four seven?"

"And comments like that are exactly why your boyfriends don't like me being around." I search around in the lower cabinets for a cheese grater.

"You searchin' for this thing?" She lifts it in the air, and the silver coating catches a glint of the overhead light.

"Yeah, how'd you know?"

"The blocks of cheese kinda gave it away. I didn't realize you were going all out. I'd have at least dressed up for you."

"You didn't?" I say, my eyes sliding up her body.

I think she blushes as I fill the largest pot she has with water, then place it on the stove. We work around the kitchen like we can predict the other's moves as we drink our wine.

She preheats the oven as I season the meat. When the oven beeps, I slide the pan of chicken in and set a timer.

"Wait, you're making homemade sauce?" She looks at the heavy cream, cheese blocks, and garlic.

"Correction, *we* are making homemade sauce."

"The last time, I burned the shit out of it, and it looked like gravy." She bursts into laughter.

"Thankfully, I'm here to make sure that won't happen."

She smiles. "Maybe you're the lucky charm then."

"Also, the only reason it looked like liquid shit is because you got distracted and forgot to stir," I remind her, grabbing the cutting board and a knife. "Come here. We'll do it together."

Grace moves beside me, and she's standing so close that I can feel the warmth of her body against mine.

I look over at her. "Let's mince the garlic, and then we'll work on shredding the cheese."

"The preshredded would've saved us so much time."

"It's not as good if you rush it though. You've got to give it care. Let it simmer. Bring it to a boil, then serve. It's kinda like a relationship in a way."

She nods. "You're right. My sauce is shit, and so is my dating life."

"You can always take cooking lessons," I tell her. "Not all is lost."

She laughs and sits on the countertop as I continue prepping. "I'm gonna make sure whoever I marry is good in the kitchen. Then I won't have to worry about it."

"Perfect partner? And go. I'm keeping my eye out."

She looks up at the ceiling like she's pondering the question, but she already knows what she wants in her dream partner. At least I do.

"Hmm. He has to be tall. Like, way taller than me. Hardworking. Not afraid to get his hands dirty. Funny. Outgoing. Sexy. Must be able to cook. Has to love his family. And strong. I need a man who can carry me if Drunkie comes out to play. Also, he has to be committed to me and me only. Oh, and if we're talking about my wish list? He needs to be able to move me with his words, you know? Be able to say stuff that takes my breath away. Snuggling every night is a requirement."

I smirk, knowing I can check every single one of those boxes. I think she knows it too.

She picks up her glass of wine and sips. "Think it's doable?"

"Sounds like a unicorn. Not sure they exist," I tell her.

"What I've learned is all the good ones are always taken." She watches me push the block of cheese down the grater.

"Want to try?" I scoot over, and she hops down and joins me. "Just go slow."

Grace takes her time, slowly shredding the cheese, keeping her grip tight on the block.

I reposition her hand on the top of the grater. "Like this. Add some downward pressure to better stabilize it. Not too much more. We just need half a cup."

"Okay," she whispers.

Once we have enough, I open the mozzarella and give it to her.

When the water begins to boil, I slide the noodles inside.

"Oh, you mean no homemade noodles?" Grace snickers.

"Maybe next time."

My arm brushes against hers as I reach for my wine. The buzzing begins, and I see goose bumps on her arms as I drop them in the water.

"So, teach me the Valentine way of making this sauce." Grace looks at the ingredients that we prepared.

"After you," I say, holding out my hand for her. "You're the chef tonight."

I move behind her, giving her plenty of space. "Put three tablespoons of butter and some oil in the bottom."

She reaches for the spatula, and that's when I notice her ass cheeks are peeking from under her shorts. Going forward, I will be keeping my eyes above the waist.

"Lord help us," she says, mixing it around.

"I was thinking the same thing."

A smile touches her lips as she slightly looks over her shoulder at me. "We'll see; maybe I won't fuck it up this time."

"I hope not," I say, knowing we're talking about two different things. Maybe one day, Grace will realize what's right in front of her.

I give her the next step, and she adds the cream and garlic, then stirs.

"So, what about you? What's on your partner wish list?"

"I'm keeping my options open. No wish list means no disappointments, ya know?"

She shakes her head. "Not good enough. There's got to be something."

"Okay, she has to be caring. Isn't afraid to be herself. Independent. Have her own style and march to the beat of her own drum."

"I'm sure there are some single elementary school teachers in town." She snickers.

"Perfect place to search for babes. Gah, I should've thought of that myself." I tap my head. "Oh, time for the final two steps. This is where the magic happens."

Grace reaches for the Parmesan and dumps it in.

"Now, stir until it's mixed and smooth. Then we'll dump the mozzarella and do it again."

After it's made, I add salt and pepper, then take the wooden spoon and lift it to Grace's lips. "You have to try it."

She tastes it, her eyes widening as she pulls away. "Wow."

"Right?"

"Should totally add that to your *trying to impress women* list."

I pop a brow. "How do you know it's not already?"

"Touché. So …" She lingers. "Kinsley told me she did a reading."

As soon as the words leave her mouth, I pull the noodles from the burner and drain them. "Not you too."

"Well, what did it say?" She sips her wine, but I see the curious look in her eyes.

"If you want her to pull your love reading, just ask her. She would be down for it, trust me. But mine? It was something about balancing forces. That's all I remember."

And I'm being honest. I don't believe in that woo-woo stuff like my sister does. But I will always stop and pick a penny up if it's heads up.

"Sounds like Jedi stuff," she says, and I laugh. "Maybe I will ask."

She pulls her phone from her pocket, and I'm honestly shocked those shorts had a pocket.

"If you open that can of worms, there's no closing it," I warn, knowing where this road leads.

She types something and presses Send.

"Well, *you* let the vampire in, okay?"

Grace leans against the counter, texting my sister as I remove the chicken. We steal glances at each other.

I shoot her a smile. "What's she saying?"

She shakes her head. "Exactly what I thought she'd say. Wait. She said we got the same exact reading. Now she's freaking out."

"I warned you," I tell her, putting garlic bread in the oven while I slice the chicken.

"Can I help you with anything?"

I shake my head. "No, babe."

Grace's phone buzzes. Text messages from my sister flood in. She glances down at it, then back at me.

"Now watch her start talking about spooky synchronicities and saying we're meant to be together," I say with a smirk.

Grace gasps. "Oh my goodness, she just did."

She turns her phone around and shows me as she grabs her glass of wine.

"Yeah, I know. I've dealt with this my entire life. Do you believe it?"

She shakes her head, but her smile lights up the entire fucking room. "Of course not."

"Okay." I playfully roll my eyes. "Then nothing to worry about."

"Yep, just like the Kiss of Death. Just a bunch of woo."

"Yeah, totally," I tell her, and then I notice a slight change in her expression. "What, is the curse working?" I lift a brow, knowing her better than she knows herself sometimes.

She grabs plates from the cabinets. "Nope. Still completely immune, just like always. But if that changes, please feel free to get me medical attention because that means something malfunctioned in my brain."

"Ouch. Harsh. But I'll keep that in mind when you start dreaming about me because I've heard that's how you know you've got it really bad."

She chuckles. "Oh good. I'm safe then. I haven't had a single dream since my parents divorced. We're good."

"Good luck." I wink and remove the garlic bread from the oven.

"Whoa." Grace scans over the counter. "This looks legit."

"Because it is. Come on."

Her eyes slide up and down my body, and I give her a look that's nothing other than a seductive dare. She licks her lips.

"A staring contest?" I ask, lifting my brows. "You know you're gonna lose. You always look away first."

I cross my arms and lean against the counter. She sets down her wine and takes several steps forward until she's standing right in front of me. The smell of her is so damn intoxicating that it nearly brings me to my knees, but my confidence doesn't flex. I've waited for this very moment for as long as I can remember, and I stand with my feet firmly planted.

"Make your move, queen," I mutter, not moving my gaze from hers. This is more than a staring contest and she knows it.

She smirks, standing up on her tiptoes, then slowly brushes her soft lips against mine before closing her eyes and whispering, "You win."

I wrap my arms around her as our mouths crash together. Her tongue swipes against mine and we're completely tangled. In the heat of the moment, I push her against the counter. Her leg wraps around my waist, and I lift her onto the flat surface as we continue to make out. Her legs are parted wide and I stand between her thighs. My heart races, and I think I've died and gone to heaven as she runs her fingers through my hair, moaning against me.

"Gracie," I growl.

"Fuck," she hisses between kisses. "We shouldn't be doing this."

"But you are." I laugh against her lips as she scoots closer to the edge. I'm hard as fuck, but I won't rush this. I won't treat her like everyone else because this woman is more than that—she's forever.

"You are," she says. "I *want* you."

I open my eyes and watch her kiss me, making sure this is real. My black-and-white world turns Technicolor.

Grace slides her shirt off and throws it on the floor, and I grab her face, kissing her again. She slides off the counter and as she grabs my hand, there's a knock on her door.

A knock that turns into a pounding.

"Why!" Grace groans.

"Grace, *please!*" Whoever it is sounds upset.

"Shit. It's Haley." Her eyes are wide, and she's rushing around, putting on her shirt and trying to fix her hair. Her lips are swollen, and she turns to me. "How do I look?"

"Guilty as fuck."

She throws her hand in the air as she rushes to the door. "Great!"

CHAPTER ELEVEN

GRACE

I suck in a deep breath and open the door.

Haley falls into my arms. "He broke up with me."

"Oh no. I'm so sorry."

"Please tell me you're not busy," she cries, and I shake my head.

"It's fine; it's fine. Come in." I open the door wider.

She looks at Harrison, then looks at me. "Look, I'm already the third wheel!"

"No, no, you're not. If anything, I'd be the third wheel because you two have a higher chance of getting together than me and him, ya know?" I tell her.

Things like that just roll so easily off my tongue that I don't have to think about it anymore. Even though he just stole my breath away and we almost went too far. We lost control—that's all it was.

"You're right," he says, agreeing with me. "Are you hungry? I cooked homemade pasta."

I look over my shoulder at Harrison, and he's in the kitchen, calm and collected.

"Yeah, you should join us. I even kinda made the sauce with a lot of help. We were just about to eat and watch some TV—that's it. We'll be the Three Musketeers."

Harrison walks into the living room and hands Haley a glass of wine. Then he returns with two plates.

I look up at him and smile. "Thank you."

"Thanks," Haley says, and we sit next to each other on the couch.

I sit in the middle, Haley is on one side, and Harrison is on the other.

"So, tell me what happened." I try to focus on Haley as Harrison's leg brushes against mine.

The temperature in the room rises, and I feel like I might internally combust. Stupid-as-fuck goose bumps trail my arm, and I rub them away.

"He … he … he called me up and told me that he didn't love me anymore and couldn't keep pretending." She sniffles, then blows her nose on her napkin. "You can't even fix that. It's over."

I wrap my arms around her. "I'm sorry you're going through this."

"Aww, but you're going through it too. It's the only reason I came over." She wipes her face.

I nod and glance at Harrison before turning to her. "I'm doing okay."

"I hate men!" she says, shaking her head.

"Me too," I tell her.

"Me three," Harrison says, and we all laugh.

"Don't act like you're innocent," Haley tells him. "You've made hundreds of women cry."

"Is it hundreds? Lost count. Might be thousands at this point." He shrugs. "There's one thing about me though, I don't lead people on. What you see is what you get, flaws and all."

I swallow hard. "Harrison is proof good guys still exist."

She laughs.

And I squeeze her. "Now, no more crying over delicious-as-fuck pasta and Daddy Kevin Costner. That cowboy hat." I fan myself. "Oh, I met someone," I tell her. "Landon."

I think Harrison tenses beside me.

"Is he single?"

I nod. "I can introduce you two. I think I'm gonna live in my single-girl era for a little while before rushing into another relationship. Next time, it has to be forever."

"Okay," she says. "He's cute?"

"Girl, like, ten times hotter than Harrison."

"Ten times?" he huffs. "Landon is a bull rider. That dude wins. Gotta have the balls to do that shit—balls that you don't mind losing. I'm good. Hundred times hotter."

I howl. "See, even Harrison approves. I'll introduce you to one another, and who knows what will happen?"

"Okay. Are your lips swollen? From Landon?"

I cover my mouth. "Are they?"

"Knowing her, she already has a new boyfriend lined up," Harrison says, and my heart rate upticks.

"Oh, who is he? A local?"

"There is *no one*. Single-girl era, *remember*? This is how rumors get started."

Haley gives me a look, and I go back to my pasta. We fall into silence, watching TV, but I'm not listening to anything. My eyes blur over as I stare at the corner of the television, completely lost in my thoughts. The only thing that brings me back is Harrison placing his hand on my back.

"Want some more?"

I shake my head, looking up at him as he stands.

"I've got it," I tell him, standing, too, taking the plates from his hands. "You cooked. Least I can do."

"Okay," he says.

I walk past Haley into the kitchen, needing the escape from being so close to him. Not knowing what I'm feeling inside. Wishing I knew if this was a mistake. It didn't feel like one, but it usually doesn't at first. It usually takes time for me to get in my head and mess up things.

"Has Hayden been as annoyingly in love lately? Because Kinsley has been intolerable." Harrison makes small talk about her older brother, who's dating his sister.

Hayden was Kinsley's high school sweetheart, the man she pretended didn't exist for years. Then, he returned to town earlier this year. After a lot of drama, the two of them decided to work it out. Now they're official again.

"Oh, grossly so. I told him I'm gonna start walking into the back room with a bucket of water in my hand because if I catch them on that couch in the bookstore one more time …" She laughs. "I have a secret to tell you that you can't fuck up."

"Okay," Harrison says, and I listen.

"My brother is planning to propose at the party on New Year's Eve. So everyone kinda needs to be at the bed-and-breakfast." Haley turns and looks at me. "You're going, right?"

I smile. "We wouldn't miss that for anything. And thanks for the heads-up."

"Oh man, she's gonna be so excited." Harrison smiles. "But now I gotta tell *you* a secret."

"Yeah?" Haley looks uneasy.

"My brothers and I will now have to threaten Hayden's life before he slides a ring on my sister's finger. The good old-fashioned Valentine way."

She bursts into laughter. "Please tell me it'll be recorded."

Harrison shoots her a wink.

Haley turns to me. "You know, I was having a shitty day, and you two helped. A lot." Then she stands. "I guess I should get going. Thanks for dinner. Was incredible."

"You're welcome to come over anytime," I tell her, meaning it.

I dry my hands and walk her to the door. She gives me a wave and walks to her car. Once she drives away, I close the door, learning to sit in the awkwardness.

"Breaking up must be in the water or something," I say as I put the dishes in the dishwasher and place food in containers.

"About what happened …" he says.

And I know he's talking about before Haley showed up.

"Yeah, we probably shouldn't do that."

He pauses for a moment, studying me. "You're right."

"We just got lost in the heat of the moment."

He laughs. "Yeah. I should probably get goin'. Had a long day."

I move around the counter and give him some to-go containers full of food. "Lunch for tomorrow."

"Thanks, princess. Have a good night. If you can't sleep, call me."

"Will do," I tell him.

He stands and hugs me, and then I follow him to the door. I lean against the frame, watching him go to his truck. He looks back at me over his shoulder, wearing a smirk. Then he turns around, pretending to lasso me as he walks backward. I play along, jolting forward and out the door. He shakes his head, then gets in his truck and leaves.

Once inside my condo, I lean against the door, holding my hand to my heart. That line should never be crossed ever again because I'm not sure we'll have Haley around to bring us back to reality. And once that cat is out of the bag, there is no putting it back in. It might already be too late.

IT'S BEEN seven days since Harrison and I crossed the line. Neither of us have mentioned it.

I carry grocery bags into my mom's house since she asked me to pick some things up before coming over. Christmas is next week, and she wanted to meet beforehand since she'll be hosting my sister and her fiancé. Plus, she's noticed I've been avoiding everyone after Joey and I broke up.

When I walk in, Mom is in her office, typing away on her laptop.

She takes her glasses off her nose and looks up at me. "You're already here?" She looks at the gold watch on her wrist, then back up at me. "Lost track of time again."

"It's fine," I tell her.

She walks over and grabs some bags from my hands, and we go to the kitchen to put them away.

"How have you been?" she asks, stacking packets of tuna in the cabinet.

"I've been fine."

"Why'd you say it like that?" She turns and looks at me, and I try not to cry. "Aww, honey. I'm sorry."

Mom wraps her arms around me, just like she did when I was a kid, and it's comforting.

"It's fine. I'm just tired of being the one who can't find someone to love them."

She sighs and wipes away my tears. "You will, honey. If I can find love again in Charles, you'll find it too. But in the meantime, you gotta live your life."

Charles is the man my mom fell in love with five years after her and my father's nasty divorce. My stepdad is a great guy.

"I'm gonna try, Mama. I am. I just really thought I'd have something other than a failed relationship to bring to my sister's wedding with me."

"Aww, sweetie. It's not a competition. I know it hurts right now, but when you get married, you'll be thankful every single one of those failed relationships happened and led you to that very moment, ya know?"

"Yes," I say, nodding, knowing as soon as I spoke to my mom, I would cry. It's why I've been ignoring her calls.

"*Oh,* honey." She gives me a hug as I wipe away my tears and put on a smile. "It's all going to be just fine. It will."

"I know. Now, about Christmas dinner."

She pushes my hair over my shoulder, and I look at her.

"Would you be opposed to somethin' like lasagna? I don't think I can eat any more turkey, or I might turn into one. Especially after Thanksgiving."

I snort. "You got a twenty-pound bird for me, you, and Charles. But honestly, I would love that." Then, I remember something. "Isn't Savannah vegetarian now?" I'm pretty sure the last time I spoke to my sister, she told me that.

Last year, she moved to California, started recycling, and then got with a surfer. In a few months, she'll be married.

"Oh, right. I'll make two lasagnas then. Thank you. I almost forgot. They're supposed to stay here that night and then go see your dad and Tanya next."

I nod. "We all know how Tanya loves a holiday feast."

"Okay, that's funny, but also, come on."

My mom caught them together on Christmas. It sucked.

I have a chuckle, and then she changes the subject. Mom has no ill will. It's just me who's harboring feelings about it—still. They killed my idea of love. I thought they were happy, but they were just playing pretend.

"You want a cup of coffee?"

"Nah, I'm good. Is that all you needed?"

"Yes, but I also wanted to see you and make sure you were doing okay. Been worried about you after Julia moved out."

"Worry about me if I cut bangs. That's a real cry for help. Until then, I'm fine. Also, Remi Valentine is moving in with me on the first of January. We spoke yesterday to confirm it all. I'm just treating it like I got to live in a two-bedroom apartment for free for a month."

She grabs the pot from the coffee maker and fills it with water before pouring it into the reservoir. "Have you thought any more about starting your business?"

"Well, yes," I tell her, tightening my ponytail and sitting on the barstool as she fills a filter with grounds. It smells good. And I'm brought back to sitting in this very spot every Saturday, waiting for my mom to drop me off at Harrison's.

"I just don't want you to get stuck working a job that's not your dream. You know, a new year is coming up. You should reach for the stars. You're single. Smart. Pretty. Talented. You can make anything happen that you want."

My phone vibrates in my pocket, and I unlock it and see a text from Harrison.

It's a picture of him in the saddle, wearing a cowboy hat, and he's blowing the largest bubble with his gum. I immediately laugh.

Mom glances at my phone and then back at me. "What's my son doin' now?"

I turn my phone around and show her, and she laughs as she reads the text he sent me under it.

HARRISON

Mine's bigger than yours.

"You'd better tell him to behave," Mom playfully warns, and I type the message and send it to him.

HARRISON

HARRISON

Do NOT let your mom read our texts. OMFG.

GRACE

There ain't nothing I'd hide in here. Totally platonic.

HARRISON

Yep, just like last week.

THE SMILE on my face widens, and Mom clears her throat as she watches me.

"What?" I ask.

"Nothing. Nothing at all," she says as she refills her mug.

It's my cue to leave.

"Gonna go, Mom. I'm pretty tired after working all day."

I walk over to her and give her a hug.

"I love you," she says, patting my arm.

"Love you too. See you next week?"

"Yep, I'll see you then."

"I'll bring a peanut butter pie," I offer, and then she walks me out.

On the way home, I stop at the gas station and buy the biggest packet of strawberry Bubblicious I can find. When Harrison and I were kids, we'd go through packages of it like our lives depended on it. I go back to my car and pop a piece in my mouth, forgetting just how sweet and juicy it is. After I blow the biggest bubble and snap a picture with my eyes crossed, I send it to him.

HARRISON

Damn.

THEN IT BURSTS, and it's all over my face, and I take another pic and send it.

HARRISON

Karma for showing off.

I SNICKER, glad that we can fall right back to how things were before.

GRACE

I'll be home soon.

HARRISON

Awesome. I'm still at work. Then, I'm meeting up with my brothers and Hayden.

I LAUGH, knowing they're going to give Hayden hell.

GRACE

You're riding and texting again?

HARRISON

What can I say? I'm a man of many talents. Chat later.

GRACE

AFTER I SEND him a heart emoji, I continue my drive home, blowing bubbles the whole way.

Maybe the single era won't be so bad after all.

Maybe it will be my best one yet.

CHAPTER TWELVE

HARRISON

"Jingle Bell Rock" blasts through my house as I place balls of cookie dough on a tray. It's tradition for Grace and me to meet every Christmas Eve in matching pajamas to exchange gifts and eat chocolate chip pecan cookies until we're sick. It's something we've done since we got our driver's license, and we haven't missed a year yet.

Headlights turn into my driveway, and I put the cookies into the oven and set an alarm.

A few moments later, the door swings open. She's carrying a huge box wrapped in silver paper, and it's so tall that I can't see her five-six frame.

"You'd better have your onesie on," I tell her, looking down at my candy-cane-striped legs and making sure my ass flap is snapped in place. This was her bad decision that I went with because, last year, I'd chosen Yeti costumes for us, and I even have pictures to prove it.

"Is that a refrigerator box?" I ask as she drags it to the corner of the room.

It's too tall to fit underneath the tree, so she sets it beside it. I walk out of the kitchen and cross my arms over my chest.

"Maybe." She turns around. "Oh my goodness. I forgot my hat! It looks adorable on you!" Her face softens, and I know she's being sincere.

It's a red-and-white Santa hat with a cotton ball on the end.

I tug it off my head, my shaggy hair going everywhere. "You want mine?"

"No, no, go ahead." She stands on her tiptoes.

I bend down for her until we're at eye level as she squishes it over my hair. "Do you remember when we were the same height?"

She meets my eyes, taking my face in her cold hand. "How could I forget? Didn't last long though." She smiles as I straighten my stance, towering over her. She looks up at me. "Now, you're ready for our picture. Let's go for it?"

"Let's do it."

She props her phone against the can opener on the counter and talks to me over her shoulder as she adjusts it. "We have ten seconds, okay?"

"Then you'd better hurry." I wave her toward me.

She jogs and slides on the floor, wrapping her arm around me. I grab her, steadying her. The fast shutter sound starts, and then we hit every pose. We have years of practice.

The Christmas playlist I created continues in the background, and we sing along in the living room.

Thankfully, Colt isn't here, or he'd have some shit to say. A few years ago, he told me he'd chill at our parents' house until midnight going forward. Makes me laugh thinking about it, because he's not here.

As we dance, Grace swings her hips around and points down to the open ass flap, revealing her cream-colored lace panties. I force myself to think about something else because these pajamas leave nothing to the imagination. And it goes both ways. Getting hard is the last thing I need.

She tries to snap the button properly, but it never clicks. "I'm kinda mad at myself for buying these. They look cute. Cheap as hell."

Her eyes slide up and down me like she just noticed how revealing it is.

"Never mind. Not upset anymore." She grabs her phone and takes a picture of me.

"That'd better not be used for blackmail later," I warn.

She shakes her head, then turns it around to show me. "You know I'd never do that to you. But there are some women online who'd pay good money for these."

"Luckily, I'm just for *your* pleasure." I meet her gaze, feeling that magnetic pull surge between us.

The oven beeps, breaking the connection as we enter the kitchen.

Taking the lead, Grace grabs an oven mitt and removes the oversized tray. "Oh my goodness, these look and smell so good."

"Hell yeah, they do."

Grace snags a cookie with her bare hands. She tosses it back and forth like a hot potato before plopping it back onto the tray. "Shit, they're too hot."

"Well, yeah, silly girl." I move her palm under the cool water. Then, I place her fingers to my lips and kiss them. "Better?"

"It always is when you do that."

"Now, can you pretty please *try* to be patient?" I tap her nose, and we lean against the counter and wait.

I open the freezer and take out a bottle of bourbon-whiskey blend, then set it on the counter.

Her brows rise. "Oh, we're going *there* tonight?"

I remove the top and take several gulps, needing to loosen up because I'm feeling the tension.

She reaches for it, reading the label. "American Honey. A bourbon-and-whiskey blend. Do I need a chaser?"

"Nope, it's smooth."

She takes a swig, then another. "Dangerous, but I likey."

This is the first time Grace has been single without immediately jumping into a relationship for the past *nine* years. It's now or never, and I've realized that every day since she broke up with her ex.

"How was the lasagna?" I take another sip. It's sweet, almost too sweet, but it does the job.

"The food was great. The conversation was fine." She shakes her head. "At least this year, I have a job, but single once again. Was so much fun announcing that."

I shrug. "You should double down on your wedding planning business and go all in next year."

"My mama said the same thing." Grace hiccups. "Oh no, I know what that means. Drunkie is coming out to play."

I snicker, shaking my head at her. "I'm happy you're in your single-girl era because we get to keep doing this."

"What do you mean?" Her brows furrow.

"Come on, Gracie. We won't be able to do this forever."

She searches my face. "Of course we will."

I take two steps forward, removing the space between us, and set my hand on her shoulder. "No, we won't. One day, you'll have a family, and that family is gonna need you to be Mom on Christmas Eve. We can't keep pretending that we'll always be able to do these types of things. I'm sure my wife won't let me go out and play with my childhood best friend if we have little ones in the house, ya know?"

"Yeah, we're getting old. Things are changing." She wraps her arms around me and squeezes. "The future freaks me out. I just kinda want to live in the moment and let future Grace figure it out."

I hug her back, smelling her hair.

"You Make It Feel Like Christmas" starts playing, and I grab her hand, and we two-step around the kitchen, laughing and singing together. The distraction is needed because if I think too much about the future, it freaks me out too.

"It's not Christmas without you," I tell her, dipping her back.

She giggles and spins around, and then we go back to one another.

"Same," she says, and we continue singing.

When it ends, she rushes over to the stovetop and grabs a cookie. They're so soft it nearly falls apart in her hand.

"These are perfection. Maybe you do have the magic touch."

"Of course I do," I say, grabbing the gallon of cold milk from the fridge and two glasses, then filling them halfway.

"Thank you. But I'm gonna have more of that." She points at the American Honey.

"Stayin' the night?" I grab another cookie. "Because that shit is gonna knock you on your ass."

"Do you want me to?"

I shrug. "Doesn't matter to me. But if you are, you're sleeping in my bed."

She smirks while she chews. "Are we snuggling?"

My head falls back on my shoulders, and I laugh. "No."

She pretends to pout, then grabs a napkin. "*Yes*, we are."

I grab her elbow, turning her toward me. "Do you want to?"

There's a small nod, but it's there, and that's all the fucking permission I need to lean forward and softly paint my lips against hers. She fists my onesie as our tongues slide together. Her hair, her touch, her mouth against mine is intoxicating. I can feel her in my veins, and it's too much. I slowly pull away.

"You taste like milk and cookies," she whispers.

I rest my forehead against hers. "You taste like my best friend."

She playfully smacks me in the stomach then tries to walk away, but I gently pull her back to me.

Slowly, I lift her chin so she can look at me. "It's not a bad thing, princess."

Her eyes flutter closed, and I study her face and pretty, puckered lips, waiting for mine. A small smile touches my lips before I meet her halfway.

Why does it feel so right? Why does she feel like home … already? I push the thoughts away.

"Should we open gifts now?"

"Abso-fuckin'-lutely," I tell her, following her to the living room. "One second," I say, grabbing what I got her.

She's already on the floor, sitting cross-legged, waiting for me next to the tree. I plop down beside her, and then we exchange packages.

"You'll never guess what I got you," she tells me.

"Uh, same. On the count of three?"

She nods. We count down, and then we begin opening them. I pull off the paper and unwrap the box, and inside of it is another box, then another. That's okay. I wrapped her gift with an entire roll of paper. And the inside layer has a roll of duct tape slapped around it.

When she gets to the middle layer, she falls back in a fit of laughter. "I'm never getting this open."

"Ugh. How many damn boxes are there?"

The living room is full of paper, but neither of us has found our prize. This is another one of our traditions.

Seeing her laugh so hard nearly has me in stitches, but she's struggling to get through the layers of duct tape.

"Okay, this is hard as fuck," she says. "No scissors?"

"You know the rules. Hands only," I remind her.

"Next year, I'm gonna get you so good," she playfully threatens.

"I look forward to it," I say, hoping this won't be our last year. It's something I've thought about a lot lately.

Three more boxes, and I'm finally to the last one. Grace has found the final layer of paper. We nod at the same time, and I pull out a photo album.

"How did you …"

She holds up the photo album I got her. "Did we get each other the same gift?"

"Did my sister tell you?" I question, even though I didn't tell Kinsley.

"No." She shakes her head. "We haven't talked about it at all. Swear."

I open the front page, and she's filled it full of pictures of us over the years. I chuckle.

"Oh, you had different pictures than me," she says, flipping through hers.

Then she crawls over next to me. Her head falls on my shoulder, and we turn pages together, pointing and chatting about memories we've shared. Then we make it to the end, and a tear falls from Grace's cheek. I turn to her, wiping it away.

"Aww, what's wrong?"

"You've just always been there."

I wrap my arm around her. "And always will be."

"I love this so much," she says.

"Love mine too."

We hug each other, holding our books of memories, and sit quietly as the music drifts in the background.

"Are you ready to watch *Elf*?"

"Yes," she says.

I stand and hold out my hand for her. She takes it, and I let her lead the way to my bedroom.

When she takes a step forward, Grace lifts her head and gasps. "You made our castle."

"After you." I shut the door.

She looks inside the lit blanket fort and sees the TV with *Elf* on the screen, waiting for her. I rearranged my room and moved my TV to the floor to make it happen.

"Oh, one second." I go to the kitchen and make a bag of popcorn, then grab the bottle of bourbon.

When I return, she's already inside it, lying down and looking back at me. "You always bring the snacks."

"You know it's impossible to watch a movie without popcorn."

"The lights are a perfect touch," she whispers, and I climb in, repositioning the pillows that I stole from my parents' house today because I didn't have enough.

Once I'm in place and we're both sitting upright, she scoots closer.

"Where's the remote?"

"I think I'm sitting on it." Grace lifts her ass and pulls it out.

I lie down and open my arms. Grace falls into them, and then we watch *Elf* together like we do every year. She throws a piece of popcorn into her mouth and catches it. At this point, we've got the movie memorized, just like her other rom-com favorites that we've watched hundreds of times over the years.

When we're finished eating, we take turns with the bourbon, passing it between us. It does make the movie funnier.

"My favorite," she says, pointing to the screen when Buddy kisses Jovie on the cheek and she tells him he missed.

I glance over at her and smile. Seconds later, she's quickly smacking her lips against my cheek.

I turn to her, grabbing her chin with my fingers, and I study her mouth. "You missed."

That's all it takes for us to be lost in one another again. We're a dangerous mixture of lips, tongue, and teeth. I nibble on her earlobe.

"We shouldn't do this." I try to be the voice of reason as she lies down, pulling me with her.

"We shouldn't," she moans out. Her fingers tangle in my hair as she pulls my mouth back to hers. "But …"

"Say it," I whisper, encouraging, hoping that this is the moment that she admits there's something between us.

Over the last few weeks, we've scaled a wall and crossed an invisible line we've been teetering for years. We can stop, but neither of us pulls away. There is no stopping this runaway train; we're too far gone.

She rolls on top of me and rocks against my cock. I'm so damn hard for her, and she knows it; she can feel it, and by the look on her face and how she grinds against me, she likes it. Leaning forward, she wraps her arms around me and kisses my neck as I dig my thumbs into her hips. I love every fucking curve of her body and feeling her pressed against mine.

I thread my fingers through her long brown hair, taking a fist of it as she slides her plump lips along my jawline. Together, we are magic as my heart rapidly beats in my chest. Desperate pants fill the room. I've dreamed of this very moment for as long as I can remember.

"Shit," she whispers, rocking against me. "*Why* are we in onesies?"

"They were your idea." I laugh against her mouth and pull away to look into her beautiful eyes.

Grace gives me Eskimo kisses, rubbing her nose against mine. "Should we stop?"

"Yes," I whisper.

"I don't want to." She grinds harder against me, and if she keeps going, she might get off. Hell, me too.

"Then don't. You're in control," I say, clenching my jaw, not wanting this to stop.

I'll let her call the shots. She is the one steering this ship, and I'd respect her decision to change her mind.

"I need these clothes off," she hisses. "Too restricting."

Lifting her leg, she unstraddles me, then props herself up on the fluffy pillows and slowly unsnaps the buttons down below her belly button. The eye contact is intense as I do the same.

Grace positions herself on her knees in front of me, and we're facing each other. Reaching forward, she slides her hands under the material, and I follow her lead. Her fingers glide down my chest, tracing my carved muscles.

She's breathless as her eyes study my body like she wants to devour every inch of me. "Harrison, I need you," she whispers, and I almost don't hear her.

Our mouths crash together, and I pepper kisses to her ear and whisper, "Say it again."

I need her to repeat it as I fist her hair. I need her to be sure as fuck about this.

"I *need* you like I need air," she says with desperation in her tone, and it's music to my ears.

I can't be the man to deny her. Not this time.

Grace reaches behind her and removes her bra, allowing her voluptuous breasts to fall free.

"Look," she whispers, and I move her hair over her shoulder. "I want you to see me."

The confident girl that I love so damn much appears, and I take my time studying every inch of her. "Gorgeous."

She smiles, leaning back on the pillows, and slides out of her clothes. I swallow hard as the lights cast a warm glow on her skin.

"This is my favorite part," she tells me.

"Fuck, mine too," I say, crawling over to her, lying on my side.

She wraps her arm around my neck, and we take our time exploring one another. I memorize her body with my hands, every smooth inch of her soft, vanilla-scented skin. Her breaths grow ragged as she parts her legs, and my fingers slide inside her.

I smile, chewing on my lip. "You're so wet, princess. I love it."

"You ... do that to me." She stills, placing her hand on my cheek as I slowly tease her G-spot. "It feels so ... good."

She rocks her hips, and I pull away, placing my fingers in my mouth.

"Delicious."

Carefully, I reposition myself so that I have the perfect view of her waxed pussy and ass. Then I lean forward and lick her clit, tasting all of her. She reaches down, tugging my messy hair as she rides my face. Her breathless pants give me life as I gently give her two fingers.

"More," she greedily whispers.

I give her a third digit. She lifts her arms above her head, arching her back, and seeing her nearly crumbling under my touch so quickly is pure fucking ecstasy.

She's close—I can tell by how tense her body is and her curled toes. Before giving her what she wants, I pull away, smirking.

The silent conversation that streams between us is almost too much.

"I need a condom. I'm sorry. One second."

She huffs, and she teeters on the edge, then laughs. Her hair is a mess as she rolls onto her stomach to watch me, showing me her beautiful ass.

CHAPTER THIRTEEN

GRACE

I turn over onto my stomach and watch Harrison as he slides the condom onto his thickness. He glances at me and then returns inside our castle made from sheets as the twinkle lights warm the space. My heart is racing, and every inch of my body is buzzing from nearly coming.

"We should probably make some rules," I explain.

I capture his lips, and he laughs against mine.

"I thought that was my job?"

I lean back, glancing over the constellation of freckles on his nose, and then I trace his lips with my finger. His eyes flutter closed, and his hot breath is on me.

"I want this. I want you, but I don't want it to change anything between us," I whisper.

"Nothing changes if you don't want it to."

He draws an *X* over his heart with his opposite hand. It's our unbreakable promise to one another, something we've always done since we were little. We've never broken the ones we've made.

I do the same back to him. We seal it with a kiss.

Running my fingers through his hair, I push him back. Then,

I lift one of my thick thighs and straddle him, letting out a huff when I feel the tip of him at my entrance. Shifting my body forward, I stay suspended above him because I know once this line is crossed, there is no going back.

"Scared?" He lifts his brows.

"You were right about little Harri. He's not little." I always knew Harrison had a package, but I'm more than scared he'll wreck me.

He places his hands behind his head and watches me with a devilish grin painted across his lips. "I've waited for this moment for a long-ass time."

"Fuck, same," I say, tugging his lip into my mouth and sucking.

Right now, nothing is off the table. There are no limits or boundaries that are keeping us away from one another. It's just us and our insatiable need to get the other out of our system. Right?

I know how being with Harrison works. It's a once-in-a-lifetime opportunity, and tonight, I feel like royalty, like his queen. He looks at me like I'm perfection with that damn female gaze. He will have anyone believing he's in love with them. Even me.

As our tongues twist together, his rough hands run up my legs, and he cups my ass.

"Mmm," he hums as I slowly sink onto him. "I fucking love your body."

Soft pants release from my mouth, and when our ends meet, butterflies swarm me.

"You feel so good," I whisper as he fills me so damn full. "I understand the addiction now."

This makes him chuckle as he slides his hands to my waist, kissing my shoulder. "Your skin against my lips—you're like a drug."

Light moans fill the space as I pick up my pace. As I throw my hair back, I feel Harrison's thumb circling my clit as I ride him, and I nearly have an out-of-body experience.

It's not supposed to feel like this. I'm not supposed to enjoy each second or wish it would last a lifetime.

"Jesus fucking Christ," I moan out, the orgasm threatening to spill over, but he doesn't give me what I crave, not yet.

He's not rushing, regardless if I'm nearly begging for it.

Harrison rocks his hips, giving me even more of him, causing more friction and force. Every part of my body goes rigid, and just as my mouth falls open, he rolls me over onto my back.

"I need it," I cry out.

So close.

Harrison pins my wrists above my head. His mouth hovers above mine as he slides out of me. "Enjoy it, princess," he whispers.

The anticipation of feeling him again is almost too much.

"Because we're a onetime thing and then we're done?" I ask, making sure I have the right expectations. I won't be like one of his obsessed ladies of the night who begs for more of him.

But I have to get him out of my system. *Now.*

"You know my rules have never applied to *you.*"

He shakes his head, and I hold my breath, eagerly waiting. I think, at this point, if he breathed on me, I'd come.

"*No?*" I tilt my head and smirk. "I knew you liked snuggling with me."

"I'm not admitting to that." He smiles, nuzzling into my neck before he returns to my mouth.

We kiss, and he slowly allows my body to adjust to his length and girth as he reenters me. His mouth captures my nipple, and he twirls the hard peak with his tongue. My eyes flutter closed, and I feel as if I'm losing my grasp on reality. Being with him feels different.

He moves hair out of my face and traces the shell of my ear

with his lips. Neither of us says a word as our breaths fill the space.

"I … *think* … I'm … close," I say, feeling the warmth spreading through my body again. It's slow and agonizing, torturous even. My back arches off the stacked blankets, and at any second, I'll lose myself.

"You *think?*" He takes my bottom lip into his mouth and sucks. "What does that mean?"

He thrusts forward, giving me all of him as my toes curl. My head rolls back on my shoulders, and then he pulls away.

"Noooo. *Please don't stop*, not yet," I beg, breathless, greedy, teetering on the edge. I'm so close that if he gave me one hard thrust, I'd crumble under him. My entire body is seized up, a cup waiting to pour over.

"Tell me what that means, or I'll edge you the rest of the night." He swipes his thumb across my cheek, wearing a panty-dropping smirk. "I've got plenty of time."

"No one other than myself has *ever* given me an orgasm," I whisper, *desperately* needing to come.

"Mmm. I'm gonna be your first? Damn, princess." He swallows hard.

"Yes. Now, can you please fuck me and give me a night I won't ever forget?"

His lips slam against mine, and Harrison quickly builds me back up.

"Be a good girl and come for me," he whispers.

"Yes," I hiss as he gives me every thick inch.

My head falls back, and my heart feels like it might stop when I finally spill over. Harrison continues to pump into me as I scratch my nails down his back. Reality shatters around me as my muscles contract.

"Fuck," he growls. "So tight," he whispers as my pussy clenches around him. And then he's groaning out his release.

We stay like this for a few minutes, and I think we're both in shock.

"That was … *intense.*" He kisses me again.

"Yeah," I say, not even sure I can form a complete sentence right now.

He rolls over on his back, and we both stare up at the soft lights strung at the top of the blankets, and then we glance at the TV that we muted at some point.

"I don't think I'll ever be able to watch that movie again without thinking about this," he admits.

"Uh, same." I roll over on my side and face him, squeezing my thighs together.

Tomorrow, I'll be sore from where he was—I can already tell. Harrison pulls me into his arms and holds me against his bare chest, and I squeeze him tight, like if I were to let go, he'd disappear.

He kisses my hair. "Want to watch *Elf*?"

"Yes," I tell him with a laugh.

Just as he reaches for the remote, there's a knock on his door, and we look at each other with wide eyes.

When the doorknob turns, Harrison jumps up and rushes forward, placing his foot in the way to stop it. Then he sticks his head into the hallway. "Can I help you?"

"Just wanted to tell Grace hello." By the sound of Colt's tone, I know he's smiling, but I feel like I can't breathe, knowing we're both butt-ass naked.

"She says hi back." He's on top of it. Probably knows my words are lodged in the back of my throat.

"Why are you being weird as fuck?" Colt asks.

"*Goodbye,*" Harrison tells him, shutting the door and locking it. He leans against it, crossing his arms over his chest until Colt's footsteps echo. "I need to remember to lock doors. That was too close," he whispers.

"I know." I burst out into laughter, twisted in the blankets. Giddy is the only way to explain it.

Harrison pulls on a pair of boxers and then lies down beside me as I slide on my bra and panties. *Elf* plays from the beginning, and I snuggle into his strong arms, listening to his heartbeat settle. The pillows and comforter feel like clouds, and my eyes grow heavy as he snuggles me.

Tonight, I had the best sex of my life.

I just hope we can keep our promise … and nothing changes.

THE NEXT MORNING, I wake to Harrison's scruff against my neck.

"Good morning."

"Mmm," I moan out, pressing my ass against his hard cock.

"Sorry," he says.

I turn and look over my shoulder at him. "Don't be."

Reaching behind me, I grip my hand around him.

"Don't you dare start something you're not gonna finish," he warns.

I let go, sliding my panties down. "What time is it?"

"Five. I've got a few hours before I have to leave for Christmas at my parents'," he growls in my ear.

As his large hand runs down my body, I part my legs, allowing him to slide his fingers between my slit.

"You're so damn wet." His voice is low and gruff.

"It's you."

"All the time?" he whispers.

I nod as he teases my clit. I'm sharing too much, but I know deep down that this can't go anywhere. That could be the fear from my failed relationships haunting me.

He moves farther down, alternating between giving me two

digits and rubbing my clit. I roll flat onto my back, giving him better access to me. The build happens even quicker, and I grab his biceps as the orgasm nearly rips me in half. I groan out, and he covers my mouth with his hand.

"Don't want my brother telling everyone at Christmas that I was making you come."

I bite down on his hand, riding it out. My breasts rise and fall as I try to catch my breath, my pussy pulsing with satisfaction.

"That was two. Shall we make it three?" he asks, and I get his smoldering gaze.

"Only if that means you'll be buried inside of me."

And then we do it all over again.

Being with him, giving him every part of my body, is earth-shattering. I realize what I've been missing—a man who knows his way in and out of the bedroom. A man who knows *me*.

When we're on our backs, gasping again, I turn to him and snicker. "I don't think I'll be able to walk today."

"Better figure it out, princess. Your dad might notice if you're limping."

I pout. "You're right. I guess that means I should head home. Soak in the tub beforehand."

An alarm goes off on Harrison's phone, and he rolls over to turn it off. "I lose time when I'm with you."

I sit up. "Time flies when you're having fun."

"True." He brushes his fingers down my neck and arm, and the goose bumps form on my body.

Harrison officially knows me at my rawest form. He's the only man who ever has.

My onesie is in a ball at the foot of the makeshift bed, and I grab it to wiggle it on. When I turn around, he's standing up and sliding on a pair of jeans. They sit low on his hips, and he catches me staring, but neither of us says a thing.

Maybe the carriage has already turned back into a pumpkin.

After a few steps forward, he reaches out his hand, helping

me to my feet, but he uses too much force. I stumble forward, crashing into him, and he catches me with a laugh. Then it fades off, and his lips are on mine.

With my eyes still closed, I pull away. "We can't tell anyone about this."

"No, we can't. Our secret."

He draws an *X* over his heart. And I do the same. Unbreakable. Until death. That was our pact we made when we were kids.

"Lots of promises," I say.

Harrison steps forward, standing behind me to snap the ass buttons for me.

"Yeah, a lot," he says, rubbing his palms across my butt cheeks before patting it. "Not a problem for me though. You know I don't share our secrets. With anyone. Ever."

I nod. "Okay. Do you think Colt knows?"

He takes a step forward, placing his hands on my shoulders, like he always does, then brushes his nose against mine. "He assumes we've been fucking for the last five years."

I gasp, and my full voice comes out to play. "What?"

"Shh," he says with a smile. "Don't wake him up." He looks over his shoulder, breathing lightly, and listens before turning back to me. "Fourth of July."

I meet his eyes. "I don't remember what happened."

"You were straddling me, pinning me down on the floor, and he walked in." He swallows. "You almost kissed me."

"Ahh, yeah, but you turned your head. That was the moment I friend-zoned you for good." I shoot him a wink, remembering that night pretty vividly.

I wanted him then, but he denied me. Mainly because I had a boyfriend, but we won't talk about my recklessness. He's loyal like that.

But it kinda hurt. I knew where I stood and was fine with it. I'm still fine with it, knowing my relationships are cursed.

He clears his throat. "I wanted you to be sure. Even if I was a rebound."

"I *was* sure. I was also really fucking nervous because it's kinda a big deal to get drunk and make out with your best friend."

He tucks his hands in his pockets, and I want to worship every inch of him.

"I'm not the one in denial." He says it like he can read my mind.

"I'm not." My tone is light. "Every person I've ever known who's dated their best friend, they became strangers. The thought of that makes me sick to my stomach. If we start something, there's a finish line somewhere."

"Not true. Maybe you're so pessimistic with love because you're searching for it in all the wrong places."

"I'm a realist, Harrison. Women whose parents divorced when they were young have a sixty-nine percent chance of also getting a divorce. That gives me and whoever I marry a thirty-one percent success rate. I'm not a mathematician, but it doesn't seem like the odds are in my favor," I breathe out. "They're not. And I can't lose you."

Within two steps, he's in front of me, wrapping his arms around me. "I'm not going anywhere. Our secrets are safe. But you have to promise me one more thing…"

"Tell me."

"If either of us gets to a point where we feel like this will destroy our friendship, we stop, no matter what. Even if the other person doesn't want to."

I cross an *X* over my heart, and he repeats it.

With his hand pressed against my cheek, he whispers, "Merry Christmas, ya filthy animal."

"Merry fuckin' Christmas," I say, and he dips down and kisses me.

CHAPTER FOURTEEN

I walk into my parents' house, whistling. It smells like cinnamon and sugar, and I can hear my family in the kitchen.

Images of last night play on repeat in my head. Grace's mouth on mine, her soft pants filling the space, the way she quivered beneath me and whispered my name …

Did it actually happen?

Yes. I smile. *Yes, it fucking did.*

And I'd do it all over again if given the chance.

"Ooh." They point at me when I walk in. "Look who's the last one here!"

"I am not." I check the time, knowing that I'm thirty minutes early. My eyes scan the room, and I count my sisters and brothers and Hayden and Summer. Guilt is written all over their faces. "Y'all planned this. What a bunch of *assholes*!"

The room bursts into laughter because the last one who arrives at our family gatherings has to do every single dish. There are so many of us that if it happens on a holiday, like Thanksgiving or Christmas, when we eat all day, it quickly becomes a full-time job.

"That's what you get for setting me up on Thanksgiving." Beckett offers me a mug of coffee, and I begrudgingly take it.

"It was his idea, but I helped execute it," Kinsley offers with a wink.

"You're gonna allow that behavior?" I say to Hayden with a grin.

He's not once mentioned the Valentine hazing we put him through. Honestly, he should be glad I'm letting him tell Beckett he's proposing instead of my brother confronting him. Unless he already knows.

Hayden shrugs. "You know she does whatever she wants."

"I'm pissed at all of you. Merry Christmas. I just created a shit list and added your names to the top. Next year, I'm gonna cross them off, one by motherfucking one."

Chatter fills the room, and fingers start pointing in all directions as each of them talks over the other. It's just noise, so I just keep shaking my head.

"No getting out of it. I don't care who put you up to it. You're all guilty."

"Okay, anyway, can we get back to the game?" Beckett waves me off.

They sit around the dining room table that easily fits fifteen with a stack of poker chips and cards. My little sister Fenix has almost all of her chips left, plus a hefty pile. Emmett is a close second.

"You're gambling this early in the morning?" I ask.

"We started at seven," Vera says and turns as I sneak a peek at her cards.

Then I continue to make my way around the table. By the time I look at their hands, I know she has the strongest with three of a kind. One more card and she'll have a full house. The odds are in her favor, so I tap on the back of her chair. She plays it really cool by going all in. I shake my head.

Kinsley scoots every chip she has forward. "Bluffin'."

Beckett and Sterling go all in too. Fenix looks at each one of them, trying to find a twinkle of a lie.

"Well, damn, this just got interesting. Guess it is true, I really am the life of the party," I say with a laugh.

"You sure are," Colt says, smirking at me over his glasses.

"Okay, let's gooooo." Fenix pushes her chips in.

Everyone slams down their cards. Then, London, who's playing dealer, plays out the last card. Three queens and two aces.

Vera stands and points at all of them. "In your face!"

"Hey, hey. Don't have to be a bad sport and rub it in all their faces," I say, patting her chair. When she sits, I point at them. "Ha ha, that's what you get, suckers!"

Vera laughs so hard that she snorts as they scowl at us. Game is officially over.

"Now, next time I'm late to a family dinner, I get to choose who does the dishes for me," she says.

"Uh, I didn't agree to that."

"Because you didn't get a vote," Remi says. "You were the rotten egg. We outvoted you."

That's one thing about my family. Since there are ten kids, we're always competing and trying to get back at one another. It makes life interesting. Considering I'm the third oldest, I feel hella responsible for my younger siblings.

Colt stands and refills his coffee. We meet each other's eye, and he nods—a silent agreement that he won't say shit about what he heard last night. It's just a part of our roommate agreement—what happens at the house stays at the house, period.

Our parents and grandparents enter through the back door, all of them wearing shawls or house robes.

"So, what time were we supposed to be here?" I ask, looking at my ma.

"Eight," she says. "It's always been eight."

"Everyone was here over an hour before that. Next year, I'm showin' up at six," I say, hearing the oven beep.

My grandma pulls out several trays of cinnamon rolls. "So, Harrison, how's Grace?"

The room grows quiet, and when I look around, everyone's eyes are on me.

"What are you all lookin' at?"

Then, I glance at Colt, who shakes his head. If he didn't tell them, I'm fine.

"She's fantastic," I say, playing it cool. "I asked her to join us today, but she had plans to go to her dad's."

London snickers. "I saw her leaving your place this mornin' when I was headed here."

"Doesn't mean anything. Can we at least go through one family dinner without someone bringing her up? Like, just one. That would be great. Nothing has changed, okay? You'll be the first ones to know if it does."

"Except the fact that you two kissed in Houston."

I groan and roll my eyes. "It was a joke, and she puked right afterward. Did she tell you that?"

Kinsley's brows furrow. "No. Kinda left that part out."

"Proof that none of you knows what you're talking about. Now, please, can we stop?"

"Yeah, y'all drop it. We don't gossip in this household," Mom interrupts, though she's not completely innocent. She and Kathy, Grace's mother, have been pairing us together for years, not that I minded.

Sterling bursts out into laughter. "Yeah, right."

Dad clears his throat, and we're still talking over each other. So he whistles, and we shut up. "All right, kids. It's time to eat and stuff your pie holes!"

Chairs scoot under the table, and the ten of us line up like we're walking through a buffet line. Colt stands behind me, and I turn to him.

"Thank you," I mutter.

"You owe me one," he says.

"Of course I do."

"Y'all don't forget about the plans at the bed-and-breakfast on New Year's Eve," Summer announces to the room when she sets a sweet bun on her plate.

"It's going to be the party of the century," Kinsley says.

I glance over at Hayden, who stays completely neutral in his expression, even though I know his secret.

My parents must know, too, because Hayden would never ask Kinsley without my father's approval. I see how easily they keep secrets. They're all too sly.

"ALMOST READY?" I ask Grace, leaning against the doorjamb of her room.

She spritzes herself with vanilla body spray, pins her bangs out of her face, then turns to me. Grace is wearing an emerald-green V-neck top that shows a sliver of side boob. It's tight around her waist, but the sparkly green skirt flares at her hips. The dark eye shadow makes her brown eyes pop, and I want nothing more than to slide my mouth across her red lips. But I decided tonight I won't make the first move. She'll have to initiate it because she's the one concerned about things changing.

And if she doesn't? Well, it was good while it lasted. But I have no doubts when it comes to us.

"How do I look?" She twirls around, placing a hand in her pocket.

"Like you're wearing my favorite color."

She doesn't say anything. She doesn't have to. I know it's just for me. It always is when she's dressed in green.

I take a few steps forward, wrapping my arm around her waist. "You look gorgeous."

"I noticed you were wearing my favorite suit," she whispers, placing her palms on my chest. Her gaze slides up to mine. "The navy makes your eyes look darker."

I move her over to the full-length mirror and stand behind her, resting my chin on her head. "We look fancy as fuck."

"It's semiformal. I think that's the point." She turns to me. "We should probably get going. If we miss your sister's engagement, you'll never live it down. Like RIP shit."

"You're right, but you wouldn't either, and we can't have that, now can we?" I step to the side, allowing her to move past me, and then I follow her down the hallway, where she grabs her coat.

As she puts it on, I speak up. "I can't believe Remi is moving in with you tomorrow. Might be kinda weird, seeing my sister so much."

The smile on her face is contagious. "It all worked out. I can't believe it."

"It always does," I remind her, just as I have a million times before.

Then I place my hand on her back, and we leave.

Neither of us has said anything about what happened on Christmas Eve. The emotions of that night stream between us, but if she wants to pretend like it never happened, then I will too. I crossed my heart for her. Made a promise I'll keep until the grave.

The truck is still running, and I made sure it stayed warm for her since the temperature has dropped.

"Kinsley's getting engaged," Grace says. "That means you're next."

I snicker. "Is there a rule I don't know about that we all gotta get married in order?"

"I hope not," she says. "You seriously can't get married before me."

"Guess we'll see what happens," I tell her, smirking, and she shakes her head.

"Who knows? You could meet the man you're gonna spend the rest of your life with tonight," I say, and she gives me her signature "yeah, right" look.

"Don't tell me I'll find love when I least expect it." She waves me off.

There's a car in the distance, and the headlights shine and light Grace's face. I keep both hands on the wheel as we drive to the Horseshoe Creek Ranch, but I'm relaxed.

Silence draws on. This always happens when things get too intense between us. A never-ending friend-zoning cycle. I'm guilty of some of that, too, especially when I thought we had no chance when things got serious with her previous boyfriends. I won't be the man who steals her from someone else, but I've thought about it.

"How're things going with Landon?"

"Well, I might've actually hooked him up with Haley."

I chuckle. "Really?"

"Yeah, I mean, he's traveling a lot right now, but I think they have potential."

"So what about you?"

She shrugs. "Single-girl era."

When we turn into the long rock driveway that leads to the ranch, I see the load of cars and trucks parked in the grass. More people showed up to the Halloween party, but it was an open invite. Summer decided to keep this get-together intimate after Hayden, who was dressed as Star-Lord, punched out some guy for harassing my sister. That party was *wild*.

The only people who should be here are locals or their

families. Summer said to expect about sixty to be in attendance, which is still a crowd.

By some miracle, I squeeze my truck right next to Beckett's. We're only a short walk from the house.

"Ready to go watch my sister get engaged?"

She laughs. "Absolutely. You know I love a good proposal. Hopefully, he nails the speech. Kinsley deserves her movie moment."

"Oh, I'm sure Hayden will give the best one any of us will have ever heard. He's a writer. And by what Kinsley said, he's good. She wouldn't lie about that, not even for him."

"I'll be the judge of that. If you see tears, then he did. If my eyes are bone-dry"—she wiggles her hand—"so-so."

"We got the Simon Cowell of wedding proposals here?" I get out of the truck and walk around to open her door.

She steps out, and we make our way toward the oversized farmhouse with a wraparound porch.

Music is blaring, and it echoes over the pasture. Before we get any closer, I stop and look up at the stars.

"It's so easy to take this for granted." I stare at the sea of them, not talking about the sky. "I realized that when we were in Houston."

"Yeah," she whispers. "It's easy to take a lot of things for granted when you're so used to them always being there."

There's an awkward pause.

"We're lucky. We have all this," I tell her, holding out my arms to the heavens.

"And we have each other," she says, grabbing my hand and leading me up the steps. "Ready?"

"As ever."

When we enter, Colt and Remi stand at the door, handing everyone a noisemaker and a glass of champagne.

"You two are in charge of the booze tonight?"

Remi snickers. "Of course. But don't drink too much. You and I have plans tomorrow."

"Sis," I tell her, wrapping my arm around her neck and giving her a noogie, "I'm not going to forget."

She slightly pushes me away and looks at Grace. "To think you're best friends with him."

"Look, don't judge me. Little kid me barely had a developed brain, and he didn't give me a choice. It is what it is," she says with a shrug.

"What she said." I grin at her. "It's Stockholm at this point. I'm holding her hostage."

Grace shakes her head. "As if you could get rid of me."

Haley walks over to us, and I can tell she's had too much to drink by the way she smiles like she's on cloud nine.

"Hi." She looks at Grace. "Why don't you date him again?"

Grace shakes her head. "Because he's my best friend. It's like kissing your brother."

"Eww," Haley tells her, looking over at Hayden and then back at us. "But is it?"

Remi hands out a few more party favors, then joins us again. She's wearing a silver sequin dress and high heels that make her nearly as tall as me. "What are we talkin' about?"

"Grace and Harrison kissing and it being like making out with a relative."

My sister makes a face and sips her champagne. "Can we talk about something else? Kinda making me sick."

Someone mentions the weather and horse training, and then Lexi, Stephanie's cousin, speaks up.

"I chatted with Steph the other day. She had a lot to say about you, *Mr. Valentine,*" she announces. And by the expression on her face, she knows we fucked.

"Yeah? Like what?" I down the rest of my champagne.

"Want another one?" Grace asks, escaping this conversation.

"Sure." I nod, smiling, then turn my attention back to Lexi, who goes through the entire conversation. Down to Stephanie mentioning us hooking up.

Remi and Haley stare at her, eating up every single word she says. This is the *last* conversation I want to have tonight. When I glance down at my phone, I realize Grace has been gone for a while. I scan the room and spot her chatting with Kinsley, laughing.

Her eyes meet mine, and there's a silent conversation that streams between us as she watches me watch her. In a crowded room, I'll always find her. Always.

"She's still in love with you, you know?" Lexi finally says.

This makes me laugh. "Yeah, well, there's a list these days."

Remi shakes her head. "The Kiss of Death. Guess you've still got it?"

"It never left," I admit. "But anyway, great chat." I lift my glass and escape.

Before I make my way to Grace, I notice Hayden and Beckett whispering in the corner, which means my brother officially knows about the engagement. And by the look on his face, he's in on it.

"Are y'all talkin' about drugs?" I look between them, still keeping my eye on Gracie. Now she's chatting with Summer as Kinsley laughs.

"Shut up." Beckett turns back to Hayden and hands him a flask from inside his jacket pocket. "Ya nervous?"

Hayden doesn't answer. He's in his head, focused. And when he sees Kinsley, he excuses himself.

"Guess it's now or never," I say.

"Oh, you know?" Beckett turns to me.

"Of course I do. Weeks ago."

He makes a face. "So you and Grace are lookin' kinda close."

I roll my eyes. "Still having this same old-ass conversation every day?"

"Probably." He lifts the flask to his lips and then hands it to me.

I take a sip. "This thing tastes like it's been passed around a hundred times in a bar. The end was wet." I wipe my mouth with the back of my sleeve. "Gross."

"It kinda has." He laughs.

"Feel like I just drank your spit directly from your mouth. I think I'm gonna throw up." I shove it back into his hands as we watch Hayden move to the front of the room.

I know what's going to happen, so I move over to Grace, who's drinking champagne by the stairs.

"Were you waitin' for me?" I ask once I'm closer.

"You know it." She hands me the extra drink in her hand with a smile, and then she leans down and whispers, "I think it's about to happen."

I place my hand on the small of her back, and she relaxes under my touch. "It is."

Hayden grabs the microphone, and the music in the room lowers. The crowd quiets, and we look up front.

"Attention, everyone. Hello? Nod your head if you can hear me."

The conversations fully stop, and people do as he asks.

"Okay, great. Hi. I'm Hayden."

Beckett cups his hands around his mouth. "Hi, Hayden!" he yells.

Hayden shakes his head, and I can see the nervousness on his face. All my brothers and sisters are here, along with most of the people our age from town. Sixty sets of eyes are on him.

"Do you see that woman right there? Kinsley, raise your hand."

She might as well have a spotlight on her when he walks toward her because she lights up the room.

He talks about how she's the most caring, beautiful woman he's ever called his girlfriend and continues on. "This woman has given me a second chance at happiness, and I want everyone here to know how much I love her."

"Aww," fills the room.

I glance at Grace, and she glances back at me with a smile. My sister blows kisses toward Hayden. People applaud, thinking it's just a simple confession, but I know better, and so do Grace, Haley, and Beckett. At this point, the whole room might know, except for Kinsley.

Then, he drops to his knee, and I pull my cell phone from my pocket and start recording.

"Kinsley Valentine. I can never thank you enough for being you and for accepting me how I am. I know what life is like living without you—it's hell. And I don't wanna go back there ever again. Hades and Persephone were made for each other, and I know for a damn fact you were made for me. I love you with all my heart, forever and always. Will you marry me?"

A tear falls from Grace's cheek, and she wipes it away. I wrap my free arm around her as we watch it play out like a movie.

Kinsley says something, and I can't hear what she says.

"Kins?" Hayden finally speaks up, and I think every person is holding their breath, waiting for her to answer. She looks around the room like she just realized we're all here waiting for *her*.

"Yes, yes, *oh my God*." Tears spill down her cheeks as he puts two different rings on two different fingers. Then, they laugh and cry and kiss.

"Get a room!" I holler before the hoorays, which earns several laughs.

They kiss and dance, and the energy is high.

"That was a great engagement speech. Seven out of ten," Grace says.

"Not a ten out of ten? I thought he was good."

I hold out my hand. "Wanna dance?"

With a nod, she interlocks her fingers with mine, and I lead her to the middle of the room, where we sway to the music.

"Shit, I love this color on you," I tell her and spin her around as she laughs.

She looks so damn happy. It's picture perfect. And this time, I hope it doesn't vanish.

The song ends, and another starts. Neither of us tries to walk away.

"Did you think of your word of the year?" she asks me as I hold her close to me.

"Hell no. I told you I'm not choosing one. Can't get me to commit to that living hell again." I meet her eyes. "Did you pick one?"

"I did. *Fearless.*"

I lift her chin and smile. "You already are."

"I will be this year. Fearless in *all* things."

"I just hope you're not *forced* to be fearless."

"Don't jinx me." She wraps her arm around my waist and squeezes.

Right now, I want to capture her mouth and make those pouty, kissable lips mine. But there are many people around. Last thing we need to do is add kindling to the rumors that already swirl around us.

When Summer grabs the microphone, my head turns in her direction. She's tipsy and wearing a goofy smile, but Beckett is right there beside her.

"Listen up, everyone! Listen up! We have two minutes until midnight. Grab your champagne and your kissing partner, and get ready to welcome in the new year surrounded by friends and family!"

People navigate through the space like ants. We get bumped around as Remi and Colt pass out glasses of sparkly. I turn on the large TV hanging on the wall so we can watch the ball drop in Times Square.

Then Grace and I move to the back of the room and stand on the stairs so we have the perfect view of the TV as Summer gives us updates by the second. Grace stands on the step above me, and I still have inches on her, but we're almost eye to eye.

"Are you ready to make a wish?" I ask when we count down from ten.

"Yes. What about you?" She places her arms on my shoulders.

I nod, knowing exactly what I *want* this year.

"Three. Two. One. Happy New Year!" everyone yells.

I place my hand on her cheek. "Happy New Year, princess." I slide the back of my fingers down her cheek as she licks her lips. I'm already drunk from the faint scent of her perfume.

"Happy New Year. Make a wish," she whispers.

As "Auld Lang Syne" plays, our mouths desperately crash together—a kiss I've wanted all night.

Slowly, I paint my lips across hers, and she opens her mouth, giving me all the permission I need to taste her tongue. Together, we're fire, burning the other to ash.

As everyone sings, I grab Grace's hand and lead her upstairs into the first empty bedroom. Once the door is closed, I press her against the cool wood, and her leg instinctively wraps around me.

"I have to have you again," she whispers.

"*Fuck. Yes,*" I mutter, needing her like I need sunshine in the winter.

My hand slides down below her skirt, and I lift it, pressing my fingertips on the outside of her panties.

My name falls from her lips in a whisper as she fists the opening of my suit jacket. She sinks against me, and her wetness seeps through the fabric. She doesn't have to admit she likes kissing me; her body gives her away every damn time.

"What are you doin' to me?" she admits shyly.

I chuckle, looking down at my hard cock. "I can ask the same thing."

Fireworks pop outside, and music plays downstairs, but in this room, it's only the two of us, and the greedy demand to have more takes over.

Lifting her, I carry her to the bed, laying her down. She looks at me, her long, dark hair splayed around her head, and I meet her on the mattress. I position myself between her legs, and we kiss as she rocks against me. The only thing stopping us from having sex is the thin fabric between us. She runs her fingers through my hair as hushed pants release from her mouth.

I nibble on her ear, and just as I'm about to say something, the door swings open. I look over at it just as Kinsley turns on the light. Our eyes meet, and then she looks at Grace. Then she flicks the lights off and shuts the door.

Grace sits up in a panic.

"Shit," I whisper, pulling away from her. "*Shit.*"

"You didn't lock the door?" Grace asks, nearly frantic. "Do you think she'll say anything?"

If my sister had walked in five minutes later, I have no doubts I'd have been buried deep inside of her.

I shake my head. "Not sure. But I do know she ain't gonna let either one of us live it down for the rest of our lives."

We sit on the bed, looking at each other in the dark. The tension is so tight that it nearly chokes me.

"Do you wanna get out of here?"

She sighs. "Fuck yes. But we can't leave the same way we came in."

"Why?"

"Because I'm not doing the walk of shame." Then she glances at the window.

CHAPTER FIFTEEN

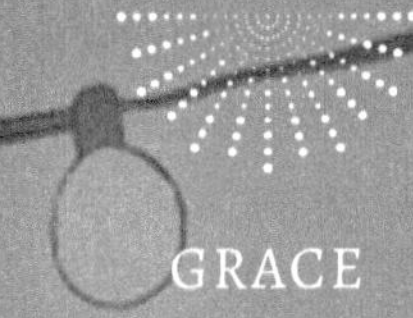

GRACE

"You can't be serious," Harrison says, looking at me like I've lost my mind.

After kissing him and nearly losing myself, I feel like I kinda have.

I slip the high heels off my feet and hold them in my hand as I walk over to the window. "I am dead serious."

Carefully, I unlock it and slide it open. The cold breeze fills the room and blows through my hair. Goose bumps coat my arms, and I shiver, but it's not because of the air or temperature.

There's just too much streaming between us right now.

"Listen, we could break arms or legs. You want to be in a cast this year?" He gives me a stern look.

I poke my finger into his chest. "Fearless, Harri. It starts now."

He shakes his head and laughs. "You wanna take risks, princess?"

"More than you know." I shoot him a wink.

"You're fuckin' adorable." He runs his fingers through his hair, thinking. "How about this? I'll go first, and then you can follow my lead. That way, if for some reason that lattice slides off the side of the house, I'll be the one on my back with broken limbs, and you can get help. Deal?"

"Okay," I whisper. "Wait." I grab his hand and put it to the pulse in my neck. "I'm kinda scared."

Harrison rests his other palm on my cheek and kisses me. *"Fearless."*

He peels his suit jacket off his body and hands it to me. Then he puts one leg out the window and reaches over until his foot is hooked into the lattice. I poke my head out, watching, trying to memorize his path.

Carefully, he climbs down until his feet are on the ground. Then he looks up at me with a smile. He made it look too *easy.*

"Incoming," I whisper-hiss, tossing his suit jacket down below, which he immediately puts on. Then I drop my heels, and they hit the grass with a plop.

My heart is still racing, and I look down at him, placing my hand on my heart.

"I can do this," I whisper.

"You can do this," he encourages, almost as if he's reading my mind.

"Get out of my head," I say.

"You first."

I hear chatter in the hallway, and I know my time is running out. It's now or never.

After releasing a breath, I climb out the window, placing my feet on the wood, and I feel like a kid again. I hold on tight, looking down at him.

"Slowly," he instructs.

"Are you lookin' at my panties?"

He shrugs. "It's a full moon tonight, and, baby, I ain't complainin' one bit."

On the next step, I lose my footing and slip. Then I'm falling so fast that I can't even scream. Of course, I'll be the one to get hurt. A million regretful thoughts flash through my mind until I land directly in Harrison's arms. He stumbles back, and we fall to the ground.

"My prince," I say, running my hand across his chest, laughing my ass off.

We're in a fit of giggles on the ground, but when our mouths are close, that vanishes. My breath is ragged as his nose brushes against mine, and he captures my mouth. His strong palm is on my ass, and I groan against him, threading my fingers through his hair.

"Harrison? Grace?" London asks from the shadows.

I didn't even notice her there. I don't notice anyone when I'm crossing the line with Harrison.

Her cell phone lights her face in the darkness, and she takes a few steps forward, then looks up at the open window. "Did you just climb down from there?"

Neither of us answers her, and I stand up, giving Harrison my hand and pulling him. Then, we take off running like the wind is carrying us. We make it to the truck, breathless, laughing. Just like we used to do as teenagers when we played pranks on his siblings.

"Shit," he huffs, opening my door, and I climb in. I sit facing him, pulling him closer to me.

"We're going to be squashing rumors for a month," I mutter as he positions himself between my legs.

"When it comes to you, I don't give a fuck." Then he's kissing me, only pulling away to buckle my seat belt. "Let's go. My place or yours?"

"Mine," I whisper. "Safer."

On the way there, Harrison and I talk about the engagement, but the cute-as-fuck smirk on his face and the sparkle in his eyes never fade.

Once we're inside, I lock the door, pushing him against it, claiming his mouth all over again.

"I want to do this forever," he whispers.

"Really?" I ask, kissing him, and he pulls away.

"You don't?" he asks.

"What?" I pull away.

"You're already trying to figure out how to move on."

"Of course I am. You're not?" I search his face.

"No." He's firm in his answer. "I don't have an inkling of doubt when it comes to you and me and what we could have. But you're already wondering how this will end without giving it a proper beginning."

I open my mouth, then close it because he's right. "Isn't that what everyone does?"

"No." He shakes his head. "It's not."

I grab his hand. "I *have* been having second thoughts, knowing this can't possibly end well. The sex is great—the best I've ever ever had. But our friendship is better. When best friends who know every single thing about the other decide to get together, sex usually *ruins* the friendship."

"Not subscribing to that bullshit. You *can* have your cake and eat it too, Grace. But you don't believe that, and you're not sure. And I told myself that if I ever crossed the line with you, you'd have to be sure *I* was what you wanted." He shakes his head.

"Because you're scared I'll fall in love with you?" I ask, knowing why he created the rules he had.

His brows crease, and he shakes his head. "No, because I'm scared of falling for *you*."

My face softens. "That's not what a fuckboy says."

"Is that what you wanted from me, princess? A fuck buddy?"

"What? You wanted more?" I look at him, confused.

Right now, we're on opposite sides of a coin, and no matter how many times it's flipped, we'll still be there. About this at least.

He crosses his arms over his chest. "I'm doing you a favor. I'm enacting our agreement right now. I don't want to actively *try* to lose you if that's where your heart already is. You know?"

I hug him, but I understand this decision. Fuck, I wholeheartedly agree. "You know that I fuck up my relationships every single time. It doesn't fail. Ever. Why would we be any different?"

"If you don't know, then I can't explain it to you. It's something you feel deep inside. When you know, you just know."

"Okay." I take in the hint of cologne on his body, and then I take a few steps back, creating space between us.

His hair is a mess, and his lips are as swollen as mine.

"I should go," he says, adjusting his suit.

"I won't stop you, Harrison. But know that when you walk out that door, you will be leaving behind your very *last* opportunity to ever be with me like this again. Because you enacted the deal. I don't break promises to you." I lick my lips, wanting to kiss him again, wanting to forget about forever and enjoy the moment, the *right now*. "Let history remember that I'm not the one denying *you*. It's the other way around."

His gaze moves from my eyes and down to my mouth before coming back to my eyes. Then, he takes several steps until he's standing inches from me.

"I'm fucked either way," he whispers. "And if it's already the end, then I don't want to regret a thing."

"Then don't."

Our desperation burns hotter than it did when we walked in. Maybe because we know it's already the end. The inevitable has already happened. It might be my record.

Emotions flood through me, and we're on each other like we might not survive through the night. He carefully peels off the green top, and I slide out of my skirt.

He gives himself space to look over every inch of me, and I feel *pretty*. He's the only man who's ever looked at me like he knows my worth and added tax.

When his mouth returns to mine, we take several steps backward until I'm falling onto the couch. I laugh, unbuttoning his shirt as he takes it off. He hovers above me, dipping down to pull my bottom lip into his mouth.

A delicious growl releases from the back of his throat, and I want nothing more than for him to *butter my biscuit.*

I tuck my fingers inside his suit pants, the suit that is my damn kryptonite, tugging him forward and unbuckling his belt. Harrison pulls it through all the loops, then drops it to the ground in a clash. His heated gaze marks the trail where his fingers will touch, and I revel in being with him like this again.

"One last time," he confirms, pulling me to my feet.

With both hands cupping my face, he leans in and kisses me, then pulls me against his chest. We slowly dance and kiss to the rhythm of our breaths and beating hearts. Slowly, he spins me around but drinks in every drop of me. Then I turn back to him, leading him to my room.

He stops at the doorway, standing with his arm resting at the top as he watches me crawl onto the bed. His suit pants hang on his waist, and that sexy *V* points down to my new favorite part of him.

When my eyes scroll down his body, I try to memorize every hard muscle that looks like it's been carved from stone. He's a Southern statue without one imperfection. As if he can read my mind, his lips curve up slightly. If I'd blinked, I'd have missed it.

I should stop this right now.

I should cut my losses while I'm ahead.

Even he knew we should've walked away when we had the chance, and now I'm scared we're already addicted. The selfish part inside me wants him and knows we could be good together, but my fear cripples me.

Sex complicates relationships—it's a fact. What we have is incredible without that.

Harrison flicks off the light, and I watch him walk toward me in the darkness. The moonlight splashes rays through the window, giving his mesmerizing body a cool glow as I look up at him like he's an archangel. Tonight, I hope he'll break me in unspeakable ways.

He crawls onto the mattress and tucks hair behind my ear. Then, he worships every inch of my body. His strong hands memorize my breasts and hips and ass. I'm everything with him and nothing without him as he brings me to the edge, nearly tipping me over until I'm panting, swearing for my release. I need him so bad that my body nearly quivers as he hovers above me, loose, messy hair falling into his face.

Mr. Perfect is my best friend. And even though being with him intimately is wrong, it feels so goddamn right. We fit together like two puzzle pieces, our curves snapping together. And as we make love, the night plays out like a silent film, without words, in black and white, under the blue light of the moon.

He slams into me, and when I finally come, I see stars. My body reaches maximum ecstasy as the orgasm rips through me, destroying me, bulldozing me down to nothing. I scream out his name as he gives me every thick inch of him, and I need him like summer needs rain.

The panic of losing him bubbles again—a reminder of why we can't continue this. But even so, no matter what, we can never take back tonight or undo what we've done. The damage has been done, and the memory has been implanted next to all the others that revolve around him.

"Fuck," he groans out as I roll him over onto his back, slide a condom on him, then go for a ride.

I whip my head back, and he gently tugs my long hair as I slide up and down him.

My ass slaps against his thighs, and our moans fill the space. He reaches up, sucking one of my nipples while palming my other breast. Every carved muscle tenses as my second greedy orgasm creeps up and takes control. Harrison has me gasping for air as I scream, bucking on top of him. He growls out when he violently loses himself, gripping my ass with his strong hands as I ride it out.

I meet his blue eyes that are full of passion and want.

"Save a horse. Ride a Valentine," I whisper.

Calling it quits is to save our friendship, the only stable thing in my life. I can't lose him among everything else.

I fall onto his chest, and he holds me. I'm so sweaty but full of satisfaction as he kisses my forehead. We're two beating hearts. That's it. With his arms around me, I close my eyes and listen to his racing heartbeat until it steadies. We stay connected until our breathing slows.

After we clean up, I climb back into bed, and a naked Harrison holds me, my ass against his cock and his arm around my waist.

"You're a great big spoon." I press against him as our bodies mold together and we relax.

"You're a great little spoon," he says, kissing my neck and nibbling on my ear.

I giggle, the scruff on his jaw tickling.

"When I wake up tomorrow and walk out that door, I'm going to pretend like none of this ever happened." I turn and look into his eyes as he continues, "I need you to be prepared for this version of us to be locked away forever. And I want you to promise me that if you ever become *certain* about us, you'll tell me."

I draw an *X* over my heart so he knows I will then settle back into position.

"I don't want to lose you," I admit into the quiet night. "It's my biggest fear."

"You'll always be my best friend," he says.

"Forever?"

"Cross my heart."

CHAPTER SIXTEEN

HARRISON

The next morning, I wake up to pounding at the door. I swear it sounds like someone might knock the shit down. I open my eyes, and Grace sits up in bed. Her room is bright as hell, but it makes her look angelic in the warm morning light.

I smile at her, pulling the covers over my head. "Make it go away."

"Oh my God, Harrison. What time is it?" she asks, frantic. "Did you oversleep?"

That's when I realize I did. It's something that *never* fucking happens either. Ever. No matter what. I don't oversleep.

I reach across to the bedside table and grab my phone in a panic. "Seven? How? Shit."

"*Grace!*" a familiar female voice yells.

"Remi," we say in unison.

Our eyes are wide as saucers.

"We're *fucked*," Grace whispers.

"We fucked around and found out," I say, glancing down at my naked body. Clothes—I need them now.

As I rush around, I wish I had the ability to stop time so last night would last forever. I push the thoughts away. What happened can't ever be discussed again. It's over, back to pretending.

I crawl out of bed to see the jacket of the suit I was wearing last night. "Do you have any of my spare clothes here? Jogging pants? T-shirt?"

My suit is scattered throughout her house. I quickly pluck up the pieces and shove them into Grace's closet.

"Where are my boxers?" I hurry and search around, but can't seem to find them. "Fuck it."

She hands me some old jogging pants that I let her borrow at some point and a T-shirt that has a *gigantic* middle finger on it.

"I look like a dickhead."

"You do." She laughs. "But you gotta go," Grace says as she hurries and wiggles into some jeans. She slides on a sports bra and a T-shirt.

I want to pull her in for a kiss but don't.

"You're distracting me. And we're not doing that anymore," she mutters as if she read my mind or can see the want written all over my face. Or maybe she's thinking about it too.

"Doin' what?" I ask with a brow popped.

She shakes her head, ignoring that and me. "You gotta go out the window," Grace whispers. "Just walk around the back."

"This new obsession with windows," I mutter, but I go with it because I don't want to experience my sister's wrath this morning, especially after she reminded me last night about our plans.

"Hello? Harrison? I know you're here!" Remi knocks some more, and I can hear her grumbling something, but I can't quite make it out. But just by her tone, I know she's pissed.

"Shit, I forgot my truck was parked out front."

Grace shakes her head. "You'll think of some reason why it's there. Now go."

She slides open her bedroom window. I sneak out like I'm a

damn teenager and cross her neighbor's backyard. Once I'm on the opposite block, I make my way to the town square. Thankfully, I have my phone, and I make my way to the coffee shop that's just a few blocks away. They're only open for a small window today, and I go in and grab three coffees. It's the perfect cover-up.

On the stroll back to Grace's, I can't stop smiling. My sister is still standing at the door when I arrive.

She turns and glares at me. "You were supposed to meet me at Mom's this mornin' to help! Thankfully, our other brothers don't suck and helped me load all of this."

"Sorry. I thought I was supposed to meet you here. It's why I got us fuel." I hand her a coffee, and then I pull the key to Grace's place from my pocket and stick it in the door.

"Why are you dressed like that?"

"Laundry day." I shrug.

"Gracie," I singsong with Remi behind me. "Hello? You up? Time to rise and shine, *bestie*!"

Moments later, she exits from the bedroom. Her hair is a mess, and there's a small hickey on her neck that I know she's very aware of right now by how she's moved her hair to the side. The guilty look on her face will always give her away.

"I was knocking so hard. You must sleep like a freight train," Remi says with a smile, taking a drink.

I think my little white lie worked.

"I do." Grace's eyes dart toward me, then down at the extra coffee I'm holding. "Are one of those for me? Please say yes."

"Yeah, thought you could use it after your night," I tell her, shooting her a wink.

Remi looks between us, shaking her head. "Okay, well, my car is full. How about we start moving my shit?" She glares at me.

Yep, she's very pissed.

"Oh, right. Here's the key." Grace slides it off the bar top and hands it to my sister. "I forgot to bring it to the bed-and-breakfast last night."

"No problem," she says. "Thanks. I'll be right back."

As soon as she's outside, Grace glares at me. "She knows."

"No, she doesn't. Just *play it cool*. You suck at this."

"I'm not a pro at acting *unbothered*, like you," she whispers and straightens her posture when Remi enters, carrying an oversized box.

"You're supposed to be helpin' me." She walks past me, bumping my shoulder.

"Oh, right." I set my coffee down. "You should help us, Gracie."

"Was totally plannin' on it."

I move outside, happy for the fresh air and sunshine. Remi wasn't lying about her car being full. My mouth falls open when I see how much she was able to stuff inside of her blacked-out Mustang.

"Tetris queen," I tell her, bowing.

"Would've been great if I'd had your truck." She narrows her eyes at me. "Also, you're both so transparent."

I roll my eyes, ignoring her, then bend over and grab a box that feels like it's full of bricks. "Not sure what you're talking about."

She doesn't say anything else as I walk inside.

When I pass Grace, I meet her eyes. "Yeah, she knows."

Grace tenses, and I laugh, knowing she feels every single inch of where I was last night. Buried deep inside her.

With the three of us unloading Remi's car, it takes less than thirty minutes. After everything is stacked against the wall in her new room, she turns to us.

"Just need to go back and get my bed, dresser, and all the clothes that are in my closet. Ready?" She turns to me.

"Yep. Let's do it," I say, holding up my hand, and she gives me a high five.

She's smiling, all of her annoyance already gone. One good thing about her, she forgives easily, even if she acts like a hard-ass most of the time. She's a little softy under that hard shell, just like Beckett.

"I'll be back," I tell Grace in my best Arnold Schwarzenegger voice.

I shoot her a wink, and she blushes, then shakes her head.

She mouths, *You're bad*.

"But in a good way."

Then I meet Remi at the truck. We back out of the driveway, the radio still on from last night. I reach forward and turn it off.

"Are you excited about Cash moving back?" she asks.

Cash Johnson is Beckett's lifelong best friend. He moved away for college and vet school and has been gone for a decade. Earlier this year, when Beckett and Summer bought the Horseshoe Creek Ranch, they offered him an opportunity to lease a slice of the ranch. He's moving back to Valentine soon and his veterinary clinic will open early next year.

I glance over at her. "That was random."

"No, it wasn't. Him moving back is all Beckett talks about every single time I see him. Thought you both shared the same sentiment."

"We don't," I tell her. "But glad to know you still have that secret crush on him. Obvious."

"Jesus. You're the last person who needs to be talking to me about secret crushes. Ya know what I mean?"

"I *don't* know. *Tell me*," I tease. I'm so used to deflecting this conversation that I'm a pro.

She shakes her head. "You're impossible."

"I've been told that a time or ten."

The sound of the gravel crunches under the tires as we turn onto my parents' ranch. Five thousand acres of pure bliss that I'm so damn grateful to live on. And one day, I hope to be able to raise my family here.

"You gonna miss it?" I turn to her, parking in front of my parents' two-story house. Then I glance at the tree house in the backyard and all the memories that come with it. "There's no place like home."

Remi furrows her brows. "I'll be ten minutes away."

"Yeah, but there's still something special about wakin' up to this every day."

"I need change. And I'm lookin' forward to livin' with Gracie."

"Don't you go stealin' my bestie away," I warn with a chuckle as we get out of the truck.

When we enter, the house smells like a freshly lit fireplace and Folgers. I can hear Mom and Dad chatting in the kitchen. The rest of the house is dark and quiet. It's still early though.

"Mornin'," I yell.

"In here," Dad hollers.

I make my way down the hallway, where they're sitting at the breakfast bar, smiling at one another with mugs in their hands.

"Howdy," I say, looking between them.

"What's going on?" Mama says, looking at the clothes I'm wearing. She gives me a look of disapproval when she sees the big, fat finger flipping her off, and then my father's eyes widen.

"What the hell is that?" He points to my shirt.

"Oh, just a good *fuck you very much* T-shirt. Ya know how it goes. Laundry day," I say with a shrug, wishing Grace had had *any* other shirt of mine. These clothes are setting the tone.

Mom looks offended.

"Anyway, I just came to fulfill my favor and help Remi move. What about y'all?"

"Nothin' much."

When I walk farther into the kitchen, I see Stephanie in the corner. She's wearing a purple sweater, and she's smiling with a cup of coffee in her hands.

"Stephie?"

"Hi, good morning."

She's the *last* person I expected to see today.

"Stephanie just told us the good news," Dad says.

Mom's expression softens as she looks back at my ex. Mama always liked her, even though she's one thousand percent Team Grace.

Remi enters the kitchen and stops when she sees we have company. She looks at me like I have answers.

"Uh," she mumbles.

Stephanie clears her throat. "I'm moving back to Valentine, and I'll be working at my parents' firm. Happy New Year!"

For once, I can't hide my shock. "What? Really?"

"*Whoa.*" Remi looks between us. She gobbled up every word Lexi spilled last night and understands what this means.

I give her a smile. "Wow, that's fantastic." I walk across the room, and she stands as I hug her. "Excited you're here."

"Me too. I was leaving my folks' place and thought I'd stop by and visit. You busy today?"

"Yeah, he's helping me move today," Remi interrupts, giving her a wave.

"Whoa, Remington? You were seriously this tall when I saw you last." She holds her hand up to her waist.

My sister grins, but I know she *hates* it when people call her by her full name.

"Yeah. Crazy what ten years can do, huh? Anyway, great seeing you." She turns to me and points her thumb over her shoulder. "We have shit to do. The sooner, the better."

Mom shakes her head. "Someone's in a mood."

I turn to Stephanie. "Call me, okay?"

"I will." She goes back to her seat as Remi leaves the kitchen.

Within a few steps, I'm right behind her. "Why are you being rude?"

"I don't like her," she admits. "You know that saying that you should never trust a skinny cook?"

I chuckle. We round the corner and take the stairs two at a time.

"If I'm choosing, I pick Grace."

"She's not an option."

"Okay." Remi huffs. "Anyone but *Stephie*."

"She's not so bad," I explain. "If you gave her a chance, you'd probably be great friends."

"No thank you."

My sister opens the door to my old bedroom, the one she took when she moved back in with my parents a few months ago. No matter our age, we always have a place to stay if something happens, so Remi temporarily took the opportunity.

Now that she's back on her feet, she's been waiting for the right chance to leave. Right now, the only two siblings that still live at home are Sterling and Vera; they're eighteen and seventeen, respectively.

I look around my old bedroom, remembering how I had it decorated as a teen, and smile. It's changed a lot. Now there's a fresh coat of paint, and the thumbtack holes where all my posters hung have been filled. However, the memories I made here are still alive. When I turn around, I glance at the tree house.

"You been in there lately?" I nod toward it.

"No. The only person who uses it is London. She's been practicing guitar in there, so she doesn't bother anyone. Said there's a lot of inspiration or something."

I smile. "Really?"

"Yeah, she wrote this new song that's so catchy. Seriously haven't been able to get it out of my head for the past week. I told her that maybe you could help her promote it since you're internet famous. Thirst trap style. Abs and a pretty face can sell anything." She pretends to throw up in her mouth. "The comments on those videos of you are gross AF."

"I'd help however I could."

"She's not going to ask," Remi admits, pulling clothes from her closet. "Maybe you can bring it up at some point."

"Yeah, I will." I hold out my arm and let her swoop the material over it until I can barely carry the weight.

She slides the handles of a tote bag up her arm and carries a box. I follow her down the stairs.

When we make it to the bottom, she reaches and struggles to open the door but eventually gets it. "All of you have something you're passionate about. You, Beckett, and Sterling are into horse shit. Kinsley has the newspaper. Fenix is about to graduate, then probably work with you fucks at the barn. Emmett and his cows. Then, there's my twin, who's got his successful handyman business. Vera and her plants. London and her guitar. And then there's me. I like puzzles, painting, and silence. I'm the Wednesday Addams of the Valentines!"

My head falls back with laughter. "You and Grace are going to have a blast."

"I hope so. Something has to give."

"She's easy to get along with. You'll have no issues." I place all of her clothes in the back seat of my truck, and she puts the boxes in the bed. "Did you pick a word of the year?"

"Yeah, but I'm not telling you because I'm superstitious about it. I only tell people after the year is over, and only then does it all make sense. What about you?"

"Nope. No way. I don't fuck with that." I shake my head. "I'm gonna put a calendar reminder in my phone to ask you in one year."

"I hope you do," she says.

We make our way back upstairs and immediately get back to work. Three trips later, her room is empty. Stephanie's still chatting with my parents in the kitchen, and they sound like they're having a good time.

When we're on the porch, Remi turns to me. "Gonna tell them bye?"

"Nah, I'm good." I walk down the steps, and then we make our way back to town.

I let out a yawn, realizing I'm tired from staying up all night.

When we pull into the driveway, I look at her. "If there's ever a point when she's not okay, will you tell me?"

She searches my face, understanding what I'm asking. "Yes. But you owe me a favor every time I do."

"That's a deal." I hold out my hand, and we shake on it because my favors are currency in this town.

CHAPTER SEVENTEEN

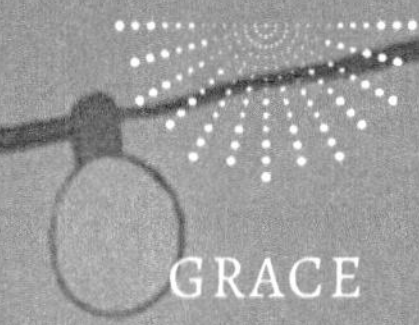

GRACE

I grab a mocha from the coffee shop and sit by the windows so I can update my dating profiles. It's a new year, and I'm searching for a new me.

After Harrison and I agreed that we couldn't cross the line anymore, it's been *awkward*. And tense as hell.

I second-guess everything I say and type and how I act, down to what I wear. He's seen me at my best and my worst and in the rawest form possible, and there is no taking it back.

It's been seven days of him staying true to his word and pretending like nothing happened. He's so convincing that, at times, even I almost believe we didn't hook up.

He's unbreakable with this shit, a master at locking emotions up and throwing away the key. I remind myself a hundred times per day that it's for the best. We made a pact and agreement to end it if our friendship was in jeopardy. Apparently, it was, or he wouldn't have called it quits. It got too serious too quickly, and now, a week later, my head is still spinning.

With a coffee in one hand, I type my password and unlock my computer. As I wait to connect to Wi-Fi, my phone rings.

It's Kinsley.

"Sorry to bother you on a Saturday—also, this is *not* work related at all."

I laugh, looking at the Ranchers Singles website, which feels very much like online shopping for men. "I'm not doing anything important anyway. What's up?"

"When I was chattin' with Harrison the other day, he mentioned you were starting your wedding planning business this year. Do you still want to give that a shot?"

A huge smile fills my face, and it almost hurts. "Are you asking me to help you plan your wedding?"

"Yes, I am! *Please?* The universe just keeps pointing me in this direction. It just feels right, ya know?"

"Kins, I don't have *any* experience." My heart races because I know this is a huge opportunity.

Kinsley Valentine knows everyone, and this could be a career launcher. The big break I've been waiting for just fell in my lap. Thanks to Harrison. He's always saving the day.

"So what? You're so organized at work. It's an incredible quality to have when dealing with something like this. I don't know anyone else who color coordinates highlighters with the tabs in their notebooks."

I chuckle. "I would love to help you."

"Oh my God, thank you! I'm already overwhelmed, and I'm trying to de-stress my life this year. Oh, if possible, can you let me know your rates so I can budget it in?"

"Rates?"

"Yes, ma'am, I'm not letting you do all of this work for free. Do some research and let me know. My brother also mentioned Weddings with Grace as a business name? It's cute. Has a double meaning. I think you should keep it."

"Wow, I told him that when we were kids." I laugh and can't

believe he remembered. "I'll let you know. Thank you so, so much."

"I'm excited! Chat soon."

I end the call and hurry and text Harrison.

GRACE

Thanks for the recommendation. Kinsley just
asked me to help her plan her wedding!!!

HARRISON

You're going to be amazing. Congrats!

GRACE

Thank you! Eek! So excited. Also, can't believe
you remembered Weddings with Grace.

HARRISON

I remember everything you've ever told me.

I READ his last message and smile, then turn my attention back to my laptop where I update my dating app radius. I'll be damned if I ever drive to Houston for dick again. Hell, I don't want to drive outside of Valentine for it.

After I upload a recent picture from Christmas, I save it, hoping for my *You've Got Mail* moment. Just as I pick up my coffee to take a drink, I notice someone walking toward me. When I look up, I give Stephanie a double take.

Shocked doesn't express how I feel, and I nearly spit out my coffee but hurry and gulp it down.

"Hey, Grace!" She sits in front of me like we're old friends. We're *not*. She dated Harrison in high school, and that's as far as our relationship went.

"Hey, good to see ya. Home visiting?" I ask, closing my laptop, not wanting her to see what I'm up to.

181

She nods, and not a single strand of blonde hair is out of place. A silver bracelet dangles on her wrist, and I realize she's put together like an adult. Meanwhile, I'm in leggings, a baggy T-shirt that I'm certain has a snarky-as-fuck saying on the front, and some Converse that have seen better days.

"Actually, I'm moving back to Valentine. Going to help my parents with their practice. Honestly, I just came to say thank you."

"For what?" I wish I could disappear and not have this conversation with her. I want to be Samantha in *Bewitched* and wiggle my nose.

She laughs. "In a roundabout way, you helped me make the big decision to return. Had you not visited Houston and brought Harrison with you, I'd have never realized how much I missed home and him. Might not even be here."

"Oh, wow. Well, I guess you're welcome. Glad I could help." I force a smile.

"Thanks. It's good to see you, Grace. Haven't changed a bit."

"Still the same small-town girl."

She smiles, and her phone buzzes. "Yeah. Oh, speaking of, I gotta go. Maybe we can hang out sometime?"

"Yeah, maybe." I give her a wave and watch her leave.

She offers me a kind smile when she passes the window, and I stare at a few crispy leaves blowing on the sidewalk. I slide my laptop off the table and shove it in my tote, grab my coffee, and head home.

She wanted to thank me for moving back for Harrison. Everyone knows that this is home, and he'll be in Valentine forever. If she wants to be with him, coming here is the only option.

When I walk in, Remi is at the table, holding a puzzle piece in her hand. She's hunched over, concentrating hard on the shape, scanning the frame.

"Did you know Stephanie is back in town?" I ask, setting my bag on the counter and playing through our conversation again.

"Yeah."

I wait for her to offer more info, but she doesn't. "Am I the only person who didn't know?"

"It's not my business, but, yeah, pretty much." She turns and looks at me. "I told Harrison he'd better not date her again."

"Dating? Why would you think that's even a possibility?"

"She was at our parents' house when he helped me move in. Did he not tell you?"

I shake my head.

"You didn't hear it from me," she says, then goes back to her puzzle. "I would give you a hug, but I'm not really a hugger."

"Thanks. It's the thought that counts." I dig my phone from my pocket and open my last text thread with him. Then I type a message.

GRACE

Are you and Stephanie trying to work things out?

I STARE at the blinking cursor, taunting me before I press Send. Then I shake my head, feeling like a jealous ex, and delete it.

It's not my damn business either.

This is why he has those rules in place with his one-night stands. I should've followed his playbook and been adamant about only doing it once. But … it was too good.

I type another message.

GRACE

Hey! Whatcha up to?

His text bubble pops up.

HARRISON

About to eat lunch.

GRACE

Yeah? Want me to join you?

HARRISON

Actually, I'm out with someone right now. What about supper?

I stare at his last message, knowing he could be with anyone, but in my heart of hearts, I know he's with her.

For as long as I can remember, we've had a pact that we'll support whoever the other is with. No matter what. And he's done that for me over the years without complaint. I'm not experienced in this because of his no-commitment rule, so keeping my end of the bargain throughout our twenties has been easy. I have a feeling it's going to get hard.

So, I do what I always do when I get stressed. I pull supplies out from the cabinet under the sink.

"Where are you going?" Remi asks as I clank the plastic bucket against the bar.

"To scrub a tub."

She smiles. "You clean when you're upset."

"Not all the time," I explain.

"I've won the roommate lottery!" She pumps her fist in the air.

"Lucky you!" I tell her as I walk away, needing the distraction so bad that it nearly hurts.

Before I get started, I change into some shorts and a tank top so my clothes don't get soaked. Then I grab my headphones, put my hair up into a high ponytail, and slide on my pink rubber gloves.

As I study the tub, I try to remember the last time I've felt this way. I'm not sure I ever have. I can't explain it.

Because I'll be on my knees, I grab a few towels and roll them up to protect me from the hard floor. Then, I turn on an audiobook, one with monsters who have eighteen dicks, and bend over the side of the porcelain with my scrub brush in hand.

Every part of me wants to escape the thoughts that are trying to pull me away from these man lizards. With every circular stroke, I put all of my weight into it, watching the grime disappear. It gives me something to focus on that has a finish line. It's a much-needed distraction from what I'm running from.

Before the dirt dries, I bend farther over and rinse away the dirty bubbles.

I let out a sigh, loving how satisfying it is to see bright-white porcelain. When I tilt my head, I can feel someone in the room, and when I turn around, I nearly gasp.

Harrison stands in the doorway with that baseball hat I've loved since we were teenagers, and he's watching me with a clenched jaw. His strong arms are crossed loosely over his chest as that fiery gaze slides over my ass, up my back, to my mouth, and then to my eyes.

I take an earbud out and look at him, drinking him in like warm whiskey on a cold winter night. "Hi."

"Hi." He glances at the supplies surrounding me. "You got a bucket and a mop for that …"

"Shut up. And don't you dare say a thing about it," I warn because he knows me and my stupid cycles.

He takes two steps forward, and I'm on my knees, looking up at him.

"You're cleaning," he whispers, lifting my chin with his fingertips.

"Yeah," I say, very much aware that his cock is at eye level right now.

I swallow hard, licking my lips, as he wraps my ponytail around his fist, forcing me to look into his eyes. I stand, and he gently lets my hair go, but we're dangerously close.

"Why didn't you text me back?" His voice is low.

His breath is hot. My heart is beating.

We're a mosaic of colors; Harrison is yellow, and I'm gray. Together, we're sunshine and midnight. And just like the moon and sun, we'll chase each other around the earth, only being in the sky together temporarily.

"You were with someone," I whisper.

His brow pops up. "Jealous?"

"No," I say breathlessly.

"Liar." He shakes his head.

I take a step back because the urge to kiss him is too overpowering. But this is the price I'll pay to keep him forever.

"Why are you here?" I finally ask.

"I came to make sure you weren't having a meltdown."

I laugh and shake my head. "Was I everything you expected?"

"Always are."

My heart flutters. "Were you with her?"

He meets my eyes and nods. "Yes."

A jab of jealousy steals my breath away, and I take a hard look at our relationship, noticing it's in shambles.

This feeling is proof that I need to find a new distraction fast before I ruin *everything* we still have and am left with nothing but my memories.

CHAPTER EIGHTEEN

HARRISON

It's been two weeks since Grace and I last crossed the line, and there hasn't been a single day I haven't thought about her.

I'm still under the influence of her, but she can't see that. No matter how fucking clear I try to make it for her. Denial should be her middle name.

"Hello?" I hear a deep voice echo through the barn, and I walk out of the stable to see Cash standing in the entryway.

"There ya are, you silly bastard." I pull him into a hug.

He's my older brother's best friend, and we all grew up together. I had Grace, and Beckett had Cash.

"Excited to see me?" He pats me on the shoulder.

"Not really," I say with a laugh.

"Beckett!" I yell, my voice carrying through the entryway.

"What?" He comes around the corner and then grins wide when he sees Cash.

"I thought you weren't gonna make it in town until tomorrow." Beckett gives him a handshake and pulls him in for a hug.

Cash shrugs, and he looks happy. "I said fuck it. Couldn't wait to be back home."

Beckett looks at me. "Must be somethin' in the water. Did you hear who else is back in town?"

"Nah, who?" He rolls the sleeves of his hoodie up.

"Stephanie Paterson."

Cash turns and looks at me. "Your ex?"

I shrug. "What can I say? The ladies can't get enough."

"That shit is gonna catch up with you one day," he warns.

"Still waitin'," I tell him with a shrug.

"Y'all want to ride over to the clinic and check it out? I've looked at pictures but haven't seen the progress in real life yet."

"Fuck yeah," Beckett says.

"I need to finish up with this horse. Can you give me five?"

They nod, and Beckett gives him a tour of the facility as I finish brushing down Deneb, an Arabian beauty I'm currently training. Once she's back in her stable and I've put the saddle and bridle in the tack room, I meet Beckett and Cash in the office.

"Sterling!" Beckett yells as we make our way toward the exit. "You're in charge."

He pokes his head from the top loft, where we keep all of the hay. "Sounds good."

Then the three of us jump in Cash's truck and drive over to the facility. When we pass the B&B, I see Remi walking to her car with her tote bag over her shoulder.

"Hey, stop," I tell Cash, then roll down the back seat window where I'm sitting.

"Hey, sis!" I whistle loud and her head turns in my direction.

"Harrison?" She looks confused. "Who are you with?"

"Join us at the clinic, doing a walk-through." I point in the direction.

"Okay!" she yells back.

Then, I roll up my window. "We can go now."

"Who was that?" Cash asks.

"Remington," Beckett tells him, keeping his gaze forward as we continue on.

"Ah," Cash says, but I see him take a second glance.

Remi has always had a thing for him, but he's too old for her. There's nearly a nine-year age difference.

As we continue on the short drive, I look out the window, looking at the dead grass and how everything from the sky to the ground looks gray. We park on the side of the building, and Remi pulls up in her Mustang and gets out of the car.

When she walks toward the truck, Cash stops walking. Their eyes meet for a brief moment, and she turns back to me.

"I was on my way home."

"I know. Now, you don't have to break in to check it out. Much easier," I explain, patting her back.

"Break in?" Cash asks, looking between us. "Like pick the lock?"

"I was kidding." She rolls her eyes. "Harrison is *Mr. Literal* sometimes. *Asshole*," she whispers, forcing a smile.

Cash unlocks the door, and Beckett follows behind him.

"After you," I tell my sister and then fall in line behind her.

The lights flicker on, and we walk through the break room, offices, and the patient rooms. In the back, there are stables for all of the equestrian appointments.

After we've had the full tour, we're all amazed, even Cash.

"I think we should celebrate. Y'all got plans tonight?" Cash looks between me and Beckett.

"Nope, and I'm off tomorrow, so I'm down to go out," I offer.

"Boot Scooting?" Remi asks.

"Don't think I can make it," Beckett tells us. "Gotta cover for this guy tomorrow on his day off."

I chuckle. "Fuck yeah, you do."

Cash checks his watch, and I see it's just past five. "How

about we meet at seven? I need to head to my parents' and get settled, then shower."

"Sounds good," I say.

He glances at Remi, waiting for her answer.

"Not sure. I got some things to do at home."

He meets her eyes. "Okay, well, if you change your mind, the invitation is open."

"Thanks." She offers him her hand, and they shake. It's very formal. "Congrats again. Thanks for showing us around."

"Anytime," Cash says.

Then Beckett steals his attention away, and they talk about the grand opening. I follow Remi to her car.

"What are you doin'?" she asks.

"Helping you out," I tell her.

She turns to me. "Don't. I don't want that kind of pressure in my life, got it?"

"Fine. Suit yourself."

Remi continues to her car. "I bet you want to know how Grace is doing."

"Nope." However, I'm dying to know because she's already started closing me out. Something I was afraid would happen.

"She seems to be moving on. Maybe you should consider it too."

Her words are like a dagger to my heart.

"How do you know?"

"Because she's going on a date tonight."

"Where?" I ask.

"Promise me that favor first."

"Scout's honor."

"Boot Scooting. Seven o'clock. It's why I'm not meeting y'all out there. I'm not getting involved in this thing going on between you two."

An evil grin slides over my lips. "Shit, you shoulda *never* told me that."

"I know."

She leaves, and I watch her headlights fade away in the dust of the gravel. Then she turns onto the country highway and makes her way to town. I'm grinning like a devil when I walk back to the guys.

"Why do you have that look on your face?" Beckett asks.

"Because I'm goin' out tonight."

Cash drives us to the barn, and when we walk in, Sterling's already finished feeding the horses and turning off the overhead lights.

"Shit, you're efficient," Beckett admits.

"I'm ready to get out of here," he says with a shrug.

I'd invite him out tonight, but he can't get into the bar because he's still underage.

"Seven, right?" Cash says, pointing to me.

"I'll be there." I slide my keys from my pocket and then I drive the short distance to my place. The day flew by quicker than I thought it would. While I'm exhausted from training all day, it doesn't stop me from going home and taking a shower.

Knowing that Grace is trying to move on and forget about us reminds me of that dull ache that's been in my chest ever since we ended things. I've pretended I don't care when we get together, but it's the hardest fucking thing I've ever had to do. Heartbreak like this is the reason I stopped seriously dating. As I rinse the soap from my hair, I think that maybe, in some fucked-up way, Grace is my karma for not giving anyone a real chance over the years.

Once I slip on my belt and boots, I check the time and button my dark-washed jean shirt with pearl buttons. As I'm tucking my phone into my pocket, Colt walks in, drops a bag full of tools onto the floor, then looks at me.

"Where are you goin'?"

"Boot Scooting, meeting Cash there. Wanna come?"

He nods. "I might, but I'm tired as hell. Did you leave me some hot water?"

"Hell no, I didn't. Emptied it." I grab my Stetson and pop it on my head. "Hope to see ya there."

I close the door behind me and stand on the porch, looking up at the stars. A meteor skims across the sky, glittering, leaving a green trail behind it.

I smile. "That'd better be a sign," I say, pointing up to it, making my wish.

On the way to Boot Scooting, I try to get my plan together and walk through exactly how I think the night will go. If Grace is on a date, I have to avoid her at all costs.

I find a parking spot on the side of the building, check the time, and walk in early. Not to my surprise, Cash is sitting at the end of the bar, away from everyone. He gives me a wave, and I join him. It has the perfect view of the entire place but also doesn't draw too much attention.

"A round," he tells the bartender, and we clink our shots together before tossing them back.

I'm not watching the door, but as soon as I see Grace enter, wearing the cutest little dress, I can't help but stare.

Cash looks at me, and then his eyes follow my gaze.

"Is that Grace? Y'all still besties?"

"Yes, but it's complicated."

"Mmm." He lifts a brow, and then he sees Grace hug another guy. "Ah. That explains it."

"No, it's a lot more complicated than just that." I point my empty shot glass in her direction with a laugh. "I can't let her see me. She'll think I showed up on purpose."

"Did you?" He looks at me from head to toe. "Because I sure as hell didn't change clothes to come up here."

I chuckle. "A little birdie might've tipped me off. So anyway, what about you? Got a girlfriend?"

"Nope," he says. "Women are trouble. I'm letting the horses occupy my time."

"Fuck yeah. I've been spending a lot of time at the barn lately. Been thinking about life. About stupid shit."

Grace and the guy sit at a high bar top on the other side of the dance floor, but I have the perfect view of her profile. He pulls out her chair for her, and then she scoots in. He says something in her ear, and she nods. Then he walks to the bar.

She's sitting alone, looking at her phone. So I pull out mine and type her a message.

HARRISON

You look gorgeous.

I see her read it, and she smiles, then looks around.

GRACE

Are you here?

I keep my head down, knowing she'll never spot me with this hat on.

Cash shakes his head. "You're both still playin' games, I see."

Just as I open my mouth to rebut him, Stephanie walks through the door.

"Shit," he says. "Now I remember why I missed being home. Small-town drama is like its own damn reality TV show."

I burst into laughter. "It is. So I guess that makes me the main character in the saga?"

"Better you than me. Not into that *other woman* drama."

Stephanie sees Grace and walks over to her. The two of them chat for a few minutes, and when Grace's date returns with two drinks, Stephanie excuses herself.

She's wearing a short skirt that shows off her long, toned legs. Step by step, she struts across the room, and then our eyes meet, and she smiles, picking up her pace. When she's close, I stand, and she wraps her arms around my neck.

"Damn, you smell good."

My hand rests on her hip. "You do too."

"Can I join you?" she asks, and I give her a nod.

Before she sits, she realizes who's with me. "Oh shit. Cash Johnson, is that you?"

He gives her a side hug.

"Are you back too?" She laughs. "Must be something in the water."

"Just couldn't stay away from this place. At least it's never boring." He looks forward.

Stephanie sits next to me, and her leg rests against mine.

"Can I get you anything?" I ask, grinning.

"Cranberry martini," she says.

I order for her. The drink comes quickly, and we chat with Cash about vet school and working at a big practice.

"Law school sucked," she admits, then glances at me, her body completely turned toward me on the stool. "I kinda wish I'd have never gone."

I shake my head, knowing she made her dreams come true. "You don't mean that."

"No, I do. I know we'd be in a different place together had I not. But I made my decision, and now I'm living with that choice."

Cash picks up his drink, pretending like he can't hear our entire conversation as Stephanie leans in and whispers in my ear.

"I came back for you," she mutters.

My gaze is focused on Grace, who excuses herself. When she's halfway across the room, walking toward the long hallway that leads to the bathroom, I pull away.

"I'll be right back," I say to Steph. "We'll finish this conversation—you have my word."

"Okay," she says and glances across the room, where Grace's date is sitting alone, but I don't care.

Stephanie is a smart woman who I'm sure has already put the pieces together.

The music plays, and people two-step across the wooden dance floor. The lights are low as I walk in the same direction she's headed, trying my best to avoid people so I don't lose sight of her.

By the time I turn the corner, she's pushing the restroom door open, so I wait.

When she comes out, she keeps her head down, not even noticing me leaning against the wall. Just as she passes me and I smell the warm vanilla on her skin, I gently grab her wrist and pull her to me. With her other hand on my chest, she stops herself from crashing into me with a ragged breath. She looks at my mouth, then up to my eyes. I adjust my hat so I can get a better view of her.

"Are you havin' fun?" I study her face.

"What do you think?" She gives me a sly smile, and it's so goddamn adorable.

"If I had to guess, I'd say you're bored, counting down the minutes, wishing you were with me." I shoot her a smirk, and I realize I'm still holding her hand.

It's as if she notices, too, and I let go of her.

"Are you expecting me to deny it?" she asks.

"No, because it's the truth."

"Of course," she whispers.

When someone turns down the hallway, she creates space,

standing with her back on the opposite side of the wall. It's the only thing that will keep our mouths apart. We both know it.

When they pass, she moves back to me. "I miss you. The old us."

"Me too."

Her perfume lingers.

"Did Stephanie find you?" she asks, and the jealousy I saw in her before is gone.

"Yes," I answer truthfully.

She smiles. "Give her a chance."

"That's what you really want?"

"I want you to be happy. We both know it's something I can't give you."

The awkward silence has me in a choke hold.

"I need to get back, okay?" Grace meets my eyes.

"Yeah."

Grace walks away and turns and looks over her shoulder, watching me watch her. "Have fun. Try to live a little, Harri."

"Plan on it." I take the advice to heart and make my way back to the bar, where Stephanie and Cash are chatting.

I slide back into place, ordering another drink as Grace leaves with the guy she met there. My thoughts race, and I wonder where they'll go next. Back to her place? A hotel?

Can he make her happy? If I can't, no one can.

Stephanie's alarm rings, and she looks at me. "Shit, I gotta get going. Have to be up really early in the morning."

"Do you have plans tomorrow night? I can pick you up around eight."

A grin fills her face. "I'd love that. What should I wear?"

"Whatever you want, darlin'."

She leans forward and softly kisses me before standing. "See you then."

"Lookin' forward to it," I admit before she walks away with a pep to her step.

Cash turns to me. "You're givin' me whiplash."

"Fuck, same."

We sit in silence, listening to the music play as we swirl the last few sips of our whiskey.

"You two were great together back in the day," Cash offers. "Prom king and queen. It's a love story that basically writes itself."

I chuckle, taking in the last swig. "We were good together. That's why I'm gonna give her a real chance this time."

Neither of us says another word.

I eventually clear my throat. "Ya know, everyone always talks about becoming friends to lovers, but not many people talk about friends to strangers."

"It's because it's depressing as fuck." Cash pats me on the back and closes out our tab. "It'll get better. Or worse. I guess we'll see how it all plays out, won't we?"

"Glad I can be your entertainment."

"Looking forward to watching the next few episodes," he says. "Was it that Kiss of Death bullshit?"

A howl of laughter escapes me. "Happy you're back, man. Also, keep this shit to yourself, got it?"

"Secret's safe with me. But fuck, what a wild ride this dramafest is gonna be."

"Don't jinx me."

He throws a few twenties on the bar. "Don't even have to."

CHAPTER NINETEEN

GRACE

As I clean the baseboards in our living room, Remi stands behind me. "Didn't you work on those last week?"

"No, I cleaned the windowsills," I tell her with a toothbrush in my pink-gloved hand.

"Look, you need to stop whatever this is." She moves her hand around. "You need to get out there, go have fun, make out with a random person, get a few phone numbers. You're making your single-girl era seem … *depressing*. You went out last weekend with that dude and haven't tried again."

"I think I'm broken," I explain, but I keep the details to myself because each time I've tried to articulate what I'm going through, it sounds ridiculous. And stupid.

Remi laughs as she dunks a tea bag into a mug and slices a lemon. "I'd agree with that."

"How do you do it? How are you okay with being alone?" I stand and stretch, and every vertebra in my back pops.

She shrugs. "When you grow up in a family like mine, you learn to love quiet time. Our house was always so loud. Something was always going on. I was never alone as a kid. So I'm making up for that now. About the partner part … I don't fuck around because as soon as I do, I tend to find out. Being independent has its perks. I know that I don't need a man … a man needs me."

"I need that attitude."

"I've been single so long that if I spot one red flag, I'm out. You eat all the food in my fridge? Buh-bye. You have a crazy ex? Bye. You argue about something trivial? See ya. Don't shower often? Outta here. No time for any of that." She blows on the top of her cup and takes a sip. "I spoke with Haley earlier. She was going to the bar tonight."

"She asked me to join her," I admit.

"And? Are you going to spend another Friday night crying on the couch? I love ya, but if I have to watch *You've Got Mail* or *13 Going on 30* one more time, I might move out." She tries to hold back her laughter but fails.

"Okay, that's fair."

She walks farther into the living room, and that's when I notice she's already in her pajamas.

"I take it you're not going anywhere tonight?"

"Nah, I'm good."

"Why? 'Cause you might see Cash out?"

She glares at me. "Out of everyone in my life, I thought you'd be the last person to pull that *secret crush* stuff on me."

"Doesn't everyone know? When he was eighteen and you were nine, I remember how you'd follow him and Beckett around like you were their shadow."

She sips her tea. "This is one of those times where I wish you weren't always around to witness all the embarrassing childhood shit that most people don't remember. It has nothing to do with *him*. Unlike you, who's avoiding every public place because you might run into your *bestie* …"

"The difference is, I can admit it. I don't want to see Harrison and Stephanie together. I'm good. I watched them choke on each other's tongues in high school enough to last me a lifetime."

She shrugs. "Fresh air and tequila will do you good."

"I'm just gonna drink wine and read in bed. I've got a why choose romance with eight guys railing and worshiping the heroine."

She bursts into laughter. "Text it to me."

"And this is why we're great friends," I offer, glancing at her, realizing she and Harrison have the same mannerisms. I guess all the Valentines do.

I miss him, but I asked for this, so it's time for me to shut the fuck up and quit crying about it. I'm even annoying myself.

When I walk into my room, I see the photo album he gave me for Christmas on my dresser. I mosey over and grab it. Moving back to my bed, I open it up. Page by page, I flip through it, glancing over the pictures we've taken together, all the memories and holidays. Wherever one of us was, the other was right there.

Once I go through it twice, I move it over and then grab my laptop. Then, I decide to open the anonymous form and submit my first question to Dear Kinsley.

As my fingers rest on the keyboard, I close my eyes, not even knowing where to begin. Too much information, and she'll figure it out. Not enough, and she won't choose it.

Sucking in a deep breath, I search for all the courage I have left.

"Fearless," I whisper.

Dear Kinsley,

That dreaded cursor continues to haunt me.

I'm in love with my best friend.

I read how stupid that sounds.

And I don't know how to admit it to myself.

This is boring.

How do I tell them before they get married?

Too much information. I delete it all and shake my head.

Dear Kinsley,

Have you ever known deep down that you're meant to be with someone but have doubts? I know I can't live without this person in my life, and the thought of losing them hurts. What do you suggest? Take the risk and potentially lose everything, or keep the boundary in place? Do stories like this ever have a happy ending, or do they all end in tragedy?

—It's Probably Too Late

She'll have no idea it's me. And it's probably best it stays that way. No talk about best friends, no talk about anything. It's basic, but hopefully not too basic.

I shut my laptop and close my eyes, hoping I'll fall asleep. As I begin to drift off, I dream about Harrison, and it's so vivid that I wake up in a panic with a racing heart. Then I realize it's the first time I've had a dream in … *years.*

Nothing like getting haunted awake and now asleep.

The Kiss of Death …

Those stupid thoughts need to go away.

Instead of forcing myself back to sleep, I roll over and check the time. It's only nine. I skipped dinner again and know I have to stop doing that.

So, I get dressed, put on a baseball hat, and grab my keys. The house is quiet and dark, and Remi is already in bed.

I'm half tempted to text Haley and see if she wants to join me for some food, but I know she's at the bar, having a good time. When I pass Boot Scooting, street parking is full, and it looks like the whole town is there tonight. I continue a few blocks and find a spot in front of the deli. Right now, I'm so thankful that they're open twenty-four hours. Just kinda sad the Mexican restaurant isn't.

The sounds of plates clattering and the smell of fried bacon grab my attention when I enter. There aren't many people inside, and I sit in my favorite booth by the windows. The server greets me, and even though I know I shouldn't drink a cup of coffee this late, I order one anyway, along with a fat stack of pancakes and extra-crispy bacon.

Fuck it all.

As I wait, I slump down in the booth, hoping no one sees me as I log in to the Ranchers Singles site. My notifications are out of control, and over a hundred messages are waiting for me. So I rest my head on my fist and scroll through, seeing if anyone catches my eye, and that's when I see I matched with Landon. Again. So I text him.

GRACE

Hey! Ranchers Singles?

LANDON

LMAO! Why are you on that site?

GRACE

The same reasons you are. How have you been?

LANDON

Good. You know, Haley and I didn't hit it off.

GRACE

No? Wow. I'm sorry. That sucks.

LANDON

Yeah, I was kinda hoping to have a chance with you.

GRACE

Not girlfriend material. I've got commitment issues.

THE TRUTH WILL SET me free.

LANDON

Me too. But, hey, maybe we can figure it out
together?

MY FOOD IS DELIVERED, and the sweet smell of pancakes pulls me away from the conversation. The server fills my coffee, and when she walks away, Harrison slides in front of me.

I stare at him like he's a figment of my imagination.

He grins. "Hi."

"How do you always seem to know where I am?" I look at him. "Do you have people spying on me?"

A bark of a laugh releases from his perfect lips. "You could fart in this town, and I'd know about it."

I smile, and it feels good. "That's true. Want to eat with me?"

He shakes his head. "Nah. I have to get going. Just saw you sitting here and wanted to see how you were doing."

"I'm good. Just been keeping busy."

"Yeah, same."

The server comes over and offers to get him a coffee, and he shakes his head. As she walks away, I can smell the hint of his cologne.

Usually, when we come here and eat, he joins me on the same side in the same booth. The one I'm in right now.

He opens his mouth and closes it.

"Just spit it out," I tell him, sipping on my coffee, hating the tension between us. "I know you have something to say. You have that look on your face."

"I can't go with you to Hawaii."

"I kinda figured that was the case. Was just waiting for you to tell me." I glance out the window that overlooks the sidewalk.

"It wasn't something I wanted to text. I'm sorry."

"Me too," I tell him. "So that was it?"

"Yeah." He studies me for a brief second, and no tears fall. I don't have any left. "It was really good seein' you."

"Don't be a stranger," I whisper.

"I won't." He pats my hand, then stands and walks away.

I watch him go to his truck, back out, and then drive into the quiet of the night.

I expected it. I did. And I know exactly what this means—*they're serious*.

I pick up my phone and message Landon.

GRACE

Want to go to Hawaii with me next month?

CHAPTER TWENTY

HARRISON

I haven't seen Grace in almost a month, since I told her I couldn't join her for her sister's wedding. A part of me hoped she would give me some sort of reaction, maybe even ask me to change my mind, but she didn't. That's one thing about Grace: she won't beg anyone to join her, not even me.

I knew that and hoped things would get back to normal between us. They haven't, but I'm getting used to the way it feels though. I'm learning to live with the loss of our friendship, already mourning it in a sense. And it's not because I want to.

It's because she's avoiding me.

It only took thirty days for me to understand my place in her world after everything we'd been through together. I'm convinced it's what she wanted, so she can easily forget about what we could've had. The silence is deafening.

I take three steps onto the porch of the gigantic brick home on the outskirts of town. With a bouquet in my hand and a smile on my face, I ring the doorbell. I hear footsteps that are followed by the door swinging open. Stephanie meets me with a sparkle in her eye, dangly pearl earrings, and a grin that could end a war.

"You remembered my favorite?" She looks down at the white roses, and I hand them to her.

She inhales, then allows me inside. Not a thing has changed in her parents' house, not even the pictures on the wall. I follow her to the kitchen, where she fills a vase with water and snips the ends of the flowers.

"What's going on?"

"Thought I'd surprise you."

She moves over to me and places a soft kiss on my lips. "Funny because I was just thinking about you. Today is our one-month-dating anniversary."

"I know," I tell her with a grin, picking up a brochure with the Eiffel Tower on the front. It's lit with lights, and they've Photoshopped stars behind it. I set it back on the counter.

"I'd like to go someday," she tells me, glancing at it. "When I went to Europe last, I didn't have time to visit, even if it was on my bucket list."

I nod. "Well, maybe that's where we'll go for our honeymoon."

She wraps her arm around me, looking into my eyes. "You're *serious?*"

"Yeah." I catch the faint hint of a familiar smell on her skin. Vanilla. And it reminds me of Grace. Or maybe I'm hallucinating because she's been on my mind so much lately.

"About that," she says. "I know I told you I didn't want to be exclusive until we knew forever was in the picture. I didn't care who you fooled around with, whatever, didn't matter."

"And that agreement went both ways," I remind her.

"Yes." She smiles. "Of course it does. And I've had my fair share of weekend flings."

I love that she's open and honest. She's not afraid to say what she thinks and backs her opinion. Maybe it's the lawyer in her, or maybe it's her low tolerance for bullshit, but it's respectable and one of the traits I love most about her.

She clears her throat. "Things seem like they're getting serious, and I guess what I'm saying is, when forever is *really* in the picture for us and *if* you decide to slide a ring on my finger, I'd like to be exclusive. Just us."

I nod. "When forever is in the picture, I want the same. No way I'd be okay with my fiancée being with anyone else."

"Okay." She lets out a relieved breath and pulls away from me, cleaning up the flower tips from the counter. "I'm just so damn scared of choosing the wrong person to spend forever with. After one failed engagement, making the wrong decision scares the shit out of me." She meets my eyes. "I also noticed how you said *when* forever is in the picture, not if."

"I chose my words wisely for a reason." I glance back at the brochure and try to imagine a life with Stephanie. "Progressing our relationship is something I've been thinking about a lot lately."

"We'll be twenty-eight soon," she reminds me. "I guess our little pact can still come true after all?"

"I think what we've got is deeper than that, don't you?"

"Oh, absolutely." Zero hesitation.

She washes her hands and then turns to me. "I think you should join Grace in Hawaii."

"Why?" I study her, not fully understanding. "And where did this come from?"

She makes a face like I'm the dumb one. "Because she's your best friend and she needs you. I don't want her to think I'm the reason you're not there. You agreed to be her plus-one. No one likes a ditcher."

"You're serious about this." I tilt my head at her.

She brushes her thumb over my bottom lip. "If you were my best friend, started dating your shitty ex that I didn't like again, and ditched me a month before a trip that we'd planned to attend together since December, I'd cut you off forever and not care how much history we had." She shrugs. "Harsh, but it's a dickhead thing to do to someone. She deserves better than that. You just don't do that to people, especially not your bestie."

"Point taken." I don't want to have this conversation, but I can see it's happening anyway. "My ticket has been canceled. I don't even have a flight there."

"So, book one." She says it like it's easy as she walks over to me. Stephanie hesitates but then finds her confidence again and clears her throat. "I just want you to be sure that when you're ready to be mine, I have *all of you*."

I lean forward, kissing her. "When I decide to slide a ring on your finger, you will."

"I'd better. I believe in us."

"Us," I whisper, the word hot on my tongue. "I kinda like the sound of that."

"Me too."

Stephanie grabs my hand. "Let's go out for dinner."

"Yes, I'd love to. I'm starving."

We return to the living room, and she grabs her coat from the rack by the door.

As I help her slide it on, she looks at me over her shoulder. "I want you and Grace to keep your friendship. I don't need you to decide on Hawaii tonight, but please think about it because the whole town's talking. You have three days."

"I promise to think about it. Now let's go eat some chips and salsa." I place my hand on the small of her back, leading her to the truck.

"And margaritas?" she asks.

"Sure." I smile.

"And guac?"

"The biggest bowl you've ever seen," I say, opening the door for her.

Before she climbs in, she turns and looks at me, and I clear my throat.

"You said the whole town's talking. What are they saying? I haven't caught wind of it yet."

"That you two are in love with each other and you're with me to get over it."

I nod. "Ah. Then I look forward to throwing everyone a curveball."

"What does that mean?" she asks when I walk around to the driver's side and get in. I crank the truck and reverse.

"You gonna make me your wife?"

"I guess we'll see."

CHAPTER TWENTY-ONE

GRACE

Love is stupid.
Lust is stupid.
Life is stupid.
Harrison Valentine is stupid.
Shit, add me to that list too.

I'm in a grumpy mood as I park at the airport and look out at the security lights, making the garage not seem so damn scary this early in the morning. It sucked to drive to El Paso alone, but I managed fine, even though I left so late at night. It was just me on the road, and it was okay, thankfully.

Once I'm through security, I find my gate and sit, kicking my feet up on my suitcase, hoping I can sleep the entire flight because hours after I get there, we'll be going straight to the rehearsal dinner.

Tomorrow, I'm supposed to give a speech about my sister and love. How am I supposed to do that when I've become very much anti-love?

I think about Joey and how Houston was one of the biggest

mistakes of my life that created a domino effect on unfortunate events.

When the sun rises, I put on my sunglasses, and I'm tired as hell. I try to get comfortable with my neck pillow as I sneak peeks of the couple in front of me being flirty. Their arms brush together. She draws circles on his palm. It reminds me of Harrison. And I wonder if they're best friends too.

Soon, it's time to board, and I scan my ticket and then get on the plane. The window seat gives me something to focus on, and the only reason I have it is because I canceled Harrison's ticket.

"We'll finish boarding in about three minutes, just waiting for one more," the attendant says.

Doesn't matter to me. I just wish they'd hurry the hell up so we can get this show on the road. I'm ready to get this over with, and the quicker this plane takes off, the better. Especially knowing that Landon couldn't join me on this trip either.

For a brief moment, I think maybe Harrison might step on and tell me he was stupid. When the flight attendant greets someone, I sit up, and my heart pounds as I wait for my movie moment.

As soon as I see an older woman boarding with a cat carrier, I slump back down. She sits in the aisle seat on my row, and I grab my sleep mask and pull it over my eyes, wanting to block the world out.

Right now, I just need to survive the next three days in Hawaii.

Never been so grateful to have canceled an extended stay at a resort in my life.

After the announcements are given and the cabin lights go off, I drift to sleep and have another *nightmare* about Harrison. Things are how they used to be, but my subconscious can't take it. I wake up in another panic with a racing heart and a heaviness I can't explain. My mouth is dry, and I'm hungry, but all I want is for my feet to be on the ground.

When the plane finally lands, I grab my suitcase and make my way to the resort where my sister's ceremony will be held. Palm trees are everywhere, random chickens are on the side of the road, and the sun is high in the sky. I got enough sleep but still feel tired.

"Can I roll down the window?" I ask the driver.

He presses a button, and the glass slides down. The warm air brushes against my cheeks, and I close my eyes, trying to take it all in. I might be in Hawaii alone, but I'll be damned if I don't have a good time.

I promise myself that I'll take some time to do whatever the fuck I want before going home. Maybe I'll get a tan and go back to Valentine glowing with sun-kissed skin. The thought brings a smile to my face.

ONCE I'M DRESSED, I go downstairs, then make my way to the bar on the beach. There's a karaoke stage and tourists sing their hearts out like they're going to be the next American Idol.

The bartender walks up, and she's smiling. "What can I getcha?"

"Laid," I say with a laugh. "But for now, I guess I'll take a lemon drop."

Moments later, the light-yellow liquid with a sugary rim is being set in front of me. I pull out my phone and snap a picture of me with my drink, then post it. I've been trying to get used to doing things alone, settling in the uncomfortableness until I learn to appreciate the loneliness of losing my bestie.

Sucking in a deep breath, I try to write the speech I'm supposed to give at my sister's dinner. I've put it off all year long, not able to find anything positive about love, not when every relationship I've had failed. I've googled it, and I even asked stupid AI to try to write me something I could use, but it was like hot garbage on a summer day. I type up a few sentences and set my phone down when a guy walks up and takes the seat next to me.

The cologne is familiar, and when I turn my head, I don't see the man I thought I'd see. It's Chip's brother, Anthony.

"You're lookin' pretty lonely over here," he says as I gulp the rest of my drink. Then he turns to the bartender. "She'll have another one of those."

"Trying to get me drunk?" I ask him.

He smirks. "Nah. You just look like you could use another one."

"It's that stupid speech I have to give. It's making me nervous," I admit. "I'm the last person on the planet who should be talking about love."

The bartender sets my drink down, then looks at me and tilts her head toward him. "Isn't this what you asked for earlier?"

I laugh and wave her away. Anthony thinks she's talking about the drink, but she's talking about him.

"Let me read what you have."

I unlock my phone and give it to him. He reads over it and hands it back.

"You're one of those hopeless romantics, aren't you?"

"How'd you guess that from this?"

"Because love is messy. It's like this ball of yarn that you're obsessed with untangling, but every time you think you've figured it out, more knots appear. What you've written is perfect love." He shakes his head. "Doesn't exist."

"Sure it does."

He laughs in my face. "With that attitude, you'll be single, like me, for the rest of your life. You'll keep searching for something you'll never find."

"Oh, so you think you have something better?"

He glances at me. "I'm going to make it up on the spot when I get there. No pressure, right?"

"Too brave. Nope. Not happening," I say, smiling, and the conversation lulls.

Anthony looks around, noticing I'm alone. "You don't have anyone with you?"

"Nope. I came alone after being ditched. Twice. Actually, three times." I shrug. "My bad luck, I guess."

"Or maybe it's your good luck," he offers. "I'm here. Had a beefhead been next to you, I'd not have walked over and chatted."

This makes me chuckle. "Beefhead. In my part of Texas, that can mean many things."

We drink for a few hours, talking about everything and nothing. He's easy to chat with, and he keeps a conversation without my effort, which I appreciate. When I talk with him, it's almost like those intrusive thoughts that have been taking over for the last few weeks vanish.

Maybe Harrison figured something out. Maybe moving on and finding someone else is the key to getting over what happened. Maybe that's the answer to this? But he also warned me that one-night stands won't fill the void.

I'm willing to try anything that will make this agonizing feeling in the pit of my stomach go away.

"What are you thinking about?" Anthony asks as I stare off into the distance, stirring the straw in the martini I switched over to.

I shake my head. "Everything. My little sister is getting married. Feel like my destiny is to be an old maid."

He pats my leg. "You're not even thirty, sweetie."

This makes me snort. "I will be in two and a half years."

"Southerners are weird as fuck with this marriage stuff. Most people don't even start living their lives until they're in their midthirties. Now, if you're forty and unmarried, call me." He orders another drink. "Another?"

I nod and tap my glass. "Might as well. What time is it?"

The clock on the wall says it's just past eleven, which means we've been at this since dark. Five hours. Shit. I lost track of time, and now I've drunk way too much.

Our glasses are set on the bar top. Then, when I turn my head and meet Anthony's dark-brown eyes, we kiss. It's sloppy and wet, and I tell myself I need this.

When we break apart, we both slam back our drinks and then he pays. I bring him back to my place, and as soon as we're alone again, I give myself a pep talk. Right now, I don't want anything other than to be fucked. For him to erase the memories of the last person.

Anthony undresses me, throws my clothes onto the floor, and leans me back on the bed. But it feels off. I kiss him, trying to push the thoughts away, wanting to be into it. Needing to be.

"What's wrong?" He pulls away. His cock is hard inside of his shorts.

I huff and lie back on the bed, holding my hands over my eyes. "I can't do this."

"Someone else?" He pulls away.

"Just a lot of baggage. I'm too in my head."

He sits next to me and laughs, pulling up his pants and grabbing his shirt. "I've been there."

I pick up my bra and panties, sliding them over my body.

"I should probably go." He runs his fingers through his hair.

"Yeah," I tell him. "I'm sor—"

He stops me. "No apologies."

Then he kisses me on the cheek. "I hope you find that happily ever after you're desperately searching for, Grace."

"*Fuck*, me too."

CHAPTER TWENTY-TWO

HARRISON

I thought about it.
I changed my mind.
I'm going to Hawaii.

Beckett *forgot* to put me on the schedule, so I took it as a sign that I needed to get on a plane. Maybe he just said that because he understood how much I needed this trip, or maybe it was a universal coincidence; either way, all signs pointed to me going. And I need to talk with Grace. A real talk, one where we can hash this shit out and really start over if that's what she wants.

I sleep the entire flight there, and when I land, I take a cab to the hotel. I walk up to the front desk, test my luck, and ask for a key to my room. When it is slid across the counter, I realize Grace didn't take my name off the reservation. Silly girl.

With my duffel tight in my grip and my suits thrown over my shoulder, I take the elevator up to the top floor. The glass elevator doors give me the perfect view of the beach, and I'm in awe as the early morning sunlight splashes across the sea. I check the time and see I have two hours before the rehearsal dinner starts, but it's on resort property so there isn't too far to travel.

At the end of the hallway is our room.

I stand outside of the door, reading the number on the outside.

With a swipe of a key, I'll be in there, and then what?

A part of me wants to turn around and book another flight home. Pretend like I didn't just fly to Hawaii to talk to her. But I don't walk away from hard conversations.

Now or never, I tell myself, pressing the key against the reader.

The door clicks open, and I walk in.

Windows fill one entire side of the room, giving the perfect view of the beach. I set my duffel down, hearing how quiet it is. I make my way through the living quarters, down a short hallway, and into the bedroom.

On the floor, I see a pair of black panties, a bra, and a dress I know she was wearing last night because I saw the picture she posted online with that lemon drop. That's her revenge drink, the one she starts with when she's trying to go home with someone.

The blankets are ruffled on top of the bed like she was rolling in them with a man last night. Maybe that's where she is right now. I stare at the rumpled sheets with a clenched jaw.

"Harrison?"

I turn around to find a wet Grace with a towel wrapped around her body. Her long, wet hair is brushed back out of her face.

"Hi." I meet her soft gaze that immediately hardens.

"What the hell are you doing here?"

Yep, *she's pissed*. But I don't blame her.

She walks past me, farther into the bedroom, and then she tosses her suitcase on the bed. I can't stop watching her as she drops the towel and proceeds to slide on a pastel-pink bra and panty set then wiggles into a flowy dress.

"What? A cat got your tongue?" She reaches behind her and tries to zip it but struggles.

I take a few steps forward, gently placing my hand on her back, grabbing the zipper, and pulling it to the top.

"I changed my mind," I say, my fingers still on her.

She turns around and meets my eyes. Her shampoo smells like summer flowers. "About what exactly?"

"About coming to Hawaii with you."

"Clearly." She presses her temple, which tells me she drank too much last night.

I grab the unopened bottle of water on the counter, then take it back to her. "Drink up. Dehydration sucks. Bet you didn't have a single glass yesterday."

"That was twenty bucks," she cries but gulps it down.

When it's half-empty, she looks up at me as I pull a twenty from my wallet and set it where the water had been.

"Look, I'm here, trying. This is me offering an olive branch."

She grabs the towel that was wrapped around her body and dries out her hair some more. "There is no trying, or however that stupid saying goes."

I chuckle at her poor attempt to quote Master Yoda. "You gotta meet me halfway, Gracie, or we'll never get back what we had."

This statement nearly steals her breath away. "You're right. But do you really think that's a possibility?"

"Yes," I say without hesitation. "I miss you."

"Which version of me?" she asks, not giving any fucks with me today.

I get the sassy, volatile version of her, and while I find it fucking hot, it sucks knowing the daggers are pointed in my direction.

"The Gracie that doesn't push me away, no matter what. *That* version. Does she still exist in there somewhere?"

"Maybe it's you who changed." She looks at me, then goes back to the bathroom. "Ever thought of that?"

"I have. Because being with you fucking changed me." I meet her in the doorway, leaning against it with my arms crossed, as I stare at her incredulously.

She doesn't say anything.

"But I'm not gonna argue with you the entire time I'm here. So, if you want me to leave, let me know right now. I will drive back to the goddamn airport and get on a plane, and you'll never have to worry about me talking to you ever again." I draw an X over my heart. And she knows it's a promise.

She stares me down, our gazes locked in the mirror, and I wait for her to tell me to leave. There's a split second where we hold a silent conversation, and no matter how badly her body wants to push me away, *she* won't. My best friend and the woman I fell in love with all those years ago is still in there somewhere. The words, the ones that demand I leave, don't come because she knows I wouldn't lie about getting the hell out of here and going home.

"That's what I thought." I let her silent admission sink in for a few seconds. "We never got to talk through this."

"There's nothing to talk about, *bestie*. We're good." She won't even look me in the eye as she puts on her makeup.

So I wait to see if she has anything else to say, but she doesn't speak. She treats me like I'm invisible.

"Don't do that." I shake my head. "I can read you like a book, princess, and I know every chapter by heart. I'm immune to your bullshit."

"So, tell me how it ends." She puts a dark-red lipstick on and then smacks her lips together, finally meeting my eyes in the reflection.

"You're doing that thing where you act tough and shut me out. Like you've *been* doing."

She adds something to her hair and scrunches the strands.

When it's fully dry, it looks like windblown beach hair. It's one of my favorite ways she wears it.

"You're with Stephanie. There's nothing to discuss." She walks past me in the doorway, going back to the bedroom.

I follow her. Memories flood in as I smell the vanilla body mist she's worn since we were teenagers. I'm reminded of driving around Valentine with the windows down on a Friday night during football season and writing stupid letters to each other in the tree house. Feels like so long ago.

"Princess," I whisper, throwing my baseball hat on the bed and shrugging off the light coat I'm wearing.

"Harrison, *please*. You're not my knight in shining armor. I don't need rescuing, okay?"

"I didn't say you did." I unzip the garment bag and take out my navy suit and my black one. "If you're gonna keep giving me the bitch version of you, you're going to get the dickhead version of me that you really don't like."

"It makes you easier to be around."

She glances at the navy suit on the bed, and I know exactly what she's thinking because the hint of pink on her cheeks gives her away. The last time I wore it was on New Year's Eve when she was ripping it from my body. And I know she fucking loves it. She swallows hard, and I wonder if she just replayed my mouth being all over her. I did.

"Why are you *really* here?"

During this trip, I will be unapologetically truthful because it's now or never. There isn't anything else to hide. I'm laying all the shit out without a sweet sugar coating. I'm done with that.

"Stephanie told me to come."

"What? Why?" She looks as confused as I feel.

I peel off the T-shirt that's sticking to me like a second skin, then walk to the bathroom. If she's getting dressed, then I guess I need to as well.

I slide the belt out of my jeans, and just as I bend over to slip off my boots, Grace moves to the door. But she doesn't look away. I glance at her over my shoulder, then turn around and cross my arms over my chest.

"You're naked." She holds up her hand to cover my junk.

"And you're not. You'd probably be happier if you were." I shrug, then turn on the water. My body slightly relaxes when I stand under the hot stream. The shower door is frosted, and I can't see her, but I see the light yellow of her dress and the color of her skin.

I continue talking. "The whole town is fuckin' talking about *me and you*. Wanted to squash that." Steam rises above as I wash my hair. "But you can finish getting ready. I'll be done in five."

She huffs.

I laugh and leave every last drop of sarcasm I have left in my tone. "Yeah, it's *really* funny. Can't believe you haven't heard that everyone thinks I'm madly fuckin' in love with you and I'm dating Stephanie to get over us. Wild, isn't it? But it's just a *stupid* rumor."

Even though it's faint, I hear her gasp. "Coming here was the stupidest move you could've made if you're trying to stop rumors. My mother will take pictures and will tell everyone you were here. You realize that, right? This is going to inflame the stupidity!"

I run my fingers through my hair, then grab her loofah and wash my body. "It's why I'm proposing to Stephanie when I get home from this trip."

"What?" She opens the shower door. Her gaze slides from my eyes down to my mouth and doesn't stop until she's staring at my cock. Then she looks up at me again. "You're getting *married*?"

I stare at her, then grab the glass door and slam it closed. "I want to settle down and start thinking about a family. I honestly have you to thank for this because you were the one who helped me realize that. I was going to tell you at the end of this trip, but you know what they say … there is *no* time like the present."

"Congrats. I'm happy for you." I see the distorted reflection of her body back away, and then she walks out of the bathroom.

After I'm done showering, I change into my black suit because I'm saving the navy one for tomorrow, for the ceremony.

I stand in front of the mirror, and I'm half tempted to drive to the airport now and book a flight back to El Paso, but I'm determined to hash this out. She might have wanted me to stay, but if we're at each other's throats the entire time, it's going to be a long three days.

I slide on my sandals because we'll be in the sand all night. Shoes would be a mistake.

Grace puts on some earrings, then turns and looks at me from head to toe. Then she smiles. "You do dress up nice."

I drink in every curve of her. "You do too."

The tension and awkwardness are enough to slice me into pieces, but I stand firm. Grace made a promise that if things changed, she'd say something. That woman has never broken a promise to me even if I'm the first person on her shit list. Her integrity runs too deep.

This weekend, she'll admit it. Or she won't. No matter what, I'm leaving this island with no regrets. Giving it my best attaboy.

"We should get going," she says, swallowing and holding out her hand like we used to do.

It's an olive branch, and I take it, even though I know she's mad as hell. Grace leads me down the hallway and into the elevator.

When we make our way onto the sand, she doesn't let go of me. The rehearsal is only supposed to last an hour.

When we're closer, her mother turns her head. Kathy's eyes meet mine then Grace's. There's an inkling of shock, and I'm sure this will all get back to Valentine before my feet land on the other side of the ocean, but right now, I don't give two fucks what anyone thinks. Do I ever?

Stephanie knew exactly what she was doing when she told me to go—ensuring I was hers.

Grace doesn't say anything, but she doesn't let go of me either. I interlock my fingers with hers and place them on my lap. Then, the officiant who's running the show arrives. Grace stands, and if I had to guess, she's seeing her sister for the first time since they arrived. The two of them immediately burst into tears.

Grace stands up front, listening to all the instructions as her mama makes her way over to me. She moves to the seat behind me and leans forward, resting her hand on my shoulder.

"How did I know you'd be here?" Kathy pats me. "Your mama know where you are?"

"Yes, ma'am, she sure does." I smirk, keeping my gaze forward, not taking my eyes off Grace as the breeze blows her long hair out of her face.

"And your *girlfriend*?" Her voice lowers.

I don't even have to turn around to know the wicked look she's giving me. That woman grounded me when I was a kid when Grace and I got into too much trouble, and I wouldn't put it past her to try it now.

"You know I've always done what I've wanted," I finally say. "But, yeah, she knows too."

Kathy squeezes my shoulder. "I just really hope you know what you're doin', honey. Before you get in too deep."

I laugh, not realizing I was going to get *this* talk this weekend. "Pretty sure it's a little late for that."

"I hope to see ya around." She stands when the music begins and goes back to her place.

Grace stands off to the side. She's the only person Savannah chose for her wedding party, and Chip's brother is up there too. As they run through how things will happen, I watch him totally eye-fucking her. But she's zeroed in on her sister, except for the few times she glances at me. When his eyes meet mine, I realize *he's* who she was with last night.

"Stupid girl." I shake my head, wishing she knew what she had, wishing she could see that I could be the man who would make her happy for the rest of her life.

After the practice ceremony ends, we're all given bracelets to drink at the tiki bar that's farther on the beach. But before we go, Grace stands with her toes dug into the sand, and I stand beside her as we silently watch the sunset.

"Another day gone," she whispers as pink and orange colors fill the sky.

"Another opportunity wasted."

We turn and walk down the beach. I grab her hand again, and she squeezes my fingers. I have no words. So I say nothing as I lead her to the bar I'm sure she got trashed at last night.

We show our passes and are served whatever we want. It's dark, and in the distance, I can hear the steady movement of waves crashing. After a few drinks, Grace has loosened up some, and things don't feel quite as tense between us.

She laughs and smiles, and she randomly touches my leg or arm as we relive old childhood memories. It *almost* feels normal, except for that unnerving urge I have to kiss her. Doing so would be the worst thing possible, considering Grace's mother is within the vicinity.

After another pink drink with an orange on the side is ordered, I lean over to her. "Want to watch the moonset? Will happen in fifteen minutes."

"We've done moonrise at the beach. Might as well watch it set too."

She pops off her stool, grabs her drink, and I lead the way. We find two loungers, and I lie back on one, crossing my feet over my ankles. I expect her to sit in the one beside me, but instead, we share. Just like in Baymont. The things I'd do differently if I could go back in time.

Our arms are pressed against each other as we stare at the moon above the horizon. It casts light across the water.

I bump into Grace, and she bumps me back.

"You're hard to stay mad at."

"I know," I say, glancing at her.

She shakes her head. "Don't get it twisted. You're not forgiven yet, but I wanted to say I'm happy for you. And for Steph. You two will be great together. I'll have to work on my speech skills before then though."

"Thanks. How'd you know I was going to ask you to be my best man?"

She shrugs and wiggles her toes. "Because there's no one else who could fill these shoes."

"Do you regret anything?" I turn to her.

She looks at me. "The way our story ended."

"You said it in past tense."

Grace says nothing else. And this very moment might haunt me for the rest of my life.

CHAPTER TWENTY-THREE

GRACE

Last night, Harrison and I slept on the edges of the mattress. It was almost like he wasn't there.

After we're dressed for the wedding, we go downstairs and wait. I honestly just want this to all be over. The faster, the better.

"So he's the reason why …" Anthony says, leaning against the bar, smirking as we wait for the ceremony to get started.

"No." I roll my eyes.

"You know you're a horrible liar." He orders me a lemon drop, and, damn, do I need it.

Harrison is sitting patiently in the third row in his navy-blue suit. Can't help but notice his messy hair blowing in the wind or the smirk that's taken up permanent residence on his stupid, perfect lips.

"Thanks." I lift the drink and slam it back. "I've been told as much."

When the officiant moves to the front of the bamboo makeshift stage, Anthony and I are given *the* look by my mother. We take it as our cue to move into position since we're the first ones up. I'm handed a beautiful bouquet of tropical flowers and dig my toes into the soft sand. When the music starts, I hook my arm with Anthony's and smile.

"Time to get this show started," I whisper.

"We've got this," he says as we make our way to the front.

While we wait to walk down the aisle, I can't seem to take my eyes off Harrison in that navy suit. He brought it on purpose. Bastard.

When I pass him, I look forward to trying to calm my racing heart. I just don't know why Stephanie would send him here. And then the realization hits me like a ton of bricks and nearly knocks the breath out of me.

I place my hand on my chest, then push it back because this ain't the damn time and place to unravel.

This is goodbye. Forever.

No.

I swallow, licking my lips, and bring my focus toward my sister, who looks so damn beautiful in her dress that's casual but elegant. She smiles at me, but when she sees Chip, her entire expression changes. It's like he's the light in her darkness, the sunshine that she wants to lie with for the rest of her life. The two of them are perfect for each other, and they love the same things. I can only hope to have that one day.

I'm lost in my thoughts as they read their own vows and exchange rings. Then, they seal them with a kiss. The tiki torches are lit, and the small group of people who joined us burst into applause. And just like that, it's over, and Harrison is by my side. But I feel numb.

"I'm so happy for you," I tell Savannah, pulling her into a hug as Harrison walks away to grab a drink. "Thank you." I turn to my new brother. "Treat her right."

"You know I will," he says kindly, and then he leans in. "So, you and Anthony?"

"No, it wasn't like that." I shake my head as Harrison returns, handing me some water.

"I'm so glad you came," my sister tells him, pulling him into a hug.

"Do I need to threaten your husband?" he asks, smirking in his six-foot-three body that towers over Chip, who nervously laughs.

"I'm actually good." Chip gives Harrison a firm handshake.

We take a few pictures, and then we're moved to the tables on the beach, where a feast is being prepared for us.

Harrison and I sit at a table with several of Savannah's surfer friends, who are also vegan. His hand rests on my thigh, and I can't find the strength to push him away.

After we eat, I stand with my glass of champagne and the microphone in front of fifty faces, many of whom are strangers. I look at my dad and his wife, then my mom and stepdad, Harrison and Anthony. Then I look at my sister and Chip. I know the faster I can get this out, the quicker I can slide out of the spotlight and disappear for a little while.

I tap the microphone to make sure it's on. "Oh, look, it works." I nervously laugh. "So, I wrote this really crappy speech about finding your one true love and how you know your partner is perfect for you. I went through all that stuff about lighting up a room and you can tell when two people are in love with one another."

I look at Harrison. "But someone recently reminded me that love is messy, even in the movies. And marriage is a pact, a promise that you'll stay with that person through the messy, through the good, and the bad. If we're lucky in life, we'll find that person who we can be messy with together, who understands the raw version of us and loves us regardless of it. Loves us *because* of it. And for everyone else, I guess we'll stay single."

I lift my glass higher. All the singles in the room raise theirs too, but when I look at Harrison, he doesn't move. His gaze is zeroed in on me and *only me*. I clear my throat, pulling myself away from him.

"When I look at Savannah and Chip, I see two people who can't survive without the other, and they're proof that true love exists. I'm so happy for you. Congratulations, lovebirds. This is your happily ever after. Make it count because you only live once."

Everyone applauds, and as I hand Anthony the microphone, he leans in. "Now that was a speech, *movie magic* shit."

"Thank you," I whisper.

"Tough act to follow," he says directly into the microphone, and as he starts his speech, I move across the room, not comprehending a word of it as my body buzzes.

I return to Harrison, and he keeps his gaze forward.

But I know there's something he wants to say by the way his jaw is clenched tight. He excuses himself, and I watch him walk to the bar. Everyone he meets lights up with a smile, even the bartender who served me last night.

Mom takes Harrison's seat and wraps her arm around me. "Oh, sweetie, why so blue?"

"I'm not blue, Mom. I'm bored," I tell her. "I'm tired of love and seeing everyone so … *happy*."

"That's not the attitude of someone who wants to plan weddings, is it? Already jaded?"

I sigh, keeping my voice low. "Did you ever forgive Dad for breaking up the family?"

She meets my eyes. "That marriage ending was the best thing that ever happened to me, honestly. I'll always be grateful for the time your father and I had, but I think we'd fallen out of love. The divorce was better than being in a loveless marriage. Who would wish for that? Not me. Sometimes, we just choose the wrong person, ya know? And we get second chances." She pats my leg, and we fall silent. "Why is Harrison here?"

"Not sure," I say. "But I have an idea."

He returns, she gets up out of his seat, and he hands me a drink. "Thought you might need it."

"You're right." I laugh and shoot it back, licking all the sugar from the rim.

One of my sister's friends, Adeline, moves next to Harrison and strikes up a conversation. I hear her ask about me, and he tells her we're just best friends.

The ceremony and reception are over, but everyone lingers around the beach, and many make their way to the minibars in their nice clothes. As Harrison chats with her, I get up and make my way to the same stool I occupied the night before when I was with Anthony. What a disaster that was.

"Cranberry and vodka," I tell her.

"Goin' for the hard stuff tonight?" She pours it and sets it down in front of me.

"I just want this weekend to be over."

She watches me spin the ice with my straw as the band plays a sad song from the '90s.

"Yeah, I hate weddings too. Especially working here."

"Have you ever been around someone that you just know would be good for you, but the timing is always wrong? Like the chemistry, the conversations, everything is exactly what you wish for, but ... it's *impossible*. Probability absolutely zero."

She nods. "Oh, is this about you and Harrison?"

Her knowing his name doesn't surprise me. "He doesn't meet a stranger, does he?"

"Tips well. Hot. Confident. Flirty as fuck though," she tells me, tossing her silver bottle opener and catching it in the palm of her hand. "But if I were you, I'd turn around because he hasn't taken his eyes off you since you walked away from him. But that's just me." She shrugs, refilling my drink. "That one is on the house."

The warm wind blows, and the tiki torches' flames flicker. I close my eyes and suck in a deep breath, chugging it back. That whole damn bottle couldn't give me the courage I need.

"Fearless," I whisper, then turn around.

As soon as our eyes meet, he gives me his perfect Valentine smirk, and then he excuses himself. Even though there are a lot of people on this beach, he's locked in on me. And as he moves toward me like the angel of death coming to take me to hell with him, I think how much I fucking love that navy suit on him. It makes his eyes look dark, like the deep sea, and I want to drown in them. He moves closer like an unstoppable magnetic force is pulling him toward me.

He holds out his hand when he's close. "Dance with me?"

"But no one is dancing," I say, shaking my head and tugging him back to me.

He leans in and whispers in my ear, "Who gives a shit? It's just me and you."

And in the moment, I believe him. Because it feels like it's just us and nothing in the world matters.

He slowly leads me to the sand, walking in front of me with our hands outstretched. When he turns and looks at me over his shoulder with that smoldering gaze, heat rushes through me. Then he turns around, placing his strong hand on my hip, resting his forehead on mine. My eyes flutter closed, our mouths dangerously close.

We're playing with fire, and it's catching up with us, chasing us like a forest fire blowing in the wind. We won't survive this—I already know—and then what?

We dance barefoot to the moody song. I interlock my fingers behind his neck, not letting him pull away, but he doesn't try. I feel him grow hard as a ragged breath escapes me.

It's too much, I think.

He's intoxicating; he's the poison in my blood right now. My utter temptation, the man who was sent to ruin me, and, fuck, do

I want to be ruined by him when his lips slide across my mouth and his tongue slides against mine.

"We shouldn't," I whisper as he fists the back of my dress.

Not only are we fighting ourselves, but we're fighting each other too. His kisses are too intense, too greedy, too hot, and I'm losing control, all willpower gone.

"I'm weak when it comes to you," he admits.

The song ends, and the lead singer of the band looks at us and gives a nod of approval. I turn and see we have an audience, eyes that shouldn't have ever seen that. Then I glance at Harrison with his swollen lips and take a few steps away. This can't get back to Valentine.

I tuck hair behind my ears, and I rush back to the resort, holding my racing heart. A few tears fall, and I hurry forward, entering the elevator. I press the top floor and sigh before the door closes. Harrison steps in, and it shuts behind him. Reaching forward, he wipes away my tears, and then he dips down and kisses me. I wrap my arms around his neck, his tongue slides into my mouth, and I feel him hard against me.

"Fuck," he says as the elevator comes to a stop and he moves to the other side of the box.

"Grace?" one of my sister's friends who lives in Alpine asks. She's from our area. "Harrison?"

She's in her bathing suit, she has a towel in her hand, and she is clearly going to the hot tub. She looks between Harrison and me with an arched brow as she pushes the floor number. "If I didn't know better, I'd say I'd interrupted something."

"Nope," I say as the elevator moves again.

We ride in silence until she exits with a wave.

Harrison leans against the wall with his arms crossed, watching me as relaxed as he can be. We've been playing this staring contest since we were kids, and I feel like I can look into his eyes without blinking for eternity. But I'm always the one to look away first.

Being together is too dangerous.

The doors open on our floor and I rush to our room. Once I open the door, our mouths crash together, and we fall into the room, greedily undressing each other. I'm on the floor, and Harrison is on top of me. He pushes his boxers down and slams inside of me, hard and rough. I cry out for more of him with my thighs pushed apart and my knees in the air, wishing he'd give me every bit of him.

"You're going to break me, and you won't be around to put me back together again," I mutter as the movements grow slower, more intense.

His hands are in my hair, his mouth is against mine, and then he's sucking my neck. I'm desperate for more, for all of him.

Our moans are music, and together, we're a symphony of need and want. My nails scratch down his back as he grabs my ass, pumping every long and thick inch of himself into me. My back arches and the quick orgasm rushes through me. I scream out his name. The ecstasy of him has me in a choke hold as every inch of me melts to nothing. His head falls back on his shoulders. He tries to pull out, and I shake my head, digging my heels into his ass as he empties inside of me.

He kisses me, and we stay connected for a few minutes. His nose nuzzles my neck, and he pushes back so he can look into my eyes.

"We can never do that again," I whisper.

"I know." I can hear the strain in his voice as he pushes himself up. He looks down at me, still on the floor, a crumpled mess.

"Come on," he whispers, standing and taking my hand, leading me to the bathroom.

He lights candles and sits on the edge of the tub to draw the water. Then he fully undresses and steps inside, holding out his hand for me again.

I look at myself in the mirror, seeing the dark bruise on my neck where his mouth was, and slide my fingers down it.

"Is this goodbye?" I meet his intense gaze, needing to know the answer.

"Goodbye to this version of us, princess, because *we can never do this again*. Your words. You chose them. You chose this. Friends forever."

I take steps toward him, knowing this is the end of us, that whatever magic we have will go back into the bottle for eternity.

As I slide down in front of him and he breathes in my hair and my skin, I close my eyes. "We tell no one."

He draws an *X* over his heart, and I do the same, knowing it's over *for good*.

Now, hopefully, we can go back to how things were before. The old us.

CHAPTER TWENTY-FOUR

HARRISON

I held her until the morning sunlight rose. Then I got up, packed my bags, and left before she woke up. We had different flights back since she'd canceled my original ticket, and it's the loneliest I've ever fucking felt. Even though I'm exhausted, I lift the window and watch the sunshine reflect on the water until it goes out of view.

It's over for us, and I've gotten the closure I needed. I take a deep breath, hoping I can move on.

My plane lands, and I grab my suit and duffel and walk through the airport, feeling like a different man.

On the way back to Valentine, I stop at a jewelry store and pick out a ring I know Stephanie would like based on what she's always enjoyed. Once I'm in my truck and on the long road home, I decide to stop by the barn. I know Beckett is still there, and right now, I need a distraction.

I walk through the barn, and Beckett comes out of a stall with a bridle in his hand.

"Well?"

"Well what?" I ask.

"I heard a rumor," he tells me.

"And how much did you bet, and which side did you bet for?" I look at him, crossing my arms over my chest.

My brother looks at me, smirking. "I bet five hundred dollars on Grace."

"Shit, you lost then."

"Bullshit," he says.

I pull the wedding ring from my pocket and show him.

His expression hardens. "What's that for?"

"I'm proposing to Stephanie."

He shakes his head. "Have you lost your fucking mind?"

I laugh. "I think I have. Grace isn't an option, and I made it very clear that I have to move on. Steph is the only other woman I think I could see myself spending forever with."

He takes a step toward me. "So that's it? You're giving up?"

"You do when love doesn't go both ways."

"You really believe it doesn't?" Beckett shakes his head and moves to the tack room. He hangs the bridle on the hook and then grabs a brush. Before he passes me in the doorway, he stops. "You need to cowboy up, little brother, or you're gonna fuck around and find out real fast. And this is going to blow up in your face."

"This is the exact talk I needed," I tell him. "Thanks."

"You're still proposing, aren't you?"

"You know it." I walk out of the barn, tossing the ring box in the air, feeling like I'm losing my mind. Knowing that I love Stephanie and maybe, one day, I will be in love with her again. I'm stubborn to a goddamn fault, and I'm angry. "You're just pissed because you lost five hundred dollars."

"I'm pissed because you're a dumb fuck who can't see what's right in front of you."

"You don't know the details," I yell back, giving him a wave.

Beckett flips me off, and I laugh.

Once I'm home, I send Stephanie a text, and she's at my house in ten minutes. I answer the door shirtless, wearing a pair of jeans on my hips. Her eyes slide over me, and I lean in and kiss her.

"Did you have fun?"

I laugh. "Yeah."

When I turn around and walk to the kitchen, she follows behind me. "Nice scratches."

"Huh?" I look over my shoulder and then go to the bathroom to see the nail marks. I shake my head and move back to the kitchen to grab a cup of water.

She lifts a brow, and she studies me. She's a fox, cunning, one of her best qualities if you ask me. Smart women are sexy as hell.

"Grace and I"—I shake my head—"we're just friends. There is nothing going on between us."

Not anymore.

A few steps and her arms are snaked around my waist. "We're going to be so good together. Like we used to be," she says, kissing my neck, nibbling on my ear, trying to steal my attention away, and it works. "I believe in us."

"Yes," I say, wishing I could erase this past weekend from my memory.

"So I have all of you?" she whispers against my chest.

"All of me," I say, pulling her into my arms, knowing we hadn't had sex since last year when we hooked up in Houston.

A WEEK LATER, Stephanie and I sit on the back porch, drinking coffee in our robes.

The stars are still out, and as we stare up at them, I turn to her, knowing nothing is going to change. "Will you marry me?"

"You mean it?" she asks.

"Be right back."

I stand and rush to the front, where my truck is parked. Then I grab the velvety box. As she's sitting in the rocking chair, looking up at me, I drop down to one knee.

"Steph. Stephie. Stephanie." I clear my throat, getting into position on my knee. "Will you marry me?"

She falls forward, wrapping her arms around my neck. "I was hoping we still had a chance."

"We always did," I say.

She pushes my back down onto the porch and slides her mouth against mine.

"Yes, I'll marry you. I'm so relieved. I love you so much."

"I love you too." I tuck loose hair behind her ear before she kisses me again.

ON THE WAY back from town, after grabbing some donuts, I stop by the vet clinic. Cash's truck is parked outside, and the lights are on inside. Since it's still dark, it glows like a beacon in the early morning. The side door is unlocked, and I walk to where he's sitting at a desk, rustling through papers.

"What are you doing here so early?" I ask, looking up at the clock and it's just past five.

"I couldn't sleep," he admits. "So, I thought I'd get started organizing shit to get ready for opening. Hey, thanks for proposing to Stephanie. I owe you a drink with the five hundred dollars I won from Beckett."

I burst into laughter. "Good. I'm glad you were the one who got the money. But also, how'd you know I'd choose Stephanie?"

He gives me a look. "I knew at the bar that night. Been there, dude. The good guy doesn't always win, and that's fine. Stephanie is really into you—always has been. Plus, she's cute."

"Well, shit, I'm glad I put a ring on her finger so you didn't steal her away."

He chuckles. "Nah. Blondes aren't really my thing."

I raise a brow. "Little brunettes with the last name Valentine your thing?"

He glares at me. "What the fuck? No."

"Okay, just making sure I don't need to shove your dick down your throat," I playfully warn. "Anyway, you want some donuts?"

"Hell yeah," he tells me and follows me to my truck, where I open the box and he snags two.

"Take another one. I got a whole other dozen."

He does.

"Congrats again," he says, ripping into the warm dough like a savage.

I give him a wave and continue to the barn, thankful the rumors stopped spreading around town once I was engaged. Even Sadie, the owner of the bakery, didn't mention Grace once. I guess everyone finally knows. And it's a fucking relief because I was growing exhausted by it all.

When I think about Stephanie, I know I could spend forever with her. And a small part of me wonders if this was the way it was always supposed to be. That in some fucked-up way, Grace and I had to happen to bring me to Stephanie.

Or am I making the biggest mistake of my life?

I guess we'll see.

CHAPTER TWENTY-FIVE

GRACE

I haven't talked to Harrison since we returned from Hawaii, but I know he proposed to Stephanie a week ago, thanks to her post on social media.

The whole town knows too. It's all anyone has been talking about, giving me congratulations like it's my wedding. But I think I've perfected smiling and telling everyone this is the happiest time of my life. I mean, why *wouldn't* I be excited to watch my best friend in the whole world marry the love of his life?

I hope everyone is buying it because if not, the rumors are going to keep flooding. Especially after I returned from Hawaii with a fucking hickey on my neck.

The truth is, I'm a mess. I've lost ten pounds because I have zero appetite. Nothing can comfort me, not even my favorite peppermint ice cream. But I'm surviving because that's what you do. I'm currently in the process of building a bridge and getting over it.

After I make a cup of coffee, I scroll through social media, and the reminder pops up on my phone that my local movie theater is having a throwback matinee of *13 Going on 30*. When I saw the announcement in the summer, I added the date to my phone. It's insane how much can change in such a short amount of time. Not sure I even know the person I used to be at this point. *Less jaded. Less angry.* Who would've thought that was possible?

I grab my keys and leave. The new me is learning how to do things alone, even if it's something I'm not used to.

Tourists are out and about, window-shopping, and I often wonder what it would be like to leave Valentine. To live in a town where no one knows anything about me or my best friend or my divorced parents. There aren't rumors about me, and people aren't waiting to get a snippet of information that I can't share. It might be a way for me to have a fresh start. Focus on my business. Myself. The thought makes me happy.

Once I arrive at the cinema, I slide three dollars under the glass partition, and I'm given a ticket. The inside smells like popcorn and old carpet, and coming here triggers memories from my childhood. Nothing has changed, not even the game room that's full of kids in the summer or the stains on the floor in front of the concessions from people spilling their drinks.

"Just one?" The attendant blocks the entrance to the theater.

I hand over my solo ticket. She glances at my neck, and even though I put a ton of makeup on that damn hickey and it's been two weeks, it's still there, like the Kiss of Death. No man has *ever* marked or taken me like Harrison did that night. No man ever will again.

"Just me." I give an awkward smile.

The paper is torn in half, and I walk down the aisle to an empty theater.

It's just me.

I find my favorite seat on row *H* and laugh because Harrison prefers *G*. Even if it's stupid, I'm perfectly in the middle with the best view in the house. I lean my chair back and play on my phone while I wait for the previews to start.

Though I've tried to avoid social media, I open it because I'm a glutton for punishment. And as predicted, my feed is full of pictures of Harrison and Stephanie. Mutuals are sharing posts of her showing the ring.

Gotta give it to them though. They look happy and perfect together. There is no denying that.

When the iconic Columbia Pictures logo flashes across the screen and the music plays, I turn off my phone.

The theme song starts, and I hum along with The Go-Go's, slowly feeling my mood change. I place my feet on the back of the seat in front of me like I used to do when I was a teenager.

Since I have every line memorized, I mumble them out loud, not missing a single one because I have the whole place to myself. The only thing that stops me is the sound of the door opening and closing. Then, seconds later, I see someone in my peripheral vision. When they make their way down my aisle, I turn and look at Harrison.

Then, he sits right next to me in his usual seat.

"What are you doing here?" My heart races when I meet his eyes under his baseball hat.

He smells like leather and sweat and hay.

"We had plans, and I always bring the popcorn." He holds it up with a smile.

I open my mouth to say something, but the words get caught in my throat. He shushes me and shakes his head, then moves his attention to the screen. Every part of my body tries to ignore his existence, but when I feel the warmth of his arm brush against mine, I can't. I move it so I don't internally combust.

When young Jenna says she wants to be thirty, flirty, and thriving, I chuckle. "Same."

We watch the entire movie, and both of us laugh where we usually do. Even though I promised myself I wouldn't cry at the end when her best friend is about to get married, elephant-sized tears pool in my eyes. I try not to blink because I don't want them to fall, but it hits differently, knowing I don't get to go back in time for a second chance.

I've kept the promise that I made. *"If either of us gets to a point where we feel like this will destroy our friendship, we stop, no matter what."*

The screen goes black, and the pink credits roll. I stand, wiping tears from my face, unable to look at Harrison, but he reaches forward and wipes my cheek.

"How did you know I'd be here?" I ask.

"Because I know you, Gracie."

I sniffle.

"To new beginnings," he says.

"New beginnings," I admit and smile, continuing to walk down the aisle.

"Where are ya headed?" he asks, throwing the empty popcorn container in the trash.

I turn around, walking backward, and look at him. "To buy myself flowers."

"I'm coming," he tells me, and we leave the theater.

The air feels different against my skin as we walk a few blocks to the nursery. It's a beautiful day, not a cloud in the sky, as we silently navigate the awkwardness. There has never been a point in our relationship where we needed to fill our time with chatter. But right now, it feels like something needs to be said because neither of us has anything to say. It's weird, and I don't know how to feel.

We enter the nursery, moving past the entrance gate, and my eyes glance over bright pink and purple flowerpots. Moments later, Harrison's little sister Vera walks over. She gives Harrison a side hug, and he smiles wide. He's a great big brother, protective, and would go to war for them.

"Whatcha doin', sis? Workin' hard or hardly workin'?"

She slaps him in his stomach. "I'm working hard after having to sell Summer a truckload of soil so she can start prepping for updating the landscaping at the B&B. I hope when Beckett marries her, it magically fixes her brown thumb."

Summer is known for killing a lot of plants. Even cacti And everyone is aware.

Harrison chuckles. It's almost easy to imagine us falling back to how we used to be. But then I think about the closeness and the boundaries we stumbled over for years. And he's right; that version where I lay on his chest, or he held me while we watched TV. It's gone. Vanished.

Friends with distance because it's easier that way—no temptation, no deep desire to do things we absolutely should never do again. Especially now that he's engaged.

Harrison Valentine is my biggest temptation, a devil who makes me want to sin and never repent.

"So"—she looks between us with her hands on her hips—"whatcha here for?"

"I'm buying myself flowers today," I explain. "He's a tagalong."

"When *isn't* he?" She nudges me, leading me over to the bouquets they have wrapped in red foil paper.

"I guess he won't be once he's married," I add with a smile and pick up the bouquet of several mixed yellow flowers.

The smirk on his face doesn't falter as he stands to the side and watches me.

I push my hair back to smell the sweetness. Every inch of my body burns under his gaze, but I avoid eye contact because it's too damn much. I don't have the energy today.

Once I've picked out my bouquet, I make my way up to the counter, where Vera finishes with another customer.

"That all?"

"Yep." I smile, and she gives me the total.

Harrison inserts his card before I can pay.

"Don't let him buy those for me," I tell Vera.

The register dings, and she hands him a receipt.

"Y'all have a nice day." She gives me a wink, then strolls off to help another customer.

I glance over at him, tucking my hair behind my ears. "You didn't have to do that."

"I know. I wanted to. A pretty girl should never buy herself flowers." He shoves his hands in his pockets.

The electricity streams between us again, and I don't like it one bit.

"Well, thanks." I hold them up as I continue down the sidewalk. He stays in line with me, and when we make it to the end of the block, I stop walking and turn to him. "It was great seeing you."

"Yeah. We should do this again soon."

"I think you have my number. Maybe you should text me sometime."

He laughs, returns my smile, and then we exchange a weird side hug. And just like that, we transform back to when we were fifteen years old, when hormones couldn't be controlled and we didn't want to touch each other.

As he turns and walks away, I watch him. He turns and looks over his shoulder at me, and I shake my head. Of course he looked back. I just wish this stupid smile on my face would go away.

Maybe we do have a chance at getting our friendship back on track and we can go back to when we weren't a runaway train heading for derailment. Who fucking knows?

ONE WEEK LATER

Kinsley comes over to my desk and sets down a stack of papers. "Can you look at these and tell me which one I should answer next?"

I force a smile and slide them toward me. "Sure."

"Going to Boot Scooting tonight to watch London play with her band?"

I shrug. "Not sure yet."

"Something wrong?"

"Nothing," I tell her honestly. "Things are fine. Just thinking about my life and how something other than the daily temperature needs to change."

I thumb through the previews of the first few questions.

Q1: Dear Kinsley ... I have a crush on my dad's best friend.

Q2: Dear Kinsley ... I know my neighbor is having an affair.

Q3: Dear Kinsley ... The person I'm in love with doesn't love me the same way.

Q4: Dear Kinsley ... My family has a dark secret that I want to share.

Q5: Dear Kinsley ... I'm in love with my best friend.

MY EYES LAND ON Q5, and I flip to the page and read it as fast as possible.

Dear Kinsley,

I have a big problem. I've fallen head over heels in love with my best friend. I don't know when it happened or how it happened, but it did, and I need to move on. I've communicated how I feel more times than I can count, but it never matters. Now, time is ticking by, and soon, neither of us will have the chance to explain how we feel because it will be too late. I've tried, and I don't regret my choices, but it seems like moving on is the only way. What would you do?

Sincerely, with an X over my heart.

I HAND the papers back to her, avoiding her gaze. "They're all juicy. Not a bad choice there."

She doesn't take her eyes off of me, and I know what she's thinking.

"I didn't write that," I explain, my entire body on fire. "I swear."

"I didn't think *you* did." She picks up the small packet. "Know anyone else who could've?"

"Nope." I wish I had a photographic memory and could recall every last word I read.

She taps the counter. "Thanks. Still *Team Grace*."

"Don't start that again. There are no teams," I correct.

Thankfully, the rest of the day flies by, and when I get home, I stare at a blank TV.

Different paintings that Remi created hang on the wall in the living room, and I love the character they add. There are bright flowers in a vase, one that looks like a galaxy, and another of some wild horses running in the wind. I lean back on the couch and stare at the ceiling, playing through everything that led me here.

I glance over at the flowers on the counter that Harrison bought me. *"A pretty girl should never buy herself flowers."*

Ugh, he haunts me.

The door swings open, and it pulls me from my thoughts.

Remi is smiling, setting her oversized purse on the couch. While she's noticed that Harrison hasn't been over in weeks, she hasn't said anything. No one has. And I feel like everyone is walking on eggshells around me. Or maybe no one notices. I feel alone.

"What are you doin' tonight?" She wiggles out of her sweater.

I look over at her. "This."

"No, you're going to Boot Scooting so we can support London. Added bonus, Cash wants to celebrate the opening of his clinic tomorrow, and he's paying for *everything*."

"Guess they don't call him Cash for no reason, huh?"

"Right. Also, I'm not giving you a choice anymore. You're going tonight. We're not sitting around and wasting your life away on this couch, okay? Now I gotta shower. We leave at seven. Oh, Haley is meeting us too."

I meet her eyes. "Anyone else?"

She shrugs, knowing what I'm asking, but doesn't say. "Not sure."

"Okay," I say with a smile, unlocking my phone, checking the time, then rushing to get ready.

"Oh, we're wearing blue jean skirts and boots," Remi says from the bathroom.

My closet is full of both. Once I'm dressed, I fix my hair. Just as I'm sliding on my signature red lipstick, it's time to go. We're leaving the cowboy hats at home tonight.

It takes us five minutes to arrive and park.

As soon as we walk in, Cash is already three sheets past the wind and tells us to order whatever we want. Beckett and Summer join us, and I see Kinsley and Hayden making out in the corner. PDA never bothered them, not when we were teenagers and not now. Some things change in this town while others stay the same.

"So London is playin' tonight? Is it her first show here?"

"Yeah! They paid to have her," Remi says, pointing to the stage. "She's right there in the wings."

London pokes her head out and waves at us. She's wearing tight-as-fuck jeans, boots, and a shirt that shows the perfect amount of stomach.

"She looks like a country star." My eyes widen.

Remi nods. "My sister is going to be famous! Wait until you hear her songs. Let's get a drink. Her set starts in ten minutes."

A stage crew goes out and checks the microphones and tests to make sure the guitars and drums are miked properly. It's a huge room, and sometimes, they get some popular musicians to come in and play, so they're set up for professional gigs.

Remi leans over the bar. "Two lemon drops," she says to the bartender, and then she points to Cash. "That guy is paying for our drinks tonight."

He looks over at Cash, who raises his hand and gives a thumbs-up. Then, we make our way back to the dance floor, where a small crowd is starting to form. I check my phone, knowing Harrison wouldn't want to miss this, and when I turn around to glance at the entrance, he enters. Alone.

I watch him, waiting for him to find me in the crowd like he always does. And like magic, our eyes meet, and I smile and wave.

He points at the bar and then gives me a thumbs-up. I smile, then face toward the stage.

Remi notices how my demeanor changes and she bumps my shoulder. "You're ridiculous."

"I'm not. I just miss my best friend. *A lot*," I admit.

CHAPTER TWENTY-SIX

HARRISON

I knew she'd be here. And when I spot her in a room full of people, I know our connection hasn't been lost. I quickly go over and say hello to Cash. He tells the bartender I'm on his tab, then returns to his conversation. Beckett and Summer are laughing their heads off while Kinsley and Hayden devour each other's faces in the corner. If I had more time, I'd bother the fuck out of them, but not tonight.

I grab my beer and head over to where Haley, Remi, and Grace are standing. When I'm closer, I notice they're all dressed the same.

"Triplets." I shake my head. "It's cute though."

"Thanks," Grace tells me, twirling the straw in her lemon drop.

The last time she drank those, we were in Hawaii, losing control. I try not to think about it.

"Where's Stephanie?" she asks.

I shrug. "She didn't feel well. Pretty sure she's stressed about the wedding."

"You know a wedding planner," Grace suggests.

"You'd help?" I ask.

"Why not? I'd love to do whatever I can for y'all. I've been getting a lot of contacts lately for Kinsley. Caterers, florists. I'm pretty sure I could plan a wedding in two weeks if I needed to."

"How did you know?"

She studies me. "Know what?"

"We want to get married in two weeks."

Stephanie and I discussed it last night. She doesn't want to wait any longer, and if I'm being honest, I don't either. The longer we wait, the more I wonder if it's the right decision, but I'm standing firm. The only person who can stop this wedding now is Grace. Period. And she won't. So we continue forward.

The ruby-red smile falters. "I was kidding, Harrison. Two weeks? That's *soon*."

"Hence why she's stressed," I say.

"If she wants my help, have her reach out to me. Right now, I need to build my client list, and it would be a good opportunity."

I smile wide, pulling out my phone. "You're sure? I'll text her right now."

"Positive. What are friends for?" she says, sipping her drink as the overhead lights begin to fade.

HARRISON

Babe! Grace said she would help you plan the wedding. Were you serious about two weeks?

STEPHIE

OMG! That would be amazing. I wanted to ask her, but I didn't want it to be weird.

HARRISON

She brought it up.

STEPHIE

Can you ask her to meet me at the warehouse tomorrow?

HARRISON

Will do. Love you. London is about to play!

STEPHIE

Take some video for me. Love you!

I SHOVE my phone in my pocket just as London walks on stage, standing right in the center. I cup one hand around my mouth and yell for her, as does everyone.

"Ladies and gentlemen, I am super excited to be here. I'm London, and we're The Heartbreakers."

The crowd goes wild as she strums her acoustic-electric guitar and belts out notes I've never heard her sing.

Remi leans forward and screams, "I told you so!"

"You were right," I say as some people in the audience sing along.

I'm not sure what shocks me more—the fact that my sister already has fans or that they have her songs memorized. When I glance around the room, it's full of people moving their bodies and watching her band play. I have a proud big-brother moment. She has the magic and the talent, and I'm turned into a believer. I understand what Remi was talking about when she said London would be a fucking star.

Grace dances in front of me to one of the slow songs, and she turns and looks at me over her shoulder. I shake my head at her, and she laughs.

"I've missed you."

"I've missed you too," I say in her ear, touching her hip.

My sister's set ends, and the sweaty crowd that was there for the band leaves the dance floor. The lights lower, and the dancing music starts.

I take Gracie's hand and swing her toward me. "Want to dance with me?"

"If you let me lead," she says.

"Be my guest."

We two-step around the building, and I press her against me. It's just like old times when we were bored and wanted to do nothing but move our bodies. The songs change and fade into others. We don't talk about anything serious, and the conversation is light, though there are eggshells sprinkled all around us. Somehow, we avoid them all. Have we been doing this all along? Playing this same game?

"Can I ask you a serious question?"

I meet her eyes. "Of course. Always."

"Did you submit a question to Dear Kinsley?"

The corner of my lips tilts up into a smile. "No. What did it say?"

Her brows furrow. "You know what it said because you wrote it, and I'm pretty sure your sister knows you wrote it."

"I submitted it at the beginning of the year. Doesn't matter now, does it? Things have changed. BFFs and all that, right?" I twirl her out, where she strikes a pose, then flawlessly comes back to me, not missing a single beat.

"Right." She nods. "Just making sure you're not having cold feet."

I shake my head. "Not yet. You?"

"No," she tells me with a laugh. "We have changed. For the better, I think."

"Yeah." I smile. "It all kinda worked out the way it was supposed to."

We finish dancing and make our way back to where Cash is standing, telling jokes. Grace and I fill in behind the crowd of people, listening to him talk about assisting in the birth of a calf.

When he gets to the placenta, I yell, "Let's talk about something else."

Everyone laughs and starts clapping.

"Disgusting," Grace mutters.

Eventually, she starts yawning, and then she turns to me. "I think I'm gonna head out."

I reach down and give her a side hug, catching the faint hint of vanilla and sweat. "Good seein' you."

"Yeah, same." She walks away and tells everyone else goodbye too. As she makes her way out the door, I follow her.

"Grace," I say, catching up to her. "I forgot to ask you a question."

She turns around, looks up into my eyes, and waits. Her arms are crossed over her chest.

"Can you meet Stephanie at the old warehouse her parents own tomorrow, around dark? She wants to see if you think it's a good location."

She searches my face and nods. I reach forward, tucking a strand of loose hair behind her ear.

"I almost thought I was going to have a *movie magic* moment." She smirks and adds a reminder to her phone. "I'll be there. Will you?"

"Maybe."

She turns and walks to her car, shaking her hips as she laughs. "Good night, Harri."

"Night, Gracie."

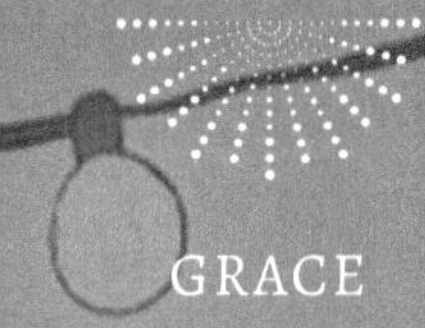

I wake up feeling like a train ran over me, but I get up and get dressed, feeling completely different about life. I feel different, knowing this wedding is happening so soon.

As I'm standing in the kitchen, drinking a cup of coffee, Remi enters the living room with her laptop. Her hair is in pigtails, and she's wearing tall socks and booty shorts. Then I realize she's wearing glasses, and I give her a confused look.

"Yes, they're real. Haven't you seen Colt wearing his? Not sure what happened. About two years ago, both of our eyesight went to shit at the same time. We chalked it up to being a twin thing."

"No, I had no idea. They look cute," I tell her.

She crosses her legs and sets her computer on her thighs. The keys click and clank, and then she stops and looks up at me. "Shouldn't you be going to work?"

"The thought makes me sick," I tell her. "Gives me the ick."

"Then quit," she says with a shrug.

I look at her like she's lost her mind. "I can't just … *quit.*"

"Why not? I hated my job, and one day, I woke up and wrote

an email to my boss. Never looked back. Also, if you really needed some help paying the bills, you know Summer would hire you. Or Haley could get you a position at the bookstore. The newspaper ain't the be-all, end-all in Valentine, especially if you ain't happy."

"It's not bad, but I just feel like there's something more out there for me. I just worry about not being able to pay my bills."

She types a sentence, then stops, and I know she's probably chatting with someone because I hear a ding each time she looks down. "You will. It always works out."

"That's the thing with all the Valentines. You just think everything is going to work out, even when the entire world is burning around you."

This earns me a laugh.

"You have your wedding planning business. You'll just have to make sure it doesn't fail."

"But what if it does?"

She smiles. "In every situation I'm in, I will always bet on *me*. And you should too. It's that easy."

I take a sip of my coffee, still in my pajamas. Then I take my mug with me, slide on my slippers, and leave my house, wearing pajama pants, a tank top, and my silk house coat.

"Grace?" I hear Remi yell from the living room after I shut the door.

But I'm already walking down the sidewalk with a smile on my face because, right now, I am the main character. The sun is hot and bright on my skin as I dodge tourists. A few of the ladies from my mama's church see me, and their eyes wander up and down my body. I'm sure everyone will be talking about me strolling downtown in my pajamas. Then I walk into the office. All the journalists are still at their desks.

When Kinsley sees me, her eyes go wide, and she looks confused. "Grace? Are you feelin' okay?"

"Feelin' just fine," I tell her with a smile, knowing they're staring as I walk into Mr. Anderson's office and sit.

I'm aware that I look like a fucking lunatic, but I'm tired of doing what everyone else thinks I should do. This job is one of them.

He looks at my wardrobe choice, and before he can say anything, I hold up a finger to stop him.

"Good mornin'. I quit."

"What?"

"Yep. I appreciate the opportunity, but this isn't for me." I hold out my hand, offering him a handshake.

He takes it, and then I walk out, feeling pure freedom.

Kinsley walks around her desk and places her hand on my head. "You don't feel hot."

"I'm done people-pleasing," I admit, and she lifts her hand and gives me a high five.

Then she bursts into laughter. "Fuck yeah!"

Mr. Anderson comes out of his office, and she gives me a quick hug as I grab the collage of me and Harrison he gave me when I got this job.

The smile that's on my face might be permanent as I walk back to my place. At the end of the block, the door is open at the hairdresser. I walk past it, then back up and walk inside.

Georgina comes over. Her bright-red hair is high up on her head, and she's smacking gum with dark-red lips. The taller the hair, the closer to Jesus, I guess.

"Do you have any openings?" I ask, checking my pocket to make sure I have my phone with me.

She lifts a brow, her eyes trailing over my outfit, and she stares at my bunny slippers. "Is this a breakup haircut?"

"Uh, no."

"Honey, I've seen thousands of women walk through that door with that same look on their faces over the years. How short?"

I hold my hand to my shoulders. "No bangs though. I'm not having a crisis—*yet*."

"We'd all be there for you if that were the case." She laughs and glances at the other stylists, who have older ladies in their chairs.

I look at all of them. "So, which one of you is Dolly Parton?"

One rolls her eyes. "We're too superstitious to pick. Ain't none of us dying."

"Oh yeah, I forgot *Steel Magnolias* was sad as hell. Never mind then," I say, sitting in the chair.

Georgina lifts and places a silk apron over my head.

"Show me again where you want me to cut," she says.

I change my mind and point to my chin. "I'm ready for a new me."

She sucks in a deep breath. "Want to donate it?"

"Yes," I say.

She separates it into different ponytails, then cuts one strand.

When I hear the first sound of the shears against my hair and she lifts up the long chunk and hands it to me, the tears start falling. I didn't mean to cry, but the emotions I'm feeling overwhelm me. I always kept my hair long for Harrison because he loved it that length. Many nights, he'd twirl strands between his fingers, and sometimes, I imagine hovering above him and my hair falling in his face. It's those images that haunt me when I try to fall asleep.

She places her hand on my shoulder.

"They're happy tears, I promise. It's just … that hair has been with me through a lot. It was kinda part of my identity."

"Sweetie, we can't undo what we've done, but know that hair grows back and hearts heal."

I nod, and she finishes, then spins me around. I stand and hold my long ponytail in my tight grip. Then she takes a picture of me with my phone. This will eventually be a memory that I look back on.

"You look happy as fuck," she whispers, leading me to the sink for a wash.

Then I'm brought back to the chair, where she does her magic and adds layers. Then she gives me the most perfect blowout, and I know I will never be able to get my hair to look like this again. When she's done, she gives me the mirror so I can see the back.

"Do you like it?"

"I love it," I tell her, shaking my head. "It feels so light."

"We just cut off what feels like five pounds of hair. I'm sure it does feel that way."

I laugh. "How much do I owe you?"

"On the house," she says.

"No, let me pay for it," I argue.

"If you don't get your ass outta here right now, I'm gonna call your mama and tell her what you did before you get the chance to," Georgina threatens, and then she gives me a hug.

I step out the door, feeling like a different woman, almost like I could fly home. By the time I walk back in the door, Remi is changed into actual clothes, and she's at the table, putting together a puzzle.

She gasps, then rushes toward me, pulling me into a hug. "Your hair looks amazing! Oh my God!"

"Thought I'd quit my job and cut my hair."

"Fearless," she says.

"How'd you know?" I ask.

"Know what?" She looks at me, confused.

"That was my word for the year."

"Then I'd say you fucking nailed it. Are you still meeting Stephanie tonight?"

I nod. "Yep. At the old warehouse."

"Can't wait to hear how that goes."

"I'll make sure to fill you in."

EVEN THOUGH I'M dressed and I look like a million bucks, I'm nervous, but I pull on my big-girl panties and make my way to the warehouse that her parents own. I drive, not knowing how long we'll stay there, and I cross my fingers and toes that Harrison is around. But I kinda have a feeling he won't make it, considering how busy he's been at work lately.

When I arrive, the lights are on inside, and the door is open. I walk in and am shocked by how gigantic it is. The building is half of the city block, and it's been used as storage for as long as I've been alive. The inside is dusty, with white drapes thrown over things, but the hardwood floor and tall ceiling give it a historic feel. There's a gigantic crystal chandelier in the middle of the room, and the lights flicker on it like flames. It's the perfect venue for a wedding.

"It was an old bank at one point, and then it was converted into a hotel," Stephanie says from behind, nearly startling me.

I turn to look at her, and she's gorgeous with her white-blonde hair, pink lips, and petite features. Her blue eyes meet mine, and I feel like the fat girl in high school, talking to the head cheerleader because my bestie is dating her again. But I put it away.

"Oh my goodness, your hair looks incredible," she says, and I smile, still not used to the way it feels. "Short suits you."

"Thanks. Is Harrison coming?"

"Unfortunately, no." She walks past me, and I follow beside her.

"I never realized you were so tall."

"It's the heels," she tells me with a smile. "I mean, I do feel like an Amazon at times. It's how I knew I needed a tall man. My only regret in life is not modeling."

I nervously laugh. Of course, this is the woman Harrison would end up with; she's perfect in every way.

She flips light switches as we pass them. "Well, let me show you around the place," she says. Her voice echoes in the room as we walk through the large, empty space.

A marble staircase that reminds me of something that should be on the *Titanic* is the showstopper.

"Wow," I say, running my hand against the marble railing.

"Right? I was thinking we could get married at the bottom. Set up all the chairs right here." She holds out her arms like she's imagining it, and I can envision it too.

"The orchestra can go over there," I say.

"Yes." She's growing giddy with excitement.

I move around her, walking the space, trying to get an idea of how many people could fit in here. "And the large windows will bring in the perfect amount of natural light if you go for an evening ceremony, like, plan to say your vows at golden hour." I smile. "It's going to be a fairy-tale wedding, Steph. Truly."

"So you think this space is a go?"

I nod. "Absolutely."

"My parents are willing to renovate it too. The entire second floor used to be hotel rooms, but they could easily be made into changing rooms for the wedding party," she says.

"That's perfect." I type a few notes on my phone so I won't forget any details. "What date are you shootin' for?"

"Two weeks from today?"

She has that nervous look on her face, and I wonder if she's having jitters. The last thing I want is for her to be nervous, not when she's marrying Harrison.

"Do you believe in miracles?" I ask.

"Sometimes. Just kinda depends."

I shift from one foot to the other, wondering if I should share this information with her. She'll find out soon enough anyway. Everyone will.

"I quit my job today, so I've got all the time in the world to focus on this and help."

She squeals, hugging me. "It's like it was meant to be. You're going to be the best wedding planner ever."

"Consider it a gift to you guys. I'm happy for you."

She continues walking through the space, and I follow her, making different notes.

"I think I've got it all. Once I get home and do some research, I'll text you some questions to make sure we're on the same page. Anything else before I go?" I ask, not wanting to linger too long.

"There is *one* thing." She clears her throat and wipes her palms on her dress. "Look, I know you and Harrison hooked up."

I open my mouth and close it but don't say anything. I crossed my heart and promised Harrison I'd never mention a word about us to anyone, and admitting it to his fiancée isn't something I can do.

But before I can jump to conclusions, she continues, "When I asked him, he looked at me the same way you're looking at me right now, but ... he didn't admit it either. But sometimes, you just know without anyone telling you."

"I'm sorry, Stephanie, but I can't have this conversation," I admit, needing to escape this place because I won't lie or deny.

"I saw the scratches on his back when he got home from Hawaii. And I know you had a hickey on your neck when you returned. Several people in town noticed too."

Now, my pulse is galloping in my chest, but I stand firm. I know I was stupid and should've worn a turtleneck to the grocery store after I returned.

She sighs. "I'm not pissed at either of you. Harrison and I had a mutual agreement that we weren't exclusive until *forever* was in the picture. And now, we're engaged ..."

I look down at the diamond ring on her finger. The chandelier casts light on it that makes it sparkle.

"He's promised me nothing is going on and that you're *only* friends, but I want a confirmation from you before I go through with this. If there is an inkling of hope, I'll call it all off. I don't want to get married just to get a divorce. Please, Grace."

I listen to every single word, and by the look on her face, I know she's being sincere. There is no way I'll be the one to stop this wedding. I'm not a home-wrecker. Harrison and I weren't meant to be together. I've realized that, and I'm more concerned with working to get him back as my friend over anything else.

I meet her eyes. "There's nothing between us. It's a line that will never be crossed—you have my word. When Harrison commits to someone, he won't cheat. He's a good man," I confirm, knowing he has integrity when he's in a solid relationship. "Plus, I'd never do anything to ruin this for you or him. You both deserve to be happy ... *together*."

I swallow hard, and I think the shards of my shattered heart crack more. Didn't even know that was possible.

A relieved sigh escapes her. "Thank you. I really want us to be friends and have a relationship. Can we have a fresh start?"

She holds out her hand, and I take it.

"I'd like that."

We shake on the promise I just gave her, and I have no hard feelings.

Or maybe I'm numb to it all?

I go home and feel like I need to puke. I rush to the bathroom and dry heave over the toilet, and Remi walks in, staring at me.

"Are you okay?"

I stand and grab a towel. "I feel like shit."

"Maybe you have a cold or something. Or you're pregnant."

My eyes go wide as I look at the calendar on my phone.

I'm late.

Remi's mouth falls open. "Holy fuck."

I grab my phone and text Harrison.

GRACE

Can we meet tomorrow for coffee around dark?

CHAPTER TWENTY-EIGHT

When I walk into the coffee shop, Grace is sitting in the corner by the large windows, sipping her coffee. She's watching two people in the town square throw a neon-green Frisbee back and forth, but she's deep in thought. The sun is beginning to set, and I suck in a deep breath when I see her skin glowing in the golden hour.

Then I notice she's cut her hair to her chin, and my mouth falls open.

When she sees me, she immediately smiles.

"Hi," she says. There's a thick spiral notebook on the table with one of her favorite gel pens.

"Hi. Your hair … it looks … incredible." I stand awkwardly for a moment too long, then nervously sit.

This woman is my kryptonite. Always has been.

"Thanks. How have you been?" she asks.

"Great. You?"

We're holding a conversation like we're strangers, and I hate it.

"Perfect." She shakes her head. "Sorry, we should probably get started with planning this wedding."

"Grace," I whisper. "You really don't have to do this, especially if it's weird."

"I know. But it's my gift to you. Before I go."

"Where are you goin'?" It catches me off guard.

"I've been doing a lot of thinking and …" She swallows. "Well, it doesn't matter. Can't worry about things before they happen, ya know?"

I meet her eyes, waiting for her to continue. To explain. Because she seems off. Something isn't right.

She swallows hard, looking at me with pain in her eyes. "I might be pregnant."

"What?" My mouth falls open, and then I realize what she's saying. Then, my mind starts spinning. "Have you taken a test?"

She shakes her head. "I didn't want to. I wanted you to be there. If …"

I can see she's visibly shaken up, and there are too many wandering eyes on her. Now, when we're together, it's like everyone is watching us to see if we cross the line so they can go back and tell Stephanie. That shit started when we returned from Hawaii. After she confronted me and asked if I'd been with Grace.

"Gracie"—I stand and hold my hand out to her—"let's get the fuck out of here."

The air feels too thick, almost as if I'm suffocating, as my mind goes through what this could potentially mean.

She takes it, and I lead her outside and to my truck.

When we get inside, I turn to her. "Who's the dad?"

Grace's jaw locks tight. "You're the *only* person I've been with."

I search her face. "I thought …"

"You thought wrong. It's only been you."

She turns her head and looks out the window, avoiding me. She's lost in her head, but I understand.

This is … not what I expected I'd be dealing with today.

I take my hat off and throw it in the back seat. "We need to find out right now."

Tears threaten to spill down her cheeks. "I can't buy a pregnancy test. Everyone in town would know, and they're all watching me. You can't buy one either. I ordered some, but they won't be delivered until next week. Right now, I just need my best friend. Okay?"

I crank the truck, understanding the assignment. I pull out my phone, knowing who will help me and won't say shit. If Grace is having my baby, this wedding is over. After I send my text, I pull out of the coffee shop parking lot.

"I've got you."

"Where are we going?" she asks when we leave town.

"Do you trust me?" I reach over and grab her hand.

"I always have." She wipes tears away, and when I pull up to Kinsley's place, she turns to me. "Please tell me you didn't tell her."

"I called in a massive favor." I search her face and kiss her knuckles. "Kins won't say anything. She keeps her promises as well as I do."

I get out of the truck and open Grace's door. Then we take the steps up to Kinsley's place. She opens the door and smiles at Grace when she passes her but glares at me like she wants to chop off my balls and shove them down my throat.

Grace stands awkwardly in the living room, and Kinsley hands her the test.

"You know how to do it?"

"I just pee on it, right?" She reads the back of the box.

"Yes, and give it the amount of time the instructions say. There are two in there. Take them both, just so you know for sure. Got it?"

Grace wraps her arm around Kinsley's neck. "Thank you."

"Bathroom's down the hall to the left," she says sweetly.

Grace makes her way there. I try to follow her, and Kinsley stops me.

"What the fuck is goin' on?" she whispers, looking at me incredulously because it's exactly what it looks like.

I shake my head. "Long story. Keep it to yourself."

"You realize if she's pregnant with *your* baby, it's going to be a clusterfuck, right?"

"Thank you, Captain Obvious. Well aware of what this means," I hiss as I walk away, not needing that right now.

I knock on the door, and the lock unlatches. Grace lets me in and then returns to the toilet with the stick in her hand. The jeans she was wearing are around her ankles.

"I'm pee shy right now. Turn around."

I laugh and do it.

"Can you please hum or something? I need a distraction."

So I pull my phone out of my pocket and play some music, and then I turn on the faucet. An entire song plays through, and I hear her flush. Both sticks are sitting on the counter, and we lean against the wall next to each other.

"How long does it take?" I ask.

"Three minutes," she says, holding up her phone.

We watch the seconds slowly click down.

"Longest three minutes of my life."

"Mine too," I admit, turning my head toward her. "What will you do if it's positive?"

She searches my face. "Are you asking me if I'll keep the baby?"

"I'll support whatever decision you make."

"Yes," she says without hesitation.

"Okay." I smile, almost coming to terms with this happening.

There's this reckless part of me that hopes it's positive even if it would be hard and people would talk. I wouldn't give two shits because we'd be parents together, raising a tiny human.

She sighs. "I don't think I'm ready to be a mom. A single mom at that."

This makes me laugh. "I don't think anyone is ready to be a parent. I'm not. You just kinda do the best you can."

The small space falls silent.

"I'll be there for everything, princess. I wouldn't let you do this alone."

"I know you wouldn't," she says, choking up. "But I'd ask you to."

"What?"

"You're getting married, Harrison."

I place my hand on her cheek. "These tests will determine that."

"No, you have to make a promise to me. If …" She looks away and glances up at the ceiling. "No matter what those tests say, please promise me that you'll get married the way you planned." She places her hand on my cheek. "Please. I can't be the reason."

I shake my head, not able to do that. "I don't make promises I can't keep."

"I don't want you to choose me. I'm not an option."

The alarm goes off, and Grace looks down at it and silences it. Neither of us takes a step forward and looks.

"I guess this is it," she says. "I'm nervous." She grabs my hand and places it on the pulse in her neck that's racing.

I open my arms and pull her into a hug, and we stand there for another three minutes. The unspoken conversation weaves through the air, and I'm ready to know the future.

"It's time to look," I whisper, and she nods.

Sucking in a deep breath, we both grab a stick, and there's a big NO on the one I have. I glance at hers, and it says NO too. She lets out a relieved sigh, then covers her face as she cries, but she's also laughing.

"It's hard for me to know how to act right now because I don't know if you're happy or upset."

She looks at the tests on the counter then wraps her arms around my neck, hugging me. "I'm happy. But for a day, I imagined a different life where we had a baby."

"I imagined the same one."

Her eyelashes flutter closed as I hold her and inhale the smell of her perfume.

The only thing that pulls me away is the knock on the door.

"Sorry to interrupt, but I'm gonna stroke out if you two don't say something. I'm a fuckin' mess out here!"

I burst into laughter, and so does Grace. I wipe away the ghost of tears that trail down her cheeks.

We open the door and let Kinsley in, and she looks down at the tests and then makes a face.

"Are you upset?" Grace asks her.

"I was hoping … never mind. Congrats. How 'bout we not see each other like this again?" Kinsley says, throwing the tests in the trash and forcing a smile. "Your secret is safe with me. I pinkie swear I won't tell a soul." She zips her mouth, makes a locking motion, and tosses the pretend key over her shoulder. "Tonight didn't happen, okay?"

"Okay," Grace says. "Thank you—again." When they pull away, Grace turns to me. "I'll wait for you in the truck?"

"Sure," I say, and she gives me a minute with Kinsley.

"I'm sorry." My sister places her hand on my shoulder.

I'm sure she's the only person in the room who sees the disappointment on my face. Not that I *wanted* Grace to be pregnant. It was never an option until it was. Another thing for me to grieve.

"I have a wedding to plan," I tell her with a smile on my face. "See ya later?"

"Under different circumstances?" She walks me to the door.

"Abso-fuckin'-lutely."

She pulls me into a tight hug, then I leave.

When I get in the truck, Grace is already inside and buckled.

"Well, that was fun." I reverse, then pull out of Kinsley's driveway. Rocks kick up in my wake as we make our way off the ranch and head back to town.

Both of us are silent; the sound of the tires on the country road fills the empty space. Neither of us says a word, too lost in our heads as we return to the coffee shop.

"Can we take a rain check?" she asks when I park next to her car.

"That's probably for the best," I say, and she grabs the handle. "Are you gonna be okay?"

She turns and looks at me, and I reach out, twirling a piece of her short, dark hair, feeling the softness of her lock wrapped around my finger.

"Yeah," she says. "Now I am. And you're still getting married. In two weeks. With no baggage."

"Right." The awkwardness drags on.

"We'll have it all planned by then," she promises. "Send me pics of your tux fitting."

"I will. Night."

"Good night."

I watch her walk away, needing a drink after that, but head home instead.

When I pass my parents' place, I see the lights are still on in the house. I park, kill the engine, then walk up the steps. The door is unlocked because no one locks anything around here. They're lying together on the couch, watching TV. There's an empty bowl of popcorn and a bottle of wine.

"I didn't just walk in on somethin', did I?"

Dad laughs. "Nah. Just catchin' up on *Yellowstone*. Have a seat."

I kick off my boots, leave them by the door, and sit in one of the recliners. We watch an entire episode before Mom starts yawning. They take one look at each other, and I know they can hold conversations without speaking.

"Did you want to talk?" Dad says.

"Yeah." I look between him and Mom. "When you two got married, did you have any doubts?"

Mom laughs. "Of course. Love ain't like the movies, honey."

"I know that." I look between them, not sure what to say.

Dad chuckles. "Son, when you find that person in your life, you know. But that doesn't mean it's gonna be easy. It's normal to have doubts in any relationship."

Mom pats Dad's leg. "I didn't know if I was ready to get married and start a family when your daddy proposed. Now, I wouldn't change my life for nothin', but marriage is a huge commitment. It can be scary as hell because it's a big life decision."

"I'm glad you woke up and stopped playin' hard to get." Dad shoots her a wink.

Mom folds the blanket they were covered with and places it on the back of the couch. "Being married to someone and spending forever with them is a choice you make every single day. I mean, I know we make it look easy, but it hasn't always been. And it won't be. But when you exchange your vows, you're vowing to work through your issues and at least try. And if you can't, divorce is the other option, but no one gets married to end things. We're all making it up as we go. From being married to being parents. Nobody is perfect, and you learn to love the imperfections."

I search between them.

"Is everything okay?" Dad asks. "You look kinda shaken up."

"I think it's just prewedding-day jitters."

"It's happening fast." Mom looks at me. "You'll be ready."

"I will. I am," I correct and stand. "This was a good chat. Thanks." As I pull my keys from my pocket, I think I hear the strumming of a guitar.

"It's London. She's been practicing in the tree house. Said she's found a lot of inspiration in there. You should go say hi."

I nod, turning toward the back door. "I think I will after hearing her play at Boot Scooting."

"Have a good night," they tell me at the same time, then laugh.

"Night, y'all." I push my hands into my pockets, listening to London sing and play from the back porch.

The starlight is so bright that it casts shadows on the ground. She sings out into the night, and I think about everything my parents said. I feel numb, thinking about the ultimatum I gave Grace … that she needed to be sure. My father wasn't even sure about my mom, and their relationship is what I strive to have. Could things have been different?

When the strumming comes to an end and I hear her sigh, I clap.

London's head pokes out from the side window. "What are you doin'?"

"I'm wonderin' the same thing," I tell her, walking down the steps and into the backyard.

She waves me up, and I take the worn wooden boards that act as a ladder. Then I pull myself up and sit on the floor and look around. The space is smaller than it used to be, but that happens when a person grows up.

"So," London tells me, lightly strumming her fingers on her guitar, "I'm kinda pissed you didn't ask me to sing at your weddin'."

"Shit." I run my fingers through my hair. "I'm sorry. What a fuckin' prick."

"That's what I was thinkin'."

"I'm sorry. I've just been …"

"Out of it? Yeah, everyone has noticed lately."

We sit in silence, and she goes through a few chords, humming over it.

"That song you were playin' when I walked up, it was depressing."

She meets my eyes. "Aren't most love songs? They're all

tragedies in three and a half minutes or less. It's why breakup songs are so popular."

"That's the one Remi was singing months ago." Then I remember the conversation we had. "I'll help you go viral. If you want that. You blew my mind the other night. Like *proud bubba* moment."

Her mouth falls open and she squeals, and it makes me jump. "Yes, thank you. I've been trying so hard, but if I had a thirst trap …"

"Consider it done. Anyway, this was a good talk. Maybe you can play at my rehearsal dinner?"

This makes her laugh. "I don't think breakup songs the night before your wedding is the vibe you're going for. But thanks. I'll let you make it up to me later."

"No hard feelings?" I ask.

She gives me a hug. "Nah."

As I hunch over, nearly hitting my head on the top of the tree house, London stops me.

"Oh, there is one more teeny-tiny thing."

"Yeah?" I look at her.

"I found this in here, and I'm pretty sure it's for you," she says, handing me a folded-up note.

"Huh?"

She shakes her head. "Read it later."

"Where was it?"

"Under a board in a small pirate treasure chest with a friendship bracelet."

I laugh, tapping it on the wood floor. "Okay. Thanks. See you at the rehearsal dinner next week?"

She nods and begins strumming again. *"I'm in love with you, and I always will be,"* she sings in perfect pitch, then waves goodbye with a pink guitar pick between her fingers.

"That might be your first hit."

She laughs. "We'll see."

CHAPTER TWENTY-NINE

"I can't believe we're at the rehearsal dinner," Remi says, looking around the open space that's been transformed into a wedding venue in record time before she eyes me.

She's wearing a pink pantsuit, and I'm certain she eats men for breakfast. No one can convince me otherwise.

Moments later, she stretches out her arms and squeezes me tight. I grab on to her, trying not to cry.

"I thought you said you're not a hugger."

"I'm not, but"—she shakes her head—"you need one."

"Please don't make my emotions spill over," I tell her.

We've never talked about it, but we don't have to for her to know what this has done to me. We're roommates. She sees me in my rawest form.

She pats me. "No man is worth tears. Because why?"

"Because we're independent women," I repeat.

Remi nods and looks me in the eye. "That's right. We're magic, baby. Love *loves* us."

"You're manifesting a relationship."

I've spent enough time with Kinsley to know this is what these woo queens do. Confidence like this just can't be bought. It runs in their entire family. But she ignores that I said anything, all she does is smirk.

"This year has felt like a decade, hasn't it?"

We move back to leaning against the wall, staying out of everyone's way, watching the room together. Her eyes dart to the door too. She must be waiting for someone. But who?

"It's March." She snickers.

The door swings open, and we both watch it with bated breath. Mr. and Mrs. Valentine enter, and I sigh. I'm waiting for Harrison, but so far, he's a no-show. Considering the importance of today, I can't believe he chose to work. Beckett would've given him off, but it's clear Harrison *wanted* to be at the barn today. Knowing each other like the back of our hands goes both ways, and I can read him like a book too. The man might be my kryptonite, but I'm his too.

"I just didn't have your brother getting married on my bingo card."

"You know what they say. Things like this happen in threes. Beckett and Summer, Hayden and Kinsley … it was destined," she tells me. "One more person gets engaged, and it's going to chain-react to two more."

As we're standing off to the side, I zero in on Stephanie as she greets the Valentines. It's hugs and smiles and *how do you do*s. The familiar conversations that never change over the years.

She walks—no, she floats around the room in a baby-blue gown she picked out to wear for this occasion. The style gives off old-money vibes, and so does the way she curled her long blonde hair. A diamond belt is cinched around her tiny waist, and her heels change colors depending on how the light hits them.

And as I stand here, holding a fresh bouquet of wildflowers for her to practice with tonight, I realize this woman is everything I'm not. My polar opposite in every shape and form. I understand why Harrison is marrying her. She's the opposite of me, which means she won't be a reminder, making me easier to forget. Maybe that's why he chose her in the first place all those years ago …

But they do have a memorable love story. They'll have their happily ever after in their perfect house with their perfect kids, living the perfect life.

I groan.

"Gracie," Remi mutters, tapping my arm just a little harder to gain my attention.

"I was staring, wasn't I?"

"Yes. And growling like a monster in one of those why choose audiobooks you listen to all the time." She chuckles.

I burst out into a fit of laughter. "Thank you. I needed that."

She bumps her arm against mine. "Anytime."

When I was always in my head, Harrison knew if he could make me laugh, I'd immediately pull out of it. And over the years, I've laughed after some fucked-up things because of him.

The thought makes me smile as I look up at the thick rolls of lace material that hang from the high ceiling. Makes me proud as fuck that I pulled off planning this event in record time.

The fact that her parents fully renovated this space just for the wedding blows my mind. The high ceiling and large area that's half the size of a city block make it ideal for events.

The elegant ambience and orange glow of the room set the perfect mood. Professionals were hired, but I found them to do it on short notice and played project manager. I worked for two weeks straight, nonstop, giving this wedding every ounce of attention I had to make sure it was everything Stephanie ever wanted.

For the first hour, we'll go through the steps of walking down the aisle with everyone. Then, starting at eight, the engagement party for three hundred people in attendance begins.

Harrison would've wanted it intimate and low key, but not Stephanie. He told me to let her do whatever she wanted.

Remi taps her pocket and pulls out *my* phone. "Oh yeah, you forgot this at home."

"I've never done that once in my adult life," I admit, grabbing it from her. "I'm losing it, aren't I?"

"You've had a lot on your mind. Give yourself a break. I tried to read all your text messages but couldn't figure out your password."

"I'm so glad you *aren't* my little sister."

The door opens, and both our eyes dart to it. When I see it's Cash, I glance over at her. While her expression doesn't change, I notice she stops breathing completely.

"Ahh," I say, nodding and leaning my head against the wall. "That's who you were waiting for."

"Hush."

I watch him scan the room and wonder if he's looking for her too.

"He looks good," I say.

He's wearing a sports jacket that fits him perfectly with dark-washed jeans.

He walks over to the open bar.

Then, the door swings open again, and I see him *in his navy suit.*

All the air in the room evaporates as I try to figure out how to avoid Harrison all night so I don't say something stupid. Because when he wears that, I can hardly form a coherent sentence. Every single time he's had it on … I've ripped it *off* his body.

"I should go double-check everything," I tell Remi breathlessly. "Can you give these to Stephanie?" I hand her the bouquet, desperately needing to walk in the opposite direction.

If Harrison scans through the people long enough, he'll spot me staring. He always finds me in a crowded room. No matter what.

As soon as she sees Harrison, she turns to me and says my name. But I keep moving away, feeling as if my heart is going to pound out of my goddamn chest. I find an empty hallway and stand there, holding my chest, telling myself I can do this.

My phone buzzes in my hand, and I flip it around.

HARRISON

Where are you?

WHEN I GO BACK into the room, he's sliding his lips across Stephanie's. He's laughing and smiling, and that's when I decide to ignore his text. Then I duck behind the faux walls, where we set up a makeshift area for the waiters and food service. My head is still spinning so I go to the restroom to calm down.

"How's everything goin'?" Fenix is at the sink, washing her hands. She looks at me in the mirror.

"Great. Everywhere I turn, there are Valentines." I smile, and it's genuine.

"Yeah, there're a lot of us." She grabs a paper towel. "You did a great job decorating. Bet my brother is happy he has you as his best friend."

"He'd better be," I tell her. I can say that I've *always* been there for Harrison … until the very, very end. The thought makes a lump form in my throat.

I go into the stall, needing her not to see the look on my face.

"Are you okay?" I hear Fenix ask, seeing her feet on the other side of the door.

"Sometimes, I need to escape," I admit.

"This isn't right." I see her weight shift from one leg to the other in her boots. "You should be out there with him. That's the way it was always supposed to be."

I turn around and open the stall door, meeting her eyes. "He made his choice. Now *we* support it."

"You love him though. And he loves you. And it's more than that."

"Fenix," I beg, knowing I can't have this conversation right now. Or *ever.*

"No lying or denying. I know the rules of your dumb promises."

"I gotta go," I tell her, then walk out of the restroom.

If I run into one more Valentine, I might scream. Two down, eight to go, including him. Then there are his parents and grandparents.

I look at my phone and notice another text message from Harrison. I open the preview.

HARRISON

I want to see you.

READING it makes my heart pound harder, but I ignore his message.

The small orchestra sets up, and I speak with the officiant, and that's the final check before we get started. I'm walking with Beckett on the day of the wedding, but tonight, I'll be standing back and making sure everything runs smoothly. When I see Stephanie is in place, I give the thumbs-up, and the orchestra plays. It's not the same music that will be used for the ceremony. I pat Beckett's shoulder, and he leads the group. I avoid Harrison's gaze that's locked in on me.

Everyone walks down, and then Stephanie and her dad step up. They're next.

"Ready?" I ask, looking at the bouquet. "Oh good, glad Remi found you."

Stephanie breaks away and hugs me. "Thank you so much for

everything. It's gorgeous in here. Because of you, I think Daddy is going to turn this into an official event center."

I glance at her dad. "Oh, wow, that's incredible. Hopefully, there will be many more happy ceremonies hosted here," I say.

The song she's walking out to for the practice round begins, and I meet her eyes. "It's time."

She nods, looking forward, then makes her way out there. I don't watch or listen; instead, I disappear.

I take the elevator to the top floor, and then I push open the door that leads to the roof of the building. The sun has already set, and the streetlights make downtown glow. All of Valentine can be seen from up here. Several blocks of cars line the street, and the back parking lot is full.

I place my hands on my head and look up to count the stars in the sky, taking in the cool spring air, even though it burns my lungs. The music eventually starts downstairs, and I can hear it on the roof. That means the engagement party has officially begun.

Everything is so well organized that it will run like a well-oiled machine whether I'm down there or not.

The door clicks closed behind me, and I turn and glance over my shoulder to see him. I bring my attention upward, wanting to get lost in the Milky Way.

"I've been searching for you all night." He walks forward and stands beside me with his hands tucked in his pockets.

"Found me." I have to avoid his eyes while the electricity buzzes between us. I let my arms drop down to my sides, trying to steady my racing heart. "You smell like old memories."

He smirks. "You do too. But anyway, I got you something." He reaches into his pocket and then gently turns me around.

Harrison stands behind me, his warm fingertips sliding against the back of my neck, moving my short hair out of the way. A cold locket presses against my chest as he clasps a necklace. His fingertips cause prickles on my skin, and goose bumps line my arms. My torturous heart upticks as I undo the clasp and look inside the locket. There's a picture of us together in the tree house. And I remember that summer like it was yesterday. We were sixteen and stupid.

I swallow hard.

"So you don't forget us," he says, leaning over my shoulder to take a peek.

His touch, his breath, his voice … are intoxicating, a true poison, and if I don't find a way to walk away, I might actually die this time.

"Never," I tell him. "Nothing can erase the memories." I close the locket and place a kiss on it.

"Gracie," he says, his voice lowering. The rasp nearly brings me to my fucking knees as he turns me around.

I meet his gaze, searching his face.

"I—"

"There you are," I hear from behind us.

Stephanie.

He turns, and the smile meets his voice. "*Babe.*"

I meet her eyes, and she grins.

"You two almost done? We have tons of pictures to take!"

"I'll be right there," Harrison says. "Ten minutes, max. Promise."

Stephanie nods and leaves us be because she trusts us, which she should. Neither of us will cross that line. *Ever.*

"Nice suit," I say, looking at him from head to toe, taking a step away from him, creating much-needed space.

"Still wearing my favorite color," he says, giving me that asshole smirk.

I move my gaze from him, focusing on the moonless sky and twinkling stars. The crowd of people down below laugh and cheer as the music blasts. Stephanie wanted a full experience, and I accomplished that by working nonstop on this project.

Tonight, my job is done. Tomorrow, there will be *I do*s, and then it will all be over.

He leans against the railing, looking down at the street, then pulls a flask from inside his suit pocket and takes a swig. Then he hands it to me.

I drink and smile. "American Honey."

"Does the job every time," he explains.

The night is still, and the party downstairs echoes throughout the streets.

"Sounds like a lot of people are having a good time down there." I hand the flask back.

"Good for them," he says.

I laugh and look at my best friend. "You should be having fun too."

"I am."

His arm brushes against mine, and those stupid butterflies still flutter, and they need to go back to their cage.

"Do you …" I shake my head.

"Ain't nothing stopping this runaway train, Gracie. Might as well say what's on your mind."

I fully turn my body toward him, leaning my back against the railing so we're facing one another. "Do you think things could've been different?"

"With us? Yes." He doesn't hesitate. "Anything else you want to share before tomorrow?"

I smile. "There's that asshole personality I've been missing so much."

"You promised," he whispers.

"And I'm keeping my promises," I state. "All of them, and I'm doing what best friends do. I'm supporting this, and then I'm moving."

His mouth falls open. "You're leaving Valentine?"

"I told you once before I'd move for love." I take a deep breath.

The silence is thick.

"You're running away," he states.

"Kinda like how you ran away in Hawaii," I say to him, knowing he left before I woke up on purpose.

There was no discussion afterward, and just like that, he was gone. Like fully giving every inch of ourselves to each other hadn't happened.

His nostrils flare, and I see the flicker in his eyes. Not even he can erase the memory of what we did, of how we burned ourselves to ash together and destroyed everything. I surely fucking can't.

The silence nearly slices me in two, and the moment passes by much quicker than it arrived. And the conversation dies, something to never be discussed.

"I should probably get going." He lifts his hand to my face and softly rubs his thumb against my cheek. "Best friends forever."

"Forever," I say, slightly choking up, trying to laugh through my tears.

Harrison hugs me, smelling my hair before pulling away. "Night, Gracie."

"Night, Harri," I whisper.

"You're still the only person I let call me that," he says as he walks away, leaving me in the cold.

The door opens, then clicks shut. And it's just me in the darkness and silence again.

I'll learn to enjoy it. Or at least I'll try.

CHAPTER THIRTY

HARRISON

I'm standing in the changing quarters on the second floor of the building Stephanie's parents miraculously converted into an event space in two weeks.

Honestly, it's beautiful inside with dark oak walls. I've already seen my parents and my brothers left me to have a moment to myself before I line up.

I check the time, and in twenty-five minutes, I'll be standing in front of a crowd, ready to say *I do* to my high school sweetheart. Funny how it all works out sometimes.

All day, I've been reminding myself that I'll be happy, that what Stephanie and I have is good. It can only get better, just like my parents.

There's a knock on the door. I adjust my bow tie, making sure it's straight.

"Come in," I say over my shoulder.

When I turn around, I see Grace.

I swallow. "Hi."

"Hi." She smiles and then stops walking, drinking in every ounce of me. "Wow. You clean up really nice."

"You do too," I tell her as she crosses the room in a light-blue dress that clings to her perfect body.

The locket I gave her last night is around her neck. When I glance at it, she reaches up and touches it.

When she's close, emotions stream between us.

It's wedding day jitters, I remind myself.

She sucks in a deep breath. "I've thought about this moment for years of my life and what I'd say to you when this day came."

"Gracie," I whisper, and it feels as if I'm dying inside as she keeps her smile, but I also see the pain in her expression. The pain she'd never fucking admit even if I called her out on it. Stubborn to the core.

"No matter what happens, know that I will always, always care about you. And I'm so happy that you found the perfect bride. She's … beautiful. And kind. And has always checked every one of your boxes. You're going to have an amazing life together." She laughs. "I was thinking that is how I'd start my speech for tonight. Did I nail it?"

I shake my head. "None of that messy love stuff that you pulled out at your sister's wedding?"

She reaches forward and adjusts my bow tie. "Not this time. There. Now you're ready." She brushes my shoulders, then looks into my eyes. "The real reason I came in here is that Colt told me you were in here, losing your shit, and I know I'm still the only one who can help cure that."

Laughter escapes me. "Do I look like I'm losing my shit?"

She takes a step back and tilts her head, chewing on the corner of her bottom lip. "Yeah."

"I'm gonna kick his ass after the ceremony, thank ya."

"You weren't supposed to get married before me." Her words come out in a whisper.

When she grabs my hand, I pull her close to me. She spins into my arms, and then we slowly dance to silence.

"I wouldn't have been able to survive it if the roles were reversed."

It's the most truthful thing I've said all week. I'd die watching Grace marry another man.

Her body is pressed against mine, and I'm so glad I can't see her face right now.

"I found the letter."

She shakes her head and pulls away from me. "I didn't write you a letter."

I pull the folded piece of paper from my pocket. It's covered in red-lipped kisses sixteen-year-old Grace wrote me. Like a flash in the dark, recognition fills her eyes as she sees it.

"I don't care that it was dated eleven years ago."

She touches the locket. Knowing why I chose *that* picture. Because *that* was the night she hid that note in that fucking treasure chest, thinking I'd find it.

Her brows crease and then straighten, and it tells me everything I need to know.

"Wait, you *just* found it?" Her nostrils flare. "I thought … you *rejected* me."

"Had I known you felt this way back then, it would've been you. It's always been *you*." I shake my head. "What is it with the older kids in families not being able to communicate properly? I love—" I swallow hard, meeting her eyes. "I *loved* you," I correct.

When she doesn't respond, I continue, "And people change, I guess."

She sucks in the heavy air that's smothering me.

I want to kiss her one last time to make sure there isn't *anything* between us, but I won't because I don't break my promises either.

But if she gave me a glimmer of hope there was an actual chance for us, I'd walk away from this wedding without looking back. I can't force her to see what's right in front of her. For this to ever work, she needs to see it for herself, now, as the woman she is today. And she still doesn't *after everything*.

Her eyes gently close, her uneasy breath flutters against my lips, and she stops.

"I should get going, okay?"

When she pulls away, I see tears threatening to spill over.

"Okay," I tell her.

The message is heard loud and clear.

There is no chance for us.

"You look … like a prince." Her words are barely audible.

"*Goodbye*, Grace," I whisper before she leaves the room. Because that's what this is … *the actual end.* The one where I get married, and she moves away, and we grow apart.

When I'm alone, I sit in one of the changing chairs and check the time.

Fifteen minutes.

The door flies open, and I think it's Grace coming back to say she realizes just how stupid she's being, but instead, it's Kinsley.

She waltzes across the room in a lavender dress like she owns the color. My older sister stands in front of me and places a hand on her hip. Gold bracelets jingle as she stares down at me like I'm one of her peasants. "You know the cards don't lie."

"Kins, please, I know you're giving queen energy today, but I can't do this right now," I groan, trying to get my thoughts under control before I make a rash decision. "Just admit it. You got it wrong. And when I kiss my wife and walk down that aisle, I'm gonna give you the biggest, fattest Valentine *I told you so* that I've ever given anyone in my entire life. And it's going to be sooooo bittersweet, rubbing it in your face how wrong you were."

She scoffs and then playfully shakes her head. "You're playin' with fire, Harrison."

"You lost. Beckett lost. Everyone lost. I'm getting married."

She clears her throat. "You should've sold tickets to the circus because, right now, you're being a clown."

"Great pep talk."

Remi enters, and my mood brightens because, out of everyone, she seems to understand both sides.

"I just came to say congrats." She shrugs. "Colt told me you were having a meltdown."

"Is he going around telling everyone that? Do I look like I'm in here losing it?" I stand and glance between them, knowing I look good as hell in my tux with the plastered smile I've faked for years.

I'm a pro at it at this point. It's how I've survived this long.

"Yes to both questions," Kinsley says. "You're doing that overcompensating thing you always do when you flick on that dickhead personality of yours."

"Sometimes, I want to give you a wet willy," I threaten, reaching for her.

"I dare you!" She rushes away, laughing, and then the mood turns serious. "I just want to make sure this is what you want."

"It is," I say.

Remi clears her throat. "Look, I'll personally explain it wasn't meant to be to every single person out there if you want to call it quits. You already know how I feel."

I gave Grace plenty of chances to admit her feelings to me, and she didn't, so I have no regrets. *I tried.*

I force a laugh and look between them. "What has gotten into you two? For real. This is the right decision for me, and I'm happy. Now, can we all pretty please put a smile on? I'm gonna make you both aunts before Beckett. So try to cut me some slack here. I'm not wasting any time after this ceremony."

This makes them grin, and I notice Kinsley's shoulders relax.

She pulls me into a hug. "Okay. But how many signs do you need before you realize this might not be the right decision?"

I don't answer her, and Remi speaks up. "I support you. This is what you want."

"Okay, great. Now, we're all on the same page." I clap my

hands together, trying to get excited. "I'm thrilled we had that little chatty chat. Oh, and know that I'm gonna try my damnedest to talk you out of getting married to your partner right before you walk down the aisle, just to make sure you're in it to win it. It's going to be a fun test. Had I not been certain about my decision, you might've cracked me with those performances. Bravo."

Kinsley turns to me. "You ruin my wedding day, and I'll chop off your balls. Then, I'll wait for someone else to put a bun in the oven and make me an aunt. You're not our only brother. I don't *need* you to deliver me a baby to spoil, thank ya very much."

"I love you, sis," I tell her and give her another hug, and Remi joins in.

"I guess it's time to get married." Remi laughs, and we leave the room.

We go our separate ways. I walk down the long hallway that leads to the stairs that Stephanie will be walking down.

Before I round the corner, I run into Beckett.

"Gotta say, all this is making me nervous about my big day."

"Dude, don't be. If we can get an entire-ass wedding together this fast, you and Summer can make it happen by the end of the year." I smile. "Also, can you tell Colt when you see him that I'm gonna fuck him up at the reception?"

"I just saw him. He told me you were having second thoughts," Beckett admits. "I'd love to get my five hundred dollars back from Cash."

I chuckle. "That money is long gone, bro."

"Well," he continues, "the horses are outside, waiting for you and Steph after the ceremony. I have a few ranch hands watching them down there."

"Thanks, bro," I tell him.

He checks his phone. "It's time to go. Congrats again." He hugs me and walks away.

When I pass the bridal room, the door swings open, and I'm

quickly pulled inside. It's almost golden hour, so there is a different glow in the room.

I cover my eyes when I see Stephanie's, not looking down at her dress.

"What are you doin'? We're not supposed to see each other before the wedding. It's bad luck."

With my eyes closed, she captures my lips. "I don't believe in superstitions," she says. "I want you to see me first, before anyone else. Makes it more special. Please look."

My eyes flutter open, and a grin touches my lips. "Fuck, you're gorgeous. I'm so lucky."

"Me too."

I smell her skin, smelling the warm vanilla on it, and it makes me think of Grace. I slam my eyes shut, pushing those thoughts away. She kisses me again, running her fingers through my hair, and things almost get too heated. The alarm I set for ten minutes before the ceremony goes off, and I silence it.

I whisper in her ear and laugh, but she pulls away and meets my eyes.

"Steph," she corrects when we break apart.

"That's what I said."

She slowly shakes her head. "No, you said Gracie."

My mouth falls open. I didn't even realize my mistake. "Shit. I'm sorry. Wedding day jitters—that's all."

She leans in, wrapping her hand behind my neck, and kisses me. "Of course. I love you."

"Love you too," I admit. "Ready?"

When we break apart, she smiles. "Yes, I'll see you out there, future hubby."

"Okay, wifey." I give her another kiss, then exit the room and stand against the door for a few seconds before sucking in a deep breath.

I make my way down the stairs and the aisle and move to the staging area as I check my watch. The place is packed, and I wouldn't be surprised if the entire town was here. When I look up and around, I see all the microphones and notice the cameras placed at every angle to capture the moment. It makes my palms sweaty, and I feel in my coat pocket for my vows since we decided to write them ourselves. I pull out the note Gracie wrote to me all those years ago.

I rub my fingers across the red kisses on the page and glance over the words she wrote again. The last sentence haunts me.

I'M *in love with you, and I always will be.*

I WAS SO focused on this that I left my vows on my dresser. *Fuck.*

When the pastor walks out, I know the show will start, and then it will be over. I'll be able to move on—forever.

Time speeds up, and everything happens fast as I go through the motions of how today will go.

The cellos give out one note and then begin to play George Strait's "Check Yes or No." I break into a smile, knowing Grace chose this song. Because Stephanie told her to plan a wedding that would make me happy. And it's already everything I imagined for my special day—from the food to the twinkle lights to the way the orange sunlight will leak through the windows when we seal our vows with a kiss.

The wedding party marches down the beautiful aisle with an elegant floor runner.

Beckett and Grace step down, and my eyes meet hers. The underlying current nearly pulls me under, and I feel like I'm drowning as she turns her head, standing up front as my best man, but she's on the bridal party side. Stephanie's request.

I make a promise to myself that I won't look at her again for the rest of the night.

When the piano begins to play and "A Thousand Years" starts, all attention goes to Stephanie. Though I've already seen her once, I notice she's wearing glass slippers and a tiara.

A smile meets my lips, and when she looks into my eyes, she grins wide. My nerves seem to disappear, and I stay focused on her.

Her father lets her go, and then she comes to me.

I take her hand, bending down, and whisper in her ear, "You're beautiful."

She grins and holds out her hand as the officiant gives the opening lines. Stephanie and I turn to one another, face to face, and right over her shoulder, I catch a glimpse of Grace.

Our eyes lock for a brief second, and her lips turn up into a smile, and I ask myself if it's really our goodbye. She swallows hard, and we hold a silent conversation. I force myself to look away. I swallow, then bring my attention back to Stephanie and smile.

The pulse in her neck upticks, and she grabs my hand and pulls me behind the staging area and down the hallway. There is commotion in the audience.

"What're you doing?" I ask her, searching her face as she pulls me with her, giving us space away from the hundreds of pairs of eyes that were watching us.

"Harrison, what are *you* doing?"

She slides the engagement ring off her finger and holds it in the air. I hold out my palm, and she places it in my hand and closes it.

"I've wanted all of my life for someone to look at me the same way you look at her."

"Stephanie," I whisper.

"I'm not letting you go through with this." She holds up her hand, stopping me from saying anything. "I know you'll keep your promises. And I know she will too. Do you want to waste your entire life playing house and pretending with me when there is more out there?"

The pastor comes to the back, where we're talking. "Everything okay?"

"Yes." Stephanie gives him a sweet smile. "We'll be right out."

When we're alone again, she grabs my face and kisses me. "Consider today the luckiest day of your life and mine too. I'm in love with the idea of us, and it's not enough. It won't ever be. I really thought you were the one who got away, but I was wrong. I love you, but … I'm not *in* love with you. And I know I'll always be your second best. I told myself I could live with that, but I can't. People like me desperately search for the love you already have."

I can't deny any of it, but I'm relieved. She sees it on my face, and she shakes her head.

"You're too stubborn and loyal for your own good sometimes, Harrison Valentine."

"I'm sorry. I'm sorry. I truly thought we'd find what we had again," I tell her. "But thank you."

"Now, don't be stupid and fuck up your second chance." She uses her stern, lawyer voice, then sighs before pulling me into a tight hug.

I hold her until she pulls away, breaking the embrace.

"Let me do the talking, okay?"

I nod, knowing it's the least I can do after this. Stephanie takes my hand, interlocks her fingers with mine, and leads us back.

I guess we're about to give everyone in Valentine something to talk about.

But I give zero fucks.

CHAPTER THIRTY-ONE

GRACE

When Stephanie interrupts the ceremony and pulls Harrison to the back, I feel like I'm having a full-blown panic attack and I might pass out. I don't know what's going on, but everyone is growing uneasy.

I look at Beckett, and he smiles.

Kinsley nods with a grin.

Remi gives a thumbs-up.

Then I realize hundreds of eyes are on me, and my cheeks are burning red.

This is a nightmare that I can't wake up from. I swallow hard, hating how the seconds feel like hours and minutes feel like days.

The pastor excuses himself, and the wedding party stands awkwardly, waiting for something to happen.

After a minute, he returns, and he seems relieved. "They're coming, and then we'll finish up. This happens sometimes. Nerves."

Everyone in this room knows for a goddamn fact that it *doesn't.*

Nothing about this is normal.

Ten long minutes pass, and Harrison and Stephanie finally

return. They're holding hands, fingers interlocked, and they look happy as hell. A good sign, I think, slightly relaxing too. I slowly let out a breath, making sure not to lock my knees so I don't fall down, even though I feel like I might.

"Is my microphone on?" Stephanie asks since they're both wearing wireless. It immediately clicks on. Feedback bounces against opposing walls, but she gives her million-dollar smile to the crowd.

I wait with bated breath for her to explain, and so does the crowd. When I look up, I see the sunlight leaking through. We planned the vows to happen at golden hour, and any more wasted time, and they'll miss their opportunity for a picture-perfect kiss.

"First of all, we wanted to thank y'all for coming out to celebrate with us."

My attention goes back to her as people move in their seats and whispers begin, but she holds the attention of the room.

There's no denying her charisma as she continues speaking. "Sometimes, we do things hastily and realize it's the wrong decision."

Her beautiful dress sparkles like a diamond in the fading sunlight, and the room glows golden.

She lifts her hand, and Harrison's is still attached. Their eyes meet and soften. "And a wrong decision at the right time results in a wedding like this one."

There is a long, awkward pause, and my heart pounds in my ears.

"The truth is, we don't belong together. And we're sorry for wasting everyone's time and figuring it out at the very last minute."

Harrison laughs and smiles, showing that adorable little dimple that only comes out when he's being genuine. And it's more than obvious he doesn't have two fucking cares in the world as the chatter grows louder.

Then she turns and looks at everyone again. "It's obvious there are two people in this room who are made for one another, and I'm just hoping this wakes them both up before it's too late."

My mouth falls open, and I drop the bouquet. It makes a loud crash on the floor. Harrison's eyes meet mine, and my vision blurs. I'm too lost in my thoughts, and nothing is making sense as she continues on. My body is on fire.

"There might not be a wedding happening, but how about we all celebrate two people not making the biggest mistakes of their lives?"

People stand from their chairs, and when I see bodies rush toward me, I need to escape.

The pressure is too much, and the air is too thick, so I push my way through the crowd and take an emergency exit outside.

When I see the buildings glowing bright, I close my eyes, trying to ground myself in the moment, trying to stop my racing heart. I might throw up as adrenaline rushes through me, but I push it back as the cool air kisses my skin.

I pick up my pace, and relief floods through me as I see my car. I climb inside, and then I drive into the sunset, needing to clear my mind as shock takes over.

CHAPTER THIRTY-TWO

HARRISON

As soon as Stephanie finishes a damn fine explanation, I expect everyone to burst into a round of applause and congratulate us for not being stupid. This is the part in those rom-coms that Grace adores where the clouds open up, the sun comes out, and the birds sing.

Instead, it's *pure fucking chaos* in the building, like someone pulled a fire alarm or something, but I don't hear anything other than my name being called. I realize how many people are rushing toward me and Stephanie. We're barricaded in by bodies. Another reason we probably shouldn't have invited five hundred people.

Kinsley rushes up to me and grabs my arm. "I get the first exclusive story, okay?"

"Are you serious right now?" I shake my head at her, trying to scan the room. "Have you seen Grace?"

"No, she rushed out," she says.

Then she turns around and immediately switches into big-sister mode. She's ready to fight every single person in the room as she tells them to mind their damn business like she's my bodyguard.

As I stand on one of the chairs, I think I see the back of her head, knowing I've always been able to find her in a crowd. Someone nearly knocks me over, and when I blink, she's gone again. It's like she vanished into thin air, nothing more than a figment of my imagination. It's how the last week feels.

Somehow, I meet Beckett's eyes, and he points toward the opposite exit. And I know that means she left.

I check my pockets for my keys, then I remember I didn't drive here like a dumb fuck. Beckett somehow convinced me to ride with him even though I always drive to events like this because something dramatic always happens. Not *cancel a whole-ass wedding* dramatic though. This is at the damn top. And now I don't have a way out. Never again.

By some miracle, I make it through the horde and push open the double doors with both palms. Across the street, Charlie, one of the ranch hands, is watching the horse that Stephanie and I were to ride away on after the reception.

"Change of plans." I jog over to him and start untying the slip knot that's in the lead rope.

He stands and looks at me like I've lost my damn mind as I slide my foot into the stirrup and pull myself into the Western saddle.

"Where are you goin'?" he asks as I move the reins and lead Tinkerbell onto the pavement.

"To find my woman," I announce, clicking my mouth.

The rumors will write themselves. I don't care anymore. The ones that involved me and her were true anyway.

Horseshoes clack, and I cut across the park that fills the town square, then break into a gallop across the grass. Tinkerbell loves to run, so I give her all the permission to open wide up, leaving dust in our wake. It's as if she knows how desperate I am to find Grace right now.

The sun is setting over the horizon, and the cool March breeze blows against my cheeks. I'll ride into the night if it means finding her because what I have to say can't wait, not anymore.

I gently tug on the reins when I turn into Grace's driveway. I hop out of the saddle, using the spare key she leaves under a plant, and walk into her house.

"Gracie?" I yell, walking down the hallway, pushing open her bedroom door at the end of the hall, and turning on the lights.

The place is *empty*. She's *not* here.

I pull my phone from my pocket and call her. It goes straight to voice mail. I try again. She turned it off so she could disappear.

"Fuck!" I run my fingers through my hair, needing to calm down.

I know where she is. She's at my house waiting for me. When we were younger and something dramatic would happen, she'd always meet me at my place. It was safe. She's there now. I'd bet anything on it.

When I walk outside, Tinkerbell is standing where I left her, grazing on the small patch of grass in front of her house. Before I mount, Remi comes around the corner like a bat out of hell, and the Mustang swings into the driveway. The lights shine against the house as she steps out, leaving the door open.

"Want to take my pony?"

I move past her. "You're the best sister ever! Timing is *perfection*."

"I'm working on my good karma these days."

I get in and have to immediately move the seat back. "Thank you. I owe you one."

"Make it ten," she says, grabbing the horn and mounting Tinkerbell in her dress. She'll bring her back to the trailer.

"You fuckin' got it." I back out of the driveway, the engine of the car roaring to life as I gun it with the windows down and drive it like I stole it.

The sound of the deep engine bounces off the buildings as I fly through the downtown area. Then I make a right and head down the country road that leads to the ranch with the mountains in the background. The car hugs every fast curve that I take, and when the tires hit the gravel on my parents' ranch, I spin out but don't stop. I rush to the ranch house on the property that I share with Colt.

Call me reckless. Call me whatever you'd like, but that's what she does to me. That woman has me in a choke hold, and she's never going to let me go. I don't want her to.

When I see Grace's car in front of my house, I let out a sigh of relief. I know her. I know her better than she knows herself. I park, then climb the steps of the porch two at a time. I push open the door and walk down the hallway.

She's standing in my bedroom, and I think I see a fucking smirk on her face right before I wrap one hand behind her head and pull her into a greedy kiss.

"You found me." She moans, her hands in my hair, and she pulls me back onto the bed.

I fall on top of her, looking down into her golden-brown eyes. Flecks sparkling just for me.

"You've got goose bumps." I kiss her shoulder, trailing my fingers down her sun-kissed skin, and glance at the locket around her neck that has a picture of us inside.

"And butterflies too. You've always done that to me," she admits, desperately sliding her mouth and tongue against mine as we try to devour one another.

"I'm so fucking sorry, princess. I almost made the biggest mistake of my life. I don't know what I was thinking. I promise to spend from now until the end of time making it up to you." I draw an *X* over my heart.

She shakes her head. "We both took it too far."

"I can't be your best friend anymore," I say, grabbing a fistful of her dress. "I need more, Gracie. I can't spend another day pretending that you're not everything I want and need in my life. Messy love—I don't give a fuck, princess, whatever you need. I'm not going anywhere. I'm stupidly and desperately in love with *you*," I mutter against her lips, hoping she understands.

"I'm ridiculously in love with you too. I learned I actually can't watch you marry someone else. I found my limit."

"I'm sorry," I whisper. "It was always supposed to be us." I rest my forehead on hers, then pull away. "You know that, don't you? Everyone else does."

"I know," she whispers. "Also, I just had my *movie magic* moment."

Gracie tilts her head at me as she sits up to undo my tuxedo coat.

We're laughing, unable to get out of our clothes fast enough to be together again. "We'll have many more."

I stand, dropping my coat to the floor, struggling to remove the stupid fucking bow tie I didn't want to wear in the first place. Seconds later, she's standing in front of me, her mouth close to mine, and I relax, resting my hands on her ass.

"Let me help you," she whispers, carefully untangling it and throwing it to the floor.

She runs her hands across my chest, undoing every button on the vest before removing my dress shirt. Her hands trace the lines of the muscles on my stomach as she peppers kisses down my body until she's on her knees before me.

"Fuck," I growl, lifting her chin with my finger and meeting her hooded eyes.

"Let me worship you the way I've always wanted to," she whispers.

Her fingers dip into the top of my suit pants, and she pulls me closer to her so she can remove my belt, unbutton my pants, and undo my zipper. My pants and boxers fall to my ankles as she sits upright on her knees, taking me into her hot mouth.

She's unraveling every thread I have left as she licks and sucks me. Fingernails lightly slide down my chest as she cups my balls and takes every inch of me down her throat. She works me so fucking good that my head falls back on my shoulders. With her palms flat against my thighs, using me as leverage, she steadies herself.

When I don't think I can take it anymore, I pull her up to me. "You make me feel so good, but I'm not giving you what you want yet."

I brush my fingertips on her neck as I fist her curled strands.

"Why did you cut your hair?" I ask, meeting her eyes.

"Because you loved it," she admits.

"Didn't work," I say, peppering kisses along her neck and jaw. "I still love it."

She grabs my cock, and it pulses in her hand.

"You've always been a tease," I whisper against her.

"Learned my best moves from you," she admits.

She lets out a ragged breath as I slide my fingers into her panties, feeling just how goddamn wet she is for me.

I kiss her, rubbing slow, agonizing circles on her needy little clit. "No more secrets when it comes to how we feel about each other."

She draws an *X* over her heart and then sinks onto my hand. "Never again. I almost lost you."

"Almost only counts in horseshoes," I whisper.

And she laughs, falling back on the bed and pulling me with her. She climbs on top of me and straddles me. I take her all in.

"I was so afraid of losing you that I pushed you away," she admits. "I'm sorry."

"And don't you ever let it happen again," I tell her with a playful wink.

"You too." She jabs me in my side, making me squirm, and then kisses me. "I'll probably fuck up a million times more, but please don't give up on me again."

"I won't." I roll her over and pin her on her back.

My face is so close to hers as I tuck hair behind her ear and slowly slide my mouth across hers. She gasps, deepening the kiss as my hand glides up her thigh. I lower the zipper on her dress, and she wiggles out of it. Her hands tangle in my hair as I peel the wet silk panties from her body and then remove her bra.

"You're gorgeous," I say, my gaze sliding over her curvy body.

As I slide my lips from her mouth to her breast, I leave a trail of kisses down to her pussy.

"Keeping up with the landscaping?" I give her a look.

"Gotta love a silky, smooth butthole." She laughs. "I was hoping I'd be able to tell you that again."

I shake my head. "Don't you ever fuckin' change. I love you just the way you are."

"Don't plan on it, cowboy," she whispers as my mouth and tongue are on her clit.

I flick and lick, loving the taste of her skin, the taste of her.

She writhes under my tongue, her fingers tangled in my hair. "More," she begs, needing me closer, deeper, harder.

I want to give her everything I have because it's always been hers anyway.

"You're mine," I whisper against her softness, then flick her hard clit, knowing she's teetering on the edge and I have complete control.

My strong hands memorize every curve of hers as I lick and suck her to oblivion. Tonight, I'll prove to her exactly why she can't live without me.

"You've always owned me," she urges, riding my mouth as I slow my pace. "Every fuckin' inch," she hisses, her body trembling.

She's on the brink of spilling over and losing herself. Her body shakes and trembles, and she nearly sets off an earthquake inside my damn heart as she rides out her release, letting me taste every inch of her.

I smile against her, and then I crawl up her body, hovering above her lips as she runs her hands through my messy hair.

"Do you think we were always destined to be like this?" I ask.

"*Yes*." No hesitation. "That wedding broke me."

"Let me put you back together, princess," I whisper.

CHAPTER THIRTY-THREE

GRACE

"You're the only one who can," I admit, inhaling his sweaty skin as he holds himself above me.

The tip of his cock is at my opening, and I eagerly wait to have him inside of me. Then I open my thighs wider, giving him the permission he needs because I can't wait any longer. I need him like I need air. My eyes crash closed, and I see colors when he's buried deep inside of me. Every part of my body craves this man so fucking much. His eyes, his mouth, his hands, his voice, the way he fills me full with every inch. The way he loves me. Has *always* loved me. He's my escape and my home. My safety. The only person who's ever gotten me, all of me.

"Harrison," I whisper between moans, and it comes out urgent because I know just how close we were to losing each other forever.

"I'll never get tired of hearing you say my fucking name like that," he says, kissing my neck and nibbling on my earlobe, giving it to me slowly.

"I want this forever," I admit breathlessly.

"Me too," he immediately says.

The energy grows more intimate as we make love in the stillness. It's just us, alone, as one, with a million silent words streaming between us. His mouth on mine is intoxicating, and I'm drunk on him. It was always supposed to be us, just like this. His muscles tremble, and his groans turn to growls. The warmth chases me, transforms me into someone who doesn't know what life could be like without this. I don't want to know ever again, not after watching him and everything we have almost slip through my fingers.

This is too good. *We're* too good *together*.

"Forever." My back arches with the insatiable pleasure he gives me every single time we're together. Emotionally and physically.

I wrap my legs around his waist tightly as we climb the mountain and repel down it together until we're lying raw and breathless at the bottom.

We are yin and yang. We are nothing without the other.

He's my other half. *My best friend.*

The orgasms rip through us, and I see stars as he nearly collapses on my chest, still buried inside of me.

I kiss his sweaty forehead, taking in the smell of the cologne on his skin, and I sigh.

Our eyes meet, and he wraps his arms around me, holding me tight.

"Go to Paris with me."

"Huh?"

"Tomorrow. The trip can't be canceled, and since I paid for it …"

"Your honeymoon?" I whisper.

"I want time alone with you, away from this place, away from the murmurs. We still have a lot of shit to hash out and talk about. And a fuckton of lost time to make up for." He props himself up on his forearms.

"I'll go with you. Messy love."

After stealing a kiss, he pushes my hair from my face. "Wouldn't want to be tangled up with anyone else."

"It's a life sentence," I remind him with a grin.

"Thank fuck for that." He captures my lips.

AT THREE IN THE MORNING, I walk into my dark condo and toss the keys to Remi's Mustang on the counter so she knows it was returned. It was sweet of her to let him drive it because she trusts very few people behind the wheel, especially men. All they want to do is hot rod it.

My car is staying at Harrison's house until we return from this trip.

Each time I take a step, I feel exactly where he was and what he claimed … every inch of me. When I close my eyes, our night together and our confession flash through my memory. It's something I never want to forget. I slowly inhale, nearly pinching myself, wondering if this happened or if I'll wake up and be back in that venue, watching him say *I do*. Losing him is what nightmares are made from.

I owe Stephanie *everything*. She was the one who saved the day, the real hero in the end.

Just as I take a step, I hear a soft moan.

Then I see a man's shoe.

A high heel.

A belt.

Pants.

A dark-gray dress shirt with pearl buttons.

I try to piece together who was wearing those clothes at the ceremony, but the whole afternoon is a blur. Too much happened, and I haven't had a chance to process any of it. My head is spinning and my body is reeling. This vacation will be good for me.

The next moan is more ragged and desperate than the first.

My eyes widen, and I freeze in place. Right now, I don't even want to breathe because I don't want to interrupt. When my phone buzzes in my palm, I look down and read a text from Harrison.

HARRISON

Be there soon.

He told me he'd let me know when he was heading this way.

I tiptoe down the hallway, trying not to be heard, but I know I need to pack for Paris. As soon as I'm in my room, I hear the deep rumble of a man's voice, followed by her giggle. I think I hear the sound again, and it's one hundred percent a sex moan. I play through all the people she could be rolling around the sheets with at this time. And while I have an idea, as of now, I have no proof, just a suspicion.

I flick on my light, pull my suitcase from my closet, and toss it onto my bed. It's still full of clothes that I packed when I went to Hawaii. For months, all of the lingerie and sexy sleepwear I'd bought to surprise Joey has lived in here. As I move things around, I see the pair of socks Harrison gave me for my cold toes. The memory makes me chuckle.

Once I'm packed, I fall back on the bed. My thighs and abs and arms and mouth are already sore.

Harrison and I almost became strangers, and now we're … *lovers?*

Five minutes later, Remi's door opens, and she walks to the

bathroom. When she's finished, she stops outside my bedroom door. "Didn't know you were home."

"I'm stealthy like that," I say, sitting up with a brow popped, looking at her messy hair and swollen lips. I smile, knowing there is someone in there. "I won't say anything," I whisper.

She smirks. "Okay." Then she walks farther into my room. "Please tell me he found you?"

"He did. Your keys are on the counter."

"And?" She glances at my suitcase.

I nod. "I'm going to Paris with him. I'll be back in a few days."

She hugs me. "Thank God." Then she looks into my eyes, searching my face. "Next time my brother is standing up there, about to promise his life to another person, it'd better be you. Got it? I don't think anyone in my entire family will be able to handle this again. Nearly destroyed us all."

"It *will* be me. I can promise you that."

Fifteen minutes later, the front door to our condo opens, and Remi turns, seeing all the clothes on the floor, then rushes around, trying to pick them up. She looks at me with clothes in her arms and fear on her face. Then I remember there's a man in her room right now.

Harrison comes closer. "Are you doin' laundry this late at night? I thought you went to bed early like a grandma."

He stands behind Remi, and I can see she's having a mini meltdown, so I do my best to distract him. The last thing I need is for him to threaten whoever is in that room and ruin their entire night. When it comes to his little sisters, he's a total asshole, and he will pull out that dickhead personality that I love and hate all at the same time. The fiercely protective one. The one who gives zero fucks.

"What's the rush?" He laughs as I push him out the door, and I wave bye to Remi.

I turn and look at him as I walk to the truck. "I'll tell you later."

He opens the door for me. "She has someone in her room, doesn't she?"

"Don't you kinda owe her one?" I pull him to me, tugging his lip into my mouth.

"I owe her ten, but I guess it's nine now."

I see the sun rising in the far distance and pull out my phone so we can take our signature road-trip selfie. "I want you to promise me something," I say.

"Anything."

"When things between us are good, we enjoy them."

"I already do that." He smiles.

As we're sitting outside of our gate, ready to board the plane, Harrison interlocks his fingers with mine. I glance over at him. A million different questions stream through me, and I feel like I've somehow slipped time lines into this alternate reality that I've only wished for.

He leans over. "Why are you lookin' at me like that?"

I shake my head. "Nothing."

He lifts my chin and forces me to meet his eyes. I stare into them, drown in the depths of them, with no need to come up for air.

"We should play a game," I tell him as he traces my bottom lip with his thumb. "While we're away."

His brow lifts, and it's seductive as fuck. "A naughty game?"

I slam my mouth against his, not able to take it anymore because the anticipation is too much. I've been pushing that feeling away for too damn long, and it nearly destroyed us in the process.

I swallow hard. "It's called *Nothing But Truths*—or at least, that's what I'm naming it. While we're away, we give each other the full truth. No more guessing. The truth, no matter what the answer is or how raw."

"And it goes both ways?" When our fingers interlock, I notice how he rubs his thumb against mine, and it makes me smile.

"Of course. Both ways."

He shakes his head. "You are *so* fucked."

A fit of laughter takes over. "Shit. I forgot that you have a better memory than me."

"Yep. So it starts as soon as the plane lands in Europe?"

"Yes, but you'd better go easy on me." I poke a finger into his side.

"No can do." He chuckles, squirming away, then pulls me close to him and whispers in my ear, "Don't tell everyone I'm ticklish. You're the only person who knows that."

I wrap my arms around his waist, inhaling him. "Your secrets are safe with me. All of them are."

An announcement is made, and then we board the plane. First class with sparkling wine and expensive chocolates. When he looks over at me in the oversized seats, I smile, and when the plane takes off, I pull him in for a desperate kiss.

We're like a bullet in the air, and I'm soaring across the sea in his arms. I hold him so tight, as though if I loosened my grip, he might disappear. When he kisses my forehead and my eyes flutter closed, I have zero doubts in my body about this choice. Being with him like this is the way it should've always been.

Kinsley was right after all … the cards *don't* lie.

CHAPTER THIRTY-FOUR

HARRISON

When we arrive in Paris, it's already dark. The city glows golden from up above, and we catch a glimpse of the Eiffel Tower before we land. Grace and I are both drowsy, and I think exhaustion from everything that's happened has finally caught up to us.

The stumble was worth her falling into my arms, and I don't regret a thing. I'll always choose the road less traveled as long as it means my best friend is by my side.

I reach out my hand, and she takes it as we make our way through the airport. There are too many stolen glances, and I know she feels the intensity by how her arms sprinkle with goose bumps. As we walk toward the baggage area, I spot our driver holding a sign that says *Mr. and Mrs. Valentine.*

Grace reads it and then meets my face with a seductive expression.

"After you, *Mrs.* Valentine," I say, and she scoots inside the limo.

Once the door shuts, we're zooming off. The partition is up, so I know we have full privacy.

She looks at the champagne and strawberries waiting for us. "Mrs. Valentine?"

"Fuck yeah," I say, bringing her in for a kiss. "Practice run."

"Not gonna lie. I kinda like the sound of that. But then again, you've always been *my* Valentine."

She grabs a strawberry and takes a bite. Then she brings it to my lips, tracing it along my bottom one before leaning forward and kissing the sweetness away. Grace offers me a bite, and as the juice runs down my chin, she straddles my lap and licks it up. My hands rest on her hips as she rocks against me.

"I started dreaming about you."

I meet her eyes. "Really? I thought you didn't dream anymore."

"It started when I knew I was losing you. You'd tell me I was being stupid, and then it'd turn sexual, and I'd wake up aching for you."

I shake my head. "The Harrison Valentine Kiss of Death strikes again. Works *every* time."

She fists her fingers through my hair and grinds against me, stealing wet kisses every chance she gets. "Did you wear that navy suit to your rehearsal dinner for me?"

"So we've started *Nothing But Truths*? You sure you're ready?" I smirk. Allowing her to back out. To stop this game before we start it. "I won't go easy on you, princess. It will get raw."

"We both need this," she confirms with a nod as I grip her ass, feeling the weight of her against me as I grow thick. "So?"

I meet her gaze. "Yeah, I did. I wanted it to destroy you. I wanted you to remember every single time I'd worn it this year and how you'd ended up beneath me."

A moan escapes her as she keeps her rhythm. "It worked. And I hated you for it," she admits. Then she's whispering in my ear, "I hope you packed it."

"I did." I take claim of her mouth. "You weren't innocent though. You wore my *favorite* color. And made damn sure that dress fit you like a second skin so I could see every torturous curve. It's like you wanted me to notice how hard your nipples got when you were around me."

"I'm a monster," she says, placing her forehead against mine. "Did it work?"

"Fuck yes," I say with a growl, loving how she feels against me. How her breaths soften and her eyes flutter closed.

Her head falls back on her shoulders, and she grabs my T-shirt. "Did you think of me when she was wearing my perfume?"

I dig my thumbs into her hips as we spiral together. "Yes. Every single time."

"I hated smelling you on her," she hisses, her breath growing more ragged. "It drove me insane."

"Take what you need, princess," I urge, rubbing my thumb against her clit as she rocks against my restricted cock. I feel like I might burst through the seams of the worn jeans as I buck against her, adding more friction against that needy little clit.

"I'm so fucking close, but I need more of you. I can never get enough. I'm addicted to you," she mutters, her body tensing as my mouth slides up her neck.

Seconds later, she's gasping and shattering with my name on her lips. I hold her against me, allowing her to come down from her high. We stay like that for a few minutes, with her on my lap, as we cruise the streets of Paris at night.

"We're almost to the hotel," I whisper, hard as a fucking rock, knowing exactly how much time we had from the airport if there was no traffic, but also not wanting her to move.

I like holding her like this, like we're frozen in a moment of time. It's almost as if she has to peel herself away from me, and I understand. I just need to be with her, to hold her, to make sure she knows that what we have isn't going anywhere.

"I owe you one." She smiles with hooded eyes and messy hair, then settles down next to me, drinking the champagne straight from the bottle before handing it to me.

I press it to my lips and sip. "For how much you fuckin' tortured me over the years, you owe me a thousand."

The limo smells like her pleasure, which is also written all over her face. Five minutes later, the car slows, and the door swings open. Our bags are carried to the front desk, and we silently take an elevator to the top floor. When I open the door to our honeymoon suite that has the perfect view of the Eiffel Tower, she smiles, but it slightly falters. She doesn't even have to say what she's thinking—I know.

I move behind her, wrapping my arms around her body and kissing the back of her head. "I'm here with you right now. That's all that matters."

She turns, and she grips my T-shirt with tight fists. "Do you always know what I'm thinking?"

"With a single glance." I set her on the edge of the bed and kneel in front of her. We're almost eye to eye. "And you know it goes both ways. One look, and you're in my damn head, reading my thoughts. Like right now, what am I thinking?"

She scrolls down to my mouth, studying it before grinning. "You're thinking about how you want to lay me down on this bed and worship my body."

"Nailed it." I shrug, placing my hands on her thighs and looking up into her eyes. "I owe you an apology."

She shakes her head. "Don't."

"You promised nothing but truths," I say, interlocking my hands with hers and kissing her fingers. "If I couldn't have you, I wanted to erase you. Every part of you. Every memory. The sound of your laugh. All of our traditions. How your hair blows with the window down in the summertime. Your perfume. The way you whisper my name when you come. Or how your body fits so perfectly against mine when we sleep. I was fucking destroyed. The thought of there not being a chance for us when I believed there was no other choice nearly killed me. I was ready to burn down the entire world without a single regret. And I would've without a distraction. I was reckless and should've never let it go so far. There was never a chance I'd have gotten over you even if I were with someone else."

She places my face in her hands. "I wanted to do the same."

"Are you still moving away?" I rub my finger against her cheek.

"No," she whispers. "I'm not going anywhere you're not. I love you too damn much."

"I love you too." I pull her into my arms, and we hold each other. "We're so lucky."

"Yeah, we are. Tonight, I just want to be with you. I need hours of uninterrupted time with you." She almost sounds desperate.

I tap my finger against her cute button nose. "I think I can make that happen. I'll order us some food. We can sit on the balcony and eat, slide into a bubble bath, then snuggle all night long."

She tilts her head. "Snuggle?" Then, a grin touches her lips. "I knew you liked it."

"No, princess, I fuckin' love it."

THE NEXT MORNING, we eat breakfast at a little café on the street. We sit in some wooden chairs with a round table that has a vase of white flowers on top. In front of me is Gracie, and behind her is a busy street full of tourists and business professionals. The thick leather menus hold one sheet of paper, and inside is a handful of choices.

She orders eggs, and I choose bagels, and we both have coffee. As I meet her eyes, I smile, still needing to pinch myself. When we're brought another mug of coffee, she wipes her red lips with the cloth napkin in her lap. The sounds of the city surround us, and the temperature is a nice seventy degrees. Right now, I don't have a care in the world, nowhere else to be but here, in the moment, with her.

"So, how many people have you been with this year?" she asks, pointing at me. "Nothing but truths."

"Going right in for it today, aren't ya?" I say, sipping my coffee, savoring the chocolate notes. "Just you. You were the be-all, end-all for me. There was no one else after we were together."

Her jaw is basically on the sidewalk. "No way."

I lean and whisper in her ear so only she can hear me, "That's the truth. Not even Stephanie. We tried to be together, but you broke my dick. The only time I ever … got *hard* was when I thought of you."

She gulps down the bite of eggs she was chewing, then brings her focus to the people walking down the street before turning back to me. "I tried to hook up with someone too. Didn't work out."

"Let me guess. At your sister's wedding," I say with a smirk.

"Wait, how'd you know that?"

"Just a guess. The weird sexual tension between you and whatever the fuck his name was, it was obvious. I knew immediately. And he knew I knew when I showed up. Almost fucked him up over it."

She shakes her head. "Jealoooouuuuuuus."

"Only when it comes to you," I admit.

"Didn't work out. I thought getting underneath someone else would fix me, but once again, you were right."

"I know." For years, I tried to forget how she always made me feel, knowing she was off-limits. We found out the hard way that being without the other is damn near impossible.

After we're finished eating, our plates are cleared from the table. Then I pay our check, and we leave.

As she takes my hand and leads me to the Eiffel Tower during the day, she whispers, "I want to remember this moment forever."

I pull her to me, kissing her in the grass.

When we pull away, she takes her phone from her pocket. "Selfie?"

"Hell yeah."

I stand behind her and duck down so our heads are close. Then, right before she takes it, I kiss her cheek. She shows me, and it's cute, and then she hands me her phone. We take pictures together—more memories for us to print and put into our photo albums.

"I'm so glad I don't have cell service right now," she admits as we continue our stroll. Our goal is to see Notre Dame today. "Very happy to have escaped with you. I'm already dreading going home. Can't even imagine what everyone is sayin' about us now."

I squeeze her fingers, bringing her knuckles to my lips as we cross the street. "I'm sure a rumor about you being knocked up will start. Shall we prove them right?"

"Oh, that reminds me of something."

She moves in front of me and pulls me onto a side street that's not quite as busy. I press her against the cool brick wall and kiss her.

"When I thought I was pregnant … what were you really thinking?"

"I imagined an entire life with you on the ranch, raising our baby together in our little house. It was a glimmer of hope that maybe we could be together, and in three minutes, it was gone. After I left Kinsley's, I felt like I'd lost you all over again. I'd never wanted to be a dad … not until that very moment."

Emotions threaten to spill over as she wraps her arms around my neck. "I felt the same way. But I also know that if that had happened, I'd have always questioned if you just wanted to be with me because of the kid. You're too loyal. Doesn't help that I'd convinced myself that I wasn't what you were into. Maybe I was too short or curvy or not girlie enough."

I study her. "You're my *only* type. Perfect height. Perfect ass. And you're not afraid to get dirty with me in all the right ways. I hooked up with people who were nothing like you to forget and replace. I didn't want anyone I was with to be like you. They'd always be a reminder of what I couldn't have."

"Wow," she whispers. "To hear you admit that. I always wondered why everyone was my polar opposite."

"Yeah, well, why did you choose Scott Eastwood as your celebrity crush?"

She leans forward, brushing her nose against mine. "Easy. He's always reminded me of you."

"That's what I thought, baby."

I grin, wrapping my arm around her and leading her to the street, loving how open we're able to be. How we can put it all out there, the old and the new. I'm learning so much and understanding all the caveats that kept us away from one another, knowing it will never happen again.

"When you made me kiss you in the tree house, what was the real reason?"

Grace chews on her bottom lip. "I wanted you to be my first, so then it would always be special. But I was too chickenshit to admit it, so I made up this elaborate story about needing to practice."

"I knew it. But you know what they say; you never forget your first." I smile.

"Who was yours again?" she asks. "I don't remember."

I look at her and confess something I've *never* told anyone. "*You.*"

Her eyes widen. "Wait, you said you'd kissed several people before that."

"I lied. I was trying to make you jealous." I shrug. "Plus, I knew you wanted it. Wanted *me*. Whatever stupid lie you made up, I didn't care. I needed to kiss you. I almost had so many times before then."

"When you used your tongue, I wanted to have sex right then. But I was always scared I'd get knocked up because of Beckett."

He'd always joked that we'd be teen parents if Grace and I kept it up, even though we were innocent teenagers who weren't fooling around like everyone suspected.

I pull her into me, laughing so loud that my voice bounces off the buildings. "My brother was a dick."

She nods. "I had the biggest, stupidest crush on you. You left me breathless. Kissing you was my first real movie moment."

"That's when I knew you'd be mine." I tuck hair behind her ear, just like I did that night when we were fourteen.

"Close your eyes," I instruct, my voice lowering.

Her eyelashes flutter closed and we go through the same motions as when I first kissed her.

"Now, part your lips slightly," I whisper, and she does.

Her chest rises and falls as I study her expression, moving close to her lips. I remember staring at her, wondering if I really had the balls to make the move. She'd brought it up; she was the one who had made a big deal about knowing how to kiss someone. And knowing she was going to be with some punk from school instead of me made me jealous.

"Now, when I kiss you, open your mouth a tiny bit wider. Okay?"

She nods, exactly like she did. When her breath is on my lips, I move forward, and our lips crash together. She opens her mouth wider, our tongues sliding together, and we make out for at least three minutes.

When I pull away, she's smiling with her eyes still closed. "It was exactly like that."

I look at the bumps that trail up and down her arms anytime I touch her. "There they are. Like clockwork."

She looks at me. "You *always* notice them?"

"Always," I say, wrapping my arm around her shoulder. "In the hot tub. At Christmas. New Year's. And a decade before then. You've pretty much always been a shitty liar."

"I just thought you didn't notice." She chuckles.

"I notice everything about you, princess."

We break apart and then do the touristy things around the city. Honestly, it doesn't matter that we're in Paris. I'd be content no matter where we were, as long as we were together.

By the time we make it back to the hotel, we're tired. So we take a nap, where I spoon the shit out of her for two hours, and then we get up and shower together. Grace dresses much faster than me, and as the sun sets, she stands in front of the gigantic windows, waiting. Tonight, we have a dinner reservation on a boat. We'll eat delicious food by candlelight as a violinist serenades us.

I drink her in, and she sips champagne, wearing that dress that nearly brought me to my knees just a few nights ago. Her chin-length hair is in loose curls that barely blow in the breeze. As if she feels my eyes on her, she turns around, memorizing my body in her favorite suit.

"Damn," she mutters.

She looks at me like I belong to her. I wonder if it's always been this way.

And I know it has. We're just both finally able to admit it.

I adjust my cuff link and walk toward her, wearing a smirk. When I'm close, I pull her into my arms, and we dance on our balcony to the sound of our beating hearts.

Eventually, we come to a stop, and I create a bit of space. "I have another truth to confess."

"Tell me," she whispers, feeling the seriousness of the moment, but I've never been more sure of anything in my entire life.

"One day, I'm gonna make you my wife." Our eyes stay locked, and I promise with an *X* over my heart.

"You'd better," she says desperately, her mouth quickly on mine as she wraps her arms around my neck.

I hold her against me, the kisses grow intense, and I can't explain the elation. I'm high on her, high on knowing that we both want the same things in life—each other.

I take her spare hand, interlocking my fingers with it. "You know I always keep my promises to you," I mutter in her ear.

"I know." She's breathless as I kiss her neck, inhaling her warm vanilla skin. "I don't want to go anywhere tonight."

"Fuck, me neither," I say, leading her back inside.

We got dressed for a night out, just to remove every single item of clothing we had on because the two of us do things our way, like we've always done before.

We make love with the balcony doors open. The sheer cream curtains lightly flap in the breeze as the lights from outside casts shadows on the suite floor. We physically and emotionally tear each other down, only to build the other up, completely losing ourselves in the moment.

And when we're *temporarily* satisfied, trying to catch our breaths and let our heart rates settle, we take turns sharing more truths and talking about the past. Confessing our sins. Revealing our fantasies. And I know that when we finally leave Paris, there will be no more secrets left between us, only our unbreakable promises.

CHAPTER THIRTY-FIVE

GRACE

I sit across the table from our mothers, the two women who have been pairing us together since we were in the womb, as I wait for Harrison to show up. He was finishing up at the stables and then would be right here. They fill the space with small talk about the weather and complain about the cost of stamps—the same familiar conversations they've had for years.

I glance out the window in the Valentines' kitchen and think about all the times Harrison has sat next to me at this table as our mothers reprimanded us. The stupid shit we used to do as kids got us in trouble, and we had plenty of discussions at this table about why we don't sneak out in the middle of the night or steal horses or climb to the top of trees. My mom learned that I didn't care if she took away my TV or my phone, and Mrs. Valentine figured out that grounding us from each other was the only thing either of us cared about. When my mom wouldn't let me see Harrison, it felt like I was dying. As an adult, it feels the same.

The sound of the front door closing, followed by boots

shuffling against the wooden floor, pulls me from my thoughts. When I turn my head, Harrison walks in wearing that baseball hat. Our eyes meet, and he immediately gives me that sexy-as-fuck smile that melts panties and steals hearts. My heart flutters when he picks up his pace just to place the softest kiss on my lips before sitting next to me.

"This is gonna be a fun conversation," he says, and he sounds excited as he places his arm around me.

When I see the dimple in his cheek appear, I know that he is being genuine.

He clears his throat. "So Grace and I are together," he announces. "Surprise!"

Our mothers cross their arms and glance at each other.

Mom clears her throat and her brow lifts. "Okay? We already knew that."

"No, you didn't," I explain. I shake my head. "We just decided to be official this morning."

They burst into laughter, and when his mama starts choking, my mouth falls open. I glance at Harrison, who shrugs. He predicted this would happen, but I was convinced they'd want to know as soon as we decided not to give a fuck what anyone in town thought. We'll hold hands, we'll kiss—hell, we'll bang on the sidewalk if we want. I don't want to hide him or us anymore, and neither does he.

"I guess I owe you twenty bucks," I tell Harrison.

"And?" He tilts his head, waiting.

"You were right," I mumble.

"Oh, I'm sorry. I didn't hear you?" he singsongs with a laugh.

I groan. "*You were right!*"

He taps my nose. "You're adorable. You still don't realize everyone already knows about us. Titles or not."

"And I was sitting here hoping you were gonna tell us that we'd be grandmas." His mom takes a sip of sweet tea. Then she narrows her eyes at him. "But since you two decided to call this very important meeting to tell us something every person in a hundred-mile radius knows, then I get to ask you two a few questions." She leans forward with that signature Valentine smirk on her lips and meets Harrison's eyes.

Suddenly, we're in the hot seat, not able to predict what she's going to say.

"When is the *real* weddin'?"

Our eyes lock, and just by the soft expression on his handsome face, I know he's remembering the promise he made in Paris. He crossed his heart. He'll keep it. Forever. I feel like I'm falling all over again as those butterflies flutter, and I bump my body against his.

His mom clears her throat to grab our attention.

Harrison interlocks his fingers with mine on top of the table so everyone can see. "Sooner rather than later. That's a promise."

"I always knew you two would end up together," Mom admits. "But Savannah's wedding confirmed it for me."

Harrison chuckles as he rubs his thumb across mine. "Ah, so you *did* see our downward spiral. Was wondering who caught a glimpse of that."

"Honey, I think everyone saw that show in the sand," she says with a chuckle, glancing down at our fingers.

Mrs. Valentine turns her head and looks at my mom. "What are ya talkin' about? You didn't tell me anything happened."

"I know something you don't know," my mom teases, just like I knew she would.

"Sometimes, I wonder why I keep you as my best friend," Mrs. Valentine says, but then she laughs.

"Because no one else would put up with you," my mom confirms.

"True." Then, his mom brings her attention back to us. "How have things been? Hopefully, not too hard."

"Just fine," I say. "There are whispers and rumors, but I'm just letting it slide off of my shoulders. No one knows what happened but us, and I'm okay with that."

When we returned from Paris, it wasn't all shits and giggles, like I'd hoped it would be. I feel awkward in public, like everyone is staring and waiting for the perfect opportunity to ask me questions, to get information, to uncover the truth. You'd think the townsfolk were solving a murder or something. I learned the hard way that running away from my problems didn't work; the issues fester and build, waiting to spill over.

"They'll move on to the next big drama soon, like always," his mom says. "So, back to my original question."

Harrison's thumb runs across mine.

"We're going to get married when we're ready," I explain with a smile. "We decided not to rush it."

He smirks. "I dunno. Twenty-seven years is a long time to be waitin'."

"It doesn't count when we were babies." I narrow my eyes.

"Okay, you two can figure out your love story later," my mom tells us. "So, was this all we needed to talk about?"

I nod. "This was it."

They chuckle like old biddies and shake their heads.

"Congrats, you two. Glad you're *official*," my mom says.

Harrison stands, and his mom looks at him.

"Where are you headin' now?"

"It's a surprise," Harrison says, kissing my fingers and pulling me with him.

I laugh as we walk away.

"Y'all behave," his mom reminds us, as she always did right before we got into some trouble.

Harrison leads me through the living room and outside onto the porch. The front door closes, and he turns around and takes a step forward. Then he smirks and softly presses me against it. I wrap my arms around his neck.

"I'll never get tired of you looking at *me* like that," I whisper.

"Fuck, same."

His lips slam against mine, and our tongues greedily slide together. Just as it grows more heated, the front door opens, and we tumble onto the floor. Harrison is on top of me, laughing his ass off as I lie on my back, making eye contact with our mothers. I feel like I'm fifteen again and just got caught ogling a shirtless Harrison.

"You okay?" he whispers in my ear.

"Just a little mortified," I mutter.

"They're both there, aren't they?" His scruff tickles my neck.

"Yes," I say, glancing back at them as condensation drips from the edge of my ma's glass of tea and drops on my forehead.

I wipe it away as he pushes himself up and grabs my hand, lifting me to him and pulling me down the porch as he continues laughing. Then we wave bye. They return the gesture and then sit in the rocking chairs since it's a nice spring afternoon.

When he opens the passenger door to the truck, I climb inside. We ride down the gravel road, holding hands as dust rises in our wake. I hope the happiness I feel stays forever as my hair whips around in the breeze. When he glances over at me and grins, I return it with an unwavering want in my eyes. There is no putting Pandora back in the box, not with us. Was pretty stupid to think that would ever be possible.

As I glance back out the window, Harrison veers off the gravel road, and then we're taking an old four-wheeler trail.

"Where are we goin'?"

"You'll see," he tells me, shifting the truck into four-wheel drive as it grows rockier.

We bounce around, and I laugh, holding on to the *oh shit* handle as he guns it. Eventually, we're at the top of the outlook. Harrison opens my door, holding out his hand, and I smile when I see the small tent and the firepit. Freshly cut logs are stacked next to it.

I take a few steps forward, resting my hands on my head as I look at the view of the valley.

He moves closer, and I wrap my arm around him, inhaling the smell of leather and soap on his skin.

"Do you remember this place?" he asks.

I look around and see exactly where we are. We used to come up here a lot, but then stopped after a while.

"Yeah, it was one of our sunset spots, a long-ass time ago. Wow," I sigh. "I haven't been here in forever."

He nods. "The last time we were here, you told me you'd given Matt your virginity. Never came back."

My mouth flies open. I don't remember that. "What?"

"I'd brought you up here, and I was going to finally make a move and tell you how I felt, but then I thought you two were serious."

"Then you brought Stephanie to prom," I whisper. "My bad timing and I strike again. But, hey, at least I was consistent over the years. It would *almost* be funny if the joke wasn't always on you."

He wraps his arms around me and kisses my forehead. "Doesn't matter. I know I'm guilty of trying to make you jealous."

"Yeah, it worked. Every time. Asshole," I whisper with a laugh.

"Well, I was thinking we could play a new game and make memories in all the places we'd wanted each other over the years. Replace it all with the good."

I grab his T-shirt in my fists. "I've got more than a few to add to that list."

His brow rises, and he grins. "Yeah? Like where?"

I lean my head against his chest, not afraid to share any truths. Not anymore. "The tree house. Your old bedroom. In the back of your truck. At the pond. In the hayloft. State fair Ferris wheel. The back of Remi's car. At church."

"Damn, girl, but those are already on my list. Just like your mom's couch and the bed-and-breakfast," he says, swaying with me, and we dance in the grass to the rhythm of our fluttering butterflies.

"Scandalous," I whisper as he spins me around. "We're going to hell."

"As long as we're together, no fucks given." His head falls back on his shoulders as he laughs. Soft fingertips brush against my face as I turn my head to kiss him. When he pulls away, he takes the smallest glance at the goose bumps that dance along my skin. He doesn't say anything, but I see a hint of a smirk. Harrison has always noticed. I just didn't notice *him*.

"Maybe I should get this fire started," he says, pulling away.

When it's fully crackling, he pulls chairs from the back of his truck for us, but I sit in his lap, and we watch the sun set below the Davis Mountains. When it's dark, he adds more wood to the fire, and then we lie on a blanket, and he points out the spring constellations as they rise. He talks about the mythology of Leo and Taurus, and when a glittering star shoots across the sky, I point it out.

"Make a wish," he says.

"It's already come true," I tell him, capturing his lips, wanting to lose control with him.

He rolls me over on my back, and the fire gives me the perfect amount of light to see him as his body casts shadows on the ground. His fingers hook into my jeans, and he pulls them off my body, the lace panties going with them. My heart thumps, and ragged breaths release from me as he slips off my shoes. When he leaves the socks on my feet, I chuckle.

"Don't want those cold nubs on me tonight," he whispers, kissing up my calf to the soft skin of my inner thigh until his tongue is on my clit.

My eyes slam closed as he slowly unravels every tangled knot in my heart. I want him to build me up and then tear me down until I'm nothing. And, fuck, he doesn't disappoint as his hands slide up my body and under my T-shirt. When my back arches off the ground, I lose myself in his touch, allowing the orgasm to take over.

My moans echo through the trees, and Harrison laughs.

"Careful. Someone might hear us," he says.

"Smart-ass," I say as he crawls up my body and slowly captures my mouth as our ends meet.

I'll never get used to how full he fills me or how he knows exactly what I like.

"Damn, do I like it hard," I hiss, letting out another loud groan.

And right now, I don't give two shits who hears us.

I hope I wake up the whole damn town.

CHAPTER THIRTY-SIX

HARRISON

The only thing that pulls me from dreamland is the sound of my phone buzzing in my jeans pocket, which is somewhere in this tent. I rustle, looking up at the fairy lights that we made love under and left on.

"No, don't go yet," Grace says as we're snuggled in the double-person sleeping bag together. "You're too warm."

With my chest to her back, her bare ass against me, I grow hard, touching her skin and kissing her neck. She lets out a whimper as I reach around and slide my fingers between her legs.

"Yes," she barely whispers.

My phone stops ringing, and then it immediately starts again.

"Fuck Beckett," I whisper, knowing I'm late to work just based on how light it is outside. I only sleep late when Grace is pressed against my body; she's my comfort.

"You're gonna be in deep shit," she says.

"Don't give a fuck," I mutter, knowing he owes me one from all the shit he and Summer put me through while they were chasing one another. He owes me a hundred after the way he acted.

Grace rolls over onto her back and faces me, but I don't stop lightly circling her clit with my fingertips. She writhes beneath me, and the softest moan releases from her mouth.

When I bend down to kiss her, she stops me. "I have morning breath."

Her hair is messy on her head, and she looks so damn adorable and beautiful.

I move closer to her. "I love your mornin' breath because it means you're waking up beside me."

"And my toots," she says with a laugh, reaching up to kiss me. "Don't forget those, snuggle buddy."

Then she unzips the bag and climbs on top of me. There's just enough morning light for me to see every inch of her as she places her hands on my shoulders, riding me, capturing my mouth. Her pants increase, and I almost wonder how we got here. How is it possible that dreams can come true, that you can be with the person you've always loved? Like this?

I'm the luckiest man in the fucking world.

"What?" She tilts her head.

"You don't know?" I ask, placing my hands behind my head and watching her take all of me.

"You were just thinking about how much you're in love with me. And have always loved me. Want me out of your head yet?"

"Never," I groan, digging my thumbs into her hips as she rides me so damn good. "How'd you know?"

"Because I feel the same," she whispers, tensing and riding out her release.

She keeps going until I follow behind her.

We lie in each other's arms, and I inhale the light vanilla on her skin and smile against the softness of her neck.

"Let's watch the sunrise," I whisper as I snuggle into her.

"Okay," she says.

We clean up and crawl out of the small tent, just big enough for us. We stand naked with the two-person sleeping bag haphazardly wrapped around us, watching it rise over the mountain.

"A new day," she mutters, and then she grins.

I wrap my arm around her waist, pull her close, and place a kiss on her forehead. "A new opportunity."

Pinks and purples splash across the sky, and there are wisps of clouds, followed by a few puffy ones.

When my phone rings again, I know it's time to go. But I turn it off. Beckett can leave me forty voice mails for all I care.

"Want me to take you back to my place or bring you home? Your decision."

She rode with her mom yesterday, so she doesn't have her car.

"Let me drop you off at work, and I'll take your truck back to your place and meet you for lunch." She waggles her brows, laughing.

"That's a damn deal," I say, knowing I don't let anyone other than her drive my truck.

BY THE TIME I'm home and dressed in some worn Wranglers and a T-shirt, I'm more than three hours late.

"Maybe I should just call in sick." I slide my lips across hers. "Lovesick."

Grace shakes her head with a laugh and turns me toward the door. "Time to go, bud. You made your bed, and now you've got to sleep in it. Beckett is gonna be *furious.*"

"Totally worth it," I say as we leave and drive the short distance to the training facility.

It's times like this I'm glad I live five minutes from work. We pull up to the barn. Beckett's truck is parked on the side, along with Sterling's. She hops out of the truck and meets me in the front, claiming my lips before she leaves me.

"Try not to drive it like you drive your car," I tell her.

"Might go for an off-road cruise," she singsongs. "Put that four-wheel drive to use. There's something sexy about a woman in something like this." She pats the dark-green paint.

I shake my head. "Go for it, but no going to DMR, okay? You know how protective I am of my baby."

She snorts. "I wouldn't fuck up your truck."

"I wasn't talking about my truck."

Davis Mountain Resort has the worst roads in the area, and there's no driving to the top without a truck that can handle it. Kinsley had to pick me up a few times when I called in favors, and it busted up her alignment. Something I paid for. But it's also where some shady individuals go to get lost.

She tries to hold back a smile but fails.

"Be good. See you in a few hours for lunch?"

"I'm gonna be the whole buffet." She smirks, then climbs in, sitting behind the wheel.

I adjust the cowboy hat on my head, taking one last look at how damn sexy she is, then shove my hands in my pockets. I make my way through the barn, smelling the sweet scent of spring while I whistle the harmony of one of London's songs that's been stuck in my head.

"You're fired!" I hear Beckett yell from his office.

I make my way through the entryway, walk past the tack and storage room, then enter the office. Beckett is sitting at the desk, and I laugh, plopping down in the chair in front of it, then kicking my boots up on the hardwood. His eyes widen when dried mud falls on a few of his papers.

"Say it to my face," I urge, staring him down with a smirk. "You can't fire me. I own half."

Moments later, I see someone enter the doorway through my peripheral vision, and when I see Grace, I immediately laugh.

"Don't be too mean," she tells Beckett, sitting on my lap, and I wrap my arms around her. "It's kinda my fault."

His face relaxes. Beckett can be pissed at me all day, but when it comes to Grace, he's a softy, and he's always treated her like she's the sixth Valentine sister.

"The only reason I'm not kicking his ass to the curb is because of you," he tells her. "But, damn, am I glad you two finally got your shit together."

Grace bursts into laughter, then shifts her weight to kiss me. "Me too."

"Gonna be completely fuckin' honest though. It's a little strange seeing you two open about it. But, damn, better than all the denial."

I chuckle and give a shitty fake cough. "Think I'm sick today."

Grace turns around and places her hand on my head. "Yeah, I think he's got a fever."

Beckett laughs. "Get the fuck outta here. Both of you. But tomorrow, be on time." Then, he studies Grace. "Make sure he's on time."

She stands and walks around the desk, giving him a tight hug. Beckett squeezes her.

"Glad you two didn't fuck this up."

"Damn, me too," I say, holding out my hand, and Grace takes it. "Thanks, bro."

"Get outta here before I change my mind," he says, but he's smiling.

Grace and I pick up our pace, and I lead her through the barn. I glance at the ladder, then lift a brow.

She chews on the corner of her lip before turning and climbing up. I follow behind her, and we tumble on top of the loose hay, and she giggles.

"Nope!" Beckett yells from the ground.

"He's down there," Grace whispers as I lay her back down.

Her dark hair is splayed around her head, and she's grinning with hooded eyes.

"No fuckin' in the loft! We had an agreement, Harrison!" he growls, and then I hear him climbing the wooden ladder.

I dip down and kiss her. "We're gonna have to take a rain check on this spot."

"Okay," she whispers. "I love that this is our life."

"Forever," I say.

"It's a life sentence," she reminds me just as Beckett's head pops up behind us.

"Down. Now." He holds on with one hand and points with the other.

"Is that your dad voice?" I turn and look at him, and his face whitens. I sit up, turning all of my attention to him, and Grace sits up with hay in her hair.

His mouth falls open and then closes.

"Is Summer pregnant?" I lower my voice, meeting his eyes, and there is no doubt about it in his expression.

"I'm not having this discussion," he says.

A roar of laughter releases from me as Beckett climbs down. I smack a kiss on Grace's mouth, and then we follow Beckett. When he turns around, I wrap him in a tight hug.

"Congrats, man. That's exciting. Starting your family with the woman of your life."

"Fuck, I knew I'd be the one to slip," he says. "But we're not telling anyone yet because it's still the danger zone, ya know. So, you'd both better keep your goddamn mouths shut. And when we announce it to the entire family, you'd both better act surprised, like I laid a golden egg or some shit. Because if Mama finds out you two knew before her …"

"We're not telling anyone," Grace says, hugging him too. "What about the wedding?"

He meets Grace's eyes. "You think you can put one together in a month? She already started talking about not having a shotgun wedding and everything else. You know how Summer gets."

"I do." Her head falls back in laughter, and she glances my way. "A month is nothing, considering what I pulled off before. We'll get you two hitched before she starts showing. Our secret. Won't say a thing. I'll call her and tell her you were so desperate to make her your wife that you *forced* me to call her."

"Plausible." I shrug. "He is an asshole and impatient."

Beckett flips me off, and he sighs. "Kinda feels good to tell someone though. Found out when you were in Paris. Pretty sure you would've figured it out had you been here."

"Sterling didn't notice you were off?"

Beckett laughs. "He's about to be nineteen, and he doesn't pay attention to us. Honestly, makes me feel old as fuck."

Grace nods. "Is the house y'all are building almost ready?"

"Yes. I love living in the one-bedroom together, but it's … tight. With a baby on the way, that shit won't fly."

"Perfect timing," I tell him, and then I meet his eyes. "If you need anything, will you let me know? Sincerely. I'm here for you, bro."

Beckett pulls me into another strong hug. "Happy for you. Now, can you please leave? Go spend the rest of the day together or something?"

I smile, wrapping my arm around Grace like we used to do all those years ago. She'd sit on a bucket and watch me muck stalls or bale hale or train. Plenty of times, we walked through the barn with my arm just like this. I lean over and kiss the top of her head as she wraps her arm around me.

"I'm glad your sister lit that love spell candle for me."

"Kinsley?" I laugh. "Oh God."

Then she cracks up as I lift her into my arms and carry her out of the barn to the truck.

"You're showing off," she says, wrapping her arms around my neck.

"I always will when it comes to you," I tell her, setting her down by the truck. Her back pressed against it.

She looks up into my eyes, and by the look on her face, I have an idea of what's on her mind. So, I wait to see if I'm right.

"The loft was a no, but …" She glances at the back seat.

"Get out of my head," I say.

"No can do," she tells me as we climb into the back like teenagers.

And when my mouth is on her, I'm thankful for tinted windows and woo-woo love spell candles.

CHAPTER THIRTY-SEVEN

GRACE

I wake up with Harrison holding me, his warm chest pressed against my back. When I move, I feel him smile.

"You're the best big spoon," I whisper, stretching my legs and rolling onto my back.

He opens his big blue eyes. "Move in with me."

"What?" I say, thinking I must still be asleep.

"Move in with me. I don't want you to have to leave me. My sister will figure it out. We'll find her another roommate," he says.

I laugh. "Okay. And be roommates with you and Colt?"

"No. Beckett and Summer are moving into the house they built on Horseshoe. That means Beckett's place will be open. We can live on the ranch, just me and you in our own space."

I search his face. "You're serious."

"As a fuckin' heart attack."

"Yes," I whisper. "But if I don't get up and pee right now…"

He chuckles and lifts his arm so I can scoot out. I slide on my pajama pants and T-shirt, then sneak to the bathroom, hoping I don't wake up Colt because it's still early. When I look in the hallway, I see my panties on the floor from where Harrison peeled them off of me last night. I hurry, pick them up, and carry them with me to the bathroom, where I empty my bladder.

Then I realize I'm in Harrison's house, and he's naked in his bed, waiting for me. I smile, not knowing how this is my life, but I'm so damn grateful it is.

As I'm washing my hands, the door swings open, and Harrison moves behind me. "What are you smiling about?"

"You. Us," I whisper.

His fingers slide against the small of my back. I meet his eyes in the mirror.

"It all worked out. Like always."

He kisses the back of my head, and as he uses the bathroom, I climb back into his bed, staring at the ceiling. A minute later, he's walking toward me, lying down next to me.

"What are your plans today?"

"I'm working on my website today, and I have a meeting with a client at the coffee shop this afternoon."

He leans over, kissing me. "I'll meet you there after work. Maybe we can grab dinner at the café?"

"That sounds so good. I'll miss you," I tell him, kissing his nose, knowing he needs to get dressed for work but also selfishly loving lying with him.

"Same," he says, pulling me to him.

I smile against his lips. "Looking forward to being your roommate, bestie."

"Hell yeah."

We pull ourselves away from one another and get dressed. Colt is awake, and I can smell the Folgers brewing in the kitchen. I open the door and walk out, seeing him standing there at the kitchen sink with his glasses on.

"You and Remi have the same frames."

"Not on purpose." He gives me a grin.

Harrison walks behind me, grinning. "It's weird twin shit." He swipes his to-go coffee mug off the counter and fills it with coffee.

"You basically took the whole pot," Colt says, shaking his head. "You suck."

"Thanks. If I'm late, Beckett is going to start throwing punches. I owe you." Harrison laughs and places his hand on his brother's shoulder. "Oh yeah, I'm moving out."

Harrison grabs his mug and walks toward me.

"Seriously?" Then Colt gives a fist pump.

"And I thought you'd be upset that I was stealing your roommate," I tell him with a laugh.

"Absolutely not. He's your problem now." Colt smirks as Harrison wraps his arm around my shoulder and leads me outside.

He leans forward and kisses me. "I love you."

"I love you, too," I whisper, then we go our separate ways.

I'm all smiles as I head home.

By the time I make it to town, everyone is waking up, and the gas station is full of people filling up their tanks. The early shoppers are parked at the grocery store, and the line of customers is pouring out of the bakery. I pass by it all, not stopping until my car is in my driveway. Now that some time has passed, everyone is aware that Harrison and I are together and that we're officially dating.

I guess no one in Valentine needed an announcement after they witnessed the wedding of the year being called off in real time. When I play back the fuzzy memory in my head, it replays like a cheap reality TV show, but hell, I'd do it again. Because now, the dust has settled, and most people have moved on to the next rumor. Our PDA doesn't even get a second glance anymore; it's like we've always been this way. And it's freeing to be openly in love with my best friend. No one questions if we're supposed to be together. I sat at a table for one for a long time, and I'm glad I woke the hell up.

I didn't know life could be like this, and each day I wake up, I get to live in my very own romance movie with my best friend. The good guy got the girl, so all that's left is our happily ever after, and we're writing that part of our story right now.

After I work on my website for a few hours, I look at all the stuff I have in my condo and smile, thinking about moving in with Harrison. I just hope Remi takes it okay because we've grown close, living together. She kept my secrets, and I'll keep hers; it's a pact we have.

When I look at the clock, I realize I need to make my way to the coffee shop. Once I grab my drink, I sit at the far table by the window so I can people-watch. I open my laptop to kill some time. I review what I did earlier, and as I get ready to close out everything, someone approaches.

I look up and see Stephanie with her blonde hair curled at the ends. I stand and pull her into a tight hug.

"I'm sorry I needed you to meet me at the last minute," she says, sitting in the chair in front of me.

"It's totally fine. Wait, let me see first," I say, and she holds out her hand and shows me the ring.

The guy she met after calling off the wedding is her *forever* person, and she's engaged again. But to someone she can't keep her hands off of, who's also obsessed with her. I know because I watched them nearly bang at the café last week when I ate breakfast with Remi.

The week after I got back from Paris, I asked to meet with her. We had a long talk. Then we both cried tears of happiness that one of us had come to our senses. We've randomly texted here and there, and there is no bad blood between us. We went through too much shit together; it's water under the bridge.

"So, you're sure about this one?" I meet her eyes with a smile, glancing down at the rock on her tiny finger.

"You've seen him. Of course I am. And there is only one person I trust who can plan a magical wedding. You've already done it once." She laughs. "And you kinda owe me."

This makes me laugh. "I owe you my firstborn and a million thank-yous."

"How is Harrison doing these days?" she asks.

"Ask him yourself," I say as soon as he walks in the door, wearing those old, worn jeans with his damp hair a mess on his head. Freshly showered—my favorite.

Stephanie turns around, and when he's close, he pulls her into a hug.

She grins and takes a step back, scanning him from head to toe. "Happy looks good on you."

"You too," Harrison tells her and takes the seat close to me, wrapping his arm around my shoulder. "We can't be late," he whispers.

Stephanie notices and starts digging into her purse. She hands me a piece of paper that's meticulously organized into boxes. "My wedding wish list."

I scan over it. Fresh flowers. Archways. Appetizers. A wine garden. "How long do I have?"

"One …"

I suck in a breath.

"Year," she says with a giggle. "Going for a *long* engagement this time. The first two didn't last six months, so I thought I'd double it or nothing with this one."

I snicker. "I'll make sure it's the wedding of the century. The third time's a charm, right?"

"Yeah. So, what about you two?" She smirks. "Not seeing a ring on that finger yet."

Harrison laughs. "Soon. Could be tomorrow. Or next week. Six months. I guess we'll see."

I look at him. "Are you chicken?"

"We can go down to the courthouse and get hitched tomorrow," he says. "First thing when they open. If that's what you want."

My mouth falls open. "Seriously?"

Stephanie knocks on the table. "Please do. I'll be your witness because what are you waiting for? To get struck by lightning?"

"Now you sound like my mama," I say, pulling my focus from Harrison and giving her a smile.

"Thanks, Grace. You're the best." She looks at Harrison. "She's the best."

"I know." He shrugs with a smirk.

She turns on her heel, laughing, and walks to the door like a runway model, still looking like a whole-ass adult with jewelry, high heels, and a pantsuit without a hair out of place.

Harrison turns to me. "You almost let me marry her."

I burst out into laughter. "Let's not forget that you slid the ring on that finger."

He nuzzles into my neck and smiles. "I love you."

"I love you. Want to grab a coffee?" I lift mine and take a sip.

"Nah, I'm good. Let's go," he says.

I place my laptop and bag in the trunk of my car, and then we walk over to the bench that overlooks the dog park. We used to sit here and talk for hours as I made friendship bracelets for him when we were kids. In the summer, it was the best, with a makeshift water park and snow cone stands. Harrison sits and opens his arm, and I lean into him as we watch people play with their dogs.

"Can we get a dog one day?" I ask him.

"If you want one," he tells me. "What kind do you want?"

"A rottweiler," I tell him and laugh. "They're cute."

He tucks hair behind my ear. "You know I wasn't joking back there," he says. "About marrying you tomorrow."

I meet his eyes, glancing down at his lips. "I'd marry you tomorrow." I smile.

Then he drops down onto one knee in front of me and pulls the box out of his pocket. My mouth falls open, and I burst out into giddy laughter because I can't find my voice.

"I'm so madly in love with you, Gracie. It's always been you. And without a doubt in my mind, you're the only woman for me. I love you. I'm *in love* with you, and I always have been. And you'd make me the happiest man on the entire earth if you'd be my best friend forever and my wife and queen. Will you marry me *tomorrow?*"

I move forward, falling in front of him, my mouth slamming against his. "Yes," I whisper. "Yes."

The ring falls out of his hand as his arms wrap around me. We roll on the grass, laughing. Nothing interrupts us or our moment.

Harrison reaches up above his head and grabs the box as we lie on the ground. Then he rolls onto his side and lifts onto his elbow, facing me. He grabs my hand and slides the ring onto my finger.

I look down, noticing the intricate carving on the side, then lift my necklace. "It matches."

He nods. "I bought the set years ago, and I thought of you when I saw it," he admits. "The hearts. Our hearts. Your Valentine."

"Years ago?"

"I knew I wanted to marry you when I was old enough to vote, Gracie. Was just waitin' for the perfect time," he whispers, his mouth dancing across mine. "I want to spend forever with you."

"I love you," I whisper. "I'm so lucky. But would you mind if we had an engagement party first?"

He holds me and smiles. "Whatever you want, babe.

Engagement party. Then we can plan a wedding. And move in together. Just really pushing the gas on it, aren't I?"

I'm giddy. "I love it. But, shit, I need a party dress, and you need—"

He shakes his head. "I'm wearing my navy suit, princess."

And he leaves me breathless.

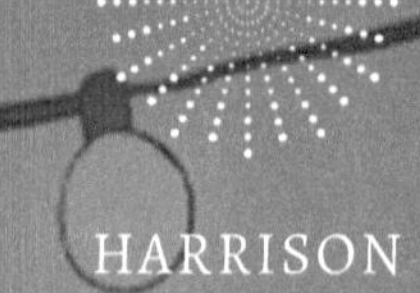

CHAPTER THIRTY-EIGHT

Grace is talking to her mom on the phone. She's been trying to calm people down all day. "I know we invited a lot of people last minute. We wanted to celebrate. Wear whatever you feel comfortable in. It seriously doesn't matter. See you in an hour."

I lean against the doorway of her room and grin because she's wearing my favorite color.

"Do you know how many people have asked me about the dress code today on top of everything else?"

I take several steps forward and cup her face in my hands. "You're wearing my favorite color."

A sly smile slides over her face as her eyes flick over me. "You make me weak."

"Feeling is mutual," I tell her, grazing my thumb across the bottom of her ruby-red lips. A ragged breath escapes her. "We should probably get goin' though."

"You're right about that because if we stand here for one more minute with you dressed like that, there's no way we'll make it," she says, adjusting my tie.

"But we'd show up fashionably *just fucked* late. Kinda worth it to me," I say, and she shakes her head as I pull her into my arms, and we dance in her bedroom. "You're sure?"

"Yes." No hesitation.

I shoot her a smirk, take her hand, and we leave.

We pull up to my parents' house and see all the vehicles parked in the front; so many that I think I might have to drop Grace off and then walk, but I squeeze in next to Emmett's truck. He might have a bitch of a time getting into the driver's side, though, because I'm close. So close that I have to climb over the passenger side.

Grace shakes her head. "Never pass up an opportunity, do you?"

"When it comes to my brothers? Fuck no," I say, interlocking my fingers with hers as we walk across the grass.

I look over at her, her hair blowing in the light breeze, and smile. As always, she returns it, and it's a snapshot that's burned into my brain forever.

We walk on the side of the house, hearing the music drifting from the backyard, where the get-together is being held. Somehow, Grace miraculously got someone to cater some snacks and booze, and she even had Sadie, my favorite woman in the world who owns the bakery, make us several strawberry cakes. Then we stop at the edge of the house and spy, like we used to do when my parents had parties that lasted through the night when we were kids.

Lights are strung above the area. The gazebo is decorated, along with every tree in their backyard. High tables are also set up for people to set their drinks on and chat. It's a mingling type of event, a simple celebration without all the bigness. Exactly the way I wanted it.

"How did you pull this off?" I ask as she leans her shoulder against the house as we continue to watch from a distance.

"I called in a few favors," she admits. "From someone who had a lot of this in storage."

I laugh, knowing she contacted Stephanie, who was probably more than willing to help out. I scan across the backyard, seeing all of our friends, family, and our parents.

Then I look at her. "You invited your dad and Tanya?"

"Yeah," she says, turning to me. "I realize people do stupid things for love. I'm over it. After nearly becoming the home-wrecker twice, I get it."

I tilt her chin up and kiss her ruby-red lips. When I pull away, I see Savannah and her new husband. "Look who else showed up."

"Wow. Everyone is here," Grace whispers and grins. "I told her she can't miss today. It's a miracle she found a flight."

Then I see London with her guitar and a microphone.

"You asked London to play?" I laugh, loving that she thought of everything. Each detail is perfection.

Grace nods, pulling me in for a kiss. "Of course I did. There's no way you can have a party without having her play. That's a dick thing to do."

"I know." I chuckle as I hear the light strum of her guitar as she tunes it. Then I wrap my arms around her. "I love you."

"I love you. Let's have some fun," she says.

She grabs my hand and pulls me with her, leading us into the crowd of smiling faces. All eyes are on us as we greet everyone, thanking them for coming. We're handed champagne from a tray, and we hear my sister's and the other guitars strumming.

"Yay! Congrats, you two," Kinsley says, lifting her glass as Hayden holds on to her. "Remember, you can't get married before me."

I give her a hug. "I love ya, but I can't make any guarantees."

As we make our way across the grass, I meet London's gaze and shoot her a wink, and she nods at me and whispers, "Thank you."

I'm so damn glad Grace asked her to be a part of this.

We pass a table with snacks, and Grace snags a tiny quiche.

"Look how cute it is!" Then she pops it in her mouth and nods. "Yep, totally suggesting these to every bride I ever meet going forward."

I try one too. "You're right. We're taking those home with us if they don't get eaten."

"Deal," she says with a laugh.

My mom and dad meet up with us, and what can I say? We're huggers in our family.

"So excited about this, sweetie," my mom says as Grace's mom walks over.

Kathy is over the moon excited. "Okay, so now, work on those grandkids," she says.

"I agree," my mom adds.

"We're goin' the traditional route. Gotta get married first," I remind them, then meet Grace's eyes with a smirk as she chats with Remi.

They seem to be having some sort of important discussion, and Grace places her hand on her shoulder. I want to eavesdrop but continue occupying our folks.

Remi smiles at me, then walks away. My phone vibrates in my pocket, and I excuse myself from the conversation and go to Grace.

"It's time, princess." I place my hand on her elbow and lean in. "Everyone is here."

She nods then meets my eyes, clearing her throat. "Attention y'all!"

The crowd hushes and turns to us. I stand back with my hands in my pockets, loving to see her in her element like this. When my eyes trail over the crowd, I see a smile on every face.

"So, hi. Wow, you all look so gorgeous out there," Grace says.

Then she looks at me, and I pull my phone out and start recording.

All eyes flick to me. "Sorry. Don't mind me. I just want to

remember this moment for the rest of my life. Because tonight, we're not here, *just* celebrating an engagement."

I can barely hold back my laugh.

"Surprise! We're getting married *tonight*. Right here, right now!" Grace says.

The crowd gasps and bursts into applause as she grabs my hand and interlocks her fingers with mine. I nearly piss myself; it's so funny. My ma is holding her hand over her chest, but she's crying and thanking Jesus, I think. Cash is on the back porch in the rocking chair, chatting with Remi. He smooths his hands down his black tailored suit and stands. Then he coolly makes his way to the front, and I'm so glad I'm recording their expressions. See, everyone thinks I don't listen to them when they talk about random shit. Beckett told me years ago that Cash had gotten his certification to marry people. It was good information to lock away, something I never forgot in a pinch. If it wasn't for him telling us to go apply for our wedding license before the courthouse closed, it wouldn't have been legal.

I take Grace's hand and kiss her fingers as we wait for Cash.

When he's close, he reaches his hand out and gives me a firm shake. "Congrats, man. Real happy for you. Love like this is hard to find."

"Thank you," I tell him as he stands in place.

I suck in a deep breath, listening to the faint sound of the crickets in the background as I face Grace. She's fucking glowing with her curls and red lips, and that's when I notice the tiara she's wearing in her hair.

My queen.

"You wore a crown," I whisper.

She nods. It takes everything I have not to bow down and unapologetically worship her right here. That's what she does to me each time I smell the warm vanilla on her skin; it drives me wild. Or maybe it's just being with her in general. Together, we're a runaway train.

Cash clears his throat and raises his voice so everyone can hear. "So, we're gathered here this evening to celebrate two people who were so clearly meant to be together …"

He continues, and I don't hear anything because I'm lost in the dark depths of Grace's chestnut-colored eyes, smiling and wiping away her happy tears. I can't help but notice how her lips slightly tilt up anytime Cash says *husband and wife*.

"The couple decided to write their vows," he continues. "Harrison, you're first."

"Gracie …" I clear my throat, holding Grace's hands, and smile. I didn't need to write down a damn word, knowing what I want to say to her by heart. Adrenaline rushes through me because I'm minutes away from having the only thing I've ever wanted, dreamed, prayed, or wished for—having my best friend as my wife. "I promised you I wouldn't get married before you. I just want to say, you get to say *I do* first."

Everyone chuckles. But Gracie looks like she hasn't taken a breath since I started talking.

"Breathe, princess," I whisper, and she smiles.

"You stole my breath away," she whispers.

I chuckle. "Articulating how you make me feel in just a few sentences is impossible; the words don't even exist. But I'll try. A life without you isn't a life worth living, and I promise you," I lean in and whisper in her ear so only she can hear, "with an *X* over my heart"—I nibble on her ear—"that I will be with you through thick and thin, through the good and the bad, through all the messy love. A lifetime isn't enough. I promise to never let you buy yourself flowers, to love your hair whether it's short or long, and, yes, I'll always watch those corny rom-com movies with you, with hopes that I can continue to give us our own movie moments. Princess, you're my everything, my forever person, my BFF, and my soon-to-be wife. Being with you is proof that dreams come true, and I will always be Team Grace. Oh, and here's your big, fat Valentine *I told ya so.*"

"The Kiss of Death," she whispers with a laugh, and I wipe more happy tears away.

"I love you."

"I love you. We're getting married," she whispers, smiling.

I reach forward and brush my thumb across her cheek. "Don't ever change."

The smile on her face doesn't falter as she tries to hold back laughter. She holds her hand out to the audience. "Sorry, I've got the giggles."

As soon as she looks at me, I cross my eyes at her, and she snorts, and then I start laughing with her. Right now, it's like no one is here but us. I've completely blocked out everything other than her. A light breeze blows in her hair, and I twist one of her curls around my finger, just like I used to do when we were kids, sitting in front of each other, coloring. Now she's going to be my wife.

"Grace," Cash whispers, bringing us back because, right now, we're love drunk. It's the only way I can explain it.

"Yes?" she asks, grabbing both of my hands and squeezing them, not giving a fuck that we're waiting on her.

It's just me and my girl.

I meet her eyes, barely lifting my brow, wearing that smirk she loves.

"That was ten out of ten."

"Really?" I chuckle.

Cash clears his throat, and Gracie smiles wide.

Something flashes in her eyes, and she says, "I've tried to think about a time when you weren't in my life, and it doesn't really exist. But I remember the moment you told me I was going to be yours. First grade. Mrs. Bailey's class. Our mothers dressed us up in matching costumes for Halloween and you were Prince Charming, and I was Cinderella, and even though I was six years old, you swept me off my feet. And you've been doing it every day since.

"I've never loved anyone as much as I love you. I didn't know this feeling was possible, and I never want it to end. I promise to be your best friend for the rest of my days. I'll be your annoying roommate too. And I promise to love you deeply and *fearlessly* with every inch of my being.

"When we crossed the line, I wasn't sure about us, but I was always afraid of losing you, and right now, I'm promising you that I will never let you go. Never again. As I am standing here right now, getting ready to be your wife, there ain't a single doubt in my mind that we were always meant to be. Just like this. Me and you. *G* and *H*—our initials are even next to each other in the alphabet. This is the way it was always supposed to be with my best friend forever. I love you and can't wait to be *your* Valentine for once."

"Always were," I whisper.

Then, we hold a silent conversation as emotions soar through me. I can see the pulse in her neck quicken as she smiles, and all I want to do is pick her up and carry her away from this, from the attention, and be alone. Because the reality is, she's all I need. She's all I want. My forever. And today, I kept my promise to her, just like all the others we've ever made.

"It's time for the ring exchange," Cash whispers, handing Grace one and me the other.

Since we filled him in on what was going to happen, we also gave him the rings. I'd already had Grace's set, but we had driven to El Paso, found a jewelry store and picked out mine.

When Grace is asked if she'll take me as her husband, she meets my eyes and a silent conversation streams between us.

"Yes." It comes out like a whispered prayer, but there is no hesitation.

"Harrison, do you take Grace to be your wedded wife?"

"Yes," I say with a promise, not able to remove my gaze from hers as we exchange rings. A magnetic force nearly pushes us together and it feels like we're the only people in the room.

Cash smiles at both of us and continues, "Harrison and Grace, you have publicly promised your love and commitment. I call upon all gathered here to witness that you are now wed. I'm so honored to introduce Mr. and Mrs. Valentine."

I don't even wait for him to give me permission before I remove the space between us.

"You can kiss your bride," he announces and begins clapping.

Excitement and joy, as I've never felt before, rush through me as I gently nibble on her lip before she claims my mouth right at golden hour, and it feels magical, everything glowing yellow. I'm so desperate to be close to her as my tongue gently slides against hers. We almost lose control.

I dip her, and she holds on to me as I softly laugh against her lips.

"My wife," I whisper.

"My husband," she says back as I bring her up, kissing her the entire way. "You're mine, Harrison."

"Forever." I draw an *X* over my heart and grin.

Everyone stands, applauding us, and we turn around, holding our interlocked fingers in the air.

"We did it," she whispers.

"You did promise me you'd be my forever princess when we were six," I tell her.

She snorts. "I always keep my promises to you."

"I want my five hundred dollars back," Beckett yells across the way to Cash, and I burst into laughter.

London starts strumming "Tennessee Whiskey." Her voice is fucking perfect for this song, and when I pull Grace into my arms, I see the goose bumps form.

"Wanna dance?" I ask Grace.

"We are," she says, slipping off her shoes, and then she smiles wide at London, who shoots her a wink.

Grace dances with me barefoot as the stars appear in my

parents' backyard. It really doesn't get any better than this. I spin her around and then bring her back to me.

"That dress, goddamn," I whisper.

She laughs, then looks up at me. "We're married."

I kiss her, resting my hand on the top of her perfect ass. "And nobody had a heart attack," I say, just as my parents dance by us, laughing.

Mom shakes her head. "I told you no more surprises at weddings or you were gonna be in big trouble."

I glance at Grace. "It was her idea."

"You're just gonna rat me out like that?" she asks.

I spin her around, bringing her back close for another kiss. She looks up at me with stars in her eyes, and I smirk.

I lean down and whisper in her ear, "Keep it up, and we might have to go to the tree house."

Her head falls back on her shoulders. "Don't tempt me with a good time."

Kinsley dances over toward us. "I knew you two were up to something."

"Nah," I say with a laugh as the song ends.

"I'll be right back," Grace says, then points to her sister and her dad.

I give her a nod, then bring my attention back to Kinsley as Beckett comes over. He pulls me into a strong hug, and Emmett walks up.

"Well, stranger. Nice to see you."

"I've been so busy with the cattle lately. I don't have a life. Going to stop being a recluse though," he says. "Didn't realize how fast shit had changed with you and Grace. Congrats, dude."

"Wild, isn't it?" Beckett says with a laugh. "Still not used to it. But I'm getting there."

Grace returns to me, smiling wide, and I'm sure she knows she is the center of our conversation. Hell, she always is. I glance around, my eyes scanning over the backyard, and see the tree house. I lean in and whisper in her ear, "Want to escape with me?"

"Yes," she says.

I lead her to the side of the house, and we hide in the dark as I press her against it.

"Fuck, you're hard," she whispers as I kiss her neck.

"Look who my wife is," I say. "Come on."

Then I take her hand, and we sneak off to the large tree where our old tree house is. I let her go up first. She turns around and looks down at me.

"Are you lookin' at my panties?" She laughs.

"No, because you're not wearing any," I tell her, climbing up behind her.

She's slightly slouched with her hands over her mouth. "You decorated."

I move closer to her, laying her down on the bed I made for us. The fairy lights above give me the perfect amount of light to see her.

"Come here, hubby," she mutters so seductively as she pulls my tie with her fist.

Her lips slam against mine, and we desperately kiss like we're doing it for the first time, but that's how it feels with her.

I unbutton the jacket of my navy suit.

She looks at me and smiles. "I think that thing might be your lucky charm."

"I think you might be right. Or your kryptonite."

"Both," she whispers against my lips. "You feel it too, right? That … electricity." She gently parts her legs, reaching forward for my belt, button, and zipper.

Sparks, electricity, every fucking time. It's never gone away. It's stronger than ever.

"Yes," I tell her, meeting her eyes as she pushes down my boxers. My cock springs free, and I impatiently wait, pausing at her entrance, kissing her all over before I give it to her inch by inch. "You're … intoxicating. Every part of you is addictive."

Grace's head falls back, and our soft pants fill the small space.

I put my finger over my mouth. "Shh." I laugh. "Our parents are down there."

"Shit," she hisses, her back arching. "More. I need more of you. *So. Fucking. Bad.*"

When her mouth flies open, I slide my lips down her face and pepper kisses along her jaw. "Come for me, *my wife.*"

CHAPTER THIRTY-NINE

His words break me, and the orgasm rips me to fucking shreds on the floor of the tree house. Then, soon, he's chasing his release, then collapsing on top of me, and we kiss and laugh.

"If I could go back in time, I'd bitch-slap younger me. Because had I found sex like that … well, I'd probably be knocked up with eighteen kids right now," I say.

He smiles against my skin. "Who says you still won't be?"

"Considering I already want you again and I barely have my breath, you're probably right, but I want to enjoy you—all of you—first. Enjoy the good, the *us, like this*," I whisper.

He nuzzles against me. "I love the sound of that, princess. I don't want to rush us either. We have forever."

I run my fingers through his hair, then trail down his biceps and see goose bumps flood his arm. "You get them too?"

That little dimple is on full display. "Of course I do."

I kiss him, and we clean up. Then he slides his pants on, and we lie back on the bed.

"Those glow-in-the-dark stars are still there?"

"Yeah," he says, reaching behind him and clicking the light off.

Then we hold each other under the plastic green-glowing stars that we stuck up there one summer.

"You know, I think the Kiss of Death has been activated since the very first time we kissed."

He chuckles. "Shit, that festered for a long-ass time."

"But we ended up here," I say, drawing circles on his skin.

Just as I'm nearly falling asleep in Harrison's arms, I hear something. His eyes fly open, and he hears it too. Then I look out the side window and see Remi in Harrison's old bedroom. She's talking to someone and shaking her head. When she turns around, I see a hand in a suit fly forward to gently grab her. Harrison's head pops up, and we sit on our knees.

"Who is she talking to?" he whispers as we hide in the shadows, like we're twelve again, spying on people.

"I don't know," I tell him, trying to make out what she's saying.

He opens his mouth to whisper, and I quickly shush him. It's a man's voice. Deep. Then I see the black suit arm and the gold cuff links, and I know who it is.

"Tell me," Harrison whispers. "I saw it on your face. You've figured out who it is."

"Sometimes, it's annoying how well you can read me."

Then Cash steps forward, and he and Remi kiss.

My eyes widen, and Harrison's jaw clenches. When it comes to his sisters, he's a terror.

I grab Harrison's hand, and I hold it tight. "Don't."

"What the fuck?" he hisses.

"Look, you told me that Remi owed you ten, right?"

"Nine," he corrects.

"Okay, then make it eight. Seriously, if you have to take away every single one of her favors based on how many times you've caught her with someone, then do it, but now is not the time. Save it."

Harrison narrows his eyes. "Sometimes, it's annoying how logical you can be." But then he slides his mouth against mine. "She does one thing to piss me off, and I'm telling Beckett. And he's gonna lose his shit. The age difference."

"It's ten years," I tell him. "It's not that big of a gap."

"For my little sister? Yes, it is."

I laugh, placing my lips against his. "You're gonna be an asshole father, aren't you?"

"Oh fuck, get the shotguns ready," he says, sliding his mouth back to mine, laying me back down on the bed. "I love you, Gracie."

"You once told me that you'd help me get my happily ever after. Did you know it'd be you?"

"Yes," he whispers. "Let's get out of here."

"Okay," I tell him, wrapping him in my arms and pulling him in for a kiss as he lifts us forward.

Once he's dressed, Harrison meets my eyes.

"How do I look?" I ask.

"Like you always do. Guilty as fuck."

"Great!" I say, throwing my hands in the air, just like I do every single time he tells me that.

I no longer have to hide kissing or touching him. Now, I get to live my fairy tale with this perfect man.

He climbs down first and holds his arms out just in case I fall. But he doesn't have to catch me this time.

I make it to the ground, and soon, I see Remi pushing open the back door of the house, meeting everyone in the backyard again. Two minutes later, Cash follows. Harrison meets my eyes.

"Make it seven," he says, and I chuckle.

"She's fucked," I mutter, swiping a glass of champagne from the table.

Then we go to the dance floor and dance with Kinsley, and we sing with London. She laughs into the microphone.

"Oh my God, there you two are," she yells.

Harrison keeps his hand on my waist.

"Sorry, we had to take care of something," he tells her.

I burst out laughing, then glance back at my husband.

Just as the song changes, he pulls me in, and we slow dance. And for a brief moment, we're in Hawaii again, toes in the sand, but this time, I don't run away.

Summer and Beckett dance beside us. Harrison and I have kept their secret, and still, Summer doesn't know that we know. We won't tell either. We promised each other.

"Thanks for setting up the cake tasting, Grace. Seriously, the chocolate was to die for."

Beckett laughs. "Yeah, I can't believe it's happening so quickly."

"What is?" Harrison asks.

Summer shakes her head but chuckles when Beckett groans. It's become a running joke where he acts like he doesn't remember they're getting married in less than two weeks, even though he's the best man. He's already been fitted for a tux, and he's hella excited for his brother. I find it cute how they've always teased each other. It's just how the Valentines are.

Emmett marches across the grass, and I can tell he's pissed.

"You're an asshole," he says to Harrison when he's closer. "I just went to get something out of my truck. Dickhead."

"I know." He chuckles. "I'm sorry. Just wanted to get a rise out of you 'cause I miss ya. That's all."

Emmett's expression softens. "I know. Sorry, man. I've been traveling a lot, and Dad is working my ass off."

"You can always come join us at Horseshoe," he tells him as we sway together.

"You two are cute," he says.

"Mainly her," Harrison tells him.

Emmett flashes him that Valentine smirk. "You know what Dad said about poaching his employees."

Harrison laughs. "Just think about it. We're a lot more fun. Now, I'm gonna go back to dancing with *my wife*."

Then he spins us around and captures my lips again.

"This feels like home," I whisper in his ear.

"And there ain't no place like it," he says, placing a kiss on my neck. "Let's go back to Hawaii. And do it right."

"You mean it?" I pull away, asking.

"Fuck yes," he says, and I laugh. "Next week?"

"Can't. Your brother and Summer are getting married."

"Oh, right," he says with a laugh.

When Harrison walks off to get a glass of champagne for us, my dad walks up and dances with me. I see my mom chatting with Tanya, and they're laughing about something. I guess it all works out, doesn't it?

My dad and I make small talk, and I see Harrison standing off to the side with his hand in his pocket, smirking. He lifts his glass at me, and I grin.

"You know, I don't think I ever got to tell you this, but I'm sorry about everything that happened between me and your mom."

"You don't have to apologize," I tell him. "After everything that's happened, I actually kinda understand it. Sucks it happened, but it all worked out. Mom is happy. You're happy. I learned that I'd rather see people in a happy relationship than pretend. That's not a way to live."

Dad chuckles. "No. It's not. I'm proud of you," he tells me.

"Thank you," I say, not knowing why I feel my emotions bubbling. Maybe because it's the realest conversation I've had with him since they sat me down and told me they were divorcing.

"Let's not be strangers anymore," he tells me. "Maybe you and Harrison can join us for dinner one night?"

In the past, I'd skip every invitation he gave. It's not that he wasn't trying; it's that I didn't give him a chance.

"Okay, yeah, I'd like that."

A few tears fall, and I wipe them away.

Moments later, Harrison is cutting in.

"May I dance with my wife?" he politely asks, and my dad gives him a firm handshake, then passes me off to him.

"You okay?" he whispers, keeping his mouth close to my ear.

"Yeah, he invited us to dinner."

"And?" Harrison meets my gaze, then smiles, knowing I actually said yes this time. "Just tell me when."

"I will," I say, swaying to the music, drowning in the smell of his cologne and his touch.

"You ready to get out of here?" Harrison finally asks, and I nod.

In one swift movement, he's lifting me up and carrying me in his arms. "Bye, y'all. Have fun."

Everyone laughs, but he's not joking as he carries me to the truck. And that's another reason why I love him. He doesn't give a shit. Not when it comes to me, to us.

Then, when we're away from the crowd, he sets me down on my feet, interlocking his fingers with mine as we look up. The sky is full of sparkling stars that look like diamonds.

"Wow, this view will never get old," I say, glancing at him, and he's looking directly at me.

"Agree."

We get to the truck, and somehow, Emmett was able to move so Harrison doesn't have to crawl through the other side.

When he cranks the engine, he looks over at me. "Ready to go home?"

"Yes," I say, but when we drive past his house, I look at him, confused.

Then, we pull up to the small cabin that Beckett lives in.

"Did he already move out?"

Harrison nods, and then we get out of the truck. As soon as he's in front of me, he lifts me in his arms again, then takes the steps to the house. Harrison reaches forward, then kicks the door open. The place is empty, except for his bed that's set up in the bedroom. He sets me on the mattress, and I push myself up on my elbows, drinking in my husband. Every single inch as he unbuttons his jacket, then throws it on the floor.

Harrison is on me, and we're desperate for each other all over again.

"Tonight, I plan on worshiping every inch of you, my queen."

"I kinda like the title upgrade." I lift a brow, remembering the last time he called me that.

"I tried it out the first time you crossed the line, but it was official when you became my wife," he whispers, kissing my shoulder, then sliding off my dress. "I can never get enough of you," he says.

"Good thing because I can't either. You're under my skin."

"And I always will be," he promises as his eyes trail over my naked body.

CHAPTER FORTY

HARRISON

Remi looks at me and shakes her head as I carry a box of Grace's shit out to my truck. When I return, she's sitting on the couch, typing something—probably chatting with Kinsley, if I had to guess. I stand in the living room with my hands in my pockets. Grace is still packing all of her clothes, but wanted to go through and donate stuff she doesn't wear anymore since we won't have tons of closet space in the house.

"Are you really pissed at me?" I ask my sister with my arms crossed over my chest.

"Yes. You stole the best roommate in the entire world from me."

"We're married now. Of course I did," I explain. "Also, she was my best friend first."

Remi does the hand puppet and mocks me.

"And don't worry; I'm on the hunt for a new roommate, and until that happens, I'm paying half the bills," I explain to her again. It's kinda my fault that Grace is leaving, and I don't want to put her in a bind or force her to move back home with my parents again. "Oh, what about Haley?"

"No, she can't. Her lease ends in six months. Bad timing." She sighs. "Maybe I'll move in with Colt in the stinky man's house, though I'm not sure I want to sleep in your old room. I can only imagine what happened in there over the years."

I chuckle. "Shut the fuck up. Not any worse than what's been happening in your room *here*."

Her gaze meets mine, but it's stone cold. If there is one good thing about her, she doesn't wear her emotions on her sleeve. It's almost impossible to know what she's thinking—unlike Kinsley, who's an open book. They're alike in many ways, but also complete opposites. I want to ask her about Cash, but she'd deny it. No way she'd admit shit.

I clear my voice. "Well, if you move in with Colt, maybe you two could start wearing the same outfits again, like how Ma used to dress you when you were kids. It would be *adorable*. Colt and Remington ... the twins would be back together again."

"You really love getting on my nerves, don't you?"

My laugh bounces off the walls. "Yeah, I actually do."

"The twin thing isn't cute when you're in your late twenties. I don't need him or Kinsley or *you* in my business."

I shrug, zeroing in on her. "It's fine because I'mma find out who you've been sneaking around with."

"Can you please, for once, mind your own damn business?"

I can tell she's growing frustrated with me, but what are siblings for?

"Oh, by the way, you only have seven favors out of ten left," I tell her.

"Actually, I still have ten because I have several banked." Her voice drops to a whisper. "You promised if I texted you about your bestie, I'd earn some favors. Remember?"

Grace enters, holding two dresses in her hand, saving Remi and stealing all of my attention away. "What are y'all talking about?" My wife looks between us.

"Oh, just Remi reminding me about all the favors I owed her from when she'd tell me when you were upset," I say, smirking.

"You're a dick." My sister slams her phone down. "Sorry, Grace. He literally paid me in IOUs, and you know those are gold around here."

Grace's mouth falls open. "I was seriously wondering how you would just randomly pop up where I was."

"Oh, I never told him where you were going."

I lock in on Grace. "I knew where you were because I know you, babe. Could write a whole-ass manual about you. Oh, but there was that one time about your date at the bar."

"Shit," Remi whispers. "Forgot about that one."

Her face softens, and then she looks at Remi. "I'm not mad at you. Honestly, thanks. I dunno if we would be here without all the little things that happened."

She lets out a breath of relief, then looks at me. "I hate you. But you're also going to tell me why you snatched two of my favors away."

Grace clears her throat because she knows if Remi continues down this path, I'll call her out and question her, which, honestly, I want to happen.

"Hubby, do you think I should keep these two dresses?" She pulls my focus back to her, like she always does.

"Hell yes," I say, remembering the last time she wore the flowered one. Fourth of July last year.

I punched a guy out for calling her a bitch. The thought makes me laugh, and she tilts her head at me.

"Was just thinking of something. I'll tell ya later."

Grace notices Remi is on the couch, scowling at me. She sits next to her and wraps her in a hug, but Remi doesn't return it.

"I'm mad at you for leaving me for him," my sister mutters, but I know she's just giving us a hard time. It's her love language.

"But you're happy for me too. That's a whole bunch of conflicting emotions if you ask me." Grace laughs. "The next person you live with is going to be a hundred times better than me."

"I doubt they'll clean *half* us much." Remi looks at me. "When she's stressed—"

I hold out my hand. "I know. One time, when we were sixteen, she detailed my entire truck in an afternoon."

Grace turns to me. "And you know why?"

"I thought it was because of a test."

"It's because I wrote you that damn letter and thought you denied me," she says with a snort.

I take three steps across the room, leaning her back on the couch, and kiss her. "Not denying you now, am I?"

Remi chuckles and scoots away from us. "Way too close for comfort. So, what are you two doing tonight?"

I shrug. "You don't want to know."

She holds up her hand and stands. "Yep, you're right. Now can you please go help your woman?"

"Yeah," Grace says. "I'm too indecisive with what I want to keep."

"You're lucky I'm not finishing this conversation," I warn Remi. "Taking another favor for that."

"You're not fair," she mutters, but doesn't say anything because I know this is a conversation she's avoiding too.

I follow Grace down the hallway and walk into her room, and it's chaos. There are a few more boxes I can carry to the truck, but instead, I join her in the closet.

"Help me pick." She pouts.

I quickly sort through one side with my keeps and donates. Smiling each time a shirt or a dress gives me a memory. They are all kept. While I finish packing my truck, Grace sorts through the clothes in her dresser.

"I'm gonna head back, okay? Start unloading things."

She sits on the floor and leans back. "Moving is hard. I could use some inspiration." Then she looks at my cock.

"Don't go there, princess," I whisper. "Because I can't say no to you."

"I know." She laughs.

I glance around, seeing all that's left are her clothes. "You pack all that, and we'll create a little reward system."

She tugs on her bottom lip, holding out her hands. I pull her onto her feet.

"Yeah?" she asks with her hands against my chest.

I lower my voice. "Fuck yeah. When you get home, we'll celebrate with you sitting on my face."

"I'm gonna pack so quick." She laughs, and when she pulls away, I smack her ass and grab a handful.

"Now, who's the one starting?" she says over her shoulder.

"You're right. I love you. See you soon?"

"I love you too. I need about an hour."

I slide a kiss across her mouth. "Make it thirty minutes."

I drive back to our place with all of Grace's stuff packed in my truck. She's going to meet me at the house after she finishes putting clothes in her car. Plus, I want to give her and Remi some time to hang out without me cramping their style. Over the last few months, they really did become great friends, which I love to see.

On the way back to my parents' ranch, I see Beckett and Cash outside, chatting at the vet clinic, so I pull in, knowing I've got at least an hour before Grace leaves.

I step out of the truck, and Beckett smiles when he sees me. They both have a beer popped open, and Cash gives me one.

"Is this legal?" I ask. "Aren't you on the clock?"

"Fuck no," Cash says. "It's a Saturday. I don't work weekends unless it's an emergency. Perks of owning the place. We're just hangin' out."

Beckett laughs. "So Cash and I were just talkin' about Grace moving out."

I smile wide. "Yeah, just finished boxing up her condo. Will be nice to unpack and get settled. I'm pretty damn excited."

"That's good news," Beckett says. "Cash here is searchin' for a place."

I meet my brother's eyes, hoping he's not insinuating Cash move in with Remi. "Okay, and?"

Cash shrugs. "I don't think I can handle staying at my parents' house any longer."

"Have you chatted with Colt?" I ask, knowing my room is now empty.

"Just found out today that Emmett's moving in with him." Beckett takes a drink of his beer. "I was thinking maybe he could move in with Remi temporarily until he finds a place. Keep an eye on our little sis. Maybe he'll scare away whoever she's been seeing," Beckett suggests.

I narrow my eyes at my brother.

"Yeah." I take a sip, not believing any of this. "Maybe he will."

Cash chuckles. "You act like I'm tryin' to date your little sister or something."

He has no idea that I saw them the night of my wedding. "No, you're not that stupid. You know we'd *fuck you up* if you *ever* crossed the line," I warn.

The seriousness in my tone has Beckett's jaw clenching. He stares Cash down for a few seconds too long, then glances over at me. The moment turns tense.

"Harrison, he wouldn't." Beckett stands firm.

I don't say anything else, and neither does Cash. I'm not falling for his bullshit, but I also don't have time for this conversation.

"I gotta go." I chug the beer, crinkle it with my fist then toss it into the garbage. "Nice talk. Don't make me kick your goddamn ass," I say directly to Cash. Then, my face transforms into a grin as I walk away.

But I'm not fucking joking. He knows I'm not. Beckett knows too.

When I get home, I start unloading all of Grace's things so

she doesn't have to. It actually doesn't take me as long as I thought it would. Once all the boxes are stacked next to mine in our small dining room, I sit back on the couch. I hear Grace's car pull up, and then the door shut. Her feet are on the steps, and then I hear a knock.

When I swing the door open, she's wearing a black trench coat. I lean against the door and smirk as she unties it, revealing the sexiest green lingerie I've ever seen. Leaves nothing to the imagination and only accentuates her curves. Within two steps, she's in my arms, and I'm growling against her lips.

"Fuck," I hiss. "I'm gonna make love to you right here on this porch."

She laughs, takes my hand, then leads me inside. Then I take her to our room, lay her down, and make love to her.

When she collapses on my chest, I hold her, kiss her, and I'm so damn grateful that this is my life.

EPILOGUE

HARRISON

TWO WEEKS LATER

Beckett stands in front of me in his tuxedo, and I've never seen him so happy in his life.

I pat his shoulder. "Man, I'm so fucking happy for you. Extra happy."

"You too," he tells me, looking into my eyes. "Never thought that either of us would be married to the love of our life."

"Fuck, me neither," I admit. "But it feels good. Right. Married life is incredible. Had I known it'd be like this, I'd have proposed when I was eighteen."

Beckett chuckles, and I can tell he's growing more excited with every passing minute.

"I worked on my speech for tonight," I tell him, patting my pocket.

"Yeah? Did Grace give approval?" He looks at me in the mirror as he adjusts his bow tie.

"Hell no. She told me I'd better not say any of it, which confirmed to me that I needed to go ahead and do that," I say.

He shakes his head. "You're never gonna change."

"Hell no," I tell him with a laugh just as the door swings open.

"Oh shit," I say when I see Kinsley. "Dude."

She's giving queen energy again, but this time, she's wearing light blue. "What are you lookin' at?" She turns to me.

"I dunno, just thinking about the last time you barged in exactly like this and tried to talk me out of getting married. Are you about to do the same to Beckett?"

"Pfft, no. Beckett isn't a dumbass," she says. "And if he even thought about leaving my best friend on the day of their wedding, well, I wouldn't be taking his side."

"Fuck," I mutter, then look at Beckett. "How does it feel to get double shit when you've pissed Summer off?"

He chuckles. "It sucks. Trust me."

"That's right," Kinsley says, and then she smiles at me. "Glad you remembered about today."

"Oh, what are we doin' today?" I ask, smirking.

They look at each other.

"I guess he's always going to be like this," Kinsley tells Beckett.

"Damn straight," I say, feeling my phone buzz in my pocket. I pull it out and see a text notification.

GRACE

Heading your way.

"MUST BE YOUR WIFE," Beckett says, recognizing the look that always fills my face when it's her.

I walk over to him and give him another hug. "Yeah, it is. I'll see you out there. Congrats."

I pass my parents in the hallway with a smile, but I'm on a mission to see my woman. As soon as I turn the corner, the door opens, and I see my best friend, wearing a red dress with pockets and crimson-red lipstick. Her mouth turns up into a smile. When I'm close to her, I gently press her against the wall.

She looks around but places her arms around my neck. "In the Lord's house?"

"Wasn't the church on your list?" I say into her neck.

Her eyes flash with want and desire, and the corner of her lips tilt up.

"You're so fucking bad. *Afterward.*"

"Okay," she whispers, looking into my eyes. "I found the perfect place."

"Five minutes," Kinsley says, walking past us, and I laugh against Grace's mouth.

"For what?" I question, not missing one of my last opportunities to annoy her.

She laughs. "You two are iconic."

"I know," I say, pressing my lips against Grace's, and she laughs. "We should go."

"Yes," she says.

I tuck hair behind her ear, then grab her hand and lead her to the back of the church.

Beckett is standing in the front of the church with Cash, who's officiating the ceremony. Kinsley is walking out alone so Grace and I can go down the aisle together.

When I turn around, Remi and Colt look directly at me with the same expression on their faces.

"Hey, twins. You two look *cute.*"

"Have I told you how glad I am that he's not my roommate anymore?" Colt tells her.

Remi bursts into laughter. "I can only imagine."

Then I see Summer line up, and Grace leans in. "Doesn't she look like a princess?"

"Yeah." I smile, so damn happy for my brother.

The music starts.

I glance over at Grace, and I bend down because I can tell she wants to tell me something.

"When you look at me like that, it gives me butterflies."

We kiss, and I feel someone push us to go. We walk out, and my eyes are on my wife. I don't want to let her hand go when we walk up front and our arms slide down each other's.

I whisper, "I love you," to her, and she whispers it back as she holds the bouquet.

Then the wedding march begins, and when Beckett sees Summer, I smile wide, knowing the elation he's feeling right now. It's the same way I still feel every single day I wake up next to Grace. My love. My wife. Mine.

As my brother and Summer say their vows, my gaze is laser-focused on Grace. Neither of us looks away. And the silent conversation is heard loud and clear. We're so damn lucky to have each other.

"The rings?" Cash asks. "Harrison?"

I pull away and check all of my pockets. "Uh …"

Beckett looks alarmed and I keep it going for at least thirty seconds.

I laugh, then pull the diamond ring from my inside coat pocket. "Oh, here it is."

The crowd chuckles, and I pat him on the shoulder. I made sure to tell Grace to fill in Summer so she didn't have a heart attack. Just him.

They exchange rings and *I love yous*, and then my brother is kissing his beautiful bride. The woman who's carrying his child. And just like that, the ceremony is over. The music plays, and I wrap my arm around Grace, kissing her on the forehead. Then she takes my hand and leads me away from everyone.

Our mouths are hot and greedy as we climb up the bell tower. It's not as big as I thought it would be, but it doesn't matter.

"We don't have much time," she breathlessly says, freeing my hard cock. "Fifteen minutes, max. I have to go to the barn to make sure everything is set up."

I drop to my knees, pushing her dress upward, noticing how hard her nipples are and the goose bumps that cover her skin. "No panties? You naughty fuckin' girl." Then I loop her leg over my shoulder, kissing the softness of her inner thigh. "You'll be trying not to scream my name within two minutes, guaranteed."

She smirks. "There's that cocky asshole I love."

But as soon as my tongue is on her, circling her clit, my name comes from her mouth like a prayer. I smile against her.

"Sometimes, I hate how right you are."

I give her two digits, and her entire body tenses, and I continue giving her exactly what she needs, what she craves, what she's demanding as she sinks onto my mouth. And in ninety seconds flat, she's coming.

I stand, and she pulls me to her, tasting herself on my lips, before she drops to her knees, pulling me out.

"My turn to worship you."

I shove my hand into her hair as she takes me in her hot mouth, nearly blinded by her touch as she devours me.

EPILOGUE

GRACE

Pleasuring Harrison is like nothing I've ever experienced before. Hearing him trying to hold back his moans as I take all of him into the back of my throat turns me on all over again. I work him so damn good and then tease him until he's ready to lose it. When his mouth falls open, I grab his thighs, continuing my pace until he's filling my mouth full, and then I happily swallow him down.

Being with him just keeps getting better and better. I stand, wiping the corners of my mouth, loving the way he tastes.

"*My wife*," he mutters against my mouth, grabbing the back of my dress in his fist.

"*My husband*. I'm so addicted to you," I whisper.

"Fuck, that lipstick is …" He runs his thumb across my bottom lip, and it steals my breath away anytime he does that.

"Magical," I tell him, demanding to have his lips on mine.

When we pull away again, he checks his watch. "Seven minutes to heaven."

I laugh. "Damn. I think we've perfected having quickies already."

"Is anyone up here?" someone calls from down below, stealing our attention away.

Harrison places a finger over his lips. I hold my breath as my heart rate increases. Just when I think we might be busted, the door snaps closed. I exhale. Then he grabs my hand and leads me down the stairs.

"We're going to hell," he tells me as we laugh.

"In a handbasket," I add.

"I'd go through the fire for you and with you," he says, pulling me closer. "I'd fuck you right in the chapel if you wanted."

"Don't you dare tempt me," I whisper.

"Hey, y'all shouldn't still be in here," one of the ladies from the church says. "We're trying to lock up."

Harrison and I run off, holding each other's hands like we're kids. Then we hop in the truck and head to the barn.

I try to smooth my hair down on my head and glance at him.

"You look guilty as fuck."

"Because I am," I say, blowing him a kiss. "No regrets."

We park on the side of the barn, and as soon as I enter, I walk around the perimeter of the dance floor that's set up in the entryway to make sure everything is exactly where it should be. The horses were moved to another barn temporarily just for this. My family plans to party until midnight, but we'll see how long they last.

"It looks incredible in here," Harrison says even though we walked through it earlier today.

With the hanging lights it just creates a completely different atmosphere. Smiles and shock fill the faces of my friends and family. I know I'm good at this, and no one can convince me otherwise.

"You're beautiful, wifey," he says, interlocking our fingers.

And I don't think I'll ever get tired of hearing it.

I smile wide. "I love you."

"Love you." He taps my nose.

The only thing that pulls me away is Summer and Beckett entering the barn. London and her band play as they dance together as husband and wife. They're completely enamored and happy to be married.

"They look at each other the same way we do," I say.

He wraps his arm around me, pulling me into a dance. "True love, baby."

"It's the best." I know the night has just begun, but I'm ready to leave so we can be together. "Did you practice your speech?"

"Yeah. And I'm keeping in all the juicy bits." He laughs.

"Don't you dare," I warn him as he gives me that look.

After they dance, Beckett and Summer find me, pulling me into a hug.

"Thank you," Beckett whispers. "Totally owe you."

When he lets me go, I laugh. "I'll remind you of that the next time I need Harrison to have a day or two off."

Summer wraps her arm around him. "I'll make sure it happens. Thank you for making sure today was … perfect."

"You two deserve it. Happy for you. Now, please go eat some of that yummy food before you get too occupied chatting with everyone." I push them toward the buffet table and continue playing wedding planner.

Then I notice Remi off to the side with Haley. Remi is expressionless, but she's always been great at pretending she's fine. The girl is like Alcatraz when it comes to expressing her emotions publicly.

"I'll be right back," I tell Harrison before making my way over to them.

"Be quick," he tells me, his hand sliding across the small of my back.

As I move to the other side of the barn, I pass Cash dancing with someone. She doesn't look familiar, and I know she's not from around here.

As soon as Remi sees me, I notice how her jaw is clenched

tight, but she forces a smile. "You're not welcome here. This is the singles' corner."

I've lived with her long enough to know she's frustrated. I squeeze between her and Haley, taking in the space. The colorful lights from the lit disco ball flash over the crowd. When I glance over, Remi is staring at the dance floor.

"Who is he with?" I ask, understanding how that feels.

"His date," Haley says, but she's not looking at Cash. She's zeroed in on Emmett.

My brows furrow. "Wait. Uh."

Remi shakes her head. "Don't ask. You'll never be able to escape the conversation."

Haley chuckles. "She's right. We'll have to plan a coffee date soon and catch up since you've been so *ocupado*."

I nod. "That's a deal. But also, sorry for ditching the single-girl era and being MIA. I've gotta lot of years of denial to make up for."

When the song finally ends, Harrison grabs the microphone and taps the top. In his hand is a glass of champagne, which means it's speech time. "Wow, it seems like we were just all together not too long ago."

I glance at his mom, who looks at me and waves.

Harrison clears his throat. "So, I wanted to chat about all the embarrassing things my brother has done over the years, but *my wife*, the only voice of reason I listen to—"

I cup my hands over my mouth. "That's right, baby!"

Everyone laughs.

"Well, she said it was a really stupid idea. So, I'll say this. Beckett, my brother, one of my best friends in the whole world, I'm so happy that you were able to marry the love of your life and didn't end up like a hermit who collects horses like we all thought you would." He meets Summer's eyes and laughs. "I'm glad you found someone who won't put up with your shit and isn't afraid to call you out."

I clear my throat, and Harrison finds me in the crowd.

"Right." He raises his glass and blows me a kiss. "I'm so happy to welcome you to the family, Summer. You're my favorite sister-in-law. Thank you for loving my brother. And if Beckett ever hurts you, all the Valentine boys will kick his ass for you. All you gotta do is ask."

Kinsley yells, "Me too!"

"Love y'all. Welcome to the family. Truly happy for you two."

Our eyes meet from across the room, and I give him a smile with a nod. Cash walks up and gives his speech, and then it's Kinsley's turn. Harrison chats with his parents, but he knows exactly where I am.

As I'm following Remi and Haley to the open bar to get another glass of wine, Cash pulls her to the side. Then I overhear him ask her for the key to the condo.

I turn to Haley with my eyes wide.

"Oh, you don't know yet?"

I shake my head. "Know what?"

She leans in and whispers in my ear.

Seconds later, Harrison is pulling me toward him, our lips crashing together, and everything seems right with the world again.

"Dance with me," he says, pulling me away.

"Okay." I wave bye to Haley, then place my hands behind my husband's neck.

This is the fairy-tale version that was always supposed to exist.

My eyes scan back to Haley and Remi before I focus on Harrison.

I whisper into his ear, "Your sister found a roommate."

His brows rise, and he laughs. "Really? Who?"

"*Cash.*"

THE END

Want to know what happens between
Cash and Remi? Continue the series in
Smooth as Whiskey: https://books2read.com/smoothaswhiskey

Harrison & Grace
Bonus Scene

BONUS CHAPTER 1

GRACE

"Did you miss me?" Harrison leans against the bathroom doorway, wearing his signature Valentine smirk with a coffee in each hand. Damn, I already *love* Hawaii.

"I always miss you." I meet his sea-blue eyes. "Even when you're gone for fifteen minutes."

"Seems like I've got perfect timing, too." Water drips down my naked body as Harrison's eyes flick up and down me, drinking in every single curve. I will never grow tired of him looking at *me* that way.

It's official. I've won the husband lottery. And I'm *so* lucky.

The urge to have him again takes over when he licks his lips. "If we don't leave in thirty, we'll miss the sunrise," I explain. It's early, but this is the first thing we're checking off on our Hawaii bucket list on our honeymoon. Before we arrived, we sat down and listed ten things we both wanted to do while visiting. A few might've been spicy, with the number one being banging on the beach. I'm unsure how we'll get away with it, but we'll try. His eyes drag over me again.

"Pretty please with sugar on top; stop *tempting me*." It comes out as a plea because I'm greedy for him. I'm living out my wildest fantasies with the man who's always been at the center of them all. I'm not taking a day or moment for granted. I don't do that anymore.

Harrison sets our coffees down on the long dresser in our room and returns to me. He grabs one of the thick, fluffy towels with his big hands and moves toward me. "Now, what were you saying again?"

"I asked you very sweetly to stop tempting me," I whisper, loving how his touch feels.

"No can do, princess," his voice drops dangerously low. "Tempting you has *always* been my favorite fucking hobby."

He takes his time drying off every inch of me.

"Trust me when I say I've *noticed*."

"Like you're innocent." He meets my eyes.

I deliver my pouty face. "I *am*. A complete *angel*."

"Yeah, *right*." A bark of a laugh releases from him. "You *wrote* the rule book on how to tease me—all those tiny shorts and silk dresses. Give me a break. Or let's talk about how you used to rub your ass against me when we'd snuggle until you felt me get hard as fuck."

Leaning forward, I kiss him. "You *loved* it."

"I *still* love it and *you*," he whispers, stealing my breath away.

The kiss deepens, and I want, no *need* him, even if we rolled around in the sheets before my shower. It's a two-way street, the desperation for one another going both ways. It's incredible to be married to someone who wants me just as much if not more. He's the perfect man in every way, and he's *mine*. *Always* has been. Always will be.

My eyes flutter open as he pulls away and returns to drying me off. "I'm positive I love you more."

He shakes his head. "Impossible. But it's pretty fucking adorable, you think so. A bit cocky, too."

I laugh, wondering if this is what royalty feels like.

We said our I DOs almost a month ago and took the first chance to break away and celebrate.

Harrison outdid himself and booked a room with a beautiful beach view. One wall is entirely windows. There's a gigantic bed that feels like it's made from clouds and a hot tub that we used last night after we landed.

When every inch of me is dry, he kisses my shoulder. "Now, better put some clothes on before we watch the sunrise from here."

"It doesn't sound like a bad idea." I put on my panties and bra, a matching set I bought for him.

"Still wearing my favorite color," he mutters, walking over and grabbing his coffee. He leans against the counter and watches me as I get the excess water out of my hair. The smile on my face hasn't left since...well, since we made *us* official. Add on the engagement party, wedding, and moving in together... I'm *always* smiling. Happiness never felt so damn good.

"What are you grinning about?" he asks, following me into the bedroom, where I pull on a pair of jeans and a T-shirt.

I meet his gaze. "I should be asking you the same thing, sir."

It's still dark outside, and if we're going to watch the sunrise, we need to go. There's no time for distractions, even though he's the *king* of them.

"Don't call me, sir. I kinda like it."

"Oh really?" I burst into laughter and deliver my best smoldering gaze. "*Sir.*"

"My wife." He stalks toward me, wrapping his arms around me, then growls against my neck. "Keep it up, and the Jeep we rented won't get used today either. *At all*," he playfully warns.

"No sunrise. No beach. No jeep. Me and you in here all day? I like the sound of that," I say.

His head dips down, and our lips crash together. I groan, grabbing his shirt in my fist. It takes every bit of strength I have to pull away.

"Fuck, princess. See what you've started." Harrison glances down, and he's *hard*.

"I'm not apologizing." I check the time because we can't miss this. "Twenty minutes." I move him to the edge of the king-sized bed with crumpled sheets.

As he opens his mouth to give me some smart-ass rebuttal, his phone buzzes in his pocket. He pulls it out, and his eyes scan over the screen.

"What?" I ask as I grab my flip-flops. Having sandals is a must here.

"Beckett is acting like a dick, per usual. But I think they're finally going to announce the pregnancy."

"Oh my God! Please tell me they'll wait until we're home so we can be a part of the celebration. It's going to be a huge deal." My eyes widen as I pull half of my hair out of my face. It's still too short to put in a ponytail after my haircut, but I've gotten used to styling it.

Harrison smirks. "That's why I said he's being a dick."

My smile fades. "Tell him he owes me! I planned their wedding in record time! Also, why isn't he asleep? Isn't it like one or two AM there?"

"You're right," he says, typing away. The time difference will take a few days to get accustomed to.

After another minute and a chuckle, he turns his phone to show me what Beckett wrote.

Beckett: Only because Grace asked. I like her more than you. Oh, and STFU. I'll go to bed and get up when I want.

"Good. I'm not sure I'd forgive him if they announced it while we're away. I know it's their moment, and they can do it whenever they want, but I want to be there. It's a big deal. The first Valentine baby!" I smile wide. "I'm super excited!"

"Ready to be the best auntie there is?" he asks.

"I doubt I'll come close to Kinsley, but I'm thrilled." I laugh. "I can't believe your brother will be a parent."

"Me neither. Kinda scary that he'll be in charge of a tiny human."

I clear my throat. "Does he know about Cash and Remi moving in together?"

Harrison sucks in air. "No. I don't think anyone does. Just us. For now. I know I owed her eight, but I feel like keeping news like that to myself deserves at least two favors taken away."

This makes me chuckle. "I think of it as one favor for not telling Beckett and another for not kicking Cash's ass, but that's just me."

"Always so logical. I wonder if I should stop this before it gets started." He sighs. "I'm sure it's nothing."

I glance away, and Harrison notices. He knows me so well it only takes one hesitation, and he's reading me like a book.

"This isn't anything new. You've caught them together before this, haven't you?" He gives me a pointed look waiting for my face to give me away.

"Oh, God. Is getting information out of people a Valentine superpower or something?" I shake my head. "It's not confirmed. I don't know. That's the honest to God's truth."

"They *have*. Wow. Now I'm *pissed*." His jaw clenches, and I know he's serious.

"Promise me you won't be the annoying big brother. At least until she's used all of her banked favors."

"You know I don't make promises to you that I can't keep."

I sigh. "When you treated *me* that way, I wanted to punch you in the dick."

Harrison stands and slides on his flip-flops, and laughs. "I should've kicked every single one of their asses."

"You *did*." I shake my head.

"Oh yeah." He shrugs. "They deserved it for treating you like shit. But honestly, their loss is my gain." He holds out his hand, and I take it as he leads me to the elevator. "I won. No regrets."

I glance at him and smile as we ride to the resort lobby.

"What?" he asks, smirking.

I shake my head. "Nothing. Glad you're mine."

I'll always be grateful for waking up and realizing I had my forever person by my side the entire time, even if it was hell getting to this point. Going through the fire was worth it, and I'll never take being in love with my best friend for granted. Ever.

He leads me past the gigantic indoor fountain and we exit through the double doors. As soon as our feet hit the sand, we take off our shoes and walk toward the wooden loungers reserved for guests. He sits first and I scoot in next to him. Like always, he opens his arms and pulls me closer as we lean back and relax.

"Let's have breakfast after this," I say, hooking my finger with his.

He leans over, nibbling on my ear. "Only if you're on the menu."

"Babe, I've already told you once. I'm the whole damn buffet. And it's all you can eat, twenty-four/seven."

BONUS CHAPTER 2

HARRISON

I hold Grace in my arms as we wait for the sun to peak over the horizon. The stars are still out. Eventually, the sky close to the water transforms into a neon pink with long brush strokes of orange. Waves crash, and I think I hear her let out a content sigh as colors fill the heavens. It makes me smile, and I squeeze her a little tighter.

My wife.

I don't know what I did in a past life to deserve to be married to my best friend, but damn, am I grateful. I lean in, smelling the vanilla on her skin, and kiss her forehead. Goosebumps cover her arms, and I grin. They've always given her away.

We've watched lots of moonsets and sunsets in the past, and now it's time for sunrises and new beginnings as we write our story.

She rests her head against my chest, and we watch the orange bursts fade into sky blue as the sun continues to rise. More people are on the beach, a couple holding hands and a woman running with her dog. I close my eyes, taking in the crashing waves as the cool breeze surrounds us, happy as fuck that this is my life, that I got my happily ever after. And so did Grace.

She sits up, tucking her short brown hair behind her ears. "Ready?"

I take her hand, lifting her knuckles and kissing them as we stroll the beach. I think I see her blush, and I'll never get over how fucking adorable she is. With our toes in the sand, we roll up the bottom of our jeans and walk on the calm water's edge, taking in the fresh sea air.

We slip our flipflops back on when we're close to the resort. Grace leads me straight to the elevator.

"I thought you wanted breakfast?" I lift a brow.

"You, first," she whispers, giving me *that* look. I love that she knows exactly what she wants...*me*.

Moments later, my lips are on hers, and our tongues tangle together as I twist her around until her back is pressed against the wall.

"Fuck," she says. "This is Fifty Shades of Grey shit."

I slide my mouth across her neck, kissing the shell of her ear. "You're so damn sexy."

With her hands shoved into my messy hair, she leans her head back, granting me more access. "You know I like a movie moment," she hisses as the elevator door opens on our floor.

It's a small miracle it didn't stop once on the way up now that the sun is up. When I glance at her, she's smiling with swollen lips and a twinkle in her eye.

As soon as the room door opens our mouths crash together. And as Grace slides one leg around mine, I lift her in the air, holding her against me as I carry her to our room.

"Still blows my mind that you're this damn strong."

I lay her down on the bed, keeping my feet planted on the floor as I kiss her. "Still underestimating me?"

Grace shakes her head, securing her fingers behind my neck, and pulls me closer. "Never."

As she wiggles out of her shirt and unbuttons her jeans, I stand, giving her more room. When she pushes them down, I pull them off her curves while she watches me. As our eyes meet again, I see the want, need, and desire written on her expression. I undress for the woman I've been in love with my entire life, and she studies me.

"All yours," I say as she hooks her finger. With two steps, I grab her ankles and pull her to the end of the before dropping to my knees.

She's greedy, writhing against me as I devour her, taking my time, allowing the orgasm to build.

Her back arches, and she sucks in air as she fists the comforter.

"Please," she urgently whispers, begging.

"Fuck, I *love* hearing you beg," I murmur against the soft skin of her inner thigh, dragging my lips back to her clit.

Seconds later, she's crumbling beneath me. "I need you," she says.

I climb onto the mattress, planting myself between her legs. Grace opens her thighs, and I glide inside her as our lips press together.

"Yes, yes," she hisses.

"You feel..." I groan out, giving her every inch of me as my words and thoughts fade off. It's just us as one, together, like this. Nothing else in the world matters. Her soft pants are music to my ears as we move in rhythm. Our bodies are like we were made for one another.

The way I feel with Grace isn't like anything else. It's emotional. It's deeper than the physical pleasure.

My grunts transform into near cries as I bury my cock deep inside of her. She arches her hips, creating more friction, the pleasure written all over her face as her mouth falls open.

"More," she begs, digging the heels of her feet into my ass. "Yes."

"Gracie," I groan out. I'm so fucking close. I'm nearing the edge of the cliff, and if she keeps rocking her perfect hips against me...

As her pussy squeezes me tight, I see stars. The orgasm rips through me, my vision blurring. Our tongues slide together as she threads her fingers through my hair.

"I can never get enough," she admits. "*Never.* Being with you feels so..."

"*Right.* Like this was always how it was supposed to be," I finish.

"Yeah. You're in my head again," she says, resting across my stomach as I draw circles on her back. "Did you always believe we'd end up like this?"

"Yes," I say without an ounce of hesitation.

Gracie sits up and brushes her lips across mine, causing the sparks to reignite. "Remember all those falling stars we wished upon over the years?"

"Mmhm." I smile, thinking about all the late nights we spent together.

"*This* is what I wished for. *Us.* Just like this."

"Me, too, princess." I kiss her forehead. "Me fucking too."

THE END

SMOOTH AS WHISKEY

Top three reasons why I shouldn't eff around and find out with Cash Johnson.

1. He's eight years older than me.

2. He's best friends with my broody, older brother who's overly protective.

3. He's hiding something.

So we become roommates. And I become his greatest temptation. I play his dangerous game of cat and mouse until we collapse between the sheets with a promise to tell no one.

The only problem is secrets don't stay hidden in our small town for long —not our forbidden relationship or the pasts we're both running from.

Smooth as Whiskey is an age-gap, secret relationship contemporary romance. If you're searching for an older brother's best friend/roommate romance set in a small Southern town, this book is for you!

https://www.books2read.com/smoothaswhiskey

KEEP IN TOUCH

Want to stay up to date with all things Lyra Parish? Join her newsletter! You'll get special access to cover reveals, teasers, and giveaways.

lyraparish.com/newsletter

Let's be friends on social media:
🤍https://tiktok.com/@lyraparish
🤍 https://www.instagram.com/lyraparish
🤍 https://facebook.com/lyraparishauthor

ACKNOWLEDGMENTS

My first thank you goes to you for deciding to pick up this book and read it to this point. Butter My Biscuit has been a top favorite book I've ever written, and I had a blast learning these characters. I felt like I'd found magic in a bottle, and I hope it felt the same for you. If I'm ever asked which book I'd like turned into a movie, it's this one. No competition (so far). But honestly, thank you. I'm so glad you're here.

Thank you to my ARC readers who were obsessed with this book before publication. Your excitement gasses me up! Best hype squad ever.

A special thanks goes to Rachel Brookes for always pumping me up and loving my words. I wish everyone were lucky enough to call you their friend. Thank you to Erica Rogers for wanting my words, even if they're in the rawest form with typos. Your encouragement and feedback means everything. Big thank you to Ashley Willd, Kelsey Uhlik, and Mayas Sanders for volunteering to beta reading and being obsessed with Harrison and Grace. Your comments were so helpful. I appreciate you and your time so much!

Oh, and I can't forget my writing buddies from my 10K group who sprinted with me until the wee hours of the night on 4thwords. You guys are amazing and were always there while I was writing this book. Thanks for joining me on this wild journey!

Jovana Shirley deserves the biggest of thanks for shining my diamonds and making this book sparkle. Big thank you to Becca

Mysoor with Fairy Plot Mother for offering your magical brain and for understanding the genre and my brain. Every book we've talked about has felt like magic in a bottle when I've written it.

Thank you to Bookinit Designs for creating a new cover, which was everything I had ever envisioned for Grace and Harrison. I appreciate you so much!

And last but not least, thanks to my hubby, Will Young (@deepskydude), for always being there and listening to me talk about all of this. You make life fun like a real-life book boyfriend should. Dreams are coming true in the comeback era. It's time to rise and shine!

ABOUT LYRA PARISH

Lyra Parish is a hopeless romantic who is obsessed with writing spicy Hallmark-like romances. When she isn't immersed in fictional worlds, you can find her pretending to be a Vanlifer with her hubby. Lyra's a Virgo who loves coffee, the great outdoors, authentic people, and living her best life.